His Darling Freckles

ALECSA KAYSER

Cover Design: Maryna Arsenieva

Character Art: Maria Rukaya or @myrcella_valentine_art

Developmental Editing: Mae Peredo @ Wildwood Author Services

Copy Editing: Kasey Kubica @ Behemoth Editing

Interior Formatting: TheBookJedi (www.thebookjedi.com)

Triggers & Content Warnings

His Darling Freckles contains themes and situations that may be distressing to some readers. I want y'all to put yourself above anything you read, so while this is a cute romance, it also explores some intense moments.

This includes:

- Fatal car accident (graphic flashback)
- Anxiety/panic attacks
- Domestic violence
- Emotional/verbal abuse
- Physical assault

All topics occur on page unless otherwise noted, but none of the harmful behaviors are committed by the main characters.
Reminder: Your mental health matters. If any of these themes feel overwhelming, please take care of yourself first and foremost. You are *never* alone, and if you need support, don't hesitate to reach out to a trusted friend, counselor, or mental health professional. I am also *always* here for any support or additional questions/concerns!

Take care, and happy reading.

Playlist

All I Want — Kodaline

right where you left me — Taylor Swift

Anyone — Justin Bieber

If You Never Call Again — Deeps, Ali Gatie

Photograph — Ed Sheeran

On My Own — Ross Lynch

I'd Rather Pretend — Bryant Barnes

I Won't Give Up — Jason Mraz

Pretty — JVKE

Alive — Austin Giorgio

So This Is Love From "Cinderella" — Ilene Woods, Mike Douglas

this is how you fall in love — Jeremy Zucker, Chelsea Cutler

The Night We Met — Lord Huron

A Sky Full of Stars — Coldplay

Stargazing – Moonlight Version — Myles Smith

Remember — Liam Payne

About You — The 1975

Two Ghosts — Harry Styles

I'm Only Me When I'm With You — Taylor Swift

I Almost Do (Taylor's Version) — Taylor Swift

This Song — Conan Gray

Tattooed Heart — Ariana Grande

Die For You — The Weeknd

PROLOGUE

Bianca

Eight Years Ago

"YOU OKAY, FRECKLES?"

I glance up at my best friend, finding his eyebrows furrow
hesitant nod leaves me, but he doesn't seem to believe it as he
his arms around my body. It seems cliché, but every time he
me, it gives this serenity that I crave even after we pull away.

"Freckles?" I hear again.

I give him a small smile. "I'm sorry. Um, what were you say

"Forget about that. What were you thinking about?"

Memories from years ago plague my mind, flashes o
and blue turning up more than once. A soft breath leaves m
remember my small, trembling hand reaching out as they carrie
away. My eyes flick down to my arms, and it's almost as if the
of glass are still in my skin. I blink to rid myself of the thou
given it wasn't the only thing weighing down on me today. "No
important. Don't worry about it," I say to reassure Liam.

He squints, but lets it go, thankfully, still giving me another one of his hugs regardless. "It's okay, you're safe. I'm here."

I sigh, hugging him harder with his statement. We pull back and his eyebrows are pinched together. "I hate that you went through *that*. If we had met earlier, maybe you would've—I don't know—not felt so alone?" he states. It sounds as heartfelt and genuine as ever, but that doesn't surprise me because that's all Liam is. At my lack of a response, he continues, "I'm sorry, Freckles. I'm here now, okay? If you want to be sad, I'm here with you."

I turn slightly to put my head on his shoulder, us both sighing in unison as he slides his fingers through mine. Today was our weekly cloud-watching day, and we were up in the tree house Dad had built for me. There is a soothing silence, and I relish it.

I love spending days with him; he always makes everything feel so much better, and I was going to miss that.

I was going to miss him.

The eviction notice we got a couple weeks ago hangs above my head, wanting to tarnish the moment. Mom has already gone through the trouble of telling everyone, but I asked her to let me tell Liam. The only problem was, I could never find the right time.

Now, I'm moving in less than twenty-four hours and my best friend has no idea.

"Liam?"

He looks at me with those captivating, forest-green eyes, and for a moment, I lose my train of thought. With determination, I shake my head, knowing I *have* to tell him today.

"Yeah?" he answers, and I falter.

How could I tell him? It was going to break his heart.

"Um, never mind. Hey, you promised me a movie and popcorn."

His pearly whites show and he stands, pulling me with him. "That I did, Freckles. Race you to my house?"

I climb down the ladder, not giving him an answer, before taking off running. He groans in the distance, and I laugh at that. Making it to his front door faster than ever, I triumphantly walk upstairs to his

room. My jaw drops when I find him already comfortably sitting on his bed while I'm basically gasping for air.

"H-how?" I stutter out.

"You took the long way, dummy." He pats my head in a condescending manner, and I swat his hand away. His little smirk turns into a full-on laugh, and after a bit, one leaves me too. His gaze connects with mine, and I revel in the look. I wish for my mind to always remember him like this. The sweetest kid who would never do anything to hurt me.

Liam

FIVE YEARS AGO

My bag hits my back as I weave through the crowded hallway. I push open the boys' locker room door, getting ready to change into my football uniform. A special vibration comes from my pocket and I check my phone, smiling. Bianca wishes me good luck with my game, my reply being I'll call her later to wish her a proper happy birthday.

Despite her being my lucky charm, I'm still antsy. It's the homecoming game, the most important one we have, and I might be called in. Nerves trickle through me at the thought.

"Parker, let's go!" Hands grip my shoulders as we crowd the entrance, getting ready to run onto the football field. A shaky breath leaves me as we rip through the paper banner. Shrieks and cheers drown out my thoughts, albeit temporarily. The sun is out, blisteringly so, and my body aches at the heaviness of my gear. I turn back, searching for my parents through hundreds of faces, hoping that they're there. Shaking my head, I jog over toward the huddle of burly players as we get the same speech from our coach.

"Win on three!" he shouts, pumping his fist in the air, and I raise mine. We count down, shouting as we break, and I move to sit on the bench with the other inactive players. Andrew, the kicker who I'm backup for, shoves me in the shoulder jokingly, and I send him an uneasy smile. He recently rolled an ankle during practice and won't be able to play. But there's a huge chance a field goal won't even be needed for the game. As the first period starts, I rest my elbows on my knees while running my hands through my hair, and I hope with everything in me that we win.

I don't feel it—the two hours that have passed. Though, a quick look at the clock and seeing we have five minutes left and are down by two points is enough to confirm. Sweat starts beading at my brow, and I hope Coach decides to go with one final play for a touchdown. Unfortunately, my name comes out of his mouth.

"Parker. You're up." My eyes snap to his, and I look between him and Andrew, my jaw hanging open slightly. Sweat runs in a full-on stream down my back and I slowly stand as I chug some water, not believing what I'm hearing. I walk closer as the shouts and cheers fade in and out. Coach is barking orders at me, and the pressure of our quarterback's hand slapping my shoulder as a sign of encouragement snaps me back to the present.

We both nod, and Coach's words, "We're counting on you," vaguely fill my ears.

I strap on my helmet as I jog behind the quarterback, and some team members cheer for me, thumbs-up sent my way. I walk to the line as our holder positions the ball, ready for me.

The clock is ticking and everyone has gone silent. *I'm not supposed to be here. I'm the backup, the second choice—not first.* This is the third game I've played in the whole season, and it just so happens that the outcome of our most important one rides on me. *Why did Andrew have to get hurt?* My breaths reverberate in my ears and I try to think of something that'll get me to be calm.

I have faith in you, always, Liam.

Bianca's voice sounds in my head and I feel a little lighter. A weight is lifted off my chest, the haze clears, and with a determined look, I kick the ball. Everyone watches as it heads straight between the goalposts; the crowd erupts in cheers.

A choked laugh leaves me and my head turns to the scoreboard, my success pushing us to win by one point. The guys run toward me and they hoist me on their shoulders as they shout about our victory. We all chant as the adrenaline soars through the roof. They put me down as Coach grabs my hand, bringing me in for a side hug. He gives me a look as if to say he knew I could do it, and I smile when the team dumps red Gatorade on him.

My stomach hurts as I laugh, and I turn to run toward one of my teammates. We jump, our shoulders clashing in midair. Twisting, I finally see Mom and Dad waving at me and jog over to them, embracing them gently, Mom squeezing me back.

"We're so proud of you, amor!" Mom hugs me once again from the side, and I'm happy for their praise. Thing is, nothing will compare to when I'll hear it from my best friend, my lucky charm.

Heading to the locker room, holding back the urge to call her right now, I stuff my things in my bag. But as I go to exit, the guys stop me.

"Parker, where are you going? We're gonna celebrate at Coach's house."

I nod, moving to give an excuse before Andrew holds a hand up. "C'mon, you gotta come, you can talk to your girl after." Everyone hoots, and exaggerated *ooh*s start while I roll my eyes.

"One hour," I relent, and they all cheer. Keeping my promise to Bianca at the forefront, I agree to not stay a minute more, which they thankfully respect. Something along the lines of hope blooms as I feel acceptance from them for the first time since joining the team. I catch a ride to Coach's house. I joke and smile as my teammates act out the plays they did, as well as my winning field goal. Thinking that it's been around an hour or so, I click my phone on, the numbers eight and thirty causing something foul to curl up behind my ribs.

Even if it's technically early for me, it's almost midnight for her in Philly.

I raise my hand. "Hold up, guys."

"Parker, wait, where are you going?" someone shouts for me, but I don't pay attention as the ringing stabs at me little by little. I head to where I left my bag, rummaging around it to take out the gift, then hurry outside. I switch to a video call, like I *promised*, my own misery staring back at me. I mean, she'll understand, right? It was an accident.

The call gets declined and my heart aches that much more. My phone rings, and it's her calling back through a normal phone call, which stings, but at least it's something.

Her sleepy voice flows through the speaker. I want to be teasing and comment on her husky voice, but now's not the time. "Hey, Freckles." The line goes silent and I close my eyes, hoping she didn't hang up. She takes a deep breath, relief filling me when I hear it, but dread still comes along for the ride. "Happy birthday."

"Thanks," she mutters, and I know there's no number of sweet nothings I can say to fix things, so I go with the truth.

"I'm sorry I didn't call earlier. I know you have a test tomorrow, which is why you wanted to talk ear—"

She cuts me off, putting a stop to my rambling. "Did your game just end?" How I wish I could say yes. I *could* say it ran late, but I can't, and I won't lie to her.

I pinch the bridge of my nose. "No. It ended around six." I can almost see her doing the math in her head when she mumbles a quiet sound of acknowledgment. "We won, and it was actually me who kicked the winning field goal, so that's why we're out celebrating. Time slipped away, even though that's not an excuse. But I didn't forget entirely, plus I wanted to show you the gift I got you over video." A small hint of giddiness starts when I remember what I got her, and I know she's going to love it.

"I'm proud of you, Liam. I knew you would do great when Coach finally gave you a chance." My heart buzzes with the praise, but then shrivels when her voice cracks on the last word. I don't bother with the details of the win, the hitch in her voice pointing to something much bigger, more important. "Now that you won the game, you're probably gonna be busier than you've been lately, huh?"

I raise an eyebrow, not knowing where she's heading. I mean, practices have been brutal since we've been prepping for this game, but I always try my best to make it up to her. "Well, possibly, but that doesn't mean I won't have time for you." She sighs sadly, and I realize I haven't been doing as well as I thought.

"Liam." She pauses and her voice wobbles as if she's stopping herself from crying. "I waited for your call for hours, trying so hard to stay awake since you said we would talk tonight." My shoulders sag, and I mentally curse myself for making her feel this way. She's my best friend—in my heart, more than that—yet she's hurting because of something I did.

"I'm sorry." I hate how shallow those words sound, but they're all I've got. "I didn't mean to, really. It's just . . ."

"*Football*," she finishes for me, lowly muttering, "it always is."

"What's that supposed to mean?"

She stays silent before sighing tiredly. "Nothing . . . Um, how's your week been besides the game?"

A little stone of guilt drops into my stomach, but I push past it. "Hectic, honestly. Coach had us doing drills, like, body-aching drills, and Andrew was making jokes to kinda help us through it. Basically, he pulled his gear over his head because of what happened last week." I laugh, shaking my head at his antics.

"Wait, I don't get the joke. What happened last week?" she asks, confusion coloring her tone.

I think back, trying to figure out how to explain it. "It's kind of a long story. I guess it's a 'you had to be there' kind of thing."

"Right." Her voice lowers to a whisper and the silence between us is thick, leaving an uneasy feeling inside me. She sighs once again, and I realize even though it may seem like she isn't upset . . .

Two sighs in the span of five minutes is never a good sign.

"Have you noticed we haven't been talking as much?" The words come out as if she's been holding them in for a while, and thinking back, she's not entirely wrong. I move to say something when she continues again. "It's either been canceled because of football or for some other thing related to that. And, I get it, I do. I just feel sick of being left behind." She isn't shouting, but she might as well be.

I sigh. "*You* feel left behind? Every time we text or talk, you're always saying how you love your life in Philly. How you're getting new friends. Did you ever stop to think about how that makes *me* feel left behind? I'm sorry I found something that helps me forget you're not here with me anymore." My voice starts controlled, but as emotions bleed through the words, it raises a bit, disbelief coursing through me as she huffs, appalled.

"At least the friends I've made here showed up for me on my birthday," she digs.

"At least the friends I've made here didn't leave me by flying two thousand miles away."

Once again, silence envelops the call, and I pant as the bubbling anger simmers, leaving me with a horrible feeling of regret.

"Well, if I'm such a bad friend, then maybe we shouldn't be friends anymore," she says dejectedly.

The words run through my head and I respond, "Maybe we shouldn't." There's a sharp intake of breath, and my heart pushes me to take back the words. The insecurities I've felt ever since she moved away are winning right now.

I screwed up, I admitted that, but to insinuate I've been leaving her behind or not thinking about her? The accusation of not taking her feelings into consideration hurts when that's all I've been doing. I think back to the times I've woken up early to talk to her, chugging an energy drink to stay awake for the rest of my day. Listening to how she's moved on, and being proud and supportive even though it's killed me inside. I started football to deal with her leaving, and now she's using that against me?

"Congrats on your win, Liam," she says sharply.

"Thanks, I'll be celebrating it with people who actually stuck around." It's the last thing said before she hangs up, and the adrenaline of the phone call wears off. I sit on the porch steps, death-staring at my phone, hoping she calls back.

An ache forms inside of me as I realize what I've done, and I press a hand to my chest while I ignore the cheering coming from inside the house. I look up, willing myself not to cry as my eyes trace each constellation in the night sky. Her birthday present stays wrapped perfectly in my hand, and I look down at it with tainted thoughts. This is a fight—we've had them prior and we always bounced back. We'll bounce back now too. We just need time to cool off, and then we'll be all good.

Bianca and Liam, forever and ever, right?

CHAPTER ONE

Bianca

FIVE YEARS LATER

"CONGRATULATIONS, CLASS OF TWENTY TWENTY-FOUR!"

Grinning, we all throw our caps upward to the sky, shrieks of laughter erupting from everyone as we finally finish our four years of high school. Moving through the crowd of people, I find Mom waving at me and I sprint toward her.

"You did it, honey!" she yells while squeezing me tightly, me returning the gesture. I pull back, seeing tears in her eyes, some of my own welling. "You know your dad would have been so proud," she says softly, and even with all the noise, I hear it loud as day and sigh. This year marks thirteen years since we lost Dad and my baby brother Ezra in a car crash. The memory never fails to leave me, holding me prisoner.

Not helping the no-crying situation, I nod once again, and she hugs me even tighter.

"Compliments on your graduation, Bianca." Pulling back, Josh, Mom's boyfriend, stands there in his suit and tie. His arm curves around Mom's waist, his wrist glinting with a watch way too expensive to be worn at a high school graduation. "Kate and I are over the moon." He gives me a small smile and I return it. She nods, placing her hand on his chest, sporting a grin as she looks up at him.

Joshua Callaway. One of the top criminal lawyers here in Philly and, unfortunately, someone Mom really cares about. They've been together for a year now, and while he's . . . nice, there's something that doesn't sit right with me. I've chalked it up to possibly being about his overall shallow nature, and I guess it's not the *worst* thing. He drags a finger along Mom's jawline, flicking the diamond earring when he reaches her earlobe. She giggles, and I roll my eyes while shaking my head.

At least he treats her right . . . That's all that matters.

"Bianca!" Jamie, my absolute best friend in the world, runs toward me, and I excuse myself as we crash into each other. "Oh my freaking goodness! We graduated!" she shrieks, and proceeds to interlace her fingers with mine as we jump up and down.

"I know, right? I can't believe it either."

She smiles, and I realize that without this girl who has the attitude of someone seven feet tall, I wouldn't have made it through high school. "And pretty soon, roomies at UPenn!"

Something passes over me, but I quickly mask it with a smile. "For sure, J."

She raises her eyebrow and opens her mouth, but I stop her before she can say anything.

Not today, we can't ruin today.

"Did anyone make it for you?" I ask, but she shakes her head, her bedazzled cap catching some sunlight in the process, and this hug we share is entirely different.

"I mean, unless little Whiskers suddenly found a way to drive a car," she says cheekily. The image of the all-black kitten she recently adopted driving a car causes me to laugh. I give her a side hug, silently affirming that *I'm* here for her at least, and hoping she knows that the people in her life who have passed are extremely proud of her.

"Bianca, we need to go!" I hear, and see Mom waving excitedly at Jamie. Josh smiles at me while tapping his watch, and I nod. Turning toward Jamie, her brown eyes gleaming with understanding, I give her one last hug.

The giddiness hasn't left my chest since I walked across the stage and switched the tassel on my cap. I open my diploma sleeve back up, eyeing my name in a bold font. As we drive home, Josh accidentally goes over a pothole, mumbling a hushed apology. I grab the door panel to steady my uneasy nerves, and a different sensation fills me. One of slight dread, where I need to shift my mind from diving back into those memories. I take deep breaths as Mom reaches her hand behind her, and I grab it, my fingers shaking slightly.

After a bit, my heart rate returns to normal. I squeeze her hand, leaning back and focusing on the scenery outside the window. When we first got here to Philadelphia, Mom and I went to live at my paternal grandma's, being that Mom's parents passed away long before I was born. It was hard starting in a new city, in a new school, but I eventually got used to it. However, after about eight months, she passed, and it hurt more than anything. Grandma was all I had left of Dad.

"Bianca."

I wake from my slight daze, and Mom is turned around in her seat as we slow in front of a fancy mansion. More specifically, Josh's *ex-wife's* mansion. I blink harshly, almost as if I'm dreaming, and then an annoyance simmers lowly in me. Mom gives me a sympathetic smile as Josh moves to get out of the car.

"Olivia's coming?" I ask curiously as he shuts the door, my eyes moving to pin Mom down with a look. "You know she doesn't like me." She rolls her eyes and waves her hand as if to say I'm being dramatic. Olivia's become tolerant of Mom over time, but only just, and I don't have the heart to tell her the truth since Mom wants to win her over. The few times Olivia and I have been in the same room, I'm either ignored completely or barely tolerated. I have no idea why, but after the first couple times, I've given up trying. Sighing, I look out the windshield to see her being spun around by Josh as he praises her for graduating after her *second attempt* at senior year.

"I'm sure that's not true, hon. Besides, Josh's wanting to take you two up to Beaumonte as a graduation present," Mom says, and my eyebrows raise at the mention of the most expensive restaurant in the area. I finally nod, as that is a really nice thing regardless.

"Congratulations! What can I get you?" The waitress looks at me with kindness in her eyes, and a small huff comes from Olivia as she flicks a black curl behind her ear. A soft guilt forms in my stomach, but given I'm the one still wearing my graduation robe, it makes sense why the waitress made the assumption. We all quickly order our drinks, and thankfully, we're able to place our dinner orders as well, and she nods before scurrying off.

Josh continues chatting with Olivia and Mom, when another person comes over with our drinks. My eyebrows raise at the service, but again, it's the Beaumonte. A waiter crosses the dining hall with a dessert cart, the portions smaller than normal. I turn back to see Josh walking off to take a call, and smile as Olivia looks up from her phone in my direction, her brown eyes connecting with mine.

"Hi," I say, waving a bit, while she nods plainly in my direction. I glance back down at my drink, embarrassment spreading through me. The waitress comes back while Josh is still away, and I gasp, surprised as a small cupcake is placed in front of me with a candle and a little note, causing me to look up at her.

"Could get fired, but here's a little something on me." She winks, and I pick up the note, seeing the words "Happy Graduation" on it. I mouth a thank you, and she nods slightly before walking off. Mom claps a little at the sweet gesture, giving me a thumbs-up.

Josh returns promptly as another waiter sets down his plate of food. Seeing it, he smiles and gently stops Mom from going for a bite. She looks up, confused, before he grabs her hand and closes his eyes. Understanding dawns on her as she grabs my hand and Olivia gives me hers, reluctantly.

Opening his eyes, he says, "Kate, you won't believe what Tony told me over the phone." I perk up at the news. Olivia turns toward him like a puppy waiting for his next words, and he sits back, adjusting his tie. "We're expanding, and *I* will be in charge of our new office." A smug smile overtakes his face.

Mom shrieks, and he looks over at her before she hugs him. Olivia and Mom crowd him with congratulations, and I offer some of my own. He thanks us before he scans the busy restaurant, seemingly looking for something. He catches the eye of someone and gives a small wave, then glances back at us with a certain look.

He clears his throat before placing his napkin over his lap. "I'm relocating to Los Angeles, Kate."

Time stops. I swear, the breeze that's continual in this place shuts off. Mom's hand freezes on his outstretched arm. My fork clatters, and his eyes home in at the sound.

"Los Angeles, *California?*" Olivia asks, and I level her with a dry look. She turns and glares once she notices my expression, then returns her attention to Josh. "But that's so far away," she whines. Josh scooches closer to her while Mom moves to rub my hand as I stare in disbelief.

"I know. Though, you'll be starting college soon. UPenn will definitely keep you busy," he says, and even though I'm hurt once again by her college news, it's nothing compared to the emotions Josh stirred up by bringing up Los Angeles.

Los Angeles . . .

That's where I used to live.

That's where he *lives.*

Josh is glancing Mom's way. "It's also in a month's time, and I really want you to come with me." She gasps. "Kate, I know we've only been officially dating for a year, but I've known you longer than that. I see a future with you, and it starts with this move." Her jaw drops open before she slides her gaze to me, and I look at her, trying not to betray anything that could sway her decision.

I know I may not wholeheartedly like Josh based on really unsubstantial things. Though, after years of hearing Mom yearn for love again, I would hate to be the reason she doesn't take the jump.

She looks back at him, and I mentally prepare myself, as I know what she'll say.

"Okay."

His eyes widen at her answer, then he pulls her in for a hug. Olivia lets out another small huff, oblivious to the deeper meaning of this decision that only Mom and I know about. Mom finds my eyes, looking conflicted when they pull back. I shake my head at her and nod, smiling. Something along the lines of relief clears in her eyes before she takes a deep breath.

"That settles it. Kate, Bianca, and I will be moving to California in a month," he announces, causing Olivia to ask to talk to him privately, leaving Mom and me as they walk off.

Her hand comes into my line of vision. "I'm trying to be happy for you, Mom. I am. It's just—" I can't even finish before she scoots closer, hugging me.

"You're such a selfless person. But you can tell me, what's really racing through your head?" Mom never fails to impress me and is truly one of the most noble people I know.

"I can't go back." My truth spills out. "My college applications have all been sent out for schools here." Every single one was sent to Pennsylvania schools, I mean, except for one. One that I sent for fun, one that even if I got accepted, I doubted I would ever take. "I already got used to Philly. I can't leave my friends here," I continue. I mean, I only have Jamie, but still—going somewhere to start over again?

Mom's hand brushes some strands of hair behind my ear as her soft fingers cup my chin. "Sweetie, it's been five years. Maybe he'll be glad to see you again." She sighs. "I don't think it's the worst news. My contract with the firm is almost over. You're done with school, and we can always apply to other colleges. California has some great options."

I nod. "You know, that's also where Dad—" I start, but I don't finish as she glances at me and she shakes her head.

"I know. That was my *first* thought. Los Angeles holds so many bad memories for me," she whispers, rubbing her stomach subconsciously. Over time, neither the redness nor the scar on her stomach ever quite went away. Now, it's like a constant reminder of what she lost. "Maybe we can create some new memories. I don't know why, but I have this feeling that things will be better this time around," she says, trying to be a little optimistic.

Josh and Olivia come back, and Mom glances at me with a look of "we'll talk more later." Besides the murmurs between Mom and Josh, it's a rather quiet rest of the meal, and we eventually reach home. Of course, Josh will be staying over, as he always does, but today I don't even care. All that's in my head is that I'm going back to the place that I wanted to forget.

As I walk into my room, emotionally exhausted, I struggle with my thoughts. How am I going to break the news to the only friend I have? I know I can't make the same mistake twice and withhold it till the very last second. I flop onto my bed as memories about that *someone* that I haven't thought about in a long time come rushing back.

I last talked to Liam five years ago, and it still hurts like it happened yesterday. We had become the best of friends, and we promised—*he* promised—that just because I had to move away, we would never lose what we had. They say long distance is hard, but I didn't listen, naively thinking our friendship could weather anything.

It didn't exactly help that on my birthday, we had a fight. He didn't call when he said he would, and I was hurt and jealous that he was moving on. That if he missed something as big as my birthday, how much more till he forgot about me completely? Yet, what hurt the most is that the door was never fully closed.

Tears gather in my eyes, but I refuse to cry about this. It's been years, and I was just a little girl who believed in promises, in Liam.

Now, I don't believe in either of those things.

I was hurt after our fight and made the mistake of blocking him. I undid it after a couple days, feeling ashamed of myself. I gave him a chance to contact me after, but he didn't, and that sent the message loud and clear.

Then, when Mom started working at the firm, she met Josh. He convinced her that our other service provider was horrible, which wasn't too inaccurate. Mom didn't have a lot of connections when Dad died, so she isolated herself. *A fresh start,* she said. And after many nights of me crying for hours, I asked for a new number along with her.

Eventually, I stopped caring and moved on. I had a new life and new friends. Thing is, I never once thought I'd be thrust back to the place I'd been trying to escape.

CHAPTER TWO

Bianca

MY ANXIETY HASN'T GONE AWAY; If possible, it's gotten worse. Jamie's on her way with a surprise, and I'm over here planning on how to tell her I'm moving. Do I just say it, or should I beat around the bush?

When the doorbell rings, I rush to get it, Mom giving me a sympathetic look before letting me open the door. I'm wrapped in a bear hug instantly.

"Hey, girl!"

I sigh, embracing her longer than usual, and a nervous chuckle leaves her as we pull apart. She looks at me quizzically. "You okay?"

"Yeah, of course. So, what's the surprise?" I switch the topic, and her face lights up again.

"I brought ice cream, cookie dough, soda, and some tissues for our movie marathon," she says, and I start giggling.

"Jamie, I don't need all this stuff." I juggle some of the items in my arms and she looks at me incredulously.

"Who said this was for you?" I slap her on the shoulder as she giggles, apparently thinking her joke was the funniest in the world.

Heading upstairs, she breaks out into conversation, but as much as I want to pay attention, my mind drifts off.

A bounce on my bed makes me snap my head in focus, and Jamie sighs.

"Okay, that's twice now." She shoves the spoon in the rapidly melting tub of ice cream, a look of concern on her face, and I give her my best innocent-looking expression.

"What?"

"You've been giving me this hurt puppy look for the past hour."

I look down, a mental groan resounding in my head as she looks at me expectantly. "Well, I . . ." I grab my star plush and hold it to my chest, the soft fibers tickling my chin as I contemplate the way to say the truth.

"Whatever it is, we're gonna get through it," she says. Her hand comes into my line of vision, her pastel-blue friendship bracelet showing, and I look at her, tears welling in my eyes.

"I'm moving in a month," I push out, heartbroken by how her face drops instantly.

"You're moving to another house? Or . . ." she says, somewhat hopeful, and I shake my head. "Okay, I mean, I'll miss the house, especially the vintage wallpaper, courtesy of Grandmama H. But we're living on campus anyway." There's a mixture of confusion and relief painting her face.

I sink farther into my pillows, not wanting to fill the silence with something that will hurt her even more. Disbelief crosses her features, her perfectly plucked eyebrows forming a small crease.

I open my mouth, confirming what she's realized. "I got rejected, J."

A wave of silence spreads through the room before she breaks it. "B, those letters have been out for months, why didn't you tell me?"

Shame swallows me because she's my best friend, and she should've been the first person I told. "I was embarrassed, and I thought maybe I could get in somewhere close, and then transfer, but I got those letters back as well."

Her eyes crinkle in concern. "Denied too?"

I don't bother answering, but she seems to understand the words I can't voice. It's silent once again, and I let it linger while I gather the courage to reply. "The last one is the one I did for fun, and I was accepted—"

She cuts me off, grinning. "*What?* Congratulations! Which one?"

A pained exhale leaves me. "Mella Colta, the one in California."

"Oh." Her voice drops at that, and I can practically see the gears turning in her head. There are different questions she wants to ask, but determination outweighs them. She looks down, and there's so much to say, yet neither of us want to take the first step. Her hope hangs by a thread, her mouth curving into a little smile. "Well, where are you moving to?"

"Los Angeles," I mutter. Jamie's eyes widen and I break eye contact, stealing the cookie dough container. Her eyes water as she finally does raise her head, and I move closer to comfort her.

Silent tears fall on my white comforter, marking her devastation, as I hold her. Her shoulders shake slightly as she sniffles. A broken whisper comes from her. "I've lost just about everyone in my life. I can't lose you too, Bianca." My heart shatters for her, and I hug her that much harder. Jamie's parents died when she was fourteen. Her grandparents took her in, but then died this year right after she turned eighteen. They left her everything, and because of that, all her aunts and uncles shunned her, leaving her all on her own, besides me.

The thoughts make me sigh as I know how I've unintentionally triggered her.

"Listen to me, you're not losing me. I'm just not gonna be living here. But nothing will change our friendship, I promise." Jamie is one of those people that no matter how much reassurance she gets, it's hard for her to truly believe it. I sigh, more so for how this is hurting the one person who helped build me up after my fallout with Liam.

She wipes a tear, more coming down subsequently. "That's what everyone says."

I shake my head, trying to reassure her with everything I've got. "But I'm not them, and I never will be. I'll always be here for you . . . for everything. I'll never abandon you, I never have, and I'm not starting today, Jamie." She nods almost absentmindedly, and I rack my brain for other things I could say for her to believe me.

"You can't leave, B. You're literally the only person I have," she replies, and I embrace her once again, her breath catching a bit.

A ragged whisper leaves me. "I'm sorry." But I know that those words aren't enough. The one thing about loving and knowing everything about someone is that you know how their brain works. Afterward, there's an awkward feeling in the air. We do everything we always do. We order a pizza and drink some of the soda Jamie brought over while we drooled over the abs of the men on TV. Yet, there was still something in the air. This tension. Even though we both do everything we can to ignore it, it stays the whole night till we eventually fall asleep.

A zipper zipping shut startles me awake, and I glance up to Jamie packing. A small headache forms, and I catch sight of my alarm clock, registering that it's three in the morning.

"You okay?" I ask, thinking she's doing her routine cleanup. After rubbing my eyes more, the strap of her backpack locked onto her shoulder comes in clearly. My heart drops to my stomach when all her belongings are gone. My sleepiness is fading and concern fills my eyes as I knew this would happen—I hoped it wouldn't.

She stops at that, and I open my eyes more, seeing she was planning on leaving. "Jamie, don't shut me out, please. I'm your B, you can talk to me," I say as she looks at me, but refuses to say anything back. All I'm met with are red-rimmed eyes and a frown.

"I know. Look, I have to go. See how Whiskers is doing. You know he's always trying to get into his catnip." I reach out for her, but she steps back, making me back up in response. "I'll talk to you later," she mutters, heading in the direction of my door.

"Oh. Um, okay—" I start as she leaves my room, no hug or anything. Following her out, I open the front door, expecting one then, but she slinks past me, heading to her car.

I look out the window in the direction of the driveway. Her bun bounces in the moonlight as she walks away. I can feel her emotionally walking away that much more, though. Something folds inside me—quietly, but achingly. Another piece of my heart cracks ever so slightly at the thought of having another person in my life no longer be in it. Though, I hold out hope thinking she'll look back and wave like she always does.

But she doesn't, and I walk to my room, already feeling the distance.

There are texts after texts I've sent to Jamie, but I've yet to hear a reply. Each unanswered message chips away at a piece of me until I'm left an aching mess. It's been a couple of days since I told her I was moving, and she's completely isolated herself; not that I blame her entirely. The feeling of helplessness, of how I can convince her that I'm not another person who'll let her down, consumes me daily.

"Jamie?" I say as I knock on her door, but no reply. Her car is out here, and she isn't working today. I knock again, discreetly looking over to Mom, but she's thankfully talking on the phone. Defeated, I walk back to the car and climb in. Mom turns to me, a question in her eyes, but she just starts driving.

Getting home, I jump out before she can ask me anything. Heading inside, but before closing my door, I hear a hushed, "What happened?"

I look around, seeing boxes already set up in my room, and tears well in my eyes at the sight of them. I don't *want* to leave either—but Jamie doesn't see that. Twirling around, I see my cork vision board and hastily grab a box. I start removing each of the pictures, tears of anguish coming down my face. My friendship bracelet jingles on my wrist, and I stop momentarily.

Setting the box down, I run my fingers over the beads, each one dedicated to something special in our lives. White for our times playing in the snow, since I had never seen it before. Purple for my favorite color. And little charms. My tears change from anguish to nostalgia, and I hope that this isn't the end of our friendship.

I don't know if my heart can handle another lost one.

A knock breaks me out of my thoughts, and I run a sleeve over my eyes and face, muttering a small, "Come in."

The door opens, and I face away from the door, pretending to throw more knickknacks into another box.

"Hey, hon." The concern in her tone is obvious, but I don't turn around, not now. "Is something up with you and Jamie?" Saying nothing, she figures it out, sighs, and approaches me. She embraces me from behind, and I scrunch my face, holding in my tears.

Nothing like a Mom hug.

"I'm sorry, honey." I nod, turning around squeezing her, when a small chuckle leaves me.

"Well, we can always let Josh go by himself." She gives me a look, making me put up my hands in mock surrender.

"I know you and Josh aren't best friends, but he's a *good* guy, honey. You'll warm up to him," she confidently states, and I nod at that. "Everything's gonna be okay. You'll see. It might be hard at first, but it'll get better."

I smile at her, feeling the pessimistic statements rising, but push them down for her benefit.

"Kate, I need you."

Smiling nervously, she retreats, practically running to him. She closes the door behind her, and I glance around once again, seeing the memories pop out from my walls. I can almost see the little ghosts of my younger self living her life in this room.

I never thought that I would fall in love with Philly, but I did. This city gave me one of my best friends after I'd lost another. Throwing myself on the bed, my mind drifts back to the moving announcement the other day, it circling my head nonstop. My mind runs through every scenario.

Seeing him.

Not seeing him.

What'll happen if I see him?

If I don't, will I be happy about it?

Should I be happy about the move?

So many questions, and I've yet to come up with any answers. On top of that, Jamie and I are in such a weird place right now, and I'm on the verge of losing yet another friend all because of moving away.

In the event of a graduation dinner, Josh, unknowingly, has managed to ruin the little life that I've tried so hard to construct. I *finally* started to consider Philly my home. The memory of Liam still stings, but I had come to terms with it, and now I have to get reaccustomed all over again.

Los Angeles is a huge city. I mean, the chances of seeing Liam are one in four million. Knowing Josh, he'll probably get the best house in the city, a place that's about showing how much you have and not about *building a home* like Liam's parents did.

Yeah, seeing him is unlikely.

Getting up with that thought, I look down at the box and see a familiar photo peeking out from the top. I sniffle slightly and slide down to the floor, gently grabbing it. Running my fingers over Jamie's and my goofy smiles, it causes me to blossom one of my own.

Putting it back, I start to pack up more things I've collected. Ever since we met in the fifth grade, it's been us against the world, but now that I'm leaving, it's just me. And even though I wish she could come with me, she has UPenn, and I won't take that from her.

Sighing, I put all the pictures in the box and move on to my closet. Outfit after outfit, I fold them up nicely, leaving some for the rest of my time here. And as I'm going through, something big and fluffy and partly dusty falls from the back shelf.

Picking it up, I'm met with Señora Bearington. The second most important plush I own. I can almost conjure the memory of when Liam handed her to me on Christmas when I was eight and revealed that he had gotten the male version to match. I hug her to my chest, and after a minute, I trace the stitching.

You'll always be my forever, Freckles.

Taking a deep breath, I put her in the box and seal it tight, placing it in the corner of my room. Glancing around, a wave of nostalgia hits me as a flashback. Ten-year-old me, coming here after a long flight, and my grandma showing me the room she prepared.

She said it was Dad's and that she would love it if I made it mine, so I did. And even though it was a rough eight years, it had its moments. After a couple of hours of packing and reminiscing, a knock makes me blink back into reality, my room feeling much colder than it did before.

"Hey, Bianca," Mom says.

She's wearing her favorite sundress. It comes down to her lower legs, the yellow color positively glowing on her skin. I raise an eyebrow in confusion as she was just wearing her lounging-around clothes.

"Your favorite dress? What's the occasion?" I ask, and she smiles.

"Josh set an appointment with a Los Angeles realtor already," she whispers. "We're flying out today, leaving in an hour or so." She claps her hands together, stars in her eyes.

I rush to my feet, rubbing my hands on my shorts. "Oh, okay. Give me a couple minutes, and I'll get ready—"

"Actually, Bianca, if you wouldn't mind, it's just gonna be Kate and me." Josh walks in suddenly as if summoned, smiling slightly, and I flinch at the statement.

Mom wrings her hands, then glances up at him. "Josh, it'll be good if she goes with us. I mean, it'll be her house too."

"Kate, we talked about this. You and I are all that's needed. Besides, Bianca looks like she has her hands full with packing." He and Mom take a glance around, a sheepish feeling passing over me.

She takes a deep breath. "Well, I guess so."

He wraps an arm around her waist. "I know exactly what I'm talking about. You don't doubt me, right?" He says it sweetly and looks at her with adoration, but there's *something else* there. There's always been something weird with Josh, something that makes me uneasy. I look at Mom, and she glances between me and him, then sighs defeatedly.

"No, of course not." She looks at me again, conflicted, and I make it easier on her.

"Yeah, I didn't wanna go anyway," I mutter, and Josh adjusts his suit jacket while looking at himself in the mirror. I slide a glance Mom's way, her eyes refusing to meet mine.

"Great. Kate, let's go. You need to get ready," he says.

Mom looks down at her outfit for a moment, then back up at him. "I *am* ready, though."

"And you look stunning as always, but I just thought you'd want to, I don't know, dress up a little more so we can make a good impression with this realtor. She's the best in Los Angeles and we don't want her thinking we don't have business to give her, right?" He tilts his head to one side and gives her a wide smile as he focuses his eyes on her face.

"Yeah, no, you're right. I'll change." Without a word, he grabs her hand while she follows him, nodding along.

Shaking my head, I look at the mess that was once my room, and a wave of exhaustion comes over me as I think about the cleaning up I have left. After another thirty minutes of taking down my wall decorations and trying to make them fit in a medium box, I give up, and instead, head downstairs for some food. When I reach the bottom of the stairs, Mom is hugging Jamie, and I rush toward them, my eyes widening in shock.

"What're you doing here?" I ask, and Mom looks between us. I give her a sad smile as I take in her new outfit. One that isn't her at all, but has Josh written all over it. The pretty sundress has been traded for a shorter, tighter version, her flats now a stiletto heel. She excuses herself, giving Jamie and me some alone time.

We look at each other, and a small sound of relief escapes me as I crash into her. Almost instantly, her arms wrap around me, causing something to make a small thudding sound on the ground.

"I'm sorry, B. Me running away like that after everything you and I have been through wasn't cool," she mumbles before backing away.

I stay silent as she runs her hands through her hair, almost if the movement helps her sift through her thoughts. "I was overwhelmed, and then I shut down, which isn't an excuse. I'm . . ." She doesn't continue, and her eyes become glassy as she glances at me. "I'm just gonna miss you . . . a lot."

She wipes at her eyes, and I mumble a soft "ditto." She chuckles sadly, and I give her a little smile while looking down at the small box on the floor. "Jamie . . . You kept this?" I pick up the very first charm bracelet I made back in the fifth grade, and she rolls her eyes.

"Of course I did. I've kept pretty much everything. I thought you needed some things to remember me by."

A faux grimace flashes across her face while I level her with my gaze so she can see the truth in my words. "I might be moving, but I'm not gonna forget about you. You're my best friend." She smiles and we hug again. I realize that no matter what happens, I'll make sure to never lose this girl.

She's too special.

Heading upstairs, we pass Josh and Mom as they're heading out to catch their private jet. He sends a polite smile to Jamie, who sends one right back, as we go straight to my room.

"I can't believe Josh and Mama Kate are going to Los Angeles right now," she mumbles, and I chuckle, nodding.

"Kudos to the company jet, you know him." We both roll our eyes as packing peanuts, plastic wrap, and flat moving boxes lie all around us. She ties back her wavy chestnut locks with a satin scrunchie as she starts to build one, and a feeling of gratitude washes over me. The newest episode of the astronomy podcast we listen to comes on, and I smile at how well this girl knows me. We hang out for the rest of the afternoon, genuine happiness filling me. This moment helps temporarily remove the anxiety that's been festering for days.

After a while, Jamie grunts as she sits on my chair, clearly wiped out. "You know, you still haven't told me how you feel about moving." I raise my eyebrows and she crosses her arms. "Isn't Los

Angeles where Mister Man lives?" she asks as if that wasn't the first thing that ran through my mind when Josh said we were moving. I send her an unimpressed expression and she shrugs innocently. Sighing, I close up the box filled with my books.

"Well, he did when I left. I have no idea now," I mumble, and she gasps, making me glance at her.

"What if you guys reconnect again? C'mon, I can tell you wouldn't be totally opposed to the idea."

Panic fills me for a bit, and I turn around briskly, losing my balance on a roll of tape on the floor. Jamie glances at me in confusion fused with concern. I play it off by grabbing another unmade box from the pile, my hand wiping a bead of sweat from my forehead. "I wouldn't go that far."

She scoffs and comes closer to me, poking me jokingly. "Bianca, puh-*lease*. I see it every time we talk about him. Your face lights up."

I stand back up to my full height. "Can we just not talk about it?" I ask sharply, and her look of defiance drops. I rub a hand over my face, feeling exhausted, my aching muscles crying out. "Look, J, yes, I've thought about it. And it terrifies me," I whisper, sitting on my bed, catching her attention, and she slides next to me. "Our friendship ended so abruptly, and it's something I never got closure on. Besides, getting denied from UPenn essentially was the kicker telling me I no longer belong here. There's so much going through my head, and while talking about Liam used to bring me so much happiness . . ." I wipe at the tears welling in my eyes. "It doesn't anymore."

Jamie looks at me with understanding and leans over to hug me. I embrace her at the same time my phone buzzes. My eyes dart down to see Mom's contact photo lighting up my screen, but I don't bother picking it up.

CHAPTER THREE

Liam

"DUDE!"

I practically slam the room door shut, wishing with everything I have that I can remove that picture from my mind. Smack-dab in the hallway of my housing building, I groan while banging my head on the wall, cringing at the noises from inside of my room that have resumed.

"Hang a sock on the handle or something next time!" I yell, getting looks from the other guys that live across from us. Rolling my eyes, I look down at my watch, seeing I have an hour or so before my next class, and no enjoyable place to study.

Well, technically . . .

No, I *refuse*.

I promised myself I would stop going to the planetarium. It brings so many memories, ones I'm trying so desperately to forget. The mind is a funny thing. I'm on a fifteen-hundred-acre campus filled with places to do schoolwork, yet I can't focus at any of them.

A gruff "thank you" falls from my lips as someone holds the door open, and I instantly miss the air conditioning as I step into the blistering sunshine en route to the library. The security guard waves at me like always, greeting me in Spanish. I return the sentiment, thankful he hasn't started a whole conversation with me yet.

While I'm technically half Colombian, I experienced a very American childhood. I can definitely understand Spanish, but speaking it is a whole other ball game. I head toward some empty desks, intent on avoiding *that* room. Though, when I see the planetarium unoccupied, I stop and fight with myself, nostalgia winning in the end. Sighing, I slip between the two large mahogany doors, the *thunk* of them shutting the only sound in the room. The smell of dust and faint lemon wafts around.

Taking a quick look, I twist the dial to darken the space and I flip a switch. Orion's Belt lights up the ceiling. A small smile starts on my face, and I adjust it slightly, with Ursa Major glowing and twinkling a bit brighter. I lean on the industrial-sized telescope that's used as a decoration after being replaced by a more expensive and updated piece.

The bliss found in silence soothes me, and after a bit of marveling at our universe far beyond our usual beautiful sky, I raise the light slightly, but don't turn off the projector. Placing my backpack on the floor and taking out my sketchbook along with a couple of pencils, I start perfecting my latest drawing.

It's always the same thing when I'm here. I get this burst of motivation, and the only signal my brain sends to my hands is for them to draw. Smudging to create a shadow along the face, I hold the notebook, sighing as I realize I once again drew blemishes in the pattern I always have. My traitorous heart and mind making sure I truly never forget.

I look down at my hand as I connect the small dots, scattering across her face—all from memory. I sigh, this girl reflecting someone who I've never been able to stop thinking about.

Bianca Harrison.

My pencil stops at the thought and I slide a hand through my hair in frustration, pulling at the strands. It's been five years since

I last talked to Bianca and eight since she left, yet I feel like it was yesterday. An ache starts in my heart as always, my mind trying to think of something else, trying to minimize the mental torture.

When I was twelve years old, I had promised my best friend I would never forget her, no matter what. How could I when she was at the root of every decision I've made? When she left, even if she had to, I refused to let life take her away mentally.

Emotionally.

I mean, we would talk almost every night for years. It was so good, *we* were so good.

Yet, on her birthday of all days, I messed up; I admitted it then and as an adult, I admit it now. What killed me was when I tried to text her a couple days later, my message didn't go through. My heart dropped, my hands almost trembled, but I held out hope. Then, when I called her and it immediately went to voicemail . . . I knew.

My best friend, the girl who I secretly loved, wanted nothing to do with me. The memory leaves a bitter taste in my mouth even all these years later.

The serene music from the speakers in the room makes its presence known, causing my thoughts to be even more nostalgic. I mean, I was hurt and lashed out by saying what I said, but to completely cut me off?

Searing my heart, I threw myself into anything and everything. It didn't matter; I needed something to stop thinking, something to redirect that ache. With lots of hard work, I graduated high school as salutatorian and was accepted into my dream school: Mella Colta University.

It was the best news I had received in a while, and with my major being aerospace engineering, it was the closest I could get to grappling with what little bit I had shared with her. Stargazing was always our thing, and now I study the machines that take others to observe everything up close.

I slightly pull again at my hair, a nervous habit, sighing at things I've been trying to forget for five years. Things I want to erase, memories I want to get rid of—but there's a part of me that won't let me. It's the reason for my suffering. I sigh, rubbing a hand over my face before beginning to fidget with the rings on my fingers, which sit there subtly emphasizing the elaborate designs on my hands.

It's been a long time since she left. I was practically a child. Turning twenty-one soon has really put a lot on me, especially when I realized my life isn't going the way I thought it would. Tracing the somewhat healed calluses on my palms, I close my eyes and think about how old habits die hard.

While football was my pride and joy, I never pursued it seriously. I had only tried out to have something that would keep my mind off Bianca's move. But at eighteen, my passion for football turned into one for tattooing. Enough pain and motivation needed to be transferred to something, and my body paid the price. It became my canvas, causing me to be covered from the neck down in tattoos.

Of course, I've heard it all from everyone.

That I've ruined my body.

I'll never get a job looking like I do.

It'll look horrible when I get older.

A stupid dare sparked it. Then, when I felt the relief of the little needles puncturing the skin, it silenced the chaos in my head. I couldn't stop; now I'm responsible for almost sixty percent of all the ink on myself. At first, it was a lot for me to get used to, especially since the bouquet of tulips on my hand was not all I wanted. Mom freaked out, and so did Dad, but it became the norm.

So, over time, I returned almost every other month for something new, and because of it, I discovered an underlying passion for drawing. The artists back home became my mentors and are the only reason I am where I am, causing me to apply to every parlor within a five-mile radius when I came to Mella Colta.

Looking back down at my sketchbook, I flip through the pages, the subtle similarities practically jumping off the paper. Orion's Belt, Ursa Major, the little freckles dotted over the bridge of every person's nose and cheeks.

It's been years, yet my mind continually tortures me. Don't get me wrong, it's been a long time, and obviously thinking about her every day isn't healthy. So, there will be days, even weeks, where I feel healed . . . Well, healed enough to ignore the hurt.

Then, a memory, a scent, a song—I'm thrust back into the abyss of our ended friendship. I guess in some sort of sick way, my subconscious always makes me draw those little freckles to feel closer to her. Hard as it is to admit, I sometimes replay our conversations in my head, but the one I remember the most is the one we had the day before it all fell apart.

I laughed as I saw Bianca put her "new" phone on her desk, then moved to sit on her bed.

"Freckles, what are you doing?" I asked, and she looked at me, facepalming herself. She must've forgotten I was here.

"Sorry, I was just trying to get comfortable."

"Ah. So, how was your day today?" I grabbed a piece of candy and she smiled.

"It was nice. We went to the space center, and thankfully, since Jamie and I are getting close, we spent the day glued to each other. The trip being a day before my birthday made it that much better. Plus, these other girls hung out with us too, I loved it." Something ached in my chest, this fear that she might be moving on without me, but I tried with all my might to not let it show.

I cleared my throat and tilted my head down. "I'm glad you had fun," I said, half meaning it. I selfishly wished that I could have been with her.

"Yeah. It would've been one hundred times better if you could have been there, though." She pouted slightly, and my eyes drifted down, but I quickly recovered. The ache shifted to a jump in my chest, and a whole-body blush washed over me. I ran a hand over my face, hoping it helped me calm down, and she noticed. "You okay? Are you thinking about the game tomorrow?"

"It's been brutal, and Andrew said he'll try to see if I can play. Coach is pushing all of us pretty hard."

She huffed and crossed her arms. "You should be first string. You're literally amazing at everything, Liam. I know you would do great if given the chance."

I shrugged, not letting the thought linger in my head so as to not build up hope. "He's the coach, he knows what's best." She stared at me with an exasperated look, but I interrupted her before she could say anything else. "C'mon, Freckles, keep telling me about the trip." That beautiful smile came back to her face and I sat there, easily listening to my girl.

"I love stars. They're so far away yet shine so bright. They light up the night sky and look small, but aren't. They're so underrated to everyone here in Philly, but I love them so much," she ranted with a sparkle in those endless blue eyes, and my heart skipped a beat.

"I love them too, Freckles," I said, completely dazed. She smiled at me, and I thought to myself, just like I love you.

The memory dissipates, bringing me back to reality. Sometimes, I wonder what she might be doing, which makes my heart ache, and I hate that.

Why can't I get her out of my head?

In the middle of my wallowing, people start shuffling in, so I slip out unnoticed and walk back to my room, hoping Chase is done. I sigh as I turn the corner to the hall, and my mind, as always, drifts back to Bianca.

Sometimes I wish she never let us go, because I sure wasn't ready to.

I mentally prepare myself for what I might witness again, shutting my eyes. Sliding my keycard through the slot, the light flashing green, I peek with one eye. Pushing inside the room slowly, I find Chase with his laptop open. Sighing in relief, I shut the door, walk to my side of the room, and get my laptop out of my backpack.

"Well, hello to you too, sunshine."

I mumble a low sound of acknowledgment. This is our normal: He talks to me while I engage with the least amount of energy possible. It's been this way for two, going on three years, and yet he still hasn't gotten the message. I don't want friends or acquaintances, and I don't even want to waste time on small talk.

A scoff escapes him, but I continue typing. A ploy he once used for me to engage in conversation that I will *never* fall for again.

"I see that the stick up your butt is still very much intact," he says sarcastically.

I slide my eyes to the mirror, glaring at him. He stares back at me, and I look down at my computer to email my boss about the new work schedule he sent out. Chase mutters to himself as I dart my eyes to the clock on my desk. I have a class in the engineering building that's about a ten-minute walk from here. I hate how time has gotten away from me this morning.

My finger subconsciously finds my favorite tattoo of Señora Bearington on my wrist, the sensation subduing me for a bit. A knock ensues, and I move to get up before Chase can, but he gets in front of me and I look at him in confusion. A giggle comes when he swings open the door, and I realize he won't be alone for much longer.

Yeah, time to go.

"Mhm, my roommate's about to leave—"

The door opens a bit more, and the redhead widens her eyes as she looks up at me. But her attention quickly returns to Chase, lust building in her gaze, and I resist the urge to gag.

Sliding past them, I make my way to class. When I got accepted into college, the original plan with my parents was to get an apartment. But because of my scholarship, I had to get a dorm room. So, I got paired with Chase—the school's golden child. His dad is on the board of directors, and apparently filthy rich. Of course, there was friction for our freshman year, but then after the horror stories I heard other guys going through, Chase didn't seem so bad, besides his persistence of wanting to be best friends.

He seems like a decent enough guy, and even offered a space I could use to study, as one of my classes is on the other side of campus. Honestly, I didn't want to accept any favors, but I eventually did since it was a shorter walk, and thankfully, he didn't make a big deal about it. It's a room in a house of the fraternity he's pledged to, and I am too by association, though I don't use it as much as he does.

Throwing open the doors to the lecture hall, seeing my usual seat empty, I quickly slide into it, beating the professor to his lecture. I do a quick scan of the space and sigh when someone plops down beside me. He opens his mouth as if to start talking, and I thank the heavens above when the professor and the TA walk in. Placing an earbud in, I start my playlist as the presentation pops up on the board.

I make a note to myself to star the information he points to as I tap my electronic pencil a couple times. Professor Baron winks dramatically to the crowd as we dive into his slides, most likely proving it will be final material.

Copying the diagram on the board, I try to drone out my unwanted thoughts with Tchaikovsky. His soft symphonies make me hyperfocus on everything the professor is teaching.

After what I thought was just a couple minutes, there is the unmistakable sound of everyone zipping up their backpacks, signaling class is over. I grab my own and walk out the door.

Once out, I walk across the street to the tattoo parlor, taking the closest shortcut. As I practically run toward the shop, my body screams blissful relief from the scorching sun outside when I enter. At the front desk, Taryn is there with her newly dyed hair, dark choice of clothing, and piercings littering her face.

"Hey, Liam," she says as she scrolls on her phone. I slightly raise my chin in acknowledgment while logging into the work computer to clock in. I see the little notification that tells me how long I've worked here, and my mouth turns up at how random it was for me to get this job.

I was an awkward freshman starting my career, but given I had some college courses under my belt, I was allowed to start on my electives. One of them being taught by my literal idol. I went to his office hours, and then, with one look at my tattoos, he offered me an internship for his tattoo parlor, and the rest is history. I thought I would be the youngest, but Tobias—the owner—has only hired college students thus far.

Taryn's sketching something on a sticky note, and I roll my eyes when Bobby throws a little paper ball at her.

"Heads up. Malibu Barbie incoming," she says, and I look at her, confused. The bell over the door jingles and I glance up, catching sight of a blonde woman with blue eyes.

Her gaze bounces around the tattoo examples on the walls. There's not a trace of ink on her skin, and I press my tongue against the side of my cheek in annoyance. Glancing over at Bobby and Luke, they shake their heads.

Sighing, I walk over to her reluctantly. "Can I help you?"

She gives me a once-over while biting her lip, and I mentally groan. "Yeah, I wanna get a tattoo."

"I figured as much. There are some designs out here and in my tattoo room, so tell me what you want and we'll get started," I say in my stern tone, starting to walk to my room as my coworkers watch me, covering their mouths as they try not to laugh.

Shaking my head, I disappear into my workspace, and after a bit, a knock ensues. She pops her head in and I wave her over.

"Um, I want this one," she says, and I look at the image on her phone. Stereotypically enough, it's a sunflower.

"Is this your first tattoo?" I ask as I walk to the edge of the room, and she nods shyly. "Alright. Well, here's the chart of where a tattoo hurts the most and least, so let me know where you want it." I look at the sketch. She picked Bobby's, so I can't copy it exactly, but I can put my spin on it.

"I want it on my forearm."

"Gotcha."

I hand her the paperwork. "So, this goes over all the basics." My pen hovers over a couple bullet points. "You understand that a tattoo is permanent, you agree that you're not under the influence of drugs or alcohol, you understand there's a chance of allergic reaction or infection. And there are the recommended guidelines on aftercare. Initial beside each item and sign and date the bottom, please." I gauge her reaction, trying to see any hesitance, but find none.

"Yeah, I'm well aware. I did my research before coming in."

My eyebrows raise and I back away to let her peruse the paperwork. Getting to the sketch, I begin working on it, and after a couple minutes, I show it to her.

"Wow, I really like it," she says, and I nod as I grab the clipboard from her, making sure everything is signed.

A small smile comes on my face as I glance down at the sketch again. I get to work prepping everything, including getting her situated in the chair. I place the stencil on her skin, and while it dries, I pack the tattoo machine and set up my workstation with color caps, green soap, and a brand-new outline needle. She sets her arm on the wide armrest. I look up at her. She nods, and I put the needle to her skin, ready to get to work, ready to distract myself from just about everything.

CHAPTER FOUR

Bianca

I NEVER KNEW HOW TRUE the expression "Get distracted enough and a lifetime will pass you by" was until one of the movers Josh hired reaches for a box I'm bringing down from my room upstairs. Smiling at him, he grabs it as others focus on moving our furniture, the place becoming emptier by the minute. At that, a guy makes his way out with an all-too-familiar photo album, and I stop in front of him.

"Can I see that, please?" He nods, and I grab it as he continues to carry everything else to the huge truck outside. I sit on the lone plastic-wrapped chair. The squeak rings out, drowning out Josh's shouts at them to be more careful.

Flipping to the last page, I'm met with Dad's freckled face, and I rub my thumb across each of the pictures. He's smiling in every single one, and I wish I could remember him more vividly, but it's been so long. Thumbing through, there's his and Mom's wedding day. He's looking at her, and you can see the immediate love in their eyes. There's a zoomed-in picture of her tired face and Dad's happy one with a little bundle in his arms.

Holding the book, I go back upstairs, being met with a bare room, and my heart constricts at the scene. The memories almost jump out from the walls, and I imagine another person making what once was my safe space theirs.

My eyes well as Jamie and I already said goodbye today since she couldn't be here on the actual day of the move. However, she did come by almost every day prior, helping me with the packing as well as keeping me company since Josh and Mom have been out of the house, jetting between here and LA.

He slapped a big for sale sign right in front of the house as soon as he could. The money that would come from either selling or renting would be a great investment for our future. *His words, not mine.*

Grabbing my backpack with all my essentials, I carry my old suitcase down the stairs. Mom and Josh are waiting for me at the front door. I look at the empty living room and an old memory overwhelms me:

"Grandma, what is it?"

She shrugged and laughed; my heart ached at how her and Dad's laughs sounded so similar.

"Please?" I pouted, and she rolled her eyes as she put her hands on her hips.

"Okay, you can open one gift. Just don't tell your mom." I nodded happily as she looked at Mom in the kitchen. After Grandma sent me a subtle thumbs-up, I giggled and moved to the Christmas tree.

A shaky breath escapes me and I turn around, the memory vanishing as I walk closer to the front door. Getting out, I twist the key and check to make sure it's locked. With one last deep breath, I walk away from a place that gave me such happy memories.

Once again.

I've got a headache bigger than I've ever had in my life. Josh's favorite pilot has his day off today, which means we've been sitting here while Josh argues with management. Though, it was the first time I've ever seen Mom roll her eyes at him, so that was pretty funny. Unfortunately, due to the maximum occupancy of the private airline lounge being at cap, we were moved to the public one right before security and Olivia has been blowing up all of their phones until Josh let her come hang with us "one last time."

She's holding on to Josh like it's the last time she'll see him while Mom sits next to them, consoling Olivia. I can't believe that today I leave Philly for good. This place became my home, and I don't want to leave. All the people I met here—well, the person I met who became such a big part of my life—is going to be left behind, and I can't bear it. I take a sip of my iced coffee and look up every time I hear something even close to my name or her voice. I hope that maybe Jamie will come, but with the way this place thoroughly vets the people allowed in, I sincerely doubt it.

Sighing at that, I look over at Mom and Josh at the desk talking to the airline employee once again, when they both cheer shortly after.

Olivia looks up from her phone as they make their way to us.

"What's going on?" I ask.

"Thankfully, we got sent his son, who is supposedly the *second-best* pilot. So, I guess he'll do," Josh reluctantly says, and Mom cups his face, giggling. He smiles. "Just want the best for my family." He leans over to kiss her, and I turn around to gag, while Olivia mirrors the expression.

"So, are we leaving soon?" I ask, and Mom wobbles her hand side to side in a so-so gesture. Making note of it, I turn on my music once more and close my eyes, drowning out life entirely.

As the songs begin fading into one another, I can subtly hear some hurrying footsteps, but I don't bother opening my eyes, chalking it up to the other passengers.

A rush of cold air hits my ears as my headphones are carefully taken off, and my eyes shoot open. Blinking to regulate my surroundings, a blurry figure is waving a hand in front of my face. "We have to get to boarding. The pilot's here," Mom says, and my eyes widen, realizing more time than I've thought has gone by.

Olivia's nowhere to be seen, and Josh and Mom are making their way to the gate. My heart deflates when I realize that this is it.

My eyes well with tears and I face away from her, grabbing my cord from the charging port. I make my way to the entrance, but as I'm going, I suddenly hear someone yelling.

"Bianca!"

Spinning, I don't see anyone calling me, and I laugh to myself, as I think I've officially gone insane. Shaking my head, I see Josh through the glass windows signaling me into the hallway. Making my way there, my steps stop when I clearly hear my name this time.

I turn around apprehensively and see a somewhat sweaty Jamie running toward me in her work uniform. I instantly put my backpack down, meeting her halfway. We collide in a hug, and my throat closes up slightly as tears well in my eyes.

"How?"

"Mama Kate added me to the vetted list. I asked her not to tell you in case I didn't make it." She pulls back, grabbing me by the shoulders. "Listen to me. You're my best friend and the only person to show me what true friendship is. You care about me more than my own family does." More tears rain down my face as she chuckles sadly. "We will *always* be best friends. No matter how far apart we are. And I swear, if you don't text and call me, I will buy a plane ticket to come strangle you." I laugh, her following along. "I'm gonna miss you so much."

"I will too, Jamie. You have no idea." I wipe my face and step back. "I actually have something for you. I was gonna give it to you earlier, but it didn't come in till this morning." I rummage around my backpack, and she holds up a rather large gift bag of her own.

"Great minds think alike," she replies, and I hand her the bag while she passes me hers. She looks at me and I nod, giving her permission to open it now. Reaching a hand in, she pulls out a light blue notebook and gel pens.

"I saw on your wish list you wanted them for studying at UPenn, so I . . ." I trail off, and a tear comes down her face as she hugs me tighter.

"You're the best, B." I hug her in response. I try to open the bag, but she pulls back, stopping me. "Do me a favor? Open it when I'm not here."

Nodding at that, I turn around as someone calls my name. Of course, Josh appears while tapping his watch, looking annoyed, causing me to roll my eyes while Jamie laughs.

"Is it wrong that I don't like that guy?"

I shake my head, giggling before muttering, "Bye, Jamie."

She puts her hand over her mouth, waving at me. "See you later, B."

Walking through security, I glance back one last time and see Jamie. She waves again, but I don't return it. Instead, I walk into the hall that leads to the cart that will drive us to the jet, having finally torn my eyes away from my heartbroken best friend.

Boarding the small plane, I'm greeted by the captain and the flight attendant, and I nod in response. The jet is what you would expect: all white leather seats, the brown lining contrasting. There's a coolness on my back as I sit next to the chilled bin filled with drinks. Mom and Josh sit comfortably on the sofa, champagne flutes in their hands as her legs rest on top of his. Bending slightly to get my journal, I turn in time to see Mom glancing back at me. I nod at her and she smiles, going back to talking with Josh while the gift bag opens up at my feet, tempting me. Multiple layers of decorative tissue paper later, I pull out a gorgeous dress.

I remember daydreaming with Jamie on the Dior website. There was a beautiful gown for twenty-five hundred dollars, and we joked that even selling our kidneys wouldn't cover it. I can't believe she went through all this trouble of recreating it. Looking at the detailing, I realize this must've taken her hours. I look back in the bag and see a card with my name on it. Tentatively, I open it.

Dear B,

If you're reading this, it means today is the day you leave Philly. I really wanted to give you something to remember me by, and ever since I saw your eyes light up at that Dior dress, I knew I had found my next project. Of course, I had no idea it would be your going-away gift, but I think it works out pretty well.

I hope you like it, and thank you for always being my biggest hype woman when it comes to following my dreams.

I love and will miss you so much,
Jamie

Folding up the letter, I clear my throat, trying not to get emotional, rubbing my thumb along the dress. It's an elegant emerald-green gown with minuscule glittering crystals. It's body hugging and strapless, and I fall in love with the soft, silky feel of it.

I mean, it's Jamie's creation. That girl is an absolute genius when it comes to this stuff. I hug it to my chest for a bit, then gently tuck it back into the bag. My journal rests on my leg, the words I've been wanting to write for days begging to be set free. The jet rumbles to life, incoherent gibberish coming through the speaker, causing me to laugh softly.

They say hope can either be your saving grace or downfall, but I hope it isn't my ruining.

I want to have hope again.

I'm going to California, and not just anywhere, but to Los Angeles. The place where I used to live. Where my ex-best friend might still live.

As always, the overthinking part of my brain starts to run as I worry about what to do with my life now that high school is over. I hate that my counselors were right and that I should've applied for safety schools. There's still time to apply to some community colleges if I really want to stay in Pennsylvania. Then, I could transfer to UPenn. It sounds like the perfect solution, and Jamie and I would finally get to do what we've been dreaming of for years. Or . . . I could just embrace that I'm moving back to California and apply to colleges there for the fall and either try to transfer to UPenn later or apply to universities there. I feel like I'm being pulled in two different directions, the right decision not seeming clear at all. As my mind wanders a bit, the hopeless romantic in me drowns out the student.

If I were to see Liam, how would he react? Would he be happy . . . or unbothered? I mean, there's a huge chance I might not ever see him, so there's that too.

And after that, my journal finally gets what it's been waiting for.

CHAPTER FIVE

Bianca

I JOSTLE AWAKE, THE RINGING in my ears still very much apparent even though I thought napping would help. I grip the armrests as the plane bounces slightly, the pain of squeezing making my head throb even harder. The flight attendant comes close to me, patting my shoulder slightly, and I smile at her kindness. Mom and Josh sit in the seats across from mine, a concerned look on her face, a questioning one on his, as a little ding echoes through the cabin.

"Callaway family, this is your captain speaking. We have now safely landed at Los Angeles International Airport in sunny Los Angeles, California. Please remain seated with your seat belts fastened until the aircraft comes to a complete stop. We wish you a pleasant day. Thank you."

I let the captain's comment slide about us being the Callaway family and focus on the fact that we're finally here.

Los Angeles, California: my hometown. The place where it all started.

After a couple of minutes, the signal for the seat belts turns off and we grab all our stuff. I wave goodbye to the captain and the nice flight attendant, making sure to leave as soon as possible when I overhear Josh mentioning he was going to talk to the captain about his overall performance.

Poor guy.

Locating my purple suitcase, I extend the handle, trying to hide my grin as Mom pulls Josh away from the captain while she apologizes profusely. I roll my shoulders and neck, feeling a satisfying pop, and walk to the rental car agencies inside the airport. I didn't think Los Angeles could get even more stereotypical or cliché than it already was. Yet, as far as the eye can see, there are people with bad fake tans, botched dye jobs, and knock-off brands of luggage.

While we wait for our car, some of the people throw looks my way. I roll my eyes at the superficiality. I exhaust myself on social media until the car finally arrives. Josh complains for a bit about how it wasn't the exact model he wanted while Mom tells him that at least we have some mode of transportation. Nerves come over me as I slide in the new car, but with deep breaths, I calm down. Josh sets up the GPS, a smile gracing his face as the new house I've yet to see is only forty minutes away, and I hide a laugh at that.

A multitude of horns blare at us and several groans come from Josh. That's right, the infamous Los Angeles traffic. We've left the airport, and our GPS is already racking up minutes like points in a video game.

"Are you serious? This added a whole hour to our ETA." Mom rubs her hand on his arm, and he sighs as he puts the car in park since no one seems to be moving. I look back to my message thread with Jamie, a giant heart bouncing on my screen. I smile at that sense of normalcy, even if I'm still freaking out. Looking out the window at the fancy cars, the huge skyscrapers . . . I'm filled with something I've missed. This sense of nostalgia. Thankfully, we make it out of the heart of LA, taking the back roads to the suburbs.

I roll my eyes as we turn right into what looks like an expensive community. There's a bright sign that reads Crystal Pines scrawled in big cursive letters. A man wearing a bulletproof vest, taller than anyone I've seen, instructs Josh to roll down his window, and I take out an earbud. He and Mom pass over their IDs, and he takes them, giving them a curt nod in appreciation.

The guard leaves while Josh murmurs, "I hope this isn't how it'll be every time we come home."

The tall security guard comes back and flashes a tight smile. "You weren't in the system. You should be fine now, Mr. Callaway, and I've added you as a resident as well."

Mom smiles at the guard. "Thank you." Something crosses his face too fast for me to perceive. His mouth even quirks up on the side before it rapidly drops. He taps the window's weatherstripping twice to signal we're good to go as the gates open. Josh zooms in while Mom turns around and squeals quietly. We pass by more and more houses until we get to a nice cul-de-sac where Josh slows down in front of one on the right.

Opening the car door, I look up at the two-story home. There are more windows than I can count, each framed with black shutters. The door looks like it weighs a hundred pounds, the light brown going well with the house's features. My jaw drops and Mom moves next to me, closing my mouth and snickering slightly. I mean, I knew that the company gave him a stipend and that he would pick the nicest house . . .

I just didn't think it would be *this* nice.

Josh stands next to Mom, and she looks up at him, a dreamy expression on her face. He stares at the house with pride. "Beautiful." They walk toward it while I trail behind. It's wild how much the company covered for us to even get this house on such short notice. Obviously, Josh and Mom pooled money together for the closing costs, but still, the place is massive. I look at the other houses around us.

My heart stills when I see a familiar-colored Jeep parked in the driveway across from our new home. The childhood memories with that car bombard my mind. Liam and me in the back seat while his mom, Ana, would drive us to and fro.

No, it can't be. Someone else must've had their car painted that color. Fuchsia is pretty common, isn't it?

Dread fills my footsteps, and I can't stop myself from looking back and remembering that same shade. She couldn't be here. They already have a house in another part of town. I sigh to myself, thinking the jet lag is getting to me, and wrap my arm around Mom's shoulders.

As soon as we walk in, my jaw drops once again. There are three chandeliers in the main hallway and an elegant, clear-glass stairway with a huge space that I assume is the living room.

Wow, Jamie would love this.

My heart deflates at the thought, and I'm slightly emotional again. But for some reason, I have this feeling that this time it'll be different. I mean, we're both adults, so we're more than capable of visiting each other. It's just weird not having her close by; now it's more like two thousand miles.

"Amazing, isn't it?" Josh says. "Our stuff will be here next week, but I'm gonna go buy some pullout couches and other things in the meantime. You guys need anything specific, Kate?"

Mom shakes her head and he glances at me. I shake my head too and he walks off, swinging his keys around his pointer finger. Curiosity getting the better of me, I start to walk down the halls while Mom goes outside, probably to get the luggage we left in the car. Back home, my room was upstairs, but now I want to switch it up. Looking around, I find there's only one bedroom on the first floor, down the hall. It's huge, displaying a large window and an expansive view of the neighborhood. It also has a sliding door which seems to lead to the backyard that has direct access to the pool and jacuzzi.

Midnight swims, here I come.

Deciding on this room, I imagine all my furniture, and I can almost see how I'm going to decorate. I start to get a little excited, but I almost feel guilty for that. I didn't want to leave Philly, or Jamie, behind, especially knowing she doesn't have many people besides me and some of her coworkers she's closer with. Thing is, there was nothing left for me in Philly. Granted, we could've moved anywhere in America, but maybe it's a sign that I need to be here right now.

I'm not that gullible little girl anymore. I've grown and I know how crappy it feels when someone forgets about you. So, I'm going to do better with Jamie. Even if she stops talking to me, I'll try and try until I know I've given it my all. Sighing, I walk back out, finding Mom still looking at the house in what looks like awe.

"You okay, Mom?" Hugging her from the back, she melts into me and gives me a slight squeeze.

"Yeah, just happy." She turns, looking at me. "For the longest time, I thought it was gonna be just you and me, but with Josh, I can really see myself being happy with him." Her eyes fill more and more as she talks about Josh, and I smile at seeing how joyful she looks. Her phone buzzes after a bit, and we both giggle when Josh sends pictures of two weird-looking futons. "I'm gonna be upstairs on the phone." She turns around before looking back. "Anything you need, let me know, okay, honey?"

Nodding, I go to the foyer—cannot believe I'm saying that—and grab my suitcase.

Unpacking back in my room, I rummage around for some things. Pulling out my bathing suit and speaker, I open the door to go relax in the hot tub.

I soak for a couple of hours as I let myself decompress from everything: leaving Philly and my best friend, moving to Los Angeles, potentially seeing Liam, and that strange moment when I saw that weirdly colored Jeep. So much has happened today, and all I want is to have some time to myself to reorganize my thoughts.

Maybe, just maybe, it'll give me some peace of mind.

My muscles lose their tension and I sigh in relief right before a door slams, and my body clenches again. I sigh as both Josh's and Mom's voices become increasingly louder. I hope with all my might that nobody will come and disturb me, but when has the universe ever respected what I want?

"Kate's calling you."

I turn back to see Josh look at me, then scroll on his phone as he opens the door.

"Got it, thanks," I mutter, turning back around to see the sun starting to set, the blue sky now covered in lovely hues of red and orange. I dry off my hands to take a picture of it, but then frown as my phone gets snatched from me.

"Now, Bianca." Josh holds my phone out of reach and I look at him, appalled at his behavior. I stand my ground and knock his arm slightly. His hand lands on the railing and he flinches. My eyes widen when I see a small cut on his finger, crimson-red liquid oozing out.

"Dad, Dad. Wake up," I said frantically, but the gash on his head kept oozing blood. I whimpered and looked up at the lady, begging for her to help him. Tears welled in her eyes, but she didn't respond.

As they carried him, the lights hit his wounds in a way that I really noticed all of the blood. I had no idea why underneath the lights, the blood on him scared me so much.

It was like I finally realized what it was, and I hated it.

I glanced down at myself and saw all the bloody wounds, which caused me to freak out. I started to move around as they tried to calm me down. I tried to get the blood off me—scratched at it, even—but all it did was smear . . .

"What is wrong with you?"

I blink rapidly, coming back to reality as Josh shakes me. Mom becomes clearer as she stands next to him with tears in her eyes.

"Bianca, breathe," she says, and I look at her, still somewhat afloat in my own body. Josh has an unreadable look on his face. Her hands are placed on me gently, and I concentrate on the scent of her perfume, breathing in and out.

Inhale.

Exhale.

"I'm okay." My voice is hoarse as if I had been screaming for hours, and Mom hugs me instantly.

"Kate, why was she freaking out over a small cut?" Josh asks while I look down, ashamed.

Mom turns around and looks at him exasperatedly. "There's a reason for it, I promise."

"A serious injury I understand, but this?" He raises his bloody finger and I stiffen. He looks at me, almost disgusted, and I shrink back; he's *never* looked at me like that. He glances toward Mom. "You need to stop coddling her, Kate." The goose bumps on my swimsuit-clad body become more apparent, the coldness from him incomparable to the slight breeze.

He throws down my phone on the table. It lands with a sharp clatter. Mom looks at him, shocked. "Josh, hon." She reaches for him, but he steps back, taking a deep breath. He walks off without another word. Mom sighs and turns back around as she passes me a towel. "The move has been stressful, and I haven't told him about your phobia. He didn't mean it that way." I nod—more so in embarrassment—and walk back into my room. I take a quick shower, then slip into pajamas. Lying down, my eyes well slightly.

What is wrong with you?

She's an adult.

Pathetic.

Pathetic.

Pathetic.

My heart stutters as the words echo, looping around in my head. Josh has never gotten that upset before. Shame comes over me at that, and I wipe away a rogue tear.

My phone buzzes next to me and I look at it. Something of a smile forms on my face.

I'm glad you got there safely, B! Call me when you get a chance. Preferably at the beach . . . on a video call . . . with your camera flipped so I can see the fineeee California men.

I turn my phone off and get up, opening my blinds, even though it's a bit dark outside. Streetlights illuminate everything and the purple-colored Jeep is still in the driveway across the street.

I bite my lip as hundreds of thoughts run through my mind. Should I go over there and see if it's them? I mean, it might not be, and instead I'll make a fool of myself. Maybe I'm making a big deal out of nothing. Crashing against my sleeping bag, rubbing my temples a bit, my phone buzzes. I smile and answer the video call.

"Hello?"

"Couldn't wait till you were at the beach." Her silliness causes me to let out a low chuckle. "Anyway, how are you?" she asks excitedly, and I momentarily forget all the stuff I was thinking about.

"Well, the house is unnecessarily huge and high-class, but it makes sense since Josh picked it—"

She interrupts me. "No, girl, I asked how *you* are. Not the house."

My heart stutters. She looks at me, waiting as emotions jumble in my throat. "Good," I squeak out before clearing my throat and repeating the word as she looks at me doubtfully. Previous events gather in my thoughts and Josh's words circle in my head. "I had another panic attack today," I mutter, and Jamie has concern crossing her features, the want to comfort me apparent in her eyes. "But I'm okay, honest. Freaked over some blood, nothing new."

She sees right through me and shakes her head.

I over explain, I over apologize for things that aren't my fault, I downplay my fears for the benefit of others, always.

She crosses her arms, setting the phone on top of her desk, little Whiskers climbing on his cardboard post behind her.

"B, it's alright if you aren't. Can I know what happened?"

I sigh, realizing my downplaying tactic didn't work. It never does, yet I never stop.

Everything spills out of me even though I don't want to burden her with it. The plane ride, the move, the incident with Josh. Her cheeks turn red and her eyebrows scrunch, causing me to look at her in confusion.

"Bianca, that wasn't right for him to say. It was an accident." She runs her hand through her hair.

"He doesn't know. Besides, it's not like he was yelling or something."

She shakes her head again. "Doesn't matter. And you better not feel ashamed about it. It wasn't your fault, okay?"

I nod, not wanting to confess that I was feeling just that. Silence fills the room and I can't even bear to look at her face.

"I love Mama Kate, but if he's saying these things—"

I wave her off. "It was this one time. I get it. It must've freaked him out."

She sighs and looks as if she wants to argue. "Fine, but if that becomes the new norm . . ." She trails off and I nod.

I run my hands through my hair, my scalp feeling my emotions as I tug and pull with my fingers. She looks at me, running her hands down her face, the helplessness transmitting through the phone.

"Talk about something else?" I ask.

Jamie looks as if she wants to keep talking about the situation, but switches topics for my sake.

CHAPTER SIX

Bianca

"I NEED YOU TO SIGN here." The movers pass the clipboard to Josh as they load our bubble-wrapped things into the new house. Mom puts her hands on Josh's shoulders, a smile on her face.

A grin finds its way to mine too, seeing her happy, knowing she deserves it—even if it's with someone whom I don't particularly like. Turning to the house once again, I'm starting to feel like I'm losing my mind.

It's been a week since we moved from Philly, and time has sped by. Yet, since that first day, the fuchsia-colored Jeep is nowhere to be seen. I've become stalkerish at this point, checking almost every day to see if it's parked in the driveway, but nothing comes of it. I made it up—I must've—and while it gives me some sense of relief . . .

I also feel disappointed, and I hate that I do.

Liam distanced himself from *me*. He didn't want anything to do with me. He had football and new friends—I wasn't needed anymore. And here I am, still wishing that car I saw was Ana's.

A squeal pulls me out of my mental daze. Mom is jumping into Josh's arms, him holding onto her tightly as another huge truck with a famous furniture store's logo printed on the side parks in

55

front of the house. Josh had told Mom he wanted to be the sole breadwinner—his words, not mine—and so she turned her focus from finding work to finding decorations for our new home. My eyes widen when the delivery drivers come out of the back with a wrapped table. Mom looks at me, waving me over, and I walk toward them.

"Bianca! It's the table I was looking at earlier." She glances between all of us. Mom hates conflict, actively seeks to avoid it, and right now, she's hoping everything is all good between Josh and me. He stares at me, and I nod, giving them both a small smile.

"Yeah, I bet it's really nice," I mumble. They head back inside and I trail behind them. I treacherously look across the street once again, but find nothing.

I walk into five or more people in the living room putting things in place for us. Entering my room, my eyes widen at the violet upholstered bed frame. Someone mutters an apology as they slip past while holding matching nightstands with glass handles. My mouth parts, words never making it out. Seeing it's starting to get crowded, I move out of the way, heading back to the living room.

I throw open the French doors leading into the kitchen, catching Mom bringing out some leftovers from yesterday. She waves me over and we sit on our beach chairs we dragged in from outside while the furniture people work on taking the bubble wrap off the new oak table.

I grab the container of noodles and look up to see Mom looking back at me with a little smile. "So, how are you liking your room so far?"

"I like it, I do, and I'm not trying to be ungrateful, but I don't know." I put my fork down, a sheepish expression coming over me. "Don't you think this is all a little much? I mean, my room—"

"That would be my doing." My head snaps up as Josh slips into a chair next to Mom, a heat of embarrassment sweeping over me. "I realize I may not have handled the incident very well the other day, so I wanted to make it up to you." I look at him hesitantly. "Kate told me you've always wanted a dark purple bedroom set, and that you felt like you outgrew your older stuff . . ." He trails off and I genuinely don't know what to say. "We're all good, then?"

My eyes slide to Mom before a pleading expression comes over her. It doesn't surprise me that this is Josh's way of apologizing, and he didn't inherently react as poorly as I thought he would.

I sigh and nod and give him a small smile. "Thanks." His chin lowers and his mood seems to improve as he grabs Mom's hand while he eats.

"Sir, I have a glass dresser for a bedroom. Would that be upstairs or—" My eyes flick upward as Josh holds up a hand. The mover— Larry, from his name tag—shuts his mouth, a smart remark on the tip of his tongue, by the looks of it.

And man, I wish he would say it.

"Upstairs." Josh answers.

Larry closes his eyes and breathes deeply as if summoning patience. Nodding, he goes over to help the others bring it upstairs.

"Some people, huh?" Josh remarks as if we'll nod along to the statement, and my face contorts in shock.

Pressing the heels of my hands to my eyes, I ask, "Can I please be excused?" But I don't stay to hear their answer before heading to my room.

After a couple hours, I press a pushpin into the last photo. A smile blooms on my face at the finished result. Jamie's and my funny faces from all our years of friendship stare back, and warmth comes over me. Walking over to my desk, I place the corkboard right above so that I can always see it, our bucket list jumping out at me with the little notes in the margins.

It's been a while since the movers left, and I can still hear Josh and Mom organizing their stuff upstairs. Their feet make hushed sounds right above my room, and I hope that won't be a problem later down the line. Decorating has taken up most of my day, being almost therapeutic, but I'm probably going to rearrange my space a couple more times.

Though, in all honesty, I've appreciated the distraction as the words from an earlier email have yet to stop spinning in my head.

Dear Bianca Harrison,

We wanted to confirm your interest in Mella Colta University for the autumn semester!

When I was applying for colleges last year, we were given a limit of ten schools since our school provided application vouchers. In the end, I only had nine options, and so for fun, I applied to Mella Colta. Honestly, being denied from everywhere else, I was fully expecting a rejection letter from MC too, but they were my one "yes." But what with my classes, graduation, the move, and everything in between, I didn't give them an answer. As I panicked a little more about my future, the need to attend Mella Colta grew, so I emailed admissions, asking—no, begging—for them to please keep a spot open for me. I assumed it was a long shot, that I'd never hear back from them. Then, this email arrived. I guess this is my second chance. Touring dates are coming soon, and from what I've researched, they tend to fill up fast. But now that my acceptance is here again, I suddenly don't know if I'll actually go.

A knock interrupts my plummeting thoughts, and I make a vague welcoming noise. Mom pops her head in as she brings me a bottle of soda with a glass of ice. She holds them up as peace offerings and I take them from her with gusto. She looks around, placing her hands in her back pockets. "It's looking good in here." I nod as I pour the yellow soda into the cup. Mom's eyes are sunken slightly, tiredness surrounding them. She's covered in dust and sweat beads along her hairline. "Honey, I know Josh has his quirks . . ." I roll my eyes at her lack of a better word. "But he really is sorry about the accident, and he's been under a lot of stress with the move and—"

"Mom, look. Josh made a mistake, it was my fault, I freaked out, we're all good." She opens and then closes her mouth quickly. She sighs, looking down at the floor, her foot nudging my rug a bit.

"I'm not saying that either, Bianca." She takes a deep breath. "I'm sorry you were triggered, honey. I know where your mind goes, but I also hope that you don't think I'm not on your side of things."

My shoulders fold inward, and I realize how harsh I'm being to her, when in reality, Josh has already apologized. I suck in a shaky breath while guiding her into a gentle hug. She stands stunned for a bit before she wraps her arms around me.

"I know, Mom."

Her comforting aroma envelops me, and I breathe her in, calming down. "I love you, Bianca."

I smile. "Me too."

There's a *thud* upstairs and we pull apart.

"Can you believe he's never decorated a room before?" she remarks.

I chuckle. "Doesn't surprise me. It's *Josh*." She glares at me and I lift my hands in surrender before she places a gentle kiss on my forehead, temporarily shushing the thoughts of my future.

I caved.

It's three in the morning and I'm on the Mella Colta website. I've scoured every club, searched every photo of the campus, and even done the virtual tour. Yet here I am hesitating on two blue buttons—one to schedule my future student orientation, or one to schedule a visitor tour.

I mean, I've never been to campus, and I've seen enough how-to college videos, and they all say to see the campus before enrolling. But I know myself—it's a cop-out. I want to go on the tour, then convince myself the whole time that I hate it. In reality, I've loved this campus ever since I can remember.

It was his and my dream college, but he probably doesn't remember that.

Going on campus as a visitor has no permanent ties; for all they know, I was denied from the school. But orientation means I commit . . . It means that I'm going to be a future student there.

I hover over both buttons as my heart seems to lead almost every decision I make. With the night sky and the constellations as my only witnesses, I accept enrollment to Mella Colta, and schedule my orientation for this weekend.

"I was accepted into a college's advanced animal science program, and I have orientation in four days." The words blurt out, and for a moment, I fear Mom and Josh don't hear me. Risking a look, they wear shocked expressions and her cutlery clatters against her plate. "It's in San Jose, by the way," I mutter even as silence envelops the dining room, and their jaws drop that much more.

"Is it Mella Colta?" Mom asks, hinting at the university she's heard about since I was a kid. I nod in agreement as she lets out a scream of happiness. Jumping up, she comes around to hug me tightly as Josh remains seated, and she shakes me slightly. "Honey! This is so great! See, I told you, rejection is merely redirection."

I can barely hear her over her slight screams in between words, and I chuckle at that, patting her back. I glance over at Josh as he straightens his tie and Mom pulls back, zeroing in on him.

"I wished you would've told us earlier, but congrats anyway." I look up while Josh doubles down. "I mean, how were you planning on getting there?" I open my mouth, but come up with nothing. I was so nervous about telling them, especially since our move here hasn't been entirely smooth. He grabs his phone, looking over his calendar. "We're supposed to have dinner as a family in Santa Clara with a business prospect. Thankfully, it's not too far."

I nod. "Oh. Well, you guys can drop me off and you two go—"

He shakes his head, cutting me off. "We'll be attending both orientation and the business dinner together. Many of my supervisors' children go to that university. Can't have them believe we let you go alone." He flits his eyes to mine. "That won't be a problem, will it?"

An innocent question, but again, there's something sharp buried underneath. I catch Mom's eyes, but she's just looking at me curiously.

"Of course not."

He smiles, no traces of the emotion he hides in the pools of his brown eyes. "Then, it's settled. Send the details to your mother and she'll give them to me." Mom squeals and grabs both Josh's and my hands. I let that bit of excitement reignite mine as I think about my brightening future.

CHAPTER SEVEN

Bianca

"SO, MOM, I HAVE A QUESTION."

She shifts in the driver's seat, simultaneously fixing the rearview mirror. The back seats are filled with our weekend luggage and Josh. He's got his arms crossed and a hat covering his face, resting. I turn toward her, and Mom looks at me for a bit before returning her eyes to the road.

"Yes?"

"Hypothetically, if Ana reappeared in your life—or if she found your new number and called you—what would your reaction be?"

A rustle sounds behind us, but I think nothing of it. Her head snaps in my direction. "Well, I'd be surprised, but I wouldn't mind talking to her again. Our relationship did end rather awkwardly considering it petered out due to you and . . ." She doesn't finish, and I don't rush to correct her.

Another rustle, and I look back, but just see Josh in a different position.

"So, what would your reaction be if I told you that I saw a fuchsia-colored Jeep in our neighborhood? Hypothetically, of course," I add the last bit, but it seems she's starting to realize that I'm not speaking in hypotheticals.

"I would be surprised, but you saw Ana's car? Where?" she asks, and I admire how quick she is to believe me.

"When we moved in, the house across the street had it in their driveway. I've been racking my brain. Ana and William already have a house," I say, and she nods. Her lips twist from side to side as they normally do when she's thinking. "But I haven't seen it since."

She sighs, laying her head slightly on her fist as she keeps the steering wheel steady with her right hand. "Why haven't you said anything?"

I shrug. "Like I said, I haven't seen it since the first day."

Her head then snaps a bit in my direction before she widens her eyes in realization. "Wait. If they were living over there, that could mean . . ."

I nod and say the sentence that's been secretly killing me inside. "There's a possibility that Liam does too."

Mom puts her hand on mine and I look out the window, trying to keep my feelings at bay. It's been five years, and I've realized that even if I did talk to them, what would it matter? They probably want nothing to do with us . . . with me.

Sighing at the thought again, I contemplate maybe leaving the topic alone. Deep down inside, while I do want to see them again, the reason I've danced around the idea is the chance of seeing him too.

Maybe he missed me, maybe it was all a misunderstanding?

I haven't thought about him so much, but once in a while, I get buried under our memories. Then, we moved back to Los Angeles and I was seeing places we would frequent. My heart wants him back in my life, but I hate that I hurt myself like this. I wish I could forget him, but I just can't.

His beautiful smile, his reassuring words that made me feel so special, and those eyes. Those forest-green eyes that captivated me with this special sparkle—it was like they told a story.

One that involved us staying friends forever, or even maybe one day becoming more.

"There it is." I look where Mom's pointing and a smile starts on my face at the university signs and humongous buildings. We keep driving, following the other cars most likely heading to the parking garage. My heart beats faster with childlike wonder as I watch all the students walking around.

Once we've parked, I jump out, Josh and Mom following suit. He takes out my duffel bag while I swing my backpack on. I look at my emails in search of the one regarding Mella Colta orientation. Mom brushes something off Josh's jacket, her pantsuit matching his. "So, where are we headed?"

"According to the email, it says the MCSU?" I reread to make sure I had it right, and then look at her exasperatedly.

"How are we supposed to know what that is?" Josh asks.

I rub my forehead before Mom playfully knocks me with her hip. "All the more reason to go exploring, we're forty-five minutes early."

She glances at Josh as he pinches the bridge of his nose and rolls his eyes. They follow me as I walk onto campus somewhat reluctantly. Finally, seeing a tent with "Information & Help" printed across it, I practically sprint there.

"Hi!" A woman with "Vanessa" printed on her name tag glances up at me while the other person barely looks my way.

"Hi, um, I'm here for ori—"

She hands me an information packet. "Orientation, yes, we have a lot of you guys today. So, what you're gonna do is head toward that huge student union building right near the hawk fountain. Trust me, you can't miss it." She smiles brightly, and I sigh in relief, giving her a thank you while dragging Mom away from being flirted with by a student, Josh glaring at the cocky kid.

I weave between a bunch of families who look as confused as we are. Mom and Josh scrunch their noses we start our journey to what I now know is the student union. Knocking into something— or rather, someone—the papers in my hand go flying.

I bend down as I say, "Sorry—didn't mean to bump into you."

His arm is outstretched and my eyes catch the tattoos that litter from his fingers all the way up. He bends down too, and a tingly feeling starts. But before I can discern what it is, I hear a low, "No problem," as he hands me the papers and disappears into the crowd. Goose bumps cover my arms and I raise my head, trying to see if I can spot the stranger. Coming up short, I sigh as my name is called. My head snaps toward the voice, and Josh and Mom are farther ahead. They wave at me, and I squeeze between people to reach them.

Mom places her hands on my shoulders. "Honey, you need to stay close."

I nod, rubbing a hand over my arms as the goose bumps still remain. As we walk with the crowd, more people with the university's logo on their shirts appear, and it causes a breath of relief. We receive wristbands to wear and find seats closer to the front—Josh's orders—causing me to look up at the crowded stage. I hear a *psst* sound as Josh mutters, "Sit up straight, stop slouching." Mom shrugs sheepishly.

The thing people don't tell you about school orientation is that they go on for hours and hours about absolutely nothing. A quick scan around and almost every single kid is on their phone while their parents write down everything. I sigh deeply, my head leaning on Mom's shoulder. She moves to grab my hand in hers in a comforting gesture, and I smile at that.

A hushed whisper comes from her. "These things drone on, don't they?" A low chuckle erupts from me, but Josh is shooting daggers, sitting perfectly proper. I nod in response against Mom's shoulder when another person comes on the stage, signaling that it's time to separate.

Mom shoos me toward my orientation leader, and I see Vanessa and a guy chatting away with someone else. "Hi, again! Are you part of the Red Hawk group?" Before I can even say anything, she grabs the paper from me and scans it intently, a smile coming on her face. "Ooh, you'll be living in Juniper Hall, so we're also temporary roommates for tonight too. Let's go!" She squeals excitedly and a sense of relief washes over me. She then grabs my hand and brings me over to the other leader, and my eyes widen as to what she might do. "Hey, Chase!"

The guy, Chase, has this popular jock thing about him as he turns around after clasping hands with someone.

"This is my new bestie—" She waits for me to fill in the blank, but I don't.

Why is he looking at me like that?

He scans me up and down, staying on my face a little longer than normal, but then snaps out of it.

"Bianca Harrison," I finally say, and he nods somewhat before shaking his head in disbelief.

He sticks out a hand with a small smile. "Have we ever met before?" I look between them before shaking my head. He sticks his hands in his pockets, and his actions seem almost shy. "I'm sorry, probably confusing you with someone else."

I nod at that and Vanessa squeals again, then Chase turns around to announce the tour is about to begin. She links her arm with mine and I'm proud that I've already found someone on this huge campus. They take the scenic route, and I act like I haven't memorized the map. After a couple hours, we stop at the dining hall, and I pile the "good" food on my plate. I scan around for any open tables when Vanessa and Chase wave me over to theirs.

I look over my shoulder, but they laugh before they point at me and wave me over once again. I rush to them, thankful I won't be sitting alone. The cold plastic sticks to the bottom of my thighs and I hiss under my breath, but I mask it with a smile.

"So, how you liking MC?" Chase dips his fries in ketchup as Vanessa smiles over at me for a bit before turning around in her seat to talk to somebody else behind her.

"It's really nice, fancier than I thought." I look down, drizzling the Caesar dressing on my salad, and he chuckles.

"Glad to hear it. So, I know it's been asked all day, but what major are you?"

"Animal science with a minor in astronomy." His eyebrows shoot up and I roll my eyes slightly. "Were you expecting something else?"

He chuckles softly again, giving me a look with his blue eyes. "See, this is me not falling for that, but you're the first person I've met with that major."

"What about you?" I counter, and he sighs deeply, running a hand through his blond strands.

"Aerospace engineering."

I nod. Engineering is definitely one of the harder majors out there. "How's that going?"

"I have two years left, and one of my professors is screwing us with the latest homework, but I guess I can't complain." I go back to eating when Vanessa turns around with a smirk.

"So, roomie, are you wanting to go to the little party tonight?" she asks, and I take a quick glance at Chase, seeing him regarding her with cool detachment. I look back at Vanessa's excited face and grimace at the question. I've never been to a party, much less a college one. "It'll be fun, that's where all the hot guys on campus are." Her smile is wide and Chase rolls his eyes.

"Well, I was planning to find out about some astronomy clubs. Plus, I don't really—"

She waves me off. "C'mon, you're in college now. Besides, there's this guy that I hooked up with a couple years ago who'll be there for sure. So, come on, be my wingwoman?"

Chase exhales sharply through his nose as the other girls she was talking to turn around and smile at me, all of them waiting for a response.

The peer pressure begins.

"It's a freshmen get-together at a frat, you should be okay," Chase speaks up. Vanessa looks back at me and I nod somewhat reluctantly. He stands. "Alright, guys, let's start to head out." We pack up our things and form a circle as we return to the tour. Leaving the dining hall, the parents walk in, and I quickly wave to Mom before seeing Josh surrounded by a bunch of stuffy-looking dads. Of course, he's already found the other social elites.

Building after building, I can feel it. This is where I'm meant to be. This has been my dream school for as long as I can remember. Liam and I both loved it, him for this place having his idol as a professor, and me for it having the largest planetarium in the whole state. There's some sort of parade going on, and we sit in the quad, watching it go by. I look around, picturing myself sitting under one of the oak trees doing my homework. Maybe even coming out at night and doing some stargazing.

"Okay, you have everything, right?"

Looking back at Mom, I say, "Yes, I'm all good, I promise."

She nods at that and looks toward the other kids checking into their overnight rooms, a wistful look on her face. "Alright, I guess this is it."

I hug her tightly, even though I'll be seeing her tomorrow afternoon, given that this is orientation and not me starting the fall semester yet.

"I'll behave, and I lov—" Josh's phone's ring cuts me off, and he answers with his lawyer tone. He nods curtly at me as he drags Mom away, and I wave at her. Shaking my head, I swing my duffel bag onto my shoulder, walking into the room and finding Vanessa smiling brightly.

"Hey! Welcome to my dorm room. That whole side over there is yours." I look around, trying to control my facial expressions at the pink splattered everywhere. Everything is either fluffy or bedazzled, and I get a good look at the Hello Kitty poster I'll be staring at tonight. Putting my bag on the small bed, I turn right when two dresses are thrust into my face.

"Red or silver?" She switches both of them so fast, I can't even tell which one will look good. Blindly pointing toward the red one, she holds it up a bit more and nods. She returns to the closet and comes back with a bunch of dresses that she throws on my bed.

"Don't think I forgot about you coming with me." I look up, ready to protest, but she holds up a hand. "You already said you would." I look at the options, knowing half of these are going to ride up, considering she's way shorter than I am. She then starts to hold some options in front of me with a pensive expression on her face, and I look at her in confusion. She's obviously popular or whatever it's called in college. She seems really nice, yet the way Chase was looking at her made me feel a bit uneasy. I mean, I just met both of them, and I believe in forming your own opinion.

She shrieks, taking me out of my thoughts, as she settles on a short navy dress with little sequins along the sweetheart neckline. A small groan comes out of me, but I shut up as she goes back into her closet. She comes back out with shoes that are surprisingly my size.

"I'm short, but have big feet. Hated them till now." I look at her in exasperation because she's too nice, and skepticism flows through me. Looking over at the clock, the party doesn't start for hours, but I already feel the need to throw up or have a panic attack. She smiles as I put the outfit together, and as much as I wanted to hate it . . .

I look nice. I look beautiful.

Vanessa tightens her grip as we stand in front of the very crowded fraternity house.

"Bianca, come on." My heart beats rapidly against my ribs as I look at the two-story house in fear. I thought this would be a small party, but from the outside, it looks like the whole school is here. "Hey, it's gonna be okay. You're nervous. I was too." I nod somewhat absentmindedly. Some of Vanessa's friends come over, and I shake their hands, but I'm in a daze.

What am I doing here?

"Harrison, you made it!" An arm wraps around my shoulders and I flinch slightly. Chase's hand drops to his side instantly, and

I look up at him as he flashes a reassuring smile. "Just me, sorry to scare you." I sigh in relief and wave him off as Vanessa chats with a bunch of other people. "You look nice." I roll my eyes at his compliment and he chuckles.

Vanessa then loops her arms around mine and drags me into the house as I look at him pleadingly. He shrugs, smirking a little, and I'm visibly shocked at his refusal to help me. She brings me to the middle of the dance floor, and I'm bombarded with the smell of sweat and the aroma of different alcohols. The song changes to one where everyone starts to line dance, and I freeze once again.

One second, I'm fine, and the next—my dress is too short and my shoes are starting to make my feet ache. The closeness of these other random people causes my anxiety to spike. The world's spinning faster than usual, and people start to resemble glowing blobs. My breaths go in and out, and the *whoosh* echoes in my head. I stumble toward the counter where a rainbow of different liquors stare up at me.

I turn them all until I finally find one that says sparkling water. The bubbles in it cause me to gag, but at least it's something. I walk away, swaying slightly, trying to gain my balance, letting the fizz tickle my taste buds. Following the chorus of thank-yous, and excuse-mes, I push through a double set of doors, hoping it leads somewhere quiet.

Success! Thank goodness.

Closing the doors behind me, I practically run to the small bench on the balcony, sipping the rest of the sparkling water, taking deep breaths. The muffled sounds of voices and music hum around me, but I manage to block it out.

"You alright?"

I flinch from the deep voice and stand a little too fast. I almost fall—my ankle rolling to the side—but not before someone grabs my hand, pulling me back up to a solid chest. I pant a bit, recognizing the tattoos I saw earlier, causing me to look up, goose bumps littering my skin.

"You," I mutter, and he looks at me in confusion. He glances down at how close we are before backing away to a respectable distance, but the warmth from his body leaving causes a shiver to run through me. "Are you following me?" A side of his mouth tics up for a millisecond at the insinuation before it goes right back down into a thin smile.

He waves his finger in the air. "My roommate is in this frat."

A blush of embarrassment zings through me, and I pop my foot, my ankle still positively throbbing.

"Oh." The one word rings out, and while there are people talking and laughing inside, out here, it's dead silent. I glance up at him once more, trying to figure out what's wrong with me. I mean, I would remember if I ever knew someone that looked like him. Yet, this doesn't feel like basic recognition, it feels deeper . . . Almost like when your heart knows and your mind is trying to catch up. "Have we ever met?" I ask, and he pushes off the wall he was leaning against. The light hits him, making his tattoos more prominent. He glances at me without a word, and surprisingly, given his aloofness, tilts his head slightly.

"Earlier, when you bumped into me."

I roll my eyes. "I meant besides that." A small smile ends before it can fully form, and I look at him, familiarity coursing through me. His eyes are the greenest I've ever seen; they're like a painter's canvas when drawing grassy landscapes. Sage green swirls around his irises, forest green poking through as well. I start to connect the dots between his familiar features before I gasp, shocked.

Of course, even with all the people here, I bump into *him*.

CHAPTER EIGHT

Liam

AS MUCH AS I HATE to admit it, this girl has made me almost smile twice, and I want to know what spell she's got me under. She's looking at me, and even though I don't want to . . .

I shamelessly stare back.

"Liam! Been looking all over—" Chase's voice rings out into what was previously a quiet space, and her expression deepens. I grimace as he shoots me a smirk, but my attention gets sucked back to her as she runs her eyes up and down the length of me.

Under her scrutiny, my skin warms, and for the first time in a long time, my heart speeds up slightly.

"Harrison?" Chase asks, confused.

My head snaps to him as he looks at her and heat pools in my stomach. This can't be—it's been years since I've even heard her name uttered. Yet, the way I want to get closer to her, since I can see how badly her ankle is hurting, to see those freckles she has . . . I remember when I was little, Bianca loved to watch romance movies with Ms. Kate. Said that since she was never going to find her Prince

Charming, she'd settle for seeing love in movies. The one time she dragged me into their little movie marathons, almost every single one had some semblance of the same scene. When the guy and girl reunite, time stops. It looks almost like it freezes slightly; the only indication that it's still running are the sounds that continue around them.

Personally, I thought all of that was a load of crap.

But today, the day I saw *her* again, was when I realized that those movies got at least one thing right. Time freezes, everything blurs, and it's just us. I stand there for probably seconds, yet it feels like it's been centuries. My mind plays out all our memories, making me find the connection between that little girl and this beautiful woman in front of me.

Her hair is no longer the pure brown that it was before, but now a long ash blonde. The dark roots make me believe her natural hair is making a comeback, but it still suits her so well. She only reaches my chin, and a flicker of a smile blooms. Traveling upward, there's a tattoo on her collarbone that she tries so hard to mask with her hair, but I notice it. Then, I meet those bottomless blue eyes and there's no mistake, it *is* her.

"Liam!"

I cringe slightly, sighing deeply at who the voice belongs to. Vanessa stumbles on the balcony, slightly tipsy, and Chase looks downright confused while Bianca freezes. Vanessa then wraps her arms around me and I recoil. She babbles and I shake my head. Chase walks over to Bianca, whose eyes widen. Something pinches in my chest, but before I can even say anything, Bianca winces, accidentally leaning more on her twisted ankle.

"What happened?" he asks her, and my blood instantly boils, not even bothering with what Vanessa is telling me as I approach Chase and Bianca. He hits my chest, confusion coloring me. "She twisted her ankle, dude. Why didn't you help her?"

I grumble, annoyed, as Vanessa gasps at Bianca's ankle turning redder by the minute.

"I was gonna," I say.

Bianca nods, backing me up. "Yeah, he was." She gives me a small smile.

"Come on, Harrison, I have some first aid stuff in my room." She limps as Chase helps her, and I'm stuck, even more frozen. The words are going around in circles in my head.

I just saw . . . Bianca Harrison . . .

My ex-best friend Bianca Harrison.

Vanessa snakes her arms around me again and I flinch. I turn around and she smiles, but I back away instantly, huffing in annoyance.

"What are you doing here?" I ask as she twirls her finger around a strand of her hair, and I do my best not to shudder at her attempts at being seductive.

"It's a Sigma Mella party. You know I never miss one of these." I sigh, knowing she doesn't. "I always hope we can have a repeat of what happened during our freshman year."

I look at her in disgust, and I'm on myself for how I could ever think about sleeping with her.

"Vanessa, we've talked about this. Please leave," I say sternly, grabbing her arms and pushing her away slightly. She looks up at me, her eyes glossier than before.

"Why?"

I scoff at that, pinching my nose in frustration, wanting to be done with the conversation as I think about Bianca being with Chase. Vanessa won't leave me alone and I truly don't know what to do.

"Vanessa, you're drunk, and I told you already, we're done. We weren't anything to begin with. It was one freaking time. How are you still hung up on that?" Lust clouds her eyes, and even more disgust fills me. "I've told you multiple times. I don't want a repeat, and I've tried to be nice, but I'm *this close* to filing a restraining order against you. Come to these parties if you want, or don't, I couldn't care less. Just stop looking for me."

She whimpers slightly at my choice of words and I roll my eyes. Leaving the balcony and her behind, my heart beats rapidly as I head back to Chase's room, to the little corner of silence and solitude, and punch in the code. Opening the door, I look around frantically, not seeing a now-familiar blonde. Chase is lying on his bed, one of the readings we have to do for class in his hands, and shock comes over me.

I shake my head. "Where is she?" He looks up at me, a smile on his face, and I raise a questioning eyebrow.

"She left."

Scoffing at him, I walk back out, searching for her, ignoring when he calls for me. Glancing at about a hundred faces, my heart drops slightly when I don't see hers. Defeat washes over me and I leave the hustle and bustle of the party, going back to the bedroom. I shut the door, preparing myself for Chase to bombard me with questions.

"I knew I recognized her from somewhere." He points to the small framed photo, one of the only things in his room that belongs to me. "Glad to see you're using the room."

Ignoring him as always, I lie down in the extra bed as my brain cycles through everything that's happened. My best friend, whom I haven't seen in eight years, showed up at my university. Coincidentally at a frat party I happened to be at, even though I'd been hiding in this room the whole time until I needed some fresh air. I've had years to think about what I would say if I saw her again, and yet, I had nothing. I was going to ask what happened between us; was I *that* bad of a friend that she stopped talking to me because of it?

In the midst of the war in my head, my phone rings, and I answer without even looking at the caller ID.

"Hello?"

"Hey, amorcito," Mom says, and I instantly feel suspicious. She only calls me her "little love" when something is up. I glare at Chase, and he raises his hands in surrender before leaving, thankfully.

"Hi, Mom. Are you alright?"

"Me? I'm good. Amazing. *Really* good. Great, even," she spills out, and I roll my eyes and smile.

"Mom, I know you. Something's up."

She tries to hold out a little longer, but then she sighs. "It's nothing really."

I clutch the phone harder to my ear. "We talked yesterday. So, either something really good or something really bad happened. What's up?"

"You'll never guess what I heard." From the sentence alone, I know what she's about to say, and it makes everything that much more real.

"What?" My voice wobbles slightly. Her lack of an immediate response probably means she's contemplating whether or not to actually tell me.

"There's a slight possibility that Kate Harrison is back in LA." I take a deep breath. "Now, I'm not one hundred percent sure, but Patty was telling me all about her new neighbors when I went to her house for book club. They moved in across from her, I think, based on how she described the woman at least. I tried to see her today, but she doesn't seem to be home."

My heart beats even faster. Orientation. She's here for orientation with Bianca, that's why she isn't home.

"Liam?" The word is muffled, and I zone back in, blinking harshly. "Li—"

"I'm here, Mom." Not only has she infiltrated my school, but now she lives in the subdivision next to mine?

We love the universe, don't we?

"Now, I didn't see Bi—well, Kate's daughter, but I assume she's there too. I mean, those two were attached at the hip." My mind flashes back to a bit ago, and I want to tell her that I saw her. Yet, I keep quiet. "Liam, I was thinking . . . and well, now with this. We should've talked about it a long time ago." When I stay silent, she takes it as a sign to continue. "It's been years, son. You're both adults now. Maybe this is a sign. You could finally get the closure you always wanted." I listen to her cautious yet hopeful tone and my heart recoils at the thought. She sighs once again, probably frustrated with my silence and with the whole situation. "Look, Liam, you're hours away, so you probably don't care about what happens here—"

I cut her off instantly because that couldn't be further from the truth. "Mom, don't say that."

"I know it's a touchy subject for you."

Scoffing at that, I lean my head back against the wall, groaning in frustration. "No, it isn't."

"I'm not stupid. I know she's a touchy subject, and I don't blame you. I wanted to tell you, so you wouldn't be caught off guard." She blows out a nervous breath. "Maybe, if I ever prove this, we can go over and say hi one day."

Something bubbles up in my chest. The irony being so ridiculous, I burst out laughing.

"What's so funny?" she asks, obviously confused.

The suggestion practically offends me. "Yeah, there's no way that I'm doing that. *She* stopped talking to *me*, remember?" My mind taunts that I didn't seem to remember all this when she was in front of me, and I mentally hush the thoughts. The thumping against the walls gets worse and I sigh, knowing this party is just getting started and is already causing a headache to form. "Look, Mom, I appreciate you telling me, but that ship has sailed. Bianca and I—" My traitorous heart clenches at what I was going to say. "We grew apart. Simple as that."

A quick flashback happens in my mind, and I get up to grab the picture of us. We're little kids on Halloween wearing our favorite costumes—I'm a knight and she chose to be Cinderella for the third year in a row. Her smile lights up the whole photo, and there I am, looking at her as if she's my whole world.

I mean, she *was* at some point.

Aiming the picture down, tears of frustration well in my eyes at how crappy my night has gone. "Anyway, I've gotta go, Mom. I, uh, have a test to study for."

"I love you, Liam," she says, and I smile.

"I love you too. Say hi to Dad for me."

"I will. Oh, and Liam?" I hum in reply, as I was about to hang up. "Not everything is always as it seems. I know you guys had a fight, and I know it hurt you. Just remember, it went both ways. Think about what I said. It really could give you that closure to truly move on." She hangs up and my hand clenches the phone. I *have* moved on, and to think I'm gonna reach out to her . . . I tried that and I was met with her voicemail. Not a single message back from her, nothing.

I hadn't been ready to give up on her, but she obviously was with me.

But . . . what if Mom's right? Maybe there's a chance we could talk it out. Hope starts a little fire in my heart, but as quickly as it started, I put it out, not wanting to think about what once was the best thing that happened to me.

We grew apart, that's it.

I know I screwed up and I tried to apologize. To this day, I hate that I made her feel less important than she actually was.

But if she truly thought our friendship was special . . . and then her response was blocking me, and not even trying?

A knock brings me out of my thoughts. Chase comes in and I groan. Faux hurt crosses his face. His hand covers his heart and there are a couple of beer bottles in his grip. "Ouch, roomie."

I take a couple Advil and lie down again. "Go away," I mutter, and he shakes his head, taking his place on the bed opposite mine. He cracks open a bottle, offering me the other, but I shake my head and he shrugs as if to say "your loss."

"So, I'm assuming Harrison is the reason I've never had to leave the room?"

I roll my eyes. "When did you get that close for the little nickname?"

He shrugs, but then raises his hands in surrender for the second time tonight. "It's not like that. She seems like a chill person, plus I'm her orientation leader." My heart eases at that, but I still give him a look of disbelief while he looks at me exasperated. "Okay, not that she paid attention to me like that anyway. She only looked at you." A blush starts on my face. "You know, I've always wondered why you weren't interested in dating. I get it now."

I shrug him off. "You know nothing."

"I know you've never looked at anyone else like you looked at her tonight, and I've known you for two years now." He doesn't back down, and the fire in his eyes is matched with mine because I don't do *this*. I don't talk about my feelings with people—I keep them to myself. Even if I wanted to, Chase wouldn't even be in my top five. "She talked about you, you know." My ears perk up at that and he looks at me with a slight smirk. "When I was treating her ankle. I asked her if she knew you and she said 'yeah, once upon a time.' I mean, based on that answer, it seems like you must've done a number on her."

At that, the soft bloom of curiosity starting in my chest shrivels at the insinuation, and *this* is why I don't talk to anyone. They assume that it's my fault. Like I didn't lose my best friend, the girl who ruined me for anyone else.

"Chase, you don't know what happened, and I'd really appreciate it if you stayed out of it. You and I are roommates—nothing more—so stop trying to butt in, please. Let it go."

His eyebrows scrunch slightly and he chuckles, somewhat annoyed. He takes the other beer and leaves the room, closing the door, and I huff. I think about our last phone call. The days following it. How horrible I felt. I couldn't believe I had messed up that bad. I thought giving her space would help.

I thought.

I thought we had something that would last forever, and while I want to be mad, to be angry at her, all that envelops my heart is regret and shame. We both felt discarded, and after what we said . . . Could we have still stayed best friends?

I throw on my jacket, ready to leave, my heart softening at the photo, and I hate the conflict going on inside me. Half of me wants to go find her—she was limping, and Chase might not have even treated her ankle correctly. The other half wants to transfer out of here to never see her again. Yet, something simmers lowly in my chest.

Yeah, hope is gonna be the death of me.

CHAPTER NINE

Bianca

"WHY DID YOU LET ME drink so much?"

Vanessa groans, glancing over as she wakes up half an hour before we need to meet at the student union, making me more nervous by the minute.

I chuckle. "I didn't *let* you, technically. Also, you sleep like the dead. I've been trying to wake you for the last ten minutes." She rolls her eyes at me as she goes over to wash her face.

Picking up her phone, her eyes widen. "Oh, we're gonna be late!" I shake my packed duffel bag and she gives me a thumbs-up. We rush out of the room and over to our destination.

Well, as best as I can rush with the whole ankle situation.

"C'mon, I know a shortcut." She grabs my hand as we tuck behind the older buildings in desperate need of renovation. Last night was a catastrophe, and while it's still affecting me, Vanessa seems fine. I drop her hand when Chase and the rest of the group come into view, as everything from last night circles in my mind.

Liam. Liam was the guy she had a thing with, who she wanted me to be a wingwoman for. She had her hands all over him, and

81

while jealousy coursed up my spine, I realized he's no one for me to get jealous over. We're practically strangers now. All night, I tortured myself as countless scenarios ran through my mind. He knew her, and for her to be on him like that, crushed me. He didn't even try to look for me—not that I made it easy. Once Chase did what he could for my ankle, I limped as fast as I could out of there. Thankfully, one of the designated drivers offered me a ride back to Juniper Hall.

Chase and Vanessa start leading us for round two of our tour, but I remain at the back with my head down. We stop at one of the humongous libraries on campus with the mascot statue having water flowing through it. Turning around, Chase shyly waves at me and I upturn my head at him.

Our reunion—Liam and mine—was probably the most disappointing one there could've ever been. Of course, my clumsy side had to show, and then Chase and Vanessa got involved. For a moment, I thought maybe I was wrong, that this brooding guy standing in front of me wasn't—*couldn't*—be the guy I remembered. Yet, when the light from inside hit him just right, the swirls in his eyes brought me the warmth I've been craving since I moved away. My ankle was swelling, and a little headache was starting due to the smell of alcohol, but with him . . .

All I wanted to do was stay there while he looked at me. It's been years since we stopped talking, and I'm over it. Or at least, I thought I was, but last night proved otherwise. Now, he'll be in my life, going to the same school as me when I start next semester.

I could always avoid him—the university is vast—but I've run into him twice already. I hear a laugh, and my attention turns to everyone taking pictures of the beautiful willow tree in the school's arboretum. Chase and Vanessa are laughing at something and my heart tugs.

They've gotten to experience Liam all these years while I haven't. I know I had overreacted back then. I was young and dumb, and was feeling left out and jealous. And now, I'm experiencing it all over again. I'm sitting at a table with Chase and Vanessa, along with some of their friends in the cafeteria, but I don't think I've ever felt more alone. I laugh in the right places, smile when someone says my name, nod when someone's talking, but my heart is bleeding inside.

It's almost time for orientation to be over, and I'm torn apart. I'm convincing myself over and over again to accept everything. At least Liam has friends—more than that, it looks like—and I'm happy for him. Sighing while stabbing my food, someone bumps their shoulder with mine and I slap on a smile, only to be met with Chase.

"You okay?" he asks, and I sag slightly because he knows what's wrong. Liam's probably told him all about me, and I hate that he knows what went down.

"Yeah, all good. Ankle's feeling better, thankfully." I divert the conversation and he shakes his head as he adjusts his hat.

"That's not what I meant." I shrug, not wanting to talk about it, and he sighs, digging his palms into his eyes. "I swear you and Liam are so alike, it pisses me off." I look at him in confusion. "You're both stubborn, and I have no idea what went down between you two. But you two should talk."

Pushing my tray away, I mutter, "Chase, I've known you for two seconds, so drop it."

He points at that, laughing. "You both even say the same thing, more or less. I think—"

"Leave it alone. He wants nothing to do with me, and neither do I. We're ghosts of each other's pasts. Please leave it at that," I remind him as I get up to go use the bathroom. Closing the door to the stall, I mentally scream.

Curse Liam for making me feel this way.

Curse Chase for reopening an old wound.

My phone vibrates in my back pocket, and I answer, putting it to my ear. "Bianca, the get-together with a business prospect in Santa Clara has been moved up, and we need to be there. Where are you?" My eyes widen at Mom's voice, and it seems the universe has decided for me, but a sad sigh still manages to filter out.

"Mom, orientation isn't over yet."

"Bianca, he really needs us there. We should want to support him, right? You're going to this school anyway."

I close my eyes at that, hanging my head. "I'll be there soon." My words betray me. She hangs up, but not before reminding me to hurry, and more weight falls on me. I wash my hands and straighten up as I go back outside. Chase and Vanessa look over at me as I smile at them.

"So, I have no idea if I can do this, but could I check out early with you guys? I need to go."

Vanessa's eyebrows furrow, her lips forming a frown. "You can, but why? Is everything alright?"

"Yeah, just family stuff." I smile again, easing her as much as I can. The memories hit, tainting the image I had of her when we first met. She puts my name down as early leave and then hugs me, and I wrap my arms around her. She was the first person who was kind to me, but now, I can't even look at her without feeling hurt.

I wave goodbye to everyone and grab my stuff before rushing out of there.

"Harrison, wait!" Chase follows behind me, a sheepish expression on his face. "I'm sorry if what I said offended you. I didn't mean—"

I stop him. "You're good, I'm not leaving because of you, I promise." He nods, but still looks at me with disbelief, and something comes over me. He seems like a really good guy, and I'm happy Liam has good friends. Even after everything, he deserves nothing but the best. "It was nice to meet you, Chase." Regret clouds his features as his eyes dart around, maybe figuring out how to get me to stay.

He sighs. "See you in the fall, Harrison." I walk away, my phone vibrating again, Mom probably wanting me to hurry up.

CHAPTER TEN

Liam

"SO, WHAT ARE WE THINKING for break coming up?" Taryn asks.

I don't even acknowledge the question, my mind still spiraling from last night. I barely got any sleep, and my entire tattoo room is filled with sketches of things, as I stayed here till four in the morning. The dark circles around my eyes are vivid and the energy drink I had has made me more irritated than awake. Summer break is a couple of weeks away, and usually I spend it with my parents back home. But now?

I have no idea what to do.

She's returned to LA, living in a subdivision so close I could throw a rock from my window and probably hit her house. There's only one grocery store close by without needing to get on the highway, so I know she'll go there.

Should I stay here in my protective bubble?

Here, it'll be a couple of months before she starts the fall semester, and with the campus being so large, it'll probably be harder to run into her. Or do I go home, knowing that there's almost a guaranteed chance I'll see her again?

Am I ready for that? Will I ever be ready to see how she moved on without me? How she forgot about me?

"Luke and I are gonna party with the sorority girls that are sticking around for the summer, so we'll be on campus," Bobby says, and expectant eyes are on me as I glance up.

My brain blanks out on Taryn's question. "I might go visit my parents back home," I say, and they roll their eyes.

"Bor-ing. Why don't you stay here and party with us, grouch?" Taryn asks and I look at her incredulously. She sighs. "God, you're *so* dull. Like, live it up for once. Aren't you a twenty-one-year-old college student?"

Sarcasm drips from her voice and I scowl at her. This is another reason why I don't want friends. "I'm twenty, and I didn't choose Mella Colta for the party scene, but because of the aerospace program. I'm content going home and sketching more—"

"Constellations and people with freckles all over their face," they say together, and my face falls at the confession. Shock and confusion flash through me.

"How do you all know that?" I ask, and Bobby and Luke look at each other knowingly while Taryn looks at me without a care in the world.

"Well, we snuck a peek at your sketchbook, and it's also pretty obvious given almost everything you draw has some relation to those two things," she says, but cringes when a pen is thrown at her head. She looks in Luke's direction, but he pretends as if nothing happened. "To be honest, I have no idea how you don't get bored. Also, there are a bunch of drawings of the same person. She has straight brown hair, blue eyes, and freckles everywhere. What's up with that?"

"That's private," I mutter, and Taryn looks like she wants to keep pushing, but the bell above the door rings. One of my regulars, Jimmy, walks in and I thank goodness for the distraction I so desperately need.

After a couple of hours, the corners of my mouth tip up as Jimmy flexes his forearm in the mirror, the fresh ink leaving his skin red, but the contrasting, stark-black lines very much apparent.

"Dude, this looks sick!"

"I'm glad you like it. It's your last session, and I was able to get you out a bit earlier." He looks over his shoulder and nods at me, and I hand him the aftercare paperwork, even though he's a pro at this point. Walking with him to my door, we shake hands, and he approaches Taryn to pay. Shoving my stuff in my bag, I grab it and lock my tattoo room this time, making a mental note that I can't trust them around my private things, given that they don't have any sort of respect.

Storming toward the front door, not looking at either of them, a hand is placed on my shoulder, and I turn around to see Bobby. He opens his mouth to say something, but I stop him.

"Don't." I leave the shop, wanting to cool off slightly. Crossing the street, I make my way toward my dorm, hoping the walk helps. Finally reaching my building and turning the corner, there's a couple talking, and they pull away slightly. I notice it's Chase and his new flavor of the day, but I ignore them. As I approach our door, I see it's wedged open with one of his shoes. I push into the room, kick the sneaker out of the way, and the door slams shut behind me. I sit on my bed, wanting to be alone.

My eyes fill with tears from the pent-up emotions and I'm practically shaking from them when I hear a knock.

"Liam?" Chase asks, and I scoff at his tone. "Dude, I don't have my key, open up. I need to talk to you." He jiggles the handle and my leg bounces up and down. I want him to be as far away as possible. "Li—"

"Go away, Chase," I struggle to say in a calm tone, and a deep breath comes from outside the door.

"Look, I get you're mad at me. I shouldn't have pried, but Bianca is leaving, and I think—"

My heart picks up when I hear her name, but it makes me want to shut down even more. "I don't care what you think, just leave me alone." The knocking ceases, and while Chase isn't my favorite person, I get he's trying to be helpful . . . in his own stubborn way.

"She's probably still in line at the parking garage. If you man up, you could catch her." He finally leaves, and I put my hands in my hair, bring my head down, and take deep breaths.

Why? Why is she still getting to me? It's been five years, but it feels like yesterday when we promised that we would always be there for each other. I look over at my keys, Chase's words staying with me even after silence fills the room.

You can still catch her.

My heart and mind fight with each other. It's almost as if I can hear what they're saying.

Go, talk to her.

Stay, let her leave.

I make the choice. Grabbing my keys, I close the door before running toward the parking garage on the other side of campus. Everyone looks at me in confusion, but I don't care. I need to see her again, talk to her, just something.

I've been given something I've been craving for five years, and my heart doesn't wanna let it go.

I cut behind buildings and skirt around some bicyclists. I almost run into a skateboarder as I see a bunch of freshmen waiting for their cars. I try looking for her blonde hair, that specific ash blonde she's dyed it now, but it's nowhere to be found.

I crash into someone and turn to apologize before those all-too-familiar watercolor eyes lock with mine. Her eyes widen and my mouth curves the tiniest bit.

"You're still here." I breathe out, my chest bumping up and down as I struggle to take in some air, while she stares at me. A man waves at her roughly and my heart cracks slightly. But not before a woman wraps her arm around him and I recognize her as Ms. Kate.

Bianca twists her lips. "Look, I get this is unconventional. I'll stay out of your way, and you stay out of mine."

I take a deep breath as her words spark ones from long ago.

"Then maybe we shouldn't be friends anymore."

My brain makes fun of me, proving that I'm right.

I made a fool of myself, again.

My reply dies the moment the guy—I assume something of Ms. Kate's, given he wasn't around when we were still in each other's lives—grabs her forearm, surprising both me and her.

He looks me up and down snobbishly. "I apologize for her." He smiles after, but the underlying irritation he has is obvious. I'm not sure whether it's directed at me or her, but I don't like it. The grip doesn't seem like he's hurting her, but shock is all over her face when facing him. "I will *not* be late because of you, *let's go*." He emphasizes the last two words, but before I can do anything, they walk off while he changes his grip.

I back away when I very clearly see Ms. Kate hug Bianca, slightly concerned, before she shrugs it off. The protective feeling doesn't lessen even when they all begin to walk away and Bianca never looks back.

I'm left with the words that she plans to stay out of my way, which I should be glad about, but for some reason, I'm not. I stay frozen to my spot. Everyone is walking around me, but I keep looking as they fade from view.

I knew I should've left it alone.

I walk to Greek Row since it's closer than my dorm room across campus. I enter the frat house, upturning my head at some of the other guys before going up the stairs to Chase's room. Emotions course through me and the energy is starting to wear off. Exhaustion comes out to play, feeding off my mental state.

The part that not many people talk about is how different it feels to be talking with someone you used to know. There was once upon a time that I couldn't imagine living life without her, and now, I can't believe I have. I sigh at the feelings swirling in my heart and mind. One of the other things I've stowed in this room, out of sight, out of mind, are my old sketchbooks, which are now peeking out from where I stuffed them in the closet. The ones Mom packed in my suitcase when I was coming up here. The ones I haven't touched since.

Standing, I move to grab each of them, beginning to flip through them, further breaking my heart, yet I don't care. There was a time I died on the hill that I would never see Bianca again, and now that I have, all our memories before the fight have been bombarding me. I look down at the hours and hours of work, tears running down my cheeks. Flipping to the last page, there's a folded piece of paper taped to it.

Confused because I don't remember what it is, I open it gently and see her writing, and more tears make their way down my face.

Dear Liam,

It's been a bit since we've written letters to each other, but I wanted to do it so you could have a more recent letter from me. I wanted to say I hope you do amazing at football tryouts, and I'll be waiting for your call. I love hearing your voice . . . always.

Love, your lucky charm and best friend,

Bianca

Instantly, I'm transported back to when I got this in the mail on my first day of high school. I trace over the writing and smile at how she would always draw something different over the I in her name.

Sometimes it was a flower, an X, a normal dot, but especially for me, she would always use a heart. My heart stutters as the little girl I'm remembering morphs into the woman I just saw leave. She looks as beautiful as ever, and I hate that I noticed. I hate how I'm going back and forth. After two hours of sitting on the bed while staring at the wall—as that's all I can emotionally manage right now—the door lock turns and Chase walks in. My face hardens at the sight of him.

"You catch her?" I don't even acknowledge the question, my brain taunting me that much more, and he sighs. "You know, we've been roommates since freshman year, and we've had a total of five conversations." I look up at him. "I've been living with someone for two years, and I know next to nothing about him. Well, until now." He walks toward the bed, sits, and leans his head against the wall. "Look, I get it. To you, we're not friends, but I *do* care about you, dude."

Clenching my hands, I stare down at the designs on them. Every single one of these tattoos has represented a time when I've thought of Bianca, when the thought of her hurt so bad that only a tattoo machine could ease the pain. In the years I've known Chase, I've never felt bad for being the way I am with him, and I hate that I do tonight.

Feeling like he's probably getting nowhere with me, he sighs again, almost hurt, and waves me off.

"I swear if you tell anyone about this, I'll castrate you." His eyes widen, and I look at him, trying to spot even a hint of malice in his gaze. I rub my neck, the muscle aching slightly. "When I was eight years old, I met this girl." His mouth drops open slightly. He beckons me to keep going, even though my pride is screaming at me. I need to tell someone what's going on in my head, or I'm going to lose it. "She was . . . well, the most amazing person you could ever meet. She was sweet, kind, selfless, and she had my heart the moment I saw her." His eyes soften slightly from the corner of my vision, but I still refuse to make eye contact.

"We grew up living right next to each other, and as the years went by, I fell more and more in love with her. I'd even tell her that I'd marry her one day. She would always laugh at that, yet she never knew that everything I told her was true. Everything I ever promised." I take a deep breath, wanting to be as emotionless as possible. I need to sound like these are just facts of my life, not the very reason I still breathe . . . the reasons I still live for. "Anyway, when I was twelve, I found out she was moving, and of course, I was crushed. I thought nothing would come between us, until her thirteenth birthday. I had a football game on that day, and I swore I would call. But I didn't, and we had a fight."

I look up, thinking that he probably isn't paying attention. I'm surprised to see him hanging on to every word. "She said she felt left out, when funnily enough, I was feeling the exact same thing. She had new friends, and I got insecure I would become someone she outgrew." I inhale sharply and chuckle self-deprecatingly. "I decided to give her space, but when I tried to call later, it didn't go through. I tried again the next day, but nothing, so I stopped." I lift my arm. "I got these tattoos because of her. She left this gaping hole in me, and this is all that's helped, but it's never gone away." I close my eyes. "*She* never went away. She stayed the whole five years, and even though there were weeks I wouldn't think of her, something would trigger it . . ."

I trail off, allowing Chase to speak up. "The universe made you remember her." I nod as I see some of my feelings mirroring back, and it makes me wonder if Chase has gone through something similar.

"Yeah, and now she's coming to MC in two months and conveniently lives a hop, skip, and a jump away from my parents." Sarcasm drips from my words, and taking a deep breath while blinking quickly, I put my head in my hands to compose myself. After a few minutes, I fully make eye contact with Chase, not knowing what to expect.

He whistles lowly. "Wow." I chuckle at that while rubbing my hands through my hair. "That's the most I've ever heard you talk." I roll my eyes and chuckle. Leave it to Chase to joke around.

"She walked away today. Said we should stay out of each other's way," I add.

A pensive look is fixed on his face, almost as if he's trying to make sense of something. "Do you still love her? After all this time?"

Ding ding ding! Ladies and gentlemen, Chase Collins really knows the right questions to ask. I think about it, and something inside of me says yes, but . . . "No. I'm chasing the comfort—the memories—of her. I have enough respect for myself, and I refuse to harbor feelings for someone who's trampled all over them. I don't wanna even be near her. Just the thought of her being next to me"—*makes me wanna melt*—"makes me wanna bolt," I finish, my mouth and heart having differing opinions.

He sighs at that, almost as if he wants to tell me otherwise. "Then be indifferent." I look at him, confused. "She's practically infiltrated your life, right?" I nod. "And, she said she wants nothing to do with you, which I think is a load of bull because eyes never lie, but that's beside the point . . ." He rambles, and I raise an eyebrow. "Honor her wishes then: If she stays away from you, then stay away from her." He takes a deep breath. "I was in love with this really popular girl. She was my sister's best friend, still is actually. I thought we were really close, and as much as it's hard to believe, I didn't look like I do now. I was bigger, not exactly overweight, but I still didn't like my body. I eventually confessed my feelings after we graduated high school, but well . . ."

"I'm sorry, Chase," I say as he shrugs, a hand mussing up his hair. "Maybe you're not as shallow as I thought." He looks at me, exasperated with faux annoyance. "I'm serious, I thought you studied on occasion and slept with anything that moved."

He chuckles. "I learned a long time ago that people don't want the real you. They expect the person tailored to them, so it's what I dish out." He does a little bowing gesture, and damn if that doesn't hit straight in the heart. We stay in a comfortable silence, and I realize he seems like a genuine person. Not that I'm ready to skip around in a circle and sing "Kumbaya" with him or anything.

"For the record, I really do think she's lying," he says.

I sigh at that and lie down while turning the lamp off. He says nothing, but rather gets on his phone while my thoughts bombard me. The girl who haunts my every thought will be a ten-minute walk from where I'll be during the summer. Yet, my mind also thinks about that guy who grabbed her and the way Ms. Kate hugged him . . . How the spite in his eyes toward Bianca makes me want to protect her, and I don't think she wants it.

She doesn't want me, and I need to learn to accept that.

Bianca

"BIANCA? WE'RE HERE, HONEY."

Someone's shaking me slightly, and the house comes into view as I open my eyes. I become that much more aware because there's no way I slept through that entire ride.

"Kate. Bianca. Little help back here!" Josh raises his voice as I drag myself out of the car. The sequins glitter under the night sky as my dress rubs against my skin rather uncomfortably. The dinner had gone longer than I thought it would, but I maintained my smile as he showed us off, and he received praise after praise. He hands me my bag and I walk inside the house, bending slightly to take my heels off. In my room, I throw the items across the space as I flop onto my bed, still somewhat tired.

Mentally, emotionally, physically, all of the above.

Said bag stares back at me, the organized person in me wanting to take all my stuff out and put it away. Though, exhaustion wins this time. I force myself up, starting on the zipper of my dress, my body screaming in relief as I let it breathe. I hadn't brought any formal clothes with me to orientation, hence, they rushed to buy me a dress before the business meeting.

My phone chimes, my heart catching. I eye the email notifications from Mella Colta. My eyes skim over the words.

Hello, Bianca Harrison,

Thank you for attending Mella Colta's new student in-person orientation! We hope you enjoyed your experience and gained helpful information that you can use as a future member of the MC community. Please be on the lookout for other announcements, and see you in the fall!

A flicker of excitement starts in my chest, and even with everything that's gone wrong, I refuse to let it taint the fact that I'm going to my dream school, that I was accepted into a prestigious program that I thought was a pipe dream. As I throw the wretched dress in the back of the closet, I hope I never have to wear it again. I grab some pajamas and shrug into them.

Plopping back down, I grab my phone, and I know I shouldn't. I really, really shouldn't, but I do. My fingers spell out Liam Parker, and after some scrolling on social media, I see his now-familiar face and click on his profile. Jamie always pushed me to look him up, but I never did. The mere thought of looking at his profile, and possibly finding *something*, would've made things that much worse.

Every single photo is of tattoos, and after stalking him for a few minutes, I realize he designed and inked all of them. I smile; he was always the better artist between the two of us. I look at his tagged posts, seeing other people raving about his work, and happiness fills me. I wish that this wasn't new knowledge to me. I wish I had already known he was a tattoo artist. I wish his friends had already known who I was. I wish we were a part of each other's lives like we once were.

A shriek cuts through the house and my heart drops. Throwing open the door, I sprint down the hall and find Mom standing in front of the opened front door.

"Hey, Kate."

Standing in the doorway is Ana—*Liam's mom, Ana*—with her hair in a messy bun and in a two-piece pajama set. Mom has her hands over her face in shock and my eyes flit between them. Ana seems nervous while I stand there, looking at them, and her expression falls. Sporting a sheepish smile, Mom wraps her old friend in a hug.

"It's been too long, Ana," Mom mumbles.

She squeezes harder. "It really has." Ana looks over at me, shock coloring her face. Nervousness courses through my veins as they pull away, but Ana keeps her eyes trained on me.

"Bianca? *Little* Bianca?" I nod, as does Mom, while Josh looks at the exchange, pensive. She comes closer to me, almost as if she's imagining me. She moves the hair away from my features and then a grin spreads across her face.

"You know, I really missed you, cupcake." I break into a grin myself at the little accent she has when she calls me "cupcake" and hug her tightly.

"I missed you too," I say, and she pulls back with a laugh. The moment is broken when Josh clears his throat, and we all look at him.

"I'm so sorry, how rude of me. I'm Ana Parker, a friend from the past." She holds her hand out, and Josh silently inspects it before he hesitantly accepts it, muttering his own introduction.

"Kate's boyfriend?" She looks at Mom for confirmation, and she leans on him. Ana grins once again. "Oh, Kate, I'm so happy for you!" Mom smiles widely while I observe Josh; the grin he sports has a hint of something else in it.

"Yes, yes. Listen, Ana, right? We just got back from a rather exhausting trip, and we're all heading to bed. You understand, right?"

All our eyes widen, and I move to stand next to Ana. "Josh, I haven't seen her in years," Mom almost begs, but when he swings his gaze in her direction, her expression falters. Though, before he can say anything, Ana interrupts.

"It's okay, Kate, I understand. It was great to see you guys, and to meet you, Josh." He nods and walks off while Mom closes her eyes in embarrassment.

"Ana, I'm so—"

Ana holds up a hand and shakes her head. "You're fine, Kate. I couldn't resist coming to see for myself if you guys were really here."

My smile only widens and Ana glances over at me. "I don't know if you still want to hang out, but I live in the next subdivision over, and well—I would love to have you over." Mom nods and hugs her, but I stay back. The invite seems to only be for Mom, and I have no idea why that stings. Though, it makes sense . . . "Both of you." I look up at that, and her eyes tell me she's sincere. She grabs both of my hands and looks at me deeply. Her eyes commanding all my attention, and the memories of this exact look have me reeling. "You're always welcome, no matter what." A couple of tears bead in my eyes, and I turn my head to wipe them on my shoulder. She pinches my cheek before walking off. When she reaches the end of the walkway, she turns and gives us the biggest wave and an air kiss. Mom closes the door and we look at each other, both shocked. Shocked this happened, shocked that after five years, Ana still wants us to be in her life.

Liam's going to *love* this.

I really need to teach the people in my life there are other reactions to have. Ones that don't involve potentially ruining my hearing. The moment I pick up the video call, Jamie takes one good look at me and *knows*, and I have to cover my ears. How do I know she knows? No idea. But *she does*.

"I'm getting a soda, and then I wanna hear absolutely everything with the most insignificant details attached, please and thank you." I open my mouth, but she's gone from the screen before I can say anything. Using the camera, I put my hair in a messy bun as my best friend plops herself in her desk chair. "Okay, hit it." She mimics pressing play on an imaginary remote and I give her my best exasperated look. She smiles and motions me to start, and I sigh, because where do I even begin?

"I had orientation a couple of days ago, and lemme tell you: *Everything* hit the fan. It was amazing, but awful at the same time."

She looks confused, but after a bit, her eyes widen. "You saw him, didn't you?" I nod, and her spinning in her chair is enough for me to know how excited she is at the news, but she stops abruptly. "Why don't you look over the moon?"

A headache is forming, and so many things want to come out all at once. "He's different. *We're* different. It's better we stay away from each other."

Oh, by the way, I'm pretty sure the only girl friend I made has been with Liam in some way.

His roommate hit a little too close to home with some of his comments.

He's completely tatted up.

But yes, in a nutshell, *he's different.*

She contemplates my answer as she goes for another sip of her drink. "Is he hot?" I facepalm as I realize Jamie—and only Jamie—would ask that type of question.

"Well—"

"Be honest, B," she warns, and I chuckle before answering honestly.

"Yes, excruciatingly. He looks like he came out of a magazine." She kicks her legs up and giggles like a little schoolgirl, and some spills out of me too. She grabs the phone from where it was propped up, and insists on looking him up. With an eyeroll, I give her his social media handle—that I may or may not have memorized, but she doesn't need to know that. Every emotion fleeting across her face from awe to surprise to plain hunger is obvious.

"Done drooling yet?" Her hand shoots up to the corner of her mouth as if to check, and I chuckle.

"I'm sorry—but he's *gorgeous.* This is Liam, that scrawny kid who you used to talk to back in the day?" I nod, and shock simmers on her face.

I lean against my fist. "Pretty wild, right?"

"Uh, yeah. He does tattoos, and oh my gosh, wait, he designs them too? This is impossible, I'm starting over." Her finger scrolls back up. I let Jamie gawk as I think about everything that went down these past few days. Being accepted into the school Dad wished for me makes the acceptance letter that much more special. Then, being accepted to their accelerated program is that much more of an honor. But while education-wise, this is the route to take, emotionally, I'm a wreck. Seeing Liam after so long, then Vanessa talking to me about him, not knowing he's someone I fell in love with way back when . . .

Then, the moment he came looking for me. His hair was disheveled, almost as if he ran his fingers through it multiple times. He was out of breath as if he had run across campus to look for me. And the look he had reminded me of when we were younger. It was the look from when he was unsure about everything in his life, *everything* except me. He would look at me like that, as if I were the only thing in that moment he was sure of, and I missed that look more than ever.

CHAPTER TWELVE

Bianca

"HE'S WHAT?"

My heart beats rapidly as I pace the room. Mom gives me a concerned expression, yet I can't concentrate on her that much. She hasn't told me everything, but what I do know is enough to blow up my world. Liam coming down from college and staying for all of summer break?

"Well, hon, she said that it wasn't a definite thing until he confirmed it a little bit ago," Mom says while I nod absentmindedly, but my mind still can't wrap around the fact that I'm going to see him.

Since orientation a couple weeks ago, my mind has been engaged in a perpetual downward spiral. Every day I wake up with his face on my mind, at how everything came together, at how he looks after so long. He's not that kid who picked daisies for me when coming over, yet when we locked eyes, the entire spectrum of green shining back, I could still see the old him under all that he is now.

I'm okay now. I got over everything . . . again.

"There's also one more thing." She nervously tugs at the loose thread on her cardigan, and I prepare for whatever the news is.

"I invited Ana and William to the event tonight, and she also asked if she could invite Liam since there's a possibility he's starting his break early . . ."

"Does Josh know?" I ask. He's currently on a business trip and will be coming home later this afternoon with Olivia for the big opening day of the new firm. Of course, there have been a couple more of his outbursts, and Ana's been the sole reason for Josh's reactions. Every time she's mentioned, this *look* comes over his face. To me, it's no secret that he doesn't like her; she's been coming over a lot and taking up Mom's time, so maybe that's why. And now, Ana has been added to the list for an event of *his*.

Mom shakes her head, answering my question. *This'll be fun.* Naively, I thought maybe I could get Ana back in my life, and even William . . . Unfortunately, the Parkers are, well, the Parkers; they're a package deal. There's always the possibility Liam might not come. I mean, he's hours away, and I know I'll have to face him eventually. At college, I could somewhat evade him, but here, I sincerely doubt it.

"Mom, what am I gonna do?" I ask, crestfallen, my mind and heart battling against each other.

"Well, hon, I know it still hurts even after all these years, but it might not be as bad as you're thinking."

I give her a flat stare. She rubs a hand over my arms, almost caressing them, and I revel in the gesture. My heart cracks with the truth seeping through.

"I think this whole time I've had hope that when we finally rekindled, it would go well, but it didn't, and shoving us in more situations won't make it better." I gently slap my hands over my face, peeking through my fingers at my traitorous romance books with the friends-to-lovers trope.

Liars.

"Bianca, I know you're scared, but if love is involved . . ." She stops as she sighs and closes her eyes. "You run the risk of experiencing every other emotion too." She places a kiss on the top of my head. I inhale shakily at that, and she raises my face to look at her. "It'll be okay, Bianca, I promise. Besides, we still need to attend to support Josh. Poor thing has been stressed out of his mind since all the attorneys from Philly will be coming too." I roll my eyes. No wonder she's pushing so hard. Josh wants to look like a devout boyfriend in front of everyone.

Ever the performer.

Though, as always, mother dearest is oblivious. I open the curtain slightly and see Ana walking in front of our house, and then she jogs to the front door. Her shriek of laughter is upon us, and a blissful memory comes over me.

"Honey, can you see who's at the door?"

I nodded and kissed her arm, as that's all I could reach. I skipped to the door and threw it open to find a short woman holding a basket, wearing a light, flowy blouse, black leggings, and black flats. But what mostly caught my attention was the boy standing next to her.

He wore a baseball cap backward on his head, a slightly faded Transformers shirt along with black shorts that went down to his knees, and new-looking white Vans. He looked to be a couple years older than me, but what most captivated me were his eyes.

They were the greenest eyes I'd ever seen. I could make out the different shades as they swirled around in his irises. Sage, spring, forest, and everything spanning the entire color spectrum of green.

"Hi, little one, is your mom or dad around?" There was an accent slipping past her lips and I broke out of my bubble as I looked at the woman who was now squatting in front of me.

"Bianca, who's—oh, hi there," Mom said as she came up behind me, and the woman rose to her full height.

"Hi! I'm Ana Parker, and this is my son, Liam. My husband isn't able to be here, but he sends his regards. We're your next-door neighbors," she said, and I looked at Liam, but he had yet to say anything. Granted, neither had I. "Liam, say hi," Ana urged him, but he stared, still not saying anything. "I'm sorry, he's usually not this shy." Ana looked between us, a small smile on her face, and Mom chuckled.

"It's okay. I'm Kate Harrison, and this is Bianca," Mom said, and stuck out her hand. Liam's face softened as he glanced back at me, but then I saw Ana's face morph into shock.

"Wait, Kate? Kate Thompson?" Ana asked with a smile, and Mom dropped her hand from my back.

"Ana Garcia?" Mom retorted, and Ana nodded quickly. They both scooted away from us slightly, hugging each other.

I looked at them, confused, but then they revealed they had been acquaintances back in high school. I looked back at Liam, who blushed slightly.

"I, um—I'm Liam," he said, and then facepalmed. "But I-I mean you already knew t-that, since you know, my mom, s-she . . ." he stuttered out, and I giggled at him as his face flushed bright red.

"It's okay, I'm Bianca," I said, repeating my name so that he didn't feel bad, and he looked at my outstretched hand before shaking it.

"Nice to meet you, Bianca." My stomach filled with this weird fluttering feeling, and I smiled at how he said my name.

"Nice to meet you too, Liam," I replied. "Do you wanna come in?" He sheepishly showed me his bright smile while nodding. He stepped in with me, and Mom realized I wanted to close the door. She stopped her conversation, closed the door, and sat beside me as Liam sat next to Ana.

"Just you wait. These two are gonna be great friends," Ana said, and I smiled at her, liking her already.

I blink, coming back to reality when Ana's rambunctious laughter fills the house, and most importantly, fills me with a happiness that her laughter used to always bring.

It's been a bit since Mom told me to get ready for the event later tonight, and all I've been doing is trying so hard not to throw up or fall into a panic attack. I shimmied into a cute, pastel-blue romper and opted for some white kitten heels. I twist my hands in my hair, making some new curls. I stand in front of the mirror, taking shallow breaths, my nerves getting the better of me. My hands smooth down the soft, buttery material, and I take one long, deep breath.

A gorgeous person stares back and I smile at her. She can do this; I know she can. I reach over to grab my gold clutch and walk out of the bedroom. As I enter the living room, Josh is admiring Mom while Olivia fixes her hair in the mirror.

"Oh my gosh, Bianca, you look amazing," Mom says, and Josh looks at me, almost analyzing the outfit; Olivia does the same. Her black hair   is tied back in a loose bun with strands falling out. Her flawless eyeshadow gives her eyes a more doe-like shape. She wears a silver dress with earrings to match.

"Thanks," I reply.

"Alright, are we ready to go?" Josh asks as he puts his arm around Mom's waist, his Rolex shining slightly, and I roll my eyes at his vanity. Nodding at that, he guides Mom to the door, and we follow behind them as I try to calm down.

Keyword: *try*.

We drive to the venue. I take some breaths as we hit potholes, Josh not bothering with apologies this time. Olivia has yet to say hi to me, and I don't even mind it at this point. As we arrive, the first thing I see is Ana's bright-colored Jeep parked, and while I want to smile, nerves attack me more.

Josh hands the key to the valet, and we all get out as Mom and I say thank you to him. Josh offers her his arm and she takes it. The venue is beautiful, and it looks like the outside is decorated as well. There are fake vines wrapped around the load-bearing columns and carefully placed flowers perfectly fitting the outdoorsy theme. Josh calls us, and I train my smile. We all shake hands with a wealthy couple—from what I can deduce, as they're dressed as if they're going to a country derby. I try not to overthink my outfit, even though everyone else looks like something out of an Armani catalogue.

He whisks us to someone else as he smiles and waves to another group, the bubbly in front of them. My mouth quirks upward as I'm faced with another couple, and I sigh in relief when I notice who they are.

"Tony. It's been a bit, hasn't it?" Mom gives him a polite hug and a small smile to his wife.

Tony—Mom's ex-boss and Josh's current one, who he's currently trying to butter up—gives her a warm grin back. "We've definitely missed you at the office." He also gives a firm handshake to Josh. "Spectacular job with the event, I'm impressed." He gives me a little wave.

"Much appreciated. I also know you haven't had the chance to meet my daughter, Olivia." She pushes past me, and I step back as she shakes Tony's hand excitedly. "She's going to UPenn in start of a very promising law degree."

He raises his eyebrows. "That's exciting. That was my alma mater, it's an amazing program. I'm sure with Joshua's influence, you'll make a fine lawyer one day." She beams at the praise, and then eyes fall on me.

"I'm also wanting to volunteer at some law firms to get some experience under my belt," Olivia brings up, and Tony's eyes once again leave me to look at her. Politely excusing myself, knowing I most likely won't be able to get a word in, I head toward the drinks table.

"Bianca!" I look up to see Ana waving at me. She has on the cutest little floral dress with beige sandals, her curls bouncing lively. She truly embodies the theme, and not in the pretentious way I've seen so far.

"You look beautiful," I say once I get close enough. She swishes back and forth and then twirls me.

"I think that's all you. Hermosa as always." I blush at the compliment, feeling more at ease in this moment than I have so far. A shadow comes to stand next to her, and I look up, gasping.

After Dad died, I never knew who to look up to, in that sense. I had Mom, of course, but the things a dad teaches you are different. I thought I would miss all of it, but because of this man standing in front of me, Mr. William Parker, I was able to still have a father figure in my life.

He wears thin-framed glasses and salt-and-pepper hair, and a couple of wrinkles line his face. He has a stoic look, yet when he makes eye contact with me, his eyes are slightly welling with tears.

"And who is this young lady?" he asks Ana.

"It's me, Will," I utter, and his face falls into that soft, familiar expression. I bite back a cry as he smiles at me, feeling like I'm six years old again.

"Come here, *you*," he says, wrapping his arms around me and I hug him back. His cologne brings back memories, and I hate how teary-eyed I'm getting. We pull away, and his eyes shine with unshed tears. Mine do too, but I blink them away, trying not to cause my mascara to streak.

"You've grown so much, pumpkin." I nearly cry out at the familiar nickname, nodding, hugging him once more. Another pair of arms snake around me, and I giggle at Ana joining in on the hug. Mom is walking over with Josh. He's not angry, but he's not happy about the scene either.

"Oh my goodness. William! How are you?" Mom exclaims, giving him a big hug while letting go of Josh's hand.

Josh wraps an arm around her waist again, reclaiming her. "Hi, I'm Josh Callaway, Kate's boyfriend."

William smiles, grabbing his hand and shaking it firmly. "Oh, nice to meet you. William Parker."

Josh pulls his hand back and fakes a smile. "Ah, you must be the husband of the woman who's been stealing Kate away from me lately."

Ana pokes her head out. "Guilty," she says.

I elbow her teasingly and look up at Josh; his expression seems to morph into one of resigned acceptance. "Well, it's a bit unexpected, but it's a pleasure to see and meet you guys."

Ana and William exchange confused glances as Josh turns to look at Mom. He grabs her chin. "Looks like you forgot to tell me, sweetie."

She smiles, but only I know it's her nervous one. "I thought it would be a nice surprise."

He raises his eyebrows. "She knows how much I love those." We all laugh again, a bit lighter than before. He swings his gaze back on the Parkers, and then I see someone else coming close to us. Josh slips on his smile, turning to begin his suck-up routine once again, before it seems to drop and my skin peppers with goose bumps when I look closer at the familiar guy.

CHAPTER THIRTEEN

Liam

TODAY'S THE DAY.

The day I've been absolutely dreading.

The day that I go home for break.

I blow out a sigh of exasperation, wishing that I didn't have to go, because technically break doesn't start for a few days. But in all honesty, I can't exactly stay here. I've finished my classes for the semester, so I have nothing to do. I thought I would have work, but no, the owner decided to close for the summer, being that most of our clientele are college students. On top of that, I'm not exactly on good terms with everyone else working there right now. I also have nothing better to do, and I promised my parents I would go see them, but that was before . . .

Before I knew who moved in close to us.

I mean, I'm thoroughly planning on ignoring her and taking Chase's advice. Besides, this will protect me in the long run. I *have* to protect my heart. I can't take any more pain. If I don't, I don't know if I would get over it a second time. I mean, I still haven't gotten over it since the first time. Contemplating the whole situation and trying my best not to freak out anymore, my hand drags down my face as I sigh. Stuffing my suitcase, I make my way to the parking lot and jog to the driver's side of the car, more than ready to roar its engine to life.

Somewhat ready to see how these months will go.

Biding my time to merge onto the busiest highway, I start to think about everything that I'm about to face.

Bianca Harrison is not only going to attend my college, but has also practically infiltrated my family. Mom called and got me up to speed. Apparently, Ms. Kate has invited us to an event, and I promised to make an appearance. Knowing Mom, she'll be acting as if nothing happened, and for a second, I want to do that. Yet seeing that rejection—that look on Bianca's face—cemented everything for me.

I refuse to go back to a place of hope. That place I dug myself out of when I realized that Bianca and I were a done deal. There's still something inside of me, though, that still can't come to its senses. This part of me that wants to give our friendship another chance, maybe one day dare to ask to be something more.

I sigh, gripping the steering wheel tightly, my knuckles turning white as I try to bury my feelings, effectively pushing them away—but they always come back. Turning on a random playlist, I raise the volume, hoping it drowns out my thoughts, but as my mind registers my getting closer to Los Angeles, music seems to be losing its usefulness.

Sighing at the restlessness in my head, and my ETA saying I have three hours to go, against my better judgment, I make a call.

"What do you want?"

I look at my phone in shock, scoffing at his tone. *This idiot didn't* . . .

"And you wonder why I never call you," I mutter, moving my thumb to hang up.

But not before he says, "Wait, no. I was joking." He bursts out laughing and I roll my eyes. Why did I become sort of friends with this guy again? He starts to calm down, and I can imagine him wiping the tears off his face. "At least now you know how you are."

I huff. "I'm not like that."

"Alright, if you say so."

I scowl at his response, and the car becomes utterly silent, to the point that all I can hear is the sound of my tires spinning along the road and the gentle hum of the motor.

"You still there?" he asks.

"Yeah, I'm here. You'd know if I hung up on you."

He chuckles. "There he is. So, what's up?"

"Nothing really," I say as I yawn, already tired of the trip.

"I don't believe you. You *never* call me. Not once. I almost dropped my phone when I saw your caller ID on my screen."

"Really? I can't imagine why," I say, and accelerate slightly as I merge into a different lane.

"Are you there yet?"

"No, still got three hours to go."

"Damn."

"Yeah."

"Okay, this small talk is sad. What did you really call me for?" he asks. "Is it about Harrison?"

"Sort of." I sigh. "I wish she hadn't come back." *Lies.* "I hate her, and her enrolling at college and moving minutes away from my home is screwing with my head." More lies, but I guess I have to convince myself somehow.

"You don't *hate* her."

"Of course I do." The words taste bitter in my mouth.

"No, you don't. You hate what went down, but not her personally. You hate that you lowered your guard. You hate that she made you feel replaceable when you tried so hard not to make *her* feel that way."

My jaw clenches and unclenches as I process his words. I mean, he has somewhat of a point, but still . . .

I hate her.

Don't I?

"Look, I get what you're going through, but do what I told you to. Ignore her."

After my talk with Chase, I feel slightly better. My feelings were out of whack, but he set me straight.

It feels weird to admit that.

My body aches from sitting in the same place for hours, but slight relief comes when I see the big sign that says, "Welcome to Los Angeles!"

Though, dread settles in as I get closer to the address Mom sent over. It's only thirty or so miles to the event, but due to a couple of accidents, there's a thirty- to forty-minute delay. I mutter silent expletives at the thought of sitting here. The long sleeves of my white shirt bother me after a bit, so I roll up the cuffs.

I unbutton the first couple of buttons of my shirt, letting out a deep breath. One thing I've always hated is being late. I promised I would be there by at least three, but that came and went. I bang my hand on the steering wheel, as for twenty minutes, all I've moved is about two inches.

Ugh, can this day drag on any longer?
Answer: Yes, it definitely can.

After about an hour, I get out of the traffic jam, but am still a little way away. I pull off to the side of the road and type a quick text to Mom, letting her know that I would be late, but the message stays on delivered. I sigh at that and get back on the road. Pulling into the fancy venue, it looks as if the event is in full swing. I get out as the valet asks for my keys and hand them to him. The ballroom looks like it costs an arm and a leg to rent. Some guests linger outside, and so do their stares, causing me to shift the cuffs of my shirt nervously. Taking a deep breath, I walk in, trying to look for someone that I know, ignoring the whispers.

I look around as I go over my game plan. Ignore Bianca, avoid the Crystal Pines subdivision at all costs, and lastly, don't let my heart get in the way.

I can do this.

Nodding, opting for a small smile as I pass by another group of men in what looks like golf attire, not taking notice of their expressions, I walk toward another huge set of doors, my mind swimming with thoughts.

She hurt you.

She ignored you. Ignore her back.

What's the deal with that girl you're always drawing?

You don't hate her. You hate what she did to you.

Maybe it was a misunderstanding.

I blink rapidly, the low symphony of the live orchestra coming at me. Guests all over are having animated conversations as I try to look for my parents. Warmth comes over me as I twist my head to the left. Squaring my shoulders, I walk closer as my eyes bounce to everyone. Mom smiles when she sees me, and I return the sentiment while she meets me halfway.

She glances up at me with a look that says, "This is it," and I nod, reassuring that I'm okay. I lock eyes on the woman who was like a second mother to me growing up. She looks at me awkwardly, mixed with confusion, and I don't blame her.

She probably doesn't even recognize me, considering that I was a little scrawny teenager the last time she saw me. Embarrassment washes over my face as she stands there. To mask it, I stick out a hand, but she shakes her head. With shame, I put it down, but then she wraps her arms around me.

The nostalgia practically rips me apart. All the times that I would go over and she would teach me how to make her famous hot chocolate, or even how to read my favorite chapter books—she was there for it all, and my inner child is so happy as her scent wafts through my nostrils.

"I'm glad we got to see each other again. You're all grown up, *little man.*"

I pull back, nodding as emotionlessly as possible, not trusting my voice when she mentions the nickname she used to have for me. Someone comes closer to her, and I recognize him from orientation. Mom always said that since I was little, I had a weird sixth sense about people. Of course, it's pretty much advanced intuition.

I haven't had that feeling in over a decade. But this guy—

This guy right here is not a good guy.

"I don't think we've properly met. I'm Josh Callaway. I'm Kate's boyfriend." He sticks out his hand, his tone clipped at the edges—almost as if I'm not supposed to be here. He gives me a knowing smile like he remembers exactly where he knows me from, yet doesn't say anything about it. I glance between him and his hand, and he looks around at the other guests as if he considers the contact a chore. I scoff slightly and begrudgingly shake.

"Nice to meet you."

He drops my hand quickly, like a pathetic show of his superiority. Though, the action falls short when he somewhat discreetly rubs it on his slacks and I realize that I make him nervous. Dad observes the interaction before wrapping me in a big bear hug, and I return the gesture. After a bit, he pulls back and smiles before it drops into a frown.

"You're late," he says, arching an eyebrow, and I give a sheepish expression.

"Traffic."

He looks at me, making sure I'm not lying, and when he's satisfied, he nods. Clapping me on the back, he says, "I've missed you, son."

Giving him a small smile, I murmur, "I did too, Dad."

He moves out of the way and she instantly comes into view; my heart constricts as if someone shot an arrow through it.

"Bianca," I breathe.

Why? *Why* is it that when I'm around her, the past five years are forgotten so easily? Five years I've been missing—hell, *pining*—for her. How do people do this? Because wrestling with your head and heart is damn near exhausting.

My eyes meet those bottomless blue ones, and I clear my throat, avoiding them. The very eyes that are in my *every* drawing, those eyes that I would look into for years of my life. My inner child jumps with joy once again, but before either of us can say something, even though I see it in her eyes that she is about to—someone speaks.

"Bianca, say hello, don't be rude," Josh scolds.

She looks around, and I hate to admit that I miss her gaze on mine. I swivel my head, a glare sent his way as he clears his throat before I look back at her. She flushes in embarrassment, making me almost wince at the familiar expression. I realize no one except Josh has said something. I stay rooted in place as she raises her head. We lock eyes, and I almost smile as I see those familiar gold specks once again. And if only for a tortured moment, one I will later regret, I *bask* in it.

"Hi."

CHAPTER FOURTEEN

Bianca

A WHISPER LEAVES HIS LIPS, forming the word, yet I can't bring myself to say anything. After everything that happened these past couple of weeks, I assumed he wouldn't come home for summer break. Yet, I was wrong, and I hate how my heart rejoices at that. It thinks he came for me.

Delusional as per usual.

I clear my throat and look around, seeing different emotions everywhere. Ana and William look like they're holding their breaths, concern etching their faces. Mom looks as though she wants to step in, but doesn't.

"Hi," I say back.

I swear that his eyes soften slightly, but it's probably my mind playing tricks on me. Microphone feedback fills the air and Josh closes his eyes in forgetfulness.

He mutters a soft curse. "Excuse me a moment." He swings his gaze toward Mom and smiles almost bitterly. "Entertain our guests." He speaks through clenched teeth as she nods before he whispers something. Her face flushes in what looks like embarrassment. Josh nods curtly before he walks off. A leggy blonde announces her appreciation for the attendance. Everyone claps softly, and I roll my eyes at the snobs that lawyers are. We all turn to the stage where she's standing and Mom grabs my arm, linking hers with mine. A shadow comes to my other side and I try not to glance in his direction. There's a crick in my neck, so I roll my shoulders and turn my head.

Our eyes find each other again; he looks like he came from a photo shoot. From his white button-up that brings out his tan skin, to the tattoos going up his neck, the silver rings on his fingers, and those gorgeous, emerald eyes.

Time has really done him well.

I snap my head forward as they continue the announcements. Seeing Olivia coming toward us, I excuse myself, knowing that the only reason she's coming over here is because of Liam.

Mom beams. "Olivia! I wanna introduce you to some people." I squeeze between attendees in search of the appetizer table, feeling the need to fill my stomach with something. Being that Josh was one of the head organizers, he was also in charge of the food, and very apparently so.

I can't read half of the names, them being seemingly in French or something, and the waiter looks at me expectantly. My eyes scan the placards, and for a moment, I despise that I chose to learn Spanish in high school. I think I see salmon, and a queasiness is already bubbling in my stomach.

Halfway through middle school, and after a terrible incident on a field trip where we went to a seafood boil place, I discovered that I hated it. Salmon, shrimp, crab—the lot of it. Any type, all freaking types, it makes me want to throw up.

"Miss?"

I glance up as he holds out the plate and I give him a sheepish smile.

"Um . . ." I trail off, hating the pressure of choosing something soon due to the rapidly forming line. Another attendee appears beside me and I wave off the worker to take them next.

"Can I have the ham and cheese quiche?" The voice makes the hairs on the back of my neck stand, and again, I risk a glance. Liam has a small smile—something different from his usual scowl—as he grabs the plate from the guy. He doesn't look at me, and instead walks off, and I huff.

He's doing what I'm doing: staying away.

I realize that what he ordered is something that doesn't have seafood. I thank my lucky stars before the guy comes back, and I ask for the same quiche. My mouth waters as I smell the decadent mix of cheeses and ham. Smiling, I make my way back, though Mom's nowhere to be found.

The woman on the stage is no longer announcing anything, and I look closely to see Josh has scooped Mom up to talk to more people. Potential partners for the new firm, potential clients, and so on. I make my way to stand next to William as Olivia chats Liam's ear off about something. I ignore the feeling in my heart when she twists her hair around her pointer finger, probably giving him her innocent little doe eyes. Not paying attention, someone pushes my shoulder playfully, and I gaze up to see William's eyes meeting mine, waiting.

"So?" he asks while fully facing me. I gulp as my anxiety starts to rise at that, since I didn't hear the question.

I try to salvage the moment, chuckling softly. "Sorry, Will, I didn't really hear the question." He chuckles right back.

"It's alright, Bianca. I repeat myself to Ana all the time. The only reason she remembers her head is because it's attached to her neck," he says, and Ana looks over at him, pulling away from the group of ladies she's already infiltrated. She walks over before looking up at William.

"You talking bad about me, Will?" Ana asks.

He feigns hurt. "Never, my love." She rolls her eyes as he plants a kiss on her forehead before they both look at me. "I was asking Bianca if she's excited to start Mella Colta in the fall."

Liam seems to stiffen; it must be regarding whatever Olivia's said. I smile as I flit my eyes back to them.

"Yeah, for sure. Mella Colta has been my dream school since I was little."

William chuckles. "I remember, you and Li—"

His sentence is stopped short when Liam's voice joins in. *"Dad."*

His deep voice causes me to shudder slightly, but I rub my arms as if to blame the cool draft. Looking over, I catch sight of Olivia, who's walking away. She slides next to Josh and he looks like he's already started scolding her. Mom stands there, appearing uncomfortable, but the moment her eyes meet mine, she smiles.

Ana clears her throat, bringing my attention back. "Liam, you think you could get me more of that quiche you didn't want?"

My eyes widen in shock and he grabs her plate before I say something. Ana and William seem to feel a bit of the tense energy between him and me.

"I thought the quiche was for you," I say to him.

He stops, and for a moment, I think he won't answer. "I don't really like quiche all that much. Besides, it's the only thing without seafood." He leaves it at that, and Ana furrows her eyebrows.

"Bud, if that's the case, get me something with some then." She rolls her eyes. "I love when quiche has shrimp and crab."

My heart beats a little irregularly as I remember Ana's guilty pleasure is seafood, but *mine* isn't. I rack my brain trying to remember if I ever told him, and I could only seem to recall when I said it in passing.

Did he remember, and when he saw me struggling, wanted to help?

I shake my head, cursing myself for being so dumb. He probably forgot or just got the first thing he saw. Nothing he does has anything to do with me anymore. I need to keep convincing myself of that.

Mom comes back over before she sighs slightly. "I'm sorry, guys. Josh has been presenting me to absolutely everyone."

Ana waves her hand in the air. "You're fine, Kate. I didn't know your boyfriend organized this party."

Mom flushes in embarrassment. "Yeah, he's been so stressed, and I've had to tell him it's going fine." They laugh, and I look over to see Josh staring Mom down. Though, when he catches me looking, he smiles and waves politely.

I nod curtly before William says, "Thanks for inviting us, Kate. It's definitely been a while, and I'm glad we got to see you again."

Ana smiles like the cat who got the cream. "Well, I've been seeing her way before you, Will. Both of them."

He shakes his head, the corner of his lips quivering. "I would've joined you if I wasn't working, beautiful." I smile, and there's a sense of peace and comfort coming over me. These two were always such important people in my life, and while their son and I are no longer amicable, I hope I can still keep a piece of them at least.

Liam finally returns and hands Ana a plate of good food. Her eyes light up and a small smile starts on his face before it drops. Mom rubs her arm, a nervous tic I got from her. "So, I heard you're in college, little man." She winces. "Liam, I mean."

He doesn't look like he minds the nickname, but before he can respond, Josh squeezes through.

He forces a smile. "Sorry, guys, need to steal Katie from you."

Mom can't even respond before he whisks her away, and Ana looks at me with a confused expression. "I thought she hated that nickname."

Shrugging, I say, "She does." Her eyes widen slightly before she nods, then looks down.

At that, the orchestra stops playing and we all look up to see Josh on the stage with a big, controlled grin. "Thank you all for coming and giving me five hours of your Saturday. I know these days are crucial for us attorneys." The haughty laughter isn't missed, and I chuckle to go along with everyone else. "When Tony offered me the relocation position to open the Los Angeles office, I was nervous, but I want to extend my gratitude for his faith in me." He raises a flute of champagne and Tony raises a glass of what looks like scotch. "And, I have enjoyed getting to know many of the people here. However, I have one more surprise left." The tall blonde from earlier brings Mom to the bottom of the stage and everyone watches her. "Katie, my beautiful girlfriend, would you mind coming up here?" Her eyes widen, and I instantly become uneasy at the sight. He grabs her hand, then looks back to the crowd. "All through the evening, I've seen people I respect with their significant others. And it's fueled something I've been planning for a while." We all wait with bated breath when Josh gets down on one knee, and a collection of gasps echo out.

Mom covers her mouth with both her hands as Josh grabs the ring from his suit jacket. He gives her a small smile. "Kate Harrison, I don't want to merely be your boyfriend anymore. I was once your coworker back in Philly, but even then, I knew I wanted more. I want you to be Kate Callaway, my partner in all ways."

He looks down, and the women say "aw," Ana being part of them as I lowly scoff.

Josh glances up. "Marry me?"

I love Mom, I do, and I want her to be happy, but I also want her to say no. She deserves someone better. Someone who doesn't let his stress dictate his emotions, someone who can be more like Dad.

She gives a shallow nod before he confirms through the microphone, "She said yes!" He hugs her and everyone claps. Olivia stays stunned and Josh looks over at her. Within a minute, her face changes to a smile and she runs up to hug them both. He slips the ring on Mom's finger and she looks at it in shock. When she looks up to find me in the crowd, I shrink back.

William and Ana don't move out of the way, and I thank goodness for it. William is clapping, but Ana's arms snake around mine, comfort behind the gesture. She doesn't say anything, and I don't know what to do either. She then pats my arm and warmth spreads through me. Liam clears his throat, causing me to look up at him. William and Ana turn back as well.

"I think it's time for me to get going. I'm exhausted, so I think I'll tuck in for the evening. Long drive and all," he says while fixing the sleeves of his shirt. He focuses his eyes on me. "Let Ms. Kate know I say congrats." I nod, and he looks as if he wants to say something else, but decides against it. "Mom. Dad. I'll see you guys later." He turns around and starts to walk off, and I deflate like a leaky balloon. He stops and turns. "Also." Those gorgeous, emerald eyes, instead of holding gentleness as they had before, hold anger, resentment, and *hurt*. "Consider your request granted."

There are hands on my shoulders, and I flinch at the feel of them.

Turning around, I say, "I'm sorry."

William shakes his head. "It isn't your fault, pumpkin. Liam's just a hothead. He's in that stage." I appreciate him trying to make me feel better, but I still feel horrible. Mom rushes to us while I watch Josh and Olivia talking to Tony and his wife, who seem to be congratulating him. Mom hugs me with the biggest smile on her face, and I give her one right back. I thank goodness for Ana's bubbly behavior as I'm not able to muster up that much excitement while my mind drifts back to Liam.

He's staying out of my way, like I wanted. Then why does my heart feel heavy in my chest? Why do I want to rewind time to orientation when his eyes didn't have the tint of hurt clouding them?

Because no matter what, he'll always be my best friend, and I love him. It's been five years and every beat of my heart still belongs to Liam freaking Parker.

"You're awfully quiet, sweetie," Mom says as she turns around to get a better look at me, but I refuse to make eye contact. I stare out the window, my heart and mind completely jumbled. She sighs and Josh starts whispering stuff to her, making me cringe slightly. Pulling into a gas station, Mom gets out to pay, and I'm stuck in the car with Josh and Olivia.

"Bianca," he starts, and I look up as he fixes the rearview mirror to stare directly at me.

"What?" I mumble, not giving him the least bit of attention.

"Aren't you happy about the proposal?"

He's baiting me, and I make sure to nod while Olivia looks over at me. "Of course," I say, and he looks at me like he doesn't believe it, but I stand my ground.

"Good. I know Katie's very happy too. Let's try not to ruin that." I mentally scoff, but only give him a small nod.

Mom gets back in. "Josh, can you pump the gas? I already paid for it." He nods before getting out of the car. "I got you some Skittles," she says, passing them into the back seat. I smile gratefully as Olivia lifts the sparkling water she grabbed before we left the event earlier. Mom looks like she wants to talk about everything, but I shake my head. She gives me a confused look. I flick my eyes to Olivia and her face clears in understanding.

Josh opens the door, hopping back into the driver's seat. "Alright, car's all filled up."

The conversation ends and we drive back to our home where Josh and Mom are returning as an engaged couple. Something sours in my mouth, and I have a feeling it's not from the candy. We all go to our respective rooms, but before I close my door, Mom's telling Josh something. He nods and kisses her cheek, and she comes down the hall to me. She slips into my room with me and I sit on the bed, waiting. I pop some more candies in my mouth, my eyes drifting down to the huge rock on her finger winking up at me.

"Bianca, you're my daughter, so I know how your mind works." She takes a deep breath. "It's been thirteen years since David died, hon. And it's time to seek other things in my life. Don't get me wrong, he was and will *always* be the love of my life, but I know that he wouldn't want me to be alone forever. We just . . ." Clearing her throat, she continues. "We loved each other so much that we wanted to make sure we were both happy."

I sniffle a bit. Mom has had so much happen to her, from losing Ezra and the love of her life to trying to find a way to raise me on her own. She deserves all of the good things that come to her.

Even if Josh is one of those good things.

"I love you, Mom," I say, and she smiles and gives me a bear hug, practically suffocating me.

"I love you more, hon." I squeeze her in response. She leaves, and when the door closes, I make a move for my phone to call Jamie.

"Hello?" she answers, and I sigh, leaning against my headboard.

"Girl, you won't believe what happened today . . ."

CHAPTER FIFTEEN

Liam

UNEASE ROLLS OFF ME IN waves as I constantly decrease my speed. Using one hand, I undo the buttons near my neck, feeling instant relief. The deal with Mom was that I was supposed to stay the whole event, and I did. But I didn't exactly go back home when I left. I take deep breaths as my emotions course through me, given my interaction with her. I feel everything, yet nothing at all.

On one hand, I'm so mad at myself, considering how my brain seems to malfunction when she's nearby. After coming up with ways to avoid her this summer and all of the fall semester, I even asked Chase for advice, for God's sake. But no—my heart refuses to understand she's not good for me anymore.

She wants me to stay out of her way, so why can't I listen?

I'm not the same kid I was all those years ago, but when I see those eyes—the most *gorgeous* eyes I've ever had the privilege of looking into—every single thought I have about protecting myself goes out the damn window. How can she still have so much power over me? I have a promising career, I'm studying one of the hardest majors out there, and yet, she still occupies space in my brain, though I'm not putting up much of a fight.

So, without even thinking, I call probably the only person I can talk to about this.

"Second time in one day, Parker. I'm honored." I say nothing. How is it that I spent semesters hating this guy, and now I'm calling him out of my own free will? "Sooo, how did it go? You making out with Harrison yet?" His suggestive tone lights a fire in me, and I merge in front of some idiot who has no concept of what a blinker means.

"First off, the nickname is *not cute*. Secondly, I wouldn't tell you that anyway."

A chuckle sounds through the phone. "I'll take that as a no." Exit signs light up and fade away as I drive by them, silence enveloping my car, even though Chase is still on the line. "Dude, I know you're new to the concept of phone calls, but when you call someone, talking is involved."

"You think we should take orbital mechanics in the fall?"

"I'd love to, but my father's wanting me to start getting some finance courses under my belt. Though, I heard Dr. Anders is the best."

I thank goodness he goes along with the stupid small talk. "Is he grooming you to be the next millionaire?"

He snorts. "Since birth, but yeah, this is another way to make sure I know who's paying my tuition every semester."

A sad smile starts on my face. "Brutal, man."

"Story of my life, unfortunately." He huffs before redirecting the conversation. "So, was she flirting with someone else, or . . ."

A frustrated sigh leaves me, my thumbs drumming on the wheel as my pent-up emotions stir up something. "It didn't go the best. Look, I called to say thanks for the advice. That's it."

He mumbles "No problem," but it doesn't feel like the end of what he has to say. "You're such an idiot."

My hand clenches the steering wheel as disbelief fills me. "Excuse me?"

"I know you did something moronic."

"I followed your advice."

He doesn't miss a beat. "Again, moronic. You should never follow my advice."

My heart drops at the admission. "Chase, what the hell?"

He chuckles. "It's good advice if you were in a situation where the other person also hates you. That's why it doesn't work in this case."

I shake my head as I start to inch right, the exit I want coming up. "Why would you . . .? Never mind." The jerk dares to laugh at me. When I head back to campus, I'm strangling the life out of him.

"I knew you were still in love with her," he says, and my lips purse at the true statement. I almost miss my exit, and I think long and hard as to why I called him, of all people.

"Shut up." My heart clenches at the words, the stupid organ not knowing when to keep itself in check.

Another chuckle ensues. "Look, here's some real advice, since your head is so far up in the clouds. Either man up and tell her everything you're feeling or suck it up and forget about it." My heart beats that much faster at the idea. He hangs up before I can reply, and my music picks up from where it left off. I scoff at the guy I've started to become sort of friends with, and I regret everything thus far.

I see the familiar street names.

Left.

Right.

Left again, till you hit a fence.

I park in my usual spot as the night sky shines above me, my mind already mapping all the constellations. I take out my portable telescope and slam the trunk. I walk into the field I've visited hundreds of times over the years. Finding the old willow tree, I set up the telescope, my hands flowing with ease as I adjust everything so I can have a direct view of the cluster of stars near and dear to my heart.

As I peek through the lens, a flash lights up the night sky, and with it, a flashback.

"Freckles, I'm gonna catch you!" I exclaimed, trying to keep up with her as I surged ahead in our race. She stuck her tongue out playfully, urging me on. In the end, she won, but before she could boast about her win, I gently tackled her to the ground, and we both dissolved into laughter. As we laid side by side, our eyes met and our hands naturally found each other. Locking our fingers together, I brought them to my lips, planting a delicate kiss on her soft skin, causing a slight blush to creep across her cheeks. I adored how I could make her blush so easily.

"I beat you," she teased, but I wasn't listening, I was getting lost in her eyes, not caring about the outcome of the race whatsoever. "The sun's setting," she said nervously, looking over to Ms. Kate, but I got up, wrapping my hands around her.

"Hey, I'm here. I won't let anything happen, okay?" I reassured, hoping my words and gentle touch eased her nerves. When I asked if she wanted to stay, she hesitated briefly before nodding.

"I feel safe when you're with me," she admitted, and my heart burst with happiness.

Taking a deep breath, we laid back down, looking up at the night sky, and then we started naming the constellations and the stars we learned about in school.

Suddenly, a bright streak lit up the sky—a shooting star. Her gasp drew my attention. "Liam, did you see that?" she exclaimed. "It was a shooting star!" I nodded. "Well, we have to wish for something. Dad told me that when you see a shooting star, you always make a wish."

"One, two, three," we counted in unison, closing our eyes. In that moment, my heart wished for something I'd longed for.

I wish you would love me back someday in the future, *I thought, silently sharing my deepest desire, speaking the words with my heart.*

"Done," she said, opening her eyes while I was already looking at her.

Intertwining our fingers again, I leaned in to kiss her temple, whispering, "Me too, Freckles."

I pull at the strands at the base of my neck in frustration, bringing me back to the present. I scoff at how much I cared about her, *loved her*, even. Then for her to end our friendship without even giving me a chance to prove her wrong. She left like we were nothing, and even came back like it's nothing. A ding comes from my phone and I grab it; it's probably Mom wondering where I went off to. Seeing the social media logo, I hold down, thinking it's another batch of likes on the official page for InkedAcademia. I hesitate a bit, seeing Mom's handle instead, a new photo of her and the bane of my existence.

Bianca's smiling so hard you can't even see her blue eyes, and for some reason, my heart starts beating so fast. I force my smile to drop and chuck my phone down on the ground, wanting to calm myself, trying not to rile myself up again at the reaction of my treacherous heart.

God, what's wrong with me? How could she do that? Be there like nothing's wrong. Go along with it all when I'm broken over everything.

We're broken.

I sigh at that, and my conversation with Chase comes back to my head.

Either man up and tell her everything you're feeling or suck it up and forget about it.

I know this. My brain knows this.

I can pass astronomical science principles in my sleep. I've passed every mathematical theory class in the aerospace curriculum and then some. But when it comes to Bianca—basic philosophical truths have different answers, and everything I know to be true blurs together. It's like I can't stop myself from throwing out my brain and letting my heart guide all my actions.

Mom once told me that I had the biggest heart she had ever seen in someone, and that it would be both a blessing and a curse. She told me to protect it, but how can I do that when all I want to do is give it to someone who doesn't want it?

Someone whom I, unfortunately, still love with everything I've got.

CHAPTER SIXTEEN

Bianca

SOUNDS OF BARKING AND MEOWING come through the door as I glance through the window, seeing all the little guys. My heart fills that much more when one of the vet assistants comes out holding a precious little chihuahua, whispering the words, "You'll be better soon."

As if my heart wasn't already full, it's now bursting at the seams.

"Hi! I'm Rachel, the volunteer coordinator." She shakes my hand. "Bianca, right?" I nod. "Great, you came at just the right time. We're always severely understaffed during the summer." She passes by a hand sanitizer station and I quickly follow after her. "Alright, your attire is absolutely perfect. Closed-toe shoes always along with clothes you don't mind getting stained." She smiles at some of the girls who pass by us, who look at me with curious stares. "You'll get a free T-shirt when I can go find one for you. Let me know the size."

I nod as she writes it down on her clipboard and starts explaining all the steps to follow every shift.

Clock in on the computer in the break room.

Find a team member who needs assistance.

129

"Now, I saw on your application you're wanting to volunteer for our vet office, right?"

"Um, yeah. I'm going to college for animal science in the fall, so I wanted to get some experience under my belt." She smiles and pushes through a door to the kennel, and my heart breaks and repairs itself at seeing all of the furry faces.

Compared to some of the other places I visited, this was the only one near me that doesn't euthanize any of their animals. Skipping past a bunch of them, she seems not to want to stop as she's explaining everything. But we pass by the last kennel, and my heart expands that much more at the sight of a golden retriever sleeping on a bed with a blanket.

"Sam," she says, and points to his doggie card.

My eyes run down everything. The number seven pops out and I look at her in shock. "He's seven years old?"

She nods with a sad smile. "Yeah, he's been here for a while, the owner's wife passed away and he couldn't take care of him after, so he dropped him off here." My heart breaks for Sam, and I knock on the kennel door softly. He raises his head, looks at me curiously, then sleepily puts it back down.

"He's tired." She checks her watch, then looks up at the digital clock, shaking her head and muttering something to herself. "Tell you what, you can start today. Kennel duty first, and when it's downtime, come find me and I'll introduce you to our vet. Sound good?" I nod at that and she sends me off. I wave at her as she walks away.

I find one of the full-time kennel keepers, who puts me on cleaning duty. It may not be the most fun work, but as each of the animals' furry faces look at the suds with curiosity, I can't help but think about every single life I'll save one day, and that . . .

That's what gets me through it.

I wake up from my nap to a car revving in the neighborhood, causing me to sigh exasperatedly. I flip onto my stomach with my pillow over my head, hoping it helps, but it doesn't. The car revs again and I huff in anger. Walking over to my window, I open it, seeing a bunch of cars in front of Patty's house. That's when understanding dawns on me: Her book club is tonight.

At that, someone climbs out of a beautiful white BMW. *He* slides out of his car, and when he does, he's wearing a warm beige linen shirt, shorts somewhat of the same color. I gawk, but when he glances over, I quickly scamper and close my curtains. Sneaking another peek, he seems completely oblivious, and I giggle at that. My eyes widen when they flick to my alarm clock, seeing my "ten-minute nap" turned into a four-hour one.

I was at the shelter for over seven hours; sue me for taking a little nap that might've lasted longer than I planned. Making my way to the bathroom, stretching out my weary muscles, I try to make myself a little bit presentable. After, I head to the living room to find Mom, but much to my dismay, all I'm met with is Josh on the couch with a laptop in hand.

"She's not here."

I stop, glance back, and see Josh looking at me. "What?"

"She's still . . . at the neighbor's." His words slow down as he looks at his watch. Something akin to annoyance passes over his face as he looks up at me. I nod, slipping my shoes on when he closes his laptop slowly. "I'll come with."

Josh comes up behind me, the house keys already on his pointer finger. He shouts to Olivia that we'll be back, her not bothering to respond. I swallow as we walk ever so calmly across the street. All the ladies are talking outside, but my face starts to warm slightly as Liam locks his eyes with mine.

Almost tripping, I keep my head down, trying to somewhat hide behind Josh as we walk toward Ana and Mom.

"Josh, honey." Her eyes widen as Josh plasters a fake smile while slithering an arm around her waist, and I grimace at that.

"*Missed you*. I thought you said you would be back ten minutes ago." Some ladies turn around and they're all holding what looks like a romance book to their chests. Mom chuckles, a nervous wobble, causing me to look at her in confusion. Everyone smiles at the cute couple. But he can't fool me anymore.

Josh is a master at hiding how he truly feels, especially around other people. I thought it was a fluke the first time I saw it, but ever since we got to California, it's been showing more and more. I risk looking up at Liam, finding him already looking at me. We stare off for a bit, almost daring each other to look away, before he loses and whips out his phone as he leans against his car.

"Of course." Mom looks at Patty, nodding at her. "Thank you for letting me join. I can't wait for next week's meeting."

"You're welcome, and Josh, next time we'll make sure she's not late home, ya hear?"

He chuckles and squeezes Mom around the waist, smiling at Patty. "Ana, always a pleasure, as well as you ladies. Get home safe," he calls out as he starts to drag Mom back to the house. As he passes by, he turns up his head at Liam. I sigh, looking over at Ana, who has a weird expression on her face. It leaves when she catches me looking at her, though.

"He seems to really love your mom," she mumbles, and I nod, not knowing what to say. She walks over to Liam, telling him something and he nods. She walks off, leaving him and me, and I glance up, my heart taking off—like always.

"We meet again," he mumbles.

I nod before cutting eye contact. "Well, our moms are in the same book club now. And Ana's been coming over a lot, so . . ." I trail off, and surprisingly, his mouth wears a small smile.

"Just like old times, huh?"

Memories flash of how it really was like old times. Both of our moms practically sleeping over at each other's houses, Ana dragging Mom to social outings while Mom begged her to stay in. But Liam and I would be happy with it . . . *We loved to hang out with each other.*

His sigh brings me back to reality, and I realize that as much as I wish it to be, this isn't like old times. Him and me, we're standing no more than a couple of feet apart, but emotionally, we're a chasm away. He used to be my best friend, the person who knew me probably better than myself, and I miss that. He clears his throat a bit before he shakes his head and I hug myself a little as a gust of wind blows by.

"Not exactly, but at least they got their friendship back." Something flickers in his eyes at my comment. Something like doubt or regret, and he sighs dejectedly.

"Yeah. Um, have a good night, Bianca."

I nod, and he stalks back to his car before Ana comes to my side.

"See you later, cupcake." She hugs me, then heads toward Liam's car. When she jumps in, he locks eyes with me for a brief moment, then starts the car and drives off. With a final wave to Patty and everyone else, I make my way back home, a hand over my heart as I try to calm it down.

I hear Mom and Josh before I see them, and I push open the door as quietly as I can.

"Josh, please don't do that again. It was embarrassing."

"You said six fifty is when those *little meetings* end. The clock says differently, sweetheart."

Mom chuckles in disbelief, and I freeze, as the whole time I've been around her and Josh, they've never fought. "It's ten minutes. I didn't need the claiming moment you just did."

"You're my fiancée, I believe"—he shrugs almost innocently, walking toward her—"I can do what I want."

"No, you ca—"

He cuts her off. "Listen, *hon.* Next time, don't lie about the time, and everything will be fine, okay?"

She shakes her head. "But I did—"

"*We're. Done. Talking.* Okay?" The "okay" sounds so sweet, uncannily so. His voice wavers from the emphasis he puts on certain words, and a chill runs down my spine. He's holding her chin, and with a closer look, his fingers are turning white.

"Okay, Josh," she says before looking over at me. She breaks free from him and comes to hug me. "Hey, sweetie, sorry we left you back there. Thought you were behind us." She turns back around and Josh's eyes dart between the both of us.

"All good, Mom," I mumble. She kisses me on the forehead while Josh keeps looking at us, tension climbing slowly but surely. His phone rings. He fishes it out of his pocket and exhales at the welcome distraction.

"Callaway." He turns around, heading toward the kitchen, and I look at Mom when he finally vanishes from view.

"Are you okay?" I ask.

She smiles, but there's something building in her eyes. Something is going on, I know it. "Of course, baby." Narrowing my eyes at her, she relents a bit. "Really, it's all good. We're going through some growing pains, it's completely normal."

Scolding her for being ten minutes late? Not even letting her fully express herself? I've never been in a relationship, but even *I* know that's wrong.

"Mom—" I start before she grabs my hands.

"It's fine, honey. When you love someone, you love them through their flaws. Plus, I'm so thankful for everything he's done, and if . . ." She sighs. "For me to be able to give you the peace of not having to worry about me. I can deal when there's some friction." I want to shake my head as I realize why she just takes it and takes it before she finally waves me off. "I know I had to leave right after dropping you off earlier. How was your first day at the shelter?" She grabs my hands excitedly, sitting us down, and I start talking about my day, but her eyes say something different.

As they say, the eyes never lie.

CHAPTER SEVENTEEN

Liam

I SHARPEN MY PENCIL ONCE again as I draw another tattoo idea on the very last page of a notebook. I've been a fountain of ideas right now, all due to a certain blonde. I smudge the shadows a bit, moving to create contrasting lines, a white pencil between my lips. My leg starts to bounce up and down as more ideas pop in my head to try to keep me from thinking about anything else. I begin the freckle pattern, noticing it looks severely similar to hers, and I crumble up the piece of paper, not wanting to even look at my past designs, knowing I'm probably going to make the same connections.

I'm conflicted. I'm unsure. I . . . I don't even know what to call it anymore, and I'm *this close* to losing my mind. I'm sad, and hurt, because Bianca now just brings back horrible feelings. But then, she's also part of almost every single childhood memory I have. From ice cream trips with my parents to having picnics segueing into stargazing later at night. Memories where I have the biggest smiles on my face, ones where I thought we would be in each other's lives forever.

Pushing off my chair, I head to my bed and run a hand through my hair. A knock comes at the door and I mutter, "Come in."

Mom enters the room and takes a deep breath. "Amor mio, you really are your father's boy." I look at her in confusion. "Your hotheadedness. That's how your father used to be before we started dating." She comes to sit next to me, squeezing my hand reassuringly. "How are you, bud?" I shrug noncommittally. "The only way I can help is if you tell me what's up. You know, I thought Bianca coming back was like fate for you." She sighs. "Aren't you happy?"

"I don't know. I wanna be, but I also don't. She blocked me, she didn't even want to give me a chance to explain, to be better for her since she felt like I didn't—" I sigh. "I mean, she doesn't even wanna be around me."

"And you believe that?" She rolls her eyes. "That girl, no matter what she says or does, looks at you as she always has. With affection and everything in between. It looks like she *misses* you more than anything," she says, and I scoff. "You miss her. You wish you were best friends again, right?" I nod at that, and then catch myself. "You're twenty years old, yet when it comes to her—" I look down in embarrassment. "You're both hurting each other because you're both the most stubborn people I've ever met."

"You're right," I say, sighing while running a hand down my face. "But I can't risk telling her anything. You didn't really hear her, Mom. I'm not gonna get hurt again. I can't."

She looks at me with sympathy. "Well, I'll respect that. You're an adult, and you can make your own decisions." She gets up to walk away. I put my face in my hands.

How can I run back when she's hurt me so badly? How can we fix what we have when we're so broken, when the pieces aren't even visible anymore? I tried at Mella Colta, and she shut me down. Why is it that I want to keep trying for our friendship till I can get through to her?

A couple of hours later, I rush to the animal shelter for my shift. The bell rings above the door, the coldness wrapping around me instantly. A couple of waves are sent my way and an upturn of my chin is sent theirs. I clock in on the volunteer laptop when someone walks into the break room.

"Liam! Back from college already?" I'd recognize that voice from miles away. I turn to see Rachel, the one who's let me volunteer here since I was sixteen years old. She comes over to hug me, and I pat her shoulder awkwardly as she pulls back, chuckling.

"I see your social skills have improved."

That elicits a laugh from me and I shake my head. Crossing my arms, I say, "It's summer break, Rachel. Besides, I had to volunteer, had to keep my record as *volunteer with the most hours* intact."

She rolls her eyes, propping a hand on her hip. "My boys are all grown up, so pardon me if I don't remember college breaks." She saunters out and I follow behind her. I swivel around the dog food tray as we get ready to begin evening feeding. She's blabbering about something, and I nod, trying to piece certain words together. "Besides, you're practically a veteran of this place. So, you'll be perfect for her to shadow." I nod before she waves someone over. "Oh, here she is. Bianca, here's the person you'll be shadowing tonight." I close my eyes in subdued pain, taking a deep breath before turning around. Maybe it's a different Bianca.

Nope. It's most definitely her.

A frown forms on my face, as does one on hers. She rubs her arms up and down before crossing them.

Old habits die hard, I guess.

No. I don't remember her nervous tics.

Rachel looks between us. "I'm sorry, have y'all met before?"

"Yes," she answers.

"No," I counter at the same time, not knowing if she wanted me to lie at all.

For a split second, there's hurt in her eyes, but it's gone before I can prove that's what it was. A closed-off expression grows across her face as she instantly becomes on guard. It's as if I can physically envision her building her wall that much higher, and that tugs at my heartstrings. She said she wanted me to leave her alone. I mean, she definitely meant it all these years, yet she's got me feeling things that she probably doesn't think about.

Rachel looks between the two of us, confused. "I—well. Liam's been volunteering with us since he was younger. He's our top volunteer with more than three thousand hours. He probably knows this place better than I do." Bianca looks at me, but I refuse to meet her eyes.

She finally speaks up. "In the vet lab as well?"

Rachel moves to answer, but I beat her to it. "I've volunteered extensively in every position." Bianca blinks at me, almost in slow motion.

Static from Rachel's radio cuts through the tension, and I look away from Bianca's eyes. She speaks a mile a minute—the Rachel norm—before I hear the words, "Kenny" and "escaped." She sighs and I chuckle as she shoots me a slight glare.

"On it," she mumbles back as she facepalms. "The smallest dog, yet he gives the biggest headaches." She looks back at Bianca as if she almost forgot about the conversation we were having before the Kenny fiasco derailed her train of thought.

I put a hand on her shoulder. "I got it, Rachel." She looks up at me, doubt clouding her eyes as she squints. "I'll take care of her, you go find Kenny. He could be trying to free the others," I whisper, and she rolls her eyes before scurrying off, barking orders at the staff through the radio.

"So . . ."

My head snaps toward the sound of her voice. Last night . . . What I said, I dug too deep. I opened something I'm sure she doesn't want to revisit—that's on me.

I just have to be professional.

Polite.

She's like a regular intern . . . who I also know inside and out.

"Um, so what exactly should we start with?" I ask. She probably realizes the route I'm taking and quickly gets on board.

"I know morning feedings, I've never done an evening shift before, though." At that, I walk her through our whole schedule. I rattle off everything she's supposed to do, pointing to things at lightning speed. I hurry her along, wanting to get through things as fast as I can, pushing back and burying every single emotion she makes me feel.

Professional, nothing personal. *Yeah, I got this.*

I take the route that'll have us pass the vet's office, for what reason I'll never admit, even though it's the longest way to get to the kennel. Putting my hand under the sanitizer dispenser, I slow as I know she probably stopped in front of the window, looking into the clinic. And, I know I shouldn't. I really shouldn't.

I look back, and true to what I assumed, she's standing in front of the window, a hand pressed against the glass. I take these few seconds to look at her. Even in a T-shirt and jeans, she still wins the prize for being the girl who takes my breath away. Even after five years, you would think these feelings had diminished, positively dulled.

I walk back, rubbing my hands, as one of the nurses holds a cute little golden dachshund.

"Bruno," I state. She flinches slightly as I appear next to her, looking through the window too. "Found him while I was jogging around my neighborhood." I barely glance at her and clear my throat. "He has a fractured leg and was limping for who knows how long. So, I brought him here."

I keep looking ahead, not wanting to fall into old habits. Though, as always, I cave. Turning around to face her, she flicks her eyes toward mine, and I'm drowning in the different saturations of blue. I probably sound like a broken record, but she's changed more than I ever thought.

She's different, and I'm a fool to think that maybe after all these years, everything would be what it once was. It would be so much easier if I hung on to the sadness I've had this whole time. Yet, when her eyes connect with mine, it simply fades away. But I need to stop.

What we had is gone, we're basically strangers now.

"I always thought if I had a dog, I'd name him Bruno," she whispers.

"From your favorite movie, *Cinderella*," I finish. Something stirs in me, before I clear my throat, avoiding it. The chipped paint on the wall becomes more interesting.

She whispers, shock evident in her tone, "I haven't watched that in so long. How do you even—"

I shake my head, a noncommittal shrug. "You seem to forget that we watched the movie almost every time we hung out."

So much for being professional.

I tilt my head to one side, motioning for her to follow me as we continue with the tour. After another half an hour of showing the most trivial things possible, we stop at the kennels. I keep my back to her as I smile, hearing her blowing a couple of kisses to some of the dogs.

A cough later, I ask, "Alright, you got everything?" The air conditioning kicks on, the rumble of it filling the awkward silence between us.

I focus on her as she rubs her arms and mumbles, "Uh-huh."

I look at the motion, my stupid heart wanting to give her my hoodie, hell—the damn shirt off my back.

"Bring a jacket next time." She moves toward the supply closet, looking over at the clock, and I realize it's time for the last walks of the day. My eyes follow her movements for a bit before I sigh and walk off, just like that. She smiles brightly at the other volunteers, and I push open the door, hating how much I missed that simple gesture.

It's been a few hours, and I'm almost done with cleaning the kennels. I toss down the brush, seeing my wrinkled fingers, and my music starts to fade out. A bead of sweat starts on my brow and I raise my shirt to wipe it off.

The dogs are currently being walked when Bianca suddenly shouts, "Coming out!"

My heart stops as the last one to be taken out is Zorro, our most aggressive and volatile dog. The only volunteer that can really go near him would either be me or Micheal, but that's definitely not his voice. My eyes widen and I sprint as quickly as I can outside. Yells and gasps fill the open space, amplifying the surefire heart attack I'm about to have.

Please, please don't get hurt. Please.

My heart's beating a mile a minute and I'm taking short bursts of breath, wanting to get there before anything happens.

I push open the door leading outside and watch in slow motion as Zorro snaps at her, then roughly drags her as she struggles to disentangle herself from the leash. He goes after a squirrel, and I rush toward them, but am too late when a piece of the fence wiring that *I* was supposed to fix today cuts the skin on her arm.

A ringing starts in my ears, her shouting reverberating as the blood starts to flow out of the wound.

Grabbing Zorro's leash before he can continue dragging her, I yell for someone to take him from me. At once, someone comes and takes him as he pulls against his collar, wanting to get back to his chase, not knowing what he did.

Bianca exhales shakily, whimpering once again as tears well in her eyes. My heart breaks and disgust fills me when I see the stupid wire hanging out.

I was supposed to get to it.

I was supposed to fix it, and because of me . . .

Crouching, I get close to her, and her eyes are dissociating as she looks at the wound.

"Hey, hey," I whisper, gripping her face in my hands, not caring if this screws with my initial plan.

Screw professionalism.

Screw not being personal.

Whispers and low voices begin behind me as a crowd forms. Her eyes are glazed over, and I know she's thinking about *that* night, and my heart begins to ache. After all this time, it still haunts her. "Bianca, hey. Don't look at them. Don't look at the wound. *Look at me*," I whisper over and over, rubbing my thumbs across her cheekbones as she blinks, her eyes coming back into focus. She squeezes her features, no doubt in pain, but she trains her gaze on mine. "What were you thinking?" I ask lowly. "He's our most violent dog, and you started not that long ago. It takes months and months of practice before you can even go . . . near him." I choke slightly on my words, but she doesn't waver from my gaze.

She winces. "I'm sor—I'm sorry, Michael said it would be fine. I'm sorry." I shake my head, hating how she's blaming it on herself. From what I know, Michael started almost a year ago, and for him to encourage this is incredibly irresponsible. Her gaze begins to stray, but I keep her looking at me. Distress courses through me as I grab her arm gently to see what the damage is, but she pulls back. The murmuring is still very much happening behind me, but it all fades as I figure out how to help her.

Rachel fights her way through the crowd before focusing on the scratch. "Liam, what happened?"

"I got her." Looking back down at Bianca, I say, "I'm gonna pick you up, okay?" She's still shaking.

It's for me. I need to have her close right now.

She nods, and I don't hesitate to wrap my arms around her body. She nods at Rachel too, almost as if she's trying to reassure her that she's okay, that it was an accident. I walk through the crowd, most of them being courteous and getting out of the way.

"Bianca, I'm so sorry. I thought you could handle stronger dogs—"

I cut off Michael, keeping my anger and frustration at bay. "You made a mistake." Inhaling shakily, I continue, "She's hurt, so go, please." He visibly pales, but nods anyway. I glance down at Bianca in worry before moving forward, even though I have more words for Michael. Coming inside, she shivers, and I hug her closer to my chest, hoping that it warms her. I skirt past the curious stares, heading to our first aid room. Closing the door, I set her down on the makeshift bed, her hissing in pain once again. I reach for her arm and she flinches, startled.

"I need to see it," I whisper, trying to get close to her, but she moves back, making me stop in my tracks. I wait a bit, not wanting to force her into anything. Glancing away from me, she holds her arm out and I grasp it gently. My heart pounds against my rib cage as I wrap my hand around hers, extending it slightly. Dropping my eyes to her wound, I analyze it, thanking everything above it isn't as deep as it looks. She looks up right when I'm ready to say something, and I lose my train of thought.

"Is it bad?"

A simple question, but again, one look from her and I've been absolutely derailed.

"Um, I don't think so. I'll get the first aid kit." I motion to the shelf next to us. I grab some antiseptic, bacitracin, and gauze. She stares at the cut and I rush to raise her head before she can go back into a panic. Clutching her arm, I start dabbing at the wound with some alcohol, but she flinches. "Hey," I say, hesitantly putting my hand on the side of her face. "I'm trying to help, Bianca." Fear is etched onto her pale face and she's still shaking like a leaf even though it's warmer in this room.

I continue to dab at the wound, trying with everything not to move her arm too much or press too hard. After disinfecting and applying a thin layer of ointment, I wrap the gauze and gently put the end under the wrap so it stays in place. Her eyes lock with mine and a small smile blooms across her lips. Clearing my throat, I blink rapidly, hoping my face isn't red as I scan her body to make sure this is the only place she's hurt. She looks at me in curiosity, but I ignore her. I want to commit her to memory because I might not have another chance to be this close. I frown as I remember this is all my fault. Fixing up that fence should've been the first thing I did when I clocked in.

She looks down before mumbling, "You think the dogs will sign my wrap?" A small chuckle leaves me and we exchange genuine smiles. Even in pain, she's the only girl who can fully capture my attention, and I run my eyes greedily all over her face.

Though, guilt overtakes me completely as I remember how I was partially at fault. "Bianca—"

The door opens and Rachel pops her head in. "Everything okay?"

"Yes," I say.

"No," Bianca counters, and I look at her, pleading her not to walk away. She clears her throat, avoiding my face. "Could I leave my shift early today?"

CHAPTER EIGHTEEN

Bianca

AFTER RACHEL LETS ME LEAVE, I try my best to avoid Liam as I wait for Mom to pick me up. I was partly successful before I open my locker to get my bag when I see his hoodie, folded nicely, with a little note.

So you don't get cold next time. —L

Debating, I bite my lip before grabbing it and heading to the parking lot. Mom's eyes widen, and I already know how this drive is going to go.

"I get it," I mumble as Mom has been—for the better part of the thirty-five-minute drive—ranting about what happened at the shelter today.

"Bianca, come on. This is serious, honey." She turns the steering wheel and my body sags in relief when I see the entrance to our home. She smiles slightly at the guard and he nods at her as he presses the button to let us in. A little smile sprouts on the guy's face, Mom looks away, and I look at her in confusion before we drive through.

"It was my fault, Mom. I told you. I wanted to be helpful and decided to take out our most aggressive dog on my *fifth* shift." I shake my head at my literal stupidity. A sound of frustration leaves her, a hint of concern mixed in as she looks at the wrap on my arm. "And, I'm going back after this heals." She opens her mouth to retort, but I hold up a hand, stopping her. "Mom, I *love* that place. It was an accident, and my fault." I close my eyes, inhaling deeply. "Let it go."

There's a familiar shriek when I walk inside the house and see Josh hugging none other than Olivia, and their eyes widen as they look at me. Her eyes trail down and she squeaks surprised when she sees the white bandage around my arm. Josh turns around at the reaction and his eyes zero in on me while Mom comes inside.

"Hey, Kate." He kisses her temple before his eyes dart back to me. "What happened?" I sigh, knowing he might make a big deal out of it when I just calmed Mom down.

Barely.

"Accident at the shelter," she answers.

His eyebrows raise and his gaze shifts back to me. "Well, it's one she won't be going back to." He adjusts his tie, dropping the statement, and I look at Mom for help. She glances over to Josh, opening her mouth, yet her words seem to die on her tongue. I shake my head.

"It was my fault I got hurt." He looks at me, most likely seeing defiance in my eyes. He takes a deep breath and tugs Mom to him.

He says firmly, "You won't, and we'll be suing."

My eyes widen. "Don't you dare, Josh." I'm shocked at my tone as he moves closer to me.

"*Watch* your tone," he says, and that usually works on Mom, and surely works on Olivia, but all it does is make my blood boil.

"Or what?" I can't help but taunt.

"Kate, a little help?" His voice hardens and her eyes flick between both of us.

"She does really like that place, Josh," she defends softly, and a familiar warmth comes over me. "And, she'll be more careful, right?"

I nod, helping her out. "I will. Please don't sue. There's no need," I whisper. He looks unmoved. Mom places a hand on his arm before his face relaxes.

"I'll consider it. Be careful with that tone, you don't want to be perceived as disrespectful, hm?" Finality floats between his words, and I nod before he turns away. Olivia follows him like a little puppy, no longer paying any attention to me.

Mom gives me an embarrassed look. "Ignore Josh, hon. He's just—"

"Stressed?" I finish, and she flushes brighter while I look down. The rock she's wearing flashes slightly, and it makes me wonder if this is the price I'll have to pay for her to wear the thing. I let out a deep breath before smiling at her. "It's fine, Mom. He wants to protect me, right?"

She opens her mouth before closing it again, no words coming out, and resigns herself to a nod. Giving her a small smile, I walk away to my little corner of peace in the house before I make the mistake of telling her what I *really* think. The mistake of telling her that Josh is not the same guy he used to be.

Or that he possibly was this man the whole time.

"Mmm, I can feel my metabolism speeding up," Olivia says as she takes big bites out of her protein bar. I give her the biggest side glare. She's wanting to rush for some sororities since she's starting college in a couple weeks. I know because she's been repeating it over and over, positively shoving it in my face that she was accepted to UPenn while I wasn't. "*And* they're gluten free!" she squeals excitedly, flipping over the package, and I glance at her in disgust. I don't bother entertaining anything as I subtly open the pantry door in search of my sugary cereal.

"What are you girls up to?" Mom asks as she comes in and kisses me on the forehead and goes to hug Olivia. Turning around, she proceeds to tell Mom her whole spiel while I pour some Frosted Flakes into a bowl. I feel someone's eyes boring holes into my back, and I know it's Miss She-Devil. She subtly jabs by saying it's a sorority at UPenn, and I scoff at that. I place a spoonful in my mouth as her smug smile drops. Mom chuckles softly while Olivia death stares at me, and I smile at her innocently, walking out of the kitchen with a smirk.

Heading to my room, I'm greeted with darkness and I slide open my curtains with my free hand. I take in my surroundings as I bring another spoonful to my mouth. The whole encounter with Liam yesterday has been fluttering through my thoughts like moths to a flame. I fear my heart has been replaying it over and over, wishing it hadn't. His wall crumbled a bit, and I saw the old him—that kid that was my best friend—starting to shine through. Some moments, it's like those five years never happened, and in others, they make up the rift between us. Feeling hurt for five years of my life has been fueled by his being a jerk and being nonchalant.

Though yesterday, all my defense mechanisms went down; I forgot about all the nights I cried, the feeling of being not enough for someone. Liam Jax Parker was in front of me, and he wanted to stay there. But then, it all comes down when I think about everything else we haven't faced. Our friendship was probably the strongest relationship I had in my life; I thought I would always have him in my corner; I thought there was no way we would lose it.

It's hard to think I've gone five years without him, and I hate that there's a part of me that might think there's still something worth saving. We were kids, and maybe, just maybe . . . after all this time, we could try again?

Throwing on my—his—hoodie, avoiding my wrap as much as possible, I try to make myself look a little presentable. My frustration shows at my dark roots growing back out. My phone buzzes, and I smile when I see Jamie's text message.

JAMIE:

> Hey, B! Sorry I didn't answer your message earlier, had to take my break later than usual.

> How's everything going?

ME:

> No worries, girly! Nothing much, honestly.

> Had a little accident at the shelter, but I'm okay.

The bubble appears instantly and I know she's probably starting to freak out.

JAMIE:

> Accident? What, how?

ME:

> I promise, I'm all good.

> I took out an aggressive dog and got cut on some exposed wire.

> But I'm fine, all wrapped up.

I send her a picture, my eyes flitting down, the memories of Liam's protectiveness bombarding me.

JAMIE:

> If you say so, girl. But please be careful.

I bite down on my lip as I contemplate telling her who wrapped my arm, and decide to go with it.

ME:

> Yeah, Liam actually helped wrap it for me.

Her answer doesn't come as quickly as I thought it would. I wait with bated breath. Finally, those three dots bounce up and down on my screen.

JAMIE:

> I hate that you told me this when I'm on a thirty-minute break.

> That's not nearly enough time to debrief . . . ugh.

A smile starts on my face, a small chuckle leaving me, and I promise that when she's off, I'll tell her anything and everything she wants to know. Out of nowhere, a knock at the door grabs my attention. Mom peeks her head in, and I smile at her in her pretty new athleisure wear. "I'm heading over to Ana's. And she's been begging me to get you to come over."

Knowing I should probably get out of the house, I slide my phone in the pocket of the hoodie. I hug her with my good arm as we close the door, heading out. I never noticed how close our two neighborhoods are until, within a split second, we're already at their front gate.

Ana is waiting for us as she chats amiably with the guards and waves when she spots us. A huge smile breaks out on her face and she runs over to hug me, almost knocking me down.

Well, as well as all four foot eleven of her could.

"I heard what happened, cupcake. You okay?" A frown pulls down the corners of her mouth and I shake my head in dismissal.

I lift the hoodie sleeve slightly, showing her the wrapped arm. "Promise it's not as bad as it looks. Just stings from time to time."

She reaches up to grab my chin, pouting slightly. "Always my brave girl." I knock her hand down, blushing, and she smiles. "I missed you." She hugs me once again.

My eyebrows scrunch. "You saw me a few days ago." She shakes her head as if my words are complete heresy to her.

"Too long for me." Mom and I roll our eyes as she pulls back and links arms with us. As we walk down the road of her subdivision, I notice how beautiful it is. It's more nature bound than ours. Hers are infested with these palm trees in the best way. There are some people outside in their yard tanning, and of course, Ana waves at every single one of them.

She's truly the biggest ray of sunshine.

Reaching her house, my eyes rake over her driveway for Liam's car, and my shoulders droop when I realize he isn't here. As if she can read my mind, Ana's eyes find mine, but they drift down to observe my hoodie. I pretend to be oblivious. We head inside and take off our shoes in the corner, and the elegance of this house strikes me.

Ana turns around, her hands on her hips. "Never in all my life did I think I would have you guys back in my house again."

"Well, we're here now, right?" Mom replies.

Ana's arms wrap around my midsection and Mom hugs her other arm. A solemn look comes over Ana's face. My heart stutters at that, and I realize something. When Liam and I . . . parted ways, I didn't even stop to think about how that affected Ana and William. Ana seems to notice what's going through my head before she replaces her frown with a small smile. "Exactly, plus I know how we can get this visit properly started." She pulls away, looking at Mom with the smug smile her son so often likes to use with me. "We all sit down with your infamous hot chocolate, and *you* catch me up." She points toward me as Mom groans.

"You know my hot chocolate takes forever to make. Besides, you don't have everything."

Mom makes the accusation before Ana places a hand on her heart. "You wound me with how unprepared you think I am." She then smiles. "Every ingredient is set up for you in the kitchen." Mom's jaw drops before shutting it. She knows Ana's serious, especially about hot chocolate. The smirk deepens when she knows Mom has succumbed to her plan. "Better get to it then, Kate."

Mom huffs, playfully annoyed, and heads in the direction of the kitchen. As she stomps off, Ana elbows me teasingly. In a low voice, she says, "I love to annoy her."

Laughing at her comment, I make my own confession. "Me too."

We laugh loudly at that and I wrap my arm around Ana as she leads me to the living room. She sits us down on her dark gray couch as Mom shouts, "You got the frother too?" We giggle like children as Ana sets up a little something on her TV.

We settle on some reality show, and I have to resist the urge to glance over again to make sure she's actually here. I'm really in her house after so long. She squeezes my hand, a small smile sent my way.

"You know, I never knew why you and Mom stopped talking." An awkward smile comes over her, and I realize she may not want to answer.

"Well, first it was getting harder to talk since you and Liam—" Her words are carried away; my face flushes and my heart aches at that. For so long, I never understood why they stopped talking, and it was because of Liam and me? "But don't put that on yourself. It's one of those things that happen. I don't even think about it because you're both back, and that's all that matters." She side-hugs me, and

I'm envious of how Ana looks at things. Mom walks back in after half an hour with a sour look on her face as Ana struggles to hold in her laughs. Three mugs are on the platter she's carrying, and she puts them down in front of us, bowing sarcastically.

"Your hot chocolate, Your Majesty."

Ana grabs the mug that reads "The person using this cup is annoying" and brings it to her lips. She smiles at the drink, wiping the bit of cream off her upper lip.

"Just like how you used to make it," she says, and Mom smiles back at her as she finally gets to sit.

A car revs outside, causing Ana to roll her eyes, and I hate that my head wants to look in that direction, but I play it cool.

"Oh my—Liam!"

My heart drops. The stupid handsome boy comes sauntering in, sweat prominent on his body. He has a sheepish expression on his face as he was probably trying not to make any noise. He's wearing a thin gray shirt, and my jaw drops open. I used to think my type would always be someone who was leaner, but now muscles have become a new favorite.

Wow.

His eyes widen when he sees me, and even with all the tattoos, the beads that trail down his neck are visible. He has grease stains on his hands, and—why does *that* make my stomach flutter? He wraps a small, white towel around his neck, a smirk coming on his face while I shut my mouth, taking a sip of my hot chocolate instead.

His head swivels to Ana before he forms a small pout. "Yes, Mom?"

"Amor, I thought the deal was no noise. Dad's in a meeting right now."

He scratches the back of his head, almost embarrassed. "That was my bad, I opened the door and I forgot how fast the noise travels. It was hot in the garage." He sighs. "I'm almost done, promise." He sounds almost boyish, like the way I remember him from so many years past. His eyes dart to me in my peripheral vision, but I don't give him the pleasure of making eye contact.

"Okay, hurry up. You've been at that forever," she says, and he gives her a salute.

He turns around, looking at Mom. "Hi, Ms. Kate." He gives her a small smile.

"Hi, Liam. Car giving you trouble?" Mom asks, trying to be polite, and I keep sipping at my hot chocolate as my body temperature goes up.

He chuckles. "Among other things." They look at him in confusion, but I know exactly what he means. "Nice hoodie, Bianca."

I go red because technically he wasn't supposed to see me wearing it. I blame it on the hot chocolate. He doesn't say anything more, and with that, he goes back to the garage, I assume, and Ana looks back at us. "That boy is the reason for my wrinkles."

"Well, you still look amazing, Ana," I say, and her expression contorts into a funny face. Feeling warmer with the hot chocolate, I shift slightly and the hoodie reveals a bit more of my collarbone.

Ana gasps. "Wait a minute. Is that a tattoo?" she asks, almost excited, coming close to examine it.

I nod, forgetting the little thing. "Yeah, it's all the planets aligned."

"When did you get this?"

"Earlier this year when I turned eighteen."

Mom starts laughing. "You know, I almost had a heart attack when she came home with it."

Ana strokes it, smiling slightly. "Do you have any other ones?"

"A small sun on my hip for my dad. I'm actually planning on getting the Ursa Major constellation on the back of my shoulder."

Her eyes shine. "Gotcha. So, you're still into astronomy?"

"Yeah. But Ursa Major has a special connection for me." My heart irregularly beats at the reason behind it, but I don't dare voice it to her.

Ana pulls back. "Kate, trust me, this isn't bad. Imagine seeing your child covered in tattoos. *I* almost had a heart attack." They both start laughing, but I don't. Personally, I think he looks beautiful.

"Talking about me, are we?"

Speak of the devil.

"Yes, all good things, Liam," Mom says, and he has a small smile on his lips.

"Mhm. Sure, Ms. Kate." He turns toward Ana. "I've gotta run to the auto parts store. I need something for my car. Can I take yours?"

Ana shakes her head. "Sorry, bud, but I have to have someone come look at both Dad's and mine."

Mom looks at me and smirks, and I look at her, confused. "Liam, you can take my car."

CHAPTER NINETEEN

Bianca

MY EYES WIDEN IMMENSELY. This is why moms can't know things—they turn around and do this.

His eyes widen too, and he doesn't say anything for a solid second. "Really, Ms. Kate? I mean, you don't have to." Ana looks over at her, and they stare, almost communicating with their eyes. Ana sips her drink contentedly while Mom reassures him.

"It's alright, Liam, and it's been years. You're grown now. Call me Kate."

He smiles and shakes his head. "You know I can't do that, Ms. Kate."

She rolls her eyes. "Can't say I didn't try. And don't worry, I don't mind letting you use my car."

"Um, okay. Thank you," he mumbles while a slight blush comes to his cheeks. I glare at her slightly, making note to talk her ear off about this betrayal before she digs the knife in deeper.

"No problem, the car and keys are at home, though. Bianca, you wouldn't mind going to get them with Liam, right?" I look at her in horror while I start to mentally sweat, or maybe I'm sweating in real life. I sit there, looking off into the distance like a complete moron, not understanding why I can't say something.

Freaking anything.

"Bianca? You wouldn't mind, right?" Mom asks again. I'm ready to shake my head because I have no idea what to do, and really hate that she's playing Cupid right now. She has this pleading look on her face, and I sigh.

"Nope, not at all," I reluctantly reply, standing. "Um, do you need anything?" She shakes her head. Liam and I lock eyes for a brief second. I try not to gawk at him as he crosses his arms, and I swear his blush from earlier deepens a tiny bit.

"Um, ready?" he mumbles, and I hesitate before nodding. He sends one back and walks to the door. I look behind me to see Mom and Ana whispering to each other. My eyes meet theirs and I blush even more. He holds the door open and I start the walk back to the house. I'm nearly levitating with how fast I'm walking, and I don't look back, but I know he's behind me. We don't say anything; I'm mentally preparing myself for being driven by someone new.

"How's your arm?" He gestures at the wrapped wound while I nod noncommittally. "Any updates since?" Awkwardness drips from his words, but I shake my head. He looks like he wants to say more before just sighing. Truth is, I can't stop the worrying thoughts running in my head right now.

It's been years since the accident, and even though I have most of the memory under control, cars trigger me the most. I've learned to handle Mom's driving, and now Josh's, even if it took me forever to get in the car with them. Someone new driving freaks me out—I mean, I still hyperventilate with Jamie sometimes. Finally getting to the house, I use my key to unlock the door and walk in. He stays outside, thankfully, and I close the door slightly.

Josh is on his laptop, Olivia nowhere in sight, though probably in her room. His eyes dart to mine and I send a polite nod his way as he glances past me, obviously looking for Mom. Grabbing her keys, I'm heading back outside when he clears his throat.

"What are you doing?" he asks suspiciously, and I give him my back.

"Grabbing the car keys," I mutter.

"You can't drive."

I roll my eyes. "They're not for me." I don't elaborate, as I know if I say who they're really for, Josh might not like it. He sighs in annoyance, and I already know what comes after this.

"Why are you so disrespectful, Bianca?"

I turn around, appalled. "Text Mom if you wanna know why I'm taking the keys."

"You know—I'm tired of this." He closes his laptop gently and runs a hand over it. "I've shown you kindness, and have provided your mother and you with your every whim. Therefore, you *need* to learn to respect me. Especially when I'm now engaged to Kate."

I've been studying Josh, especially how he acts with Olivia. Buying everything she desires, paying for her blind loyalty. He has these little quirks that have been growing more since Mom and him got engaged. For once, I'm sick of always looking down and taking it, chalking it up to stress.

"Respect is *earned*, and while I appreciate everything, I can't be bought and won't fall at your feet because you demand it," I say, trying to be calm, considering Liam is right outside the slightly opened door.

"You *will* respect me one way or another," he promises while I'm walking away. In response, I roll my eyes as I open the door to find Olivia getting out of her car, moving to talk to Liam.

Flirting, more like it.

His eyes snap to mine and Olivia looks over at me smugly. "Did Daddy scold you?" she mocks, and I don't even know what to say.

Liam moves away from her at that, and I don't answer as I walk off. Olivia asks where he's going, but his footsteps don't stop—in fact, they speed up. I head to the passenger side of Mom's car, but there's a gentle hand on my wrist that makes me turn around. His eyes scan me from head to toe; I don't give him the privilege of eye contact.

"How long has he treated you like that?" he asks. I shrug, not wanting to answer, but he continues. "Does Ms. Kate know? I mean, surely she wouldn't let him speak to you like that. But when I heard him say that stuff to you . . ." He looks at me as different emotions flutter in his eyes. My heart tugs as he continues. "No one should be disrespected like that."

I take a deep breath, not acknowledging it. "Here are the keys."

I slide into the car as he walks around to the driver's side. I take shallow breaths and close my eyes, trying not to freak out.

I can do this.

Liam doesn't say anything when he climbs in, and when he starts the car, I aim all the air vents toward me. He begins the drive, and I hold the side of my seat in a death grip even though he drives significantly better than Josh does. We go over a pothole and I wince.

"You okay?" he asks.

"Mhm," I mutter, trying not to show more of my freak-out.

He flicks the turn signal on and again attempts small talk. "So, why don't you drive?"

While I don't want to respond, I do. "Don't have my permit."

He looks almost shocked that I said something. "Oh, is it because of the—"

"I don't really wanna talk about it."

He nods, and I notice the subtle change—if he was driving amazing before, it's perfect now. That was the last thing he said, and even though my annoyance is with Josh, I'm still not entirely okay with Liam either. For once, I don't know how to act with him; it's awkward. It was easy at Josh's event. We said we'd stay away from each other for multiple reasons. We aren't the same people anymore, especially the whole thing with him and Vanessa, but I guess that fell through. Then, at the shelter, he was acting perfectly professional and I thought that could work. We would act like there's no history between us, no vulnerable moments or confessions, just two people volunteering.

But . . . I look down at my arm and his words bombard my brain.

Don't look at the wound. Look at me.

I'm trying to help, Bianca.

For the first time, everything melts away, and it's him and me. When he was always by my side, when he protected me more than anything else in his life. For a moment, we were Bianca Harrison and Liam Parker, the best of friends, and I recognize how much I miss that.

The neon lights are hard to miss as well as the bustling parking lot. The doors slide open, and Liam sighs as we find a line a little longer than he probably expected. We don't say anything to each other, and I'm fine until I get the feeling someone is staring at me. Discreetly, I turn and see a group of guys looking at me suggestively. Trying to hide my cringing, I stare down at the floor, counting the specks in the tiles. I desperately try to avoid eye contact with everyone, and on the cusp of feeling extremely self-conscious, I make a move in poor judgment.

I inch closer to Liam.

Though, when I touch his arm, he looks down at me, confusion swirling in his darkened eyes. His body flinches away from mine, making me retract too.

"What're you doing?" he asks, and embarrassment licks at me while I clear my throat.

"Nothing," I mumble as I glance around. While some of the men have taken their eyes off me, a lot of them haven't.

I stuff my hands in my pockets and try to make myself invisible. My body language is as closed off as possible, yet that doesn't seem to matter. There are whispers still coming from behind us, making me hate that I came here. At that, a warm arm wraps around my shoulders, and I glance up, finding Liam now looking at me with concern. He glances around, finally noting the stares. Then, he plays with the strings of my hoodie with one hand while the other settles loosely on my waist, and more whispers cease.

A beat passes and I do nothing. A frown comes onto his face momentarily, but then he gives me a gentle smile.

This is the guy I've missed for so long. Something settles in my chest; maybe there's some hope for us yet. Though, a hurtful but true memory comes to mind, and I remember something that's standing between us.

"There's this guy that I hooked up with a couple years ago who'll be there for sure." And boy, was he. I remember how Vanessa grabbed him like it was normal for them. The way she looked up at him—the way the very first friend I made had been involved with Liam. Orientation was so long ago, and my brain likes to shove it away till it needs to put me back in check. I blink rapidly, stepping back as his arm drops from my waist.

His eyebrows furrow, and he seems ready to ask what's wrong before someone shouts, "Next!"

We startle at that, and Liam quickly walks up to the register as I trail behind him. A guy around my age gives me a once-over before focusing on Liam.

"Hey, man, what can I do for you?"

"I need an oil filter for a BMW 320i." The guy smiles at me, but I don't return it. He leaves for a moment, heading to the back, and Liam stiffens slightly as his hand clenches and unclenches at his side. Waves of what seems like slight annoyance roll off him and unease comes over me. Poor guy has no idea when he comes back, whistling slightly, scanning the box.

He then looks at Liam, and with an easy smile, says, "It's gonna be fifteen fifty-nine."

Liam rolls his eyes and takes out his wallet, paying with his card. Not even wanting his receipt, he grabs my wrist and whisks me out of there. We walk through the doors heading to the parking lot and he's breathing heavily. Given that he's taller than me, I have to jog slightly to keep up with his pace. He unlocks the car and we get in. He then puts his head on the steering wheel, the ink on his skin moving along with every exhalation.

We sit there for a beat before he sighs, causing my tentative smile to not even fully form. His eyes lock with mine, regret taking over his features. "I'm sorry if I made you feel uncomfortable, I forgot, we're not—*you know*. Slipped my mind for a moment," he says.

"Right. Yeah," I mumble, putting my head against the window. He composes himself, starts the car, and we're driving back home. Looking out, I focus on all the dry land of Los Angeles behind the bougie establishments.

The silence is back again. But it's what I wanted, right?

Him to stay out of my way, me out of his. He's Vanessa's something, and I'm not his . . . anything.

But this silence hurts more than I thought it would, and I'm such a coward to even want to say something about it. I jump out of the car once we park in front of my house, making my way to the driver's side. His eyes flit between me and my outstretched hand as he chuckles in disbelief.

"Back to square one, huh?"

I roll my eyes. "We never left, right?"

He pinches his nose, chuckling almost bitterly. "This is what you wanted, right? What we both wanted," he says, and we stay still after. His shoulders have fallen and he looks tired, looks *done*. I must mirror the expression, and his eyes lock with mine, showcasing hurt above all.

His face searches mine for answers. It seems as though we have each other's hearts in our hands, yet don't know how to handle them. Much to my dismay, a tear streams down my face against my will. His eyes soften and he looks as though he wants to say something, but resists. He drops the keys in my outstretched hand, stalking off without a word.

Walking in, Olivia's on the floor while Josh and Mom are on the sofa behind her. Mom looks to be the only one interested as her eyes light up when she sees me coming into the room.

"Hey, hon, how was the trip with Li—"

I look away. "Fine. I'm going to my room."

"Bianca, let's think about being more respect—"

My blood boils, bringing back the annoyance I have with Josh. "*Respectfully*, Josh, screw off!" I yell, not caring what Mom says. I slam the door and pull the curtains together, tears running down my face. Some of the animal science books I bought crowd my bed, and I grab them, slamming them down on the floor. The only source of light in the now-dark room—the fairy lights—catches my eye. I slide down the bed, bringing my knees up when my eyes catch the corner of a familiar box, and I reach for it hastily. Opening it up, it's full of all the things representing Liam and me, things I never got rid of despite the ongoing rift between us. My hands reach for the Polaroid strip of us from years ago. It was one of the days when he came with me and Mom to the mall.

I look at the strip of photos, and the first is a cute one, then a couple ones with our tongues out, but the last one causes me to cry that much more. It's him kissing me on the cheek while I giggle. I remember that day when he whispered into my ear:

"*I'll never stop loving you, Freckles.*"

But he lied. The one person I truly believed in *lied to me.*

CHAPTER TWENTY

Bianca

THERE'S A BREEZE ACROSS MY leg and I quickly tuck it under the covers, finding warmth. I cuddle more into my pillow, but then groan as I can't seem to find that sweet spot again. Opening an eyelid to see the number nine flashing on my alarm clock, I shoot up, remembering my shift today. Mom had convinced Josh to let me volunteer at the shelter once my wound healed, and no lawsuit was pursued, thank goodness.

After a couple of weeks, the injury has faded away and you can't even tell it was there. It's also been a couple of weeks since Liam and I have talked. He hasn't come by, and every time Ana comes over, she gives me this sad mom look. I don't dare ask about him, so I tap back into the mentality I've had these past years, the years I've learned how to live without him. Mom waits for me in the car as I slide in, heading to the shelter. Even though I hated to do it, I apologized to Josh for my outburst and didn't disclose to Mom what he had told me earlier that day.

It's the way he is, and I have to accept it, right?

The sign of the animal shelter comes into focus, and even though I didn't have the best experience last time I was here, that doesn't stop me. Doesn't deter me. I just want to keep doing what I love. Pushing open the doors, Rachel is pacing, stopping only to lock eyes with me. She rushes over, hugging me quickly. "Well, I didn't think you were gonna come in. Thank goodness you're alright."

I tilt my head at her, confused. "Yeah, I'm all good, honest." She nods, placing a hand on her chest. I simply shrug. "I missed these guys." As if the dogs can understand me, some of them bark happily, and she smiles at that.

"We're glad to have you, and Zorro has been transferred, so nothing else should happen."

I nod and rub her arms as if to calm her down. "Rachel, you're good. Don't worry, it was an accident." I smile and she returns it. Her stance becomes more relaxed and I hug her again. It's been a few weeks, but she's been so unbelievably sweet to me.

I laugh when her radio grumbles on, saying a certain chihuahua has escaped. "Duty calls!"

Making my way to the kennels, I send a slight wave to the people working in our laundry room. I accidentally bump into someone. Stepping back, ready to apologize, I look up and see him. He has dark circles under his eyes and his hair is slightly mussed, and his eyes . . .

Clearing my throat, I say, "Sorry."

His eyes don't stray from my face until I cross my arms. They flick down to my once-wrapped arm, and the crease forming between his eyebrows seems to soften. He then closes his eyes, sighing, before he slides around me. I stand there, the warmth from his body leaving with him, but I don't dare look back. I keep walking, the to-do clipboard having several items unchecked. A bark catches my attention, and I look down at our newest doggy boy, Frankie, as he looks up at me happily. Sticking my hand through the spaces between the bars, he laps at it excitedly. I rub his head, as much as he lets me, and convince myself to think about this. What I'm doing to help these little guys.

Liam

A laugh pulls me out of my daze, and I look back to see Bianca talking to James, the vet intern. He hands her the box of gloves as they bathe the smaller dogs today. She begins to suds up Frankie, cooing at him, and the urge to smile is strong. James gets closer by kneeling next to her, doing the same thing. I roll my eyes as I grab another tennis ball, throwing it out in the yard. Our newest collie, Cookie, runs after it, and a shiver runs up my spine as she laughs again.

I know James is not that freaking funny.

Cookie trots back happily, dropping the green ball at my feet, and I make the mistake of looking behind me in time to see James throw soapy water at her. He guffaws as she smiles rather politely, and I'm this close to leaving Cookie in the enclosed yard. She wipes her forehead with her sleeve and something stirs within me.

The hoodie she's wearing is mine.

My body warms, not from jealousy, but due to the butterflies roaming my insides. Throwing the ball once again, I turn back when she lifts her gaze. Cookie looks at me expectantly, barking as she runs to fetch it. James chuckles again, but I smirk to myself. It doesn't matter what he does, what he says, because she's wearing my hoodie—*mine*. She has *my* scent engulfed around her. He's talking and flirting with her, but *I'm* enveloped all around her. I shake my head, wondering why I care so much.

She's . . . just someone I used to be friends with, and who I'm currently trying to stay away from.

I shouldn't care, right?

The sun sets, and it's the closing shift, meaning everyone's pretty much gone home. Walking around, I check our puppies, making sure they have more than enough toys to play with. I check their blankets, food, and water bowls, and some of them bark happily while others stay in dreamland. I run a hand over our new litter of dachshunds, and smile as I remember Bianca's reaction when Rachel dropped them off earlier today. Grabbing a squeaker toy, I throw it in there and one of the little guys goes after it.

The lights are dimmed, and soothing music plays all throughout the facility to help our animals sleep more peacefully, and for the enjoyment of those working the shift. I check on the patients in our ICU, making sure they're alright before I realize I did everything I needed to.

I close the door softly as I make my way to the last kennel of the night. I put my hand under the sanitizer dispenser, proceeding to then rub my hands together while pushing the door open with my shoulder. I scan all of the kennels, my mouth quirking up at the corners at everyone having the sleep of their life. Finally, I get to my old pal, Sam.

He's resting as always, and I bend down, tapping the glass, causing him to open his eyes instantly.

I wave. "Hey, bud." He looks at me curiously. I laugh softly before grabbing a leash and taking him to one of our playrooms. He hasn't wanted to go out all day, poor guy. He starts walking, but after a while, I carry him the rest of the way, and he lets out a tired huff. Finding the door unlocked, I walk in and sit with him in my arms before the door opens again, and I hear a yell.

She puts her hands over her heart as she looks at me in shock. "Liam!"

I close my eyes, exhaling sharply. "Bianca, what are you doing here?"

She looks at me confused. "I, um, didn't know anyone was still here. I—" She trails off before she looks down at Sam. "Guess we had the same idea." I squint involuntarily, and I sigh while running a hand through my hair, pulling at the strands at the nape of my neck. Her posture sags as an icy look passes through her eyes. The same look she's been giving me all day. "I can go." She bends down to pet Sam for a bit before she starts to walk off.

I should let her go.

Let her leave.

I reach out, grabbing her wrist gently, bringing her to a stop. "No, it's okay. *Stay*." The last word tumbles out and I can't take it back. I clear my throat, hoping she doesn't get the double meaning. She doesn't turn around and I drop her wrist instantly.

Sam lets out an insistent whine, and she chuckles softly before turning back around. "I'll stay for you, Sammie." She squats and gives Sam all her love, cooing at him like a baby. And I know I shouldn't, but I look at her.

I do, because God, she's so beautiful, both inside and out. No amount of anything can ever change that.

Sam's furry coat glides through my fingers as I pet him gently, and he whines as he stretches slightly. I look back over to her, and she pets Sam absentmindedly. Her eyes unfocus a little and her mind seems to have left this place for a bit.

She looks—*no. I don't care. I don't.*

Yes, I do.

"Your wound," I mention. She looks up at me and my train of thought derails. "Um, it healed." She nods at that and looks back down at Sam, and I deflate.

Out of everything I could've said, that's what I went with?

Come on, don't be a coward.

"Bianca." Her cerulean eyes make contact with mine, and I fall right back in like I always do. Except I'm not twelve years old anymore, I'm not a little kid anymore. We're not kids anymore. "I'm tired of this."

Her eyebrows crease together and I sigh as that did not come out the way I thought it would. I shake my head, trying to clear everything up. "Not—" I take a deep breath. "I'm tired of this back and forth." Understanding passes through her eyes, but she doesn't say anything, and I let it all go. "We were best friends, you and me.

For years. This . . . *animosity*, for lack of a better word, is getting exhausting." Her eyes widen, but I don't stop. "I've been trying to rid myself of our memories for years. Trying to put you behind me, and I thought I had, but then I saw you again, and it made me realize I didn't want to. I just—didn't know if you felt the same." I stand, Sam looking at me, as I run my hands through my hair, frustrated.

"So, I became who I am with everyone else. A jerk. An emotionless prick because I couldn't handle it when you left the first time. A second time would finish me off, yet all you have to do is look at me . . ." Her eyes raise to mine as she stands slowly, and I chuckle sadly, pathetically, as I move closer to her. "And I physically can't keep going through with it. You just look at me with those eyes I'd looked into for years, and the last thing I wanna do is stay away from you." I swallow harshly. "Even with the risk that I might get hurt again."

I'm breathing heavily, my lungs can't get enough oxygen, and she hasn't said a single word. "Tell me right now if you want me to stay out of your way. That you want me to act like I don't know you. That we're strangers. And I'll honor it, I swear I will. Because even after all this time . . . I'd still do just about anything for you." Her mouth drops open at that.

Sam squirms slightly, probably feeling the tension, and I sit back down, rubbing his head, his body loosening up instantly. I run my hand through his fur, my eyes not wanting to meet Bianca's even after she sits next to me . Her body heat is so close, it could engulf me if I wanted it to.

"Liam," she says, and my head snaps up, her face the picture of every emotion all wrapped into one. She looks conflicted, scared, hurt—and each one breaks my heart more than the last. I brace myself for the impact of her words, for her to hammer in the last nail of my coffin . . . *when she hugs me.*

Her arms wrap around as best as they can and I freeze. In one moment, she's squeezing me, and in the next, I'm wrapping my arms around her. She smells of coconut and sunny days, and my goodness, have I missed that smell. It's something so uniquely her. Something

I've never forgotten. The hug feels like it lasts for an eternity and it heals something in me that's been broken for a long time, but then she pulls back.

"I'm sorry." Two words. Words that will either put on a Band-Aid and heal my heart, or shatter it more than it already is. "I haven't been acting great either. I realized I wasn't truly over things that happened forever ago, and now, seeing you having friends and doing everything we said we would, and the whole thing with Va . . ." Her voice cracks slightly, and a sour taste starts in my mouth and I look down. "It kind of brought back the jealousy I felt all those years ago," she whispers.

She felt jealous?

"You were calling less, and when we did talk, you'd tell me all about how the football guys were accepting you. I was so happy, don't get me wrong . . ." She trails off. "I was scared that one day you'd leave me behind. I mean, where would I fit in your new life?"

I shake my head. "*You were my whole life.* I tried out for the team because you believed in me. I didn't even spend that much time with them because I wanted to hang out with you." I blow out a breath at how she didn't understand how much I cared about her.

How much I still do.

"I was jealous too, you know." Her body angles toward mine, and her face is more confused than shocked. "You were always talking about your new friends, about Jamie. I just—you had already left physically." I shrug. "I thought I was gonna have to say goodbye to my best friend once more." Tears well in her eyes, and I don't dare maintain eye contact. I confess, "I'm sorry for what I said."

She chuckles sadly. "*I'm* sorry for what I said." She puts her hands over mine, her fingers wrapping around mine tightly. "I'm sorry you felt like that. And about telling you to stay away . . . I won't tell you to." My heart beats rapidly. "I've missed you, Liam Parker, *a lot*. Every memory I have of this place—Los Angeles—has you smack-dab in the middle of it." I chuckle and she smiles. "I don't want you to stay away. Please don't. I didn't mean what I said back at Mella Colta."

I shift closer and place my finger under her chin. She raises it slightly and I look deep into her alluring eyes. "Even when you didn't want me, I was there." She looks at me confused, but I push through. "You have always got me. *Always*. Best friends, *forever and ever*, remember?" I hold out my pinky, reciting the promise we made all those years ago fresh in my mind.

She smiles and wraps hers around mine, the same words leaving her mouth with utter gentleness. My eyes trace her face, memorizing it, feeling that if I blink, she'll fade away. The slope of her nose, the little dots scattered across it, some stray outliers on her chin and upper lip. I raise my hand, my fingertips aching to trace the small dots across her face. She leans into my touch, and I swear, she moves even closer. Her beachy scent comes back to envelop me, creating a buzz around my senses. Her lips are a breath away from my own and her eyes are hooding slightly.

My eyes flick down to her lips before they shoot right back to her eyes, and I can't help the strangled whisper that leaves me.

"Freckles."

The once-beloved nickname I had for her. One she loved to hear all those years ago causes her to *flinch* now. She blinks rapidly, pulling back. "Um, it's getting late." She looks down at Sam, his head propped up as if he knows that it's time to go back to his kennel. She doesn't make an effort to move and neither do I. She keeps petting him, and I keep my hand still, because after a bit . . . Her hand hits mine and she looks up at me.

How is it that I wanted to hate her for letting me go? For forgetting about me—*damn it, us*—for five years, and yet my heart wants to give itself back to her, the scar of her leaving the first time very much prominent.

Her phone vibrates and she looks down at it, sighing. "Mom says she's picking me up late, and *Josh* is too busy, apparently." She practically spits his name and my body lights up in protectiveness. The words he told her the other day haven't left my mind, and if he wasn't Ms. Kate's fiancé, I would've confronted him then and there.

She runs her hand through her hair and it cascades back down. Her natural brown color fights against the blonde. Personally, I love the brown, *always have*, but she looks so pretty either way. A small smile blooms on my face and her eyes narrow slightly as she looks at me.

I stand, shaking my head, holding out my hand for her, and with a raised eyebrow, she takes it. "C'mon, I'll drive you home." Her words of protest die on her tongue as I stop her with a raised hand. "You're on my way, and I'm not gonna leave you here by yourself."

She closes her mouth, and after a bit, she nods, and we both look down at Sam as he looks up at us curiously. "What about the rest of your shift?"

She doesn't know I finished, but even if I hadn't, she can't really think I would leave her here, right? She bumps into my chest, and my hands cup her face lightly, giving her the option to back away if I'm crossing a line. Thankfully, she lets me put them there, and I lock my eyes with hers. For a bit, I remember all the times I used this exact gesture to calm her down.

"I'm taking you home. Okay?"

Her inhale is sharp, but her eyes seem to soften. The warmth she carries in that big heart of hers fills them, and *it's finally directed toward me.*

A small whine takes us out of our bubble, and my hands drop as we chuckle lightly. Sam stares up at us and I bend over to scratch the top of his head. "I hate leaving you here too, buddy."

"Sam's got your heart, huh?" she asks, and I almost, *almost* laugh at the irony in the question. "He's got mine too."

After putting him in his kennel, Bianca throws a fluffy blanket over him, causing a chuckle to leave my lips. I hold the exit door open for her and she slides in when we get to the car. I slip in behind the wheel and give her a little time as she geeks out. "You like it?"

She gives me a stunned look. "Duh, BMWs are my weakness, and the white is a great choice." I duck my head at that, a blush roaring its way up to my face, and I thank goodness it's dark right now. I drum my fingers nervously before I ease out of the parking lot, my mind preparing for the highway.

"You think?" I ask.

"Yeah, this is my literal dream car," she mumbles, and for a fleeting moment, my heart jumps at the idea of this car being hers one day. But I pull myself back to reality.

Scanning her to see if she's fidgeting as we drive, I say, "We have to focus on getting you your permit first." I cross into the middle lane as we get close to our exit, and I try with all my might to avoid potholes. Flitting my eyes to hers, she has her arms crossed, looking at me with the cutest expression.

"We?"

I shrug. "I could teach you." Throwing it out there, I say nothing else as we drive to her house. A couple of weeks ago, we were in this same situation, but it feels different somehow. I feel light, happy, almost giddy. She's here and she trusts me even with her fear of being in cars. We don't talk about the near kiss, and I don't want to push her. I merge into the right lane, the perfect opportunity to get another glance at her, and warmth blooms within me.

Yeah, she's worth the wait. I've always known she's worth everything.

CHAPTER TWENTY-ONE

Bianca

HE KILLS THE ENGINE BEFORE looking at me, not making a move to do anything, letting me set the pace, and I almost cry at the familiarity.

Always making sure I'm alright.

"Thanks for the ride." I'm not even sure he hears me, but he dips his chin while glancing at me. A small smile takes over his face before it leaves.

"Of course."

The streetlight outside illuminates his ink, and I blurt out something, not wanting the night to end. "How many tattoos do you have?"

He looks to actually consider the question before he pushes out a breath. "I stopped counting after a while."

I twist my lips. "Makes sense, you're"—my eyes scan him meticulously—"covered." My voice gets slightly breathless toward the end.

He smiles. "Maybe I'll show you them one day and we can count them together." My body instantly warms at the thought. Josh's

Mercedes is parked in the driveway and a groan makes its way up and out of me. His eyebrow raises curiously, and I lift a shoulder in a half-hearted gesture before pointing at the car. "You sure you wanna go in right now?" he asks, and I smile, the nostalgia hitting me as I sigh.

"Kinda have to."

He opens his mouth before closing it. "Yeah, I guess." I open the door, but he doesn't let me get far. He reaches for my wrist and grabs it gently. "Bianca." He says my name, but my heart aches for the eight-letter word . . . The nickname he always called me that caught me off guard tonight. Still, I turn around and his eyebrows furrow, his pillowy lips forming the cutest pout. "Are we . . . okay?"

He wants reassurance. Reassurance that the moment I walk out of this car, I won't act the same way. Reassurance that we're fine, that even with everything . . .

"Yeah." I smile, a downward tilt forming on his mouth. "We're okay." He lets go of my wrist almost reluctantly and I release a breath as I step out. The passenger side window rolls down as I close the door, and he looks at me with blinding jade orbs.

"Good night, Bianca."

"Night," I whisper and turn to walk to my house, hoping everyone's asleep. My cheeks burn as I haven't heard his car speed off. No, he's still there waiting for me to walk in safe and sound. I unlock the door before turning around and giving a shy wave. He sends one back as he drives off and I sigh happily as I close the door.

"Where the hell have you been?" Josh seethes and Olivia's crossing her arms smugly.

"At the shelter." I place my keys on the hook near the door.

He groans in annoyance. "So, who dropped you off?"

I turn back around, shrugging. "That's none of your business."

"It was Liam, Dad," the snitch says, and I look at Olivia in shock. Jealousy crosses her face while I stand my ground. She then looks at him with fake doe eyes. "Daddy, I would *never* hang out with someone like that." It comes out all sickeningly sweet, and I fight the urge to expose her.

Hypocrite. Absolute hypocrite.

Low whispers echo between them, my name and Liam's getting thrown around, and I sigh loudly, getting their attention. "Look, Mom gave me her permission—" I start before the door opens behind me, Mom holding some groceries from that place Josh likes that's forty-five minutes away.

"What's going on here?" she asks, confused, while putting down the bag. I move to speak, but of course, I get interrupted.

"I was reminding Bianca that she needs to be more respectful by letting me know, as her future stepfather, when she plans to get home."

I look at him incredulously. "I don't have to tell you anything. I told Mom I was gonna get a ride since she was gonna be late." Anger floods my words and Mom glances between us with a worried look. He smirks at me as he wraps an arm around her waist and I look at her in shock. "Mom?"

She doesn't say anything as Josh hugs her closer, a smug grin stretched across his face. Who is this woman, and what has she done with Mom? Mom would always side with me, *defend* me, but this woman—I don't know who she is.

"Consider this a warning, Bianca. You are *not* to get rides, hang out, or do anything with that boy again. Bad enough we have to deal with his mother." My eyes widen, and so do Mom's, but she stays mute. I scoff, shaking my head in disbelief as he continues. "You are to wait for us, no matter what, am I clear?" He hugs Mom closer to him, almost to prove a point.

"Whatever," I mumble as I walk off, closing the bedroom door in frustration and locking it. *My mom*—I stifle a cry at the thought. It was her and me against the world. No one was ever above her, and no one was ever above me. Yet now, she sides with him when I did nothing wrong.

Is this how it'll always be? Will I now be *second* to Josh and Olivia? *In that case, who will I be first for?*

I sigh at all the thoughts swirling in my mind. "Bianca?" Mom's voice comes through the door and I jump slightly, getting out of my bubble.

"Go away," I mumble.

"Honey?" she tries again, and I turn off my lamp. She seems to get the hint. Her footsteps leave and this familiar feeling of numbness comes over me. I used to feel it with Liam, and now it's bleeding through into other areas like a disease. Wanting sleep to take me away, not wanting to feel this hollow emotion, I grab my star and Señora Bearington, closing my eyes harshly.

"Come on, guys! We're gonna miss it!" I whined, and Mom laughed as she wobbled as best as she could, Dad fussing over her per usual.

He opened Mom's door, sliding his hand in hers to help her into the car. He closed the door gently after having given her a million kisses, then came over to my side to make sure I was buckled in.

"I'm all good, Dad. See?" I pointed to my seat belt, placed across my chest the right way, and he gave me the dad thumbs-up. We were finally on our way to the county fair and I was beyond excited. It was a tradition we were wanting to start, and I loved it. Soon enough, the beautiful lights appeared, the happy musical jingle blocked out the sounds of traffic, and I smiled.

Once Dad found a prime parking spot, I was the first to jump out.

"We're here." I glanced back. "WE'RE HERE!"

I knew the drill, so I quickly got in line for the wristbands, and after a couple minutes passed, we were next. I frowned slightly when Dad said Mom wouldn't be getting one, that we wouldn't want anything to happen to baby Ezra in her tummy, so I nodded.

I grabbed his much-larger hand and dragged him to the first ride of the night: the Spinning Teacups. I smiled at the very short line, and looked up at Dad with my puppy-dog eyes, as I knew he hated this ride, and he sighed.

"The things I do for our daughter," he said jokingly to Mom while she rolled her eyes.

"I'm gonna get some hot dogs. Our baby boy is really hungry," she said and he nodded before leaning in for a kiss. I cringed at them.

"C'mon, Dad!" I said, and he pulled back, laughing and shrugging at Mom, who smiled at us in turn.

After the teacups, we went on a bunch more rides and played a lot of games. Surprisingly, on top of winning Mom a prize, he got me one too. She had gotten a gigantic silver moon while I had gotten a small yellow star. He had tried for the sun one for himself, but didn't get it.

"It's okay, Dad. You can get it next year!" He smiled at that and nodded before he mussed up my hair.

"Did you have fun, honey?" he asked, and I nodded excitedly, my mouth full of funnel cake. Content with my answer, he grabbed both Mom's and my hands.

Nothing could be better than this.

We all jumped in the car after being at the carnival for three hours, and while I wanted to go on the teacups for a third time, Mom was all tuckered out. As we drove home, I played with my little star, pressing it against the window, showing it all the real stars in the night sky.

"You really like that toy, huh, kiddo?" Dad asked as he adjusted the rearview mirror to see me, and I nodded happily.

"It looks like the stars in the sky, Dad. And I'm matching with Mom because she got the moon. All we needed was the sun," I said, pouting, and he laughed. Mom hissed slightly and he glanced over at her in worry. She smiled at him as he smiled back. As cars passed by in the opposite direction, their headlights illuminating the interior, I picked up Dad mouthing "I love you" to her.

I smiled at them. Even though they grossed me out sometimes, I loved them so much.

Suddenly, before Mom could say anything back, she yelled, "David, watch out!"

Scared, I looked up. A set of headlights were really close to the windshield. Shock took over my body and I hugged my star to my chest, feeling the car crash into something. We began to spin, and it felt like the ride at the carnival all over again, except this time, it wasn't any fun.

Screeching tires and rough sounds came from every direction. The car flipped over, a small second of silence, before it was torn as the hood of the car scraped against the concrete. I screamed as Mom did too, and the glass shattered all over me.

Gravity pulled me down with each spin and I winced in pain. Dad yelled for me and Mom, and then the car hit something else. Ringing started in my ears as darkness consumed me, and I could no longer hear anything.

I groaned, my heart thumping in my ears, but I didn't make a move to wake up. There were muffled sounds, and I shuddered as the wind blew over my exposed cuts. My mouth tasted of pennies and my eyelids felt so heavy.

"Bianca? Come on, honey. Wake up, please," a muffled voice said, and I tried to open my eyes. The seat belt dug into my chest. Mom was still in the passenger seat, her wails loud even through the fuzz that was in my ears. My vision blurred once more, but through it, I was able to make out flashing red and blue lights.

A firefighter EMT wrenched open Mom's crushed door and reached in, asking her something. I blinked slowly as I watched my door being taken off too. The firefighter tried to ask me something, and I knew I needed to be polite and answer back, but I couldn't.

The lady put something spongy around my neck and I moaned in pain. She then cut off my seat belt, and my body slumped forward, but she caught me. I made out blobs, but couldn't seem to focus over the throbbing in my head. I was placed on something before I saw what looked like Mom's body being taken out, and I tried to move, but couldn't.

I blinked, hoping to focus my vision, and I winced again, my neck hurt. My ears picked up the sirens as well as the chatter of people around me. Mom cried out and put her hand on her belly.

Worry coursed through me, but I couldn't do anything. I felt paralyzed and I begged for them to put me next to Mom. Someone must have heard me because they did, and I reached out, grabbing Mom's hand shakily.

She sobbed profusely as she tried to grip my hand. I glanced around, getting used to my surroundings. My head pounded. I glanced down to the pieces of glass in my arms. There was a flurry of whispers, murmurs, and Mom's wails.

I kept holding her hand as they tended to our injuries; I realized that I didn't see Dad anywhere.

"Mom, where's Daddy?" I whispered, as that's all my voice could do, and she looked at me sadly. I looked up at the paramedics, their expressions betraying nothing.

One paramedic took Mom and another took me, both muttering they needed to get us to the hospital. The glass they couldn't remove dug deeper into my arm and the cuts on my face were burning as my tears' saltiness seeped into them.

I gasped and winced at the car's busted-up condition. I cried louder, but gasped once more when they took out a body, and my vision focused on a familiar arm with a special tattoo.

"Daddy." I tried to shout, but it fell as a flat whisper. He stayed still as dread simmered in my belly. That's not right, he always answers . . . Always.

I tried again, my voice now hoarse, my throat raw.

"Dad, Dad. Wake up," I said frantically, but the gash on his head kept oozing blood. I whimpered, and looked to the paramedic lady, begging for her to help him. Tears welled in her eyes, but she didn't respond.

As they carried him, the lights hit his wounds in a way that I really noticed all of the blood. I had no idea why, underneath the lights, the blood on him scared me so much.

It was like I finally realized what it was, and I hated it.

I glanced down at myself and saw all the blood and cuts and I started to freak out. I thrashed as they tried to calm me down. I tried to get the blood off me—scratched at it, even—but all it did was smear, and I frantically clawed at myself. They rolled me into the ambulance, and new tears had found their way onto my face.

I couldn't do it. I couldn't do it anymore.

I felt sleepy, then, and I tried to stay awake, but couldn't.

Mommy, Daddy. Please don't go.

I shoot up from the bed, panting loudly as my arms tremble beneath me. Blinking, I take in my surroundings, seeing the comfort of my room.

Not in a destroyed car, glass slowly cutting my skin.

The shock radiates through me as tears start to build in my eyes. I cry in silence as I think about the accident. It's been so long since I've thought about it, but whenever I do . . . I'll never forget how Dad looked. He was so lifeless, so dead, *so not him.*

Swiping at my tears as they run down my face, light filters into my room. The streetlamps glow under the night sky, and I grab my phone and keys, preparing to leave. Once outside, I walk some before I realize where I'm heading.

Purely due to grief, I find myself in front of the only window that has the light on. I knock softly at it, hoping. I don't hear anything and sigh, as he's probably gone to sleep and maybe left his light on. Getting ready to turn back, I hear some shuffling and come face-to-face with Liam. He's standing there in a plain, white T-shirt and gray sweats, looking at me, confused, and I suddenly want to cry.

I wave slightly, and he signals for me to wait before shutting the curtains. Crossing my arms as a gust of wind blows, it goes right through my flimsy pajamas. He walks out, coming toward me, taking in my troubled look.

"Bianca, what—"

Without thinking twice, forgetting everything that's happened with Josh, with Mom, *with Dad* . . . I wrap my arms around him and bury my face in his chest, a sob ripping from me. He stands there for a minute, probably shocked, and I start to shake as the accident flashbacks circle my brain. Embarrassed, I pull back and wipe my nose, sniffling slightly, but he doesn't let me get far as he takes me into his arms.

"Freckles, what's wrong?" he asks, and my heart beats faster as the nickname leaves his lips. I look up, expecting his expressionless face, but see concern instead. I don't answer, and instead hide my face in the warmth of his chest once again.

I mutter slowly, "I had a bad dream."

He sighs before his arms tighten a bit more. He rests his face on the top of my head, mumbling what he always has. "It's okay, you're safe. I'm here." He lets me stay in his hold as long as I need to and I lose all sense of time. His fingers continually run through the strands of my hair, whispering reassurances over and over. His breath tickles my ear and I shiver, causing him to pull me in closer. "Do you wanna come in?" he asks after a bit, and while I want to say yes, the argument I had with Josh comes into play.

"I shouldn't." He looks as if he wants to say something, but restrains himself. I whimper from the loss of contact as he takes one step back.

"Alright."

I nod at that, and think I shouldn't have come. I do want to stay, but I would get in so much trouble. I turn to walk away, my mind cursing at me.

"Bianca, wait."

His fingers wrap around my wrist, swiftly turning me around. His body and mine end up being so close that I have to look up at him. His eyebrows furrow and his eyes lock with mine.

"I get you don't want to stay. Would you wanna talk over the phone? I just—" He stops himself, sighs, and lets go of my wrist. Pinching the bridge of his nose, he looks back down. "I wanna make sure you're *really* okay."

My heart warms at the words and I nod. He grabs my phone, puts in his number, and déjà vu washes over me. He offers to drive me or at least walk me home, but I refuse, knowing it's not a good idea for him to come anywhere near the house right now. I walk back home, and the moment I know he can no longer see me, his name lights up my phone.

CHAPTER TWENTY-TWO

Bianca

A SMILE IS PERMANENTLY STAMPED onto my face. Butterflies have not stopped flying around in my stomach, and honestly, *I don't want them to.*

"Bianca, is that okay?"

I blink rapidly as I remember I'm at the breakfast table and everyone is looking at me expectantly. I cough slightly and cover my mouth. "I'm sorry, what?"

Mom looks down at her plate while Josh and Olivia roll their eyes, and I glare at both of them. Tension has been high since yesterday, and I can see it's still very much in the air.

"I was asking about Ana inviting us to William's work ball, are you wanting to—?" she asks curiously, and I nod, cutting her off.

"Of course, we have to show up for the Parkers," I say. Josh rolls his eyes, and he doesn't even care when he notices I catch him. There are a couple more sounds of clinking forks on plates. "Um, can I be excused, Mom?"

Josh sets down his cup. "We haven't all finished, have we?" I cast a harsh glance in his direction. Mom looks between us as Josh stares at her. She seems to plead with him, and he finally nods, resigned. "Bianca?" My head snaps up and he has me locked in a glare. "I realize my behavior hasn't been the best it can be. Therefore, I want to extend my apologies." My eyebrows raise and Mom grabs his hand, grinning at him. "I have something to make it up to you."

I narrow my eyes, and I want to spit out that I want absolutely nothing from him. This is what he does, *it's his game*. He releases his pent-up aggression and says something that isn't right. Then he throws in a gift in an attempt to, what, buy me back? The doorbell rings, and I don't say anything before going to answer. The corners of my mouth are pulled downward, yet the moment I open the door . . .

"You're joking."

"Surprise!" Jamie exclaims.

I practically crash into her, hugging her deeply as she rocks us side to side. My eyes water as my frustration begins to ebb away; I can't believe she's really here.

"I missed you so much." She mumbles a sound of affirmation. "I sent you a care package a couple days ago."

She giggles, waving me off. "It'll be there when I get back, no worries, girl." Footsteps come from behind me and I pull away as everyone approaches the door, Mom with a big smile on her face and a knowing look.

"Mama Kate!" Mom chuckles while throwing her arms around Jamie. I smile at seeing the two, avoiding eye contact with Josh. They pull apart and she grabs Mom's left hand, observing the sparkling teardrop diamond ring that hasn't left her finger since the engagement. "I heard you got engaged." Jamie looks over to Josh as she smiles. "Congrats to you both, and thank you for bringing me over to spend time with Bianca."

My eyes widen. *This* is what the surprise was? Conflicting feelings rise in my throat; I hate accepting anything from Josh, but this . . . "Yeah, thanks, Josh," I force out, and he gives me a curt nod. Jamie sends a wave Olivia's way, but she just upturns her head, disinterested.

"No problem. I hope this makes up for everything," Josh says while Jamie looks at me, confused, but I shake it off. "Olivia, remember to get ready, we have a prior engagement." She sighs, stalking off to her room, before he whisks Mom away.

"How was the trip?" I ask, grabbing her lone suitcase. She looks as though she wants to ask, but she doesn't, thankfully. Her expression changes to one of excitement as she retells the story of how she traveled through three different airports all to get here. I don't want to fight or even bring up that I hate that Josh didn't get her a nonstop flight, but I guess I need to be grateful. I listen animatedly, and my heart is at ease once again after these last few days. Heading into my room, she marvels at everything, her eyes staying on the strip of Polaroids on the wall. Throwing ourselves on the bed, she laughs while giving me all her exciting updates.

"Oh also, I didn't wanna tell you over the phone, but guess who was offered a scholarship for fashion design." My eyes widen and she gives me her biggest grin.

"Jamie! That's amazing!"

She shrugs. "Yeah, I knew I wouldn't have been able to afford college with the financial aid package they offered, so I applied for the scholarship. The only clause is to keep up with the program, pumping out designs and such."

I roll my eyes because that's all Jamie has done since I met her. Take anything, and she can make something beautiful out of it. "Well, no problem there. You're a genius."

Her cheeks redden, and I forgot how much of an easy blusher she is. Her phone lights up with a message and she looks down at it. A small smile makes its way on her face and I give her a playful nudge.

"Who's that?"

She rubs at the back of her neck, almost as if she's been carrying the weight of the world on her shoulders.

"It's actually my cousin, Isabelle."

I blink, confused. "Cousin?"

She nods. "Yeah. We've actually been talking for a bit, and she came over for the first time the other day." My mind works double time as I process everything. When Jamie was pushed away by her family, I remember her telling me Isabelle was the only one who stood by her. Though, being she's only sixteen, her mom's word trumps hers. She sighs, rubbing her weary eyes. "Don't get me wrong. I don't trust her. For all I know, it's some evil plan from Aunt Mary . . ."

Ah yes, Aunt Mary, the person who convinced all of Jamie's uncles and aunts to abandon her after the will reading. How could such a cruel woman give birth to such a sweet person like Isabelle? Granted, I only know bits and pieces of when Jamie would play with her when she was younger, but the fact remains. I grab Jamie's hand and she looks up. Her eyes bore into mine, and I hate that she feels ashamed. "Jamie, I think it's awesome."

"Really?"

"Of course. I've always hoped that someone would reach out after what had happened. We all want our families even if they don't want us sometimes. Besides, if she rode the Amtrak from little Greencastle without telling her mom . . . She really wants to form a relationship with you." Her head tilts as if she hadn't really considered that. "Give her a chance. She's your family, after all." She nods and grabs her backpack to pull out the notebook and pens I gifted her. Her stomach grumbles, and we both laugh before she hops off the bed, grabbing my arm in the process.

"Come on, I know you must have the best snacks in this bougie house."

My laugh echoes when we get to the foyer. "Bougie house?" She points at the three chandeliers, and I shrug, playfully defeated. "Got me there." We're padding along the heated tile—regardless of the temperature outside, Josh has it turned on since he always runs cold—when the doorbell rings. I freeze; if it was Josh and Mom, they would've just opened the door, but it stays shut. Jamie looks over at me in confusion and I mirror it back. I head to the door, but she beats me to it and throws it open.

"Whoa." One word from her, and I get closer to see Liam, standing there in all his six-foot-four glory. He gives Jamie a glance before looking toward me, a smile breaking out on his face.

"Hi."

My cheeks flush and I cross my arms, looking at him with a quirked eyebrow. "Hi." Jamie's eyes dart between us, and I rub a nervous hand through my hair. "Jamie, this is Liam." He looks at her shocked, as does she.

"Yeah, nice to meet you finally." She sticks out her hand and he shakes it politely while looking over at me. When I first met Jamie back in Philly, Liam and I were still close. They knew of one another, but their meeting was never the plan. Well, not today at least.

A sheepish expression comes over him. "I came from the shelter and wanted to swing by since I didn't see you there. I, um, didn't realize you had company." He pinches the bridge of his nose, sighing once again. "We can talk about that thing . . . another day." Jamie looks confused, but deep down, I know what he wants to bring up.

Last night, me crying in his arms.

Me skirting the lines of our friendship when we're still trying to build that trust.

"Are you sure?" I lean against the doorframe as he stands up straighter, looking down at me, a cute smile coming over his face despite the war going on in those emerald eyes.

He nods. "Catch up, okay? Don't worry about it." He sticks his hands inside his hoodie pocket, and I want to talk about it now . . . I just *can't*. And here I am, using Jamie as an easy way out.

"Okay. I'll see you later?" He nods, his eyes lighting up a tiny bit. His focus moves to Jamie, who I'm sure is gawking behind me.

He says, "Nice meeting you, Jamie." Spinning on his heel, he walks off, and I stand there like a complete idiot. Jamie closes the door while I move out of the way, still dumbfounded as she pins me down with her stare. Her arms are crossed and her expression is almost annoyed.

"*Bianca Everly Harrison*, you have five seconds to tell me everything you've been hiding from me."

"Okay, you guys are so cute," she simply says while she prepares her clothes to take into the bathroom. I grab a soda from my mini fridge, not responding. A smirk forms on her face as she locks herself in my en suite, leaving me with my thoughts. I try, but fail, to not think about the whirlwind that has been life this past month. The main twist: Liam Jax Parker.

We've gone from strangers, to sort of acquaintances, to coworkers, to I don't even know what. And the way he gazed at me the other night . . . Even in the dark, I could make out every little detail on his face. The way his long, full eyelashes—that I'm one hundred percent jealous of—fluttered as he looked at me.

Held me close and whispered those same words from all those years ago.

You're safe with me, always.

"Is this what people look like when they're in love?" I put a hand to my heart, an audible yelp leaving me as Jamie asks, standing there with her arms crossed once again. "If so, remind me never to do it." She walks toward the bed in her matching pajamas, and I roll my eyes at that. Jamie has one of the purest hearts I know, but after everything she's been through, she guards it well. While it may be hard, I know when the perfect guy comes, she'll fall even harder than I already have with mine.

CHAPTER TWENTY-THREE

Liam

MY PHONE RINGS AND I don't hesitate to pick it up, the morning light blinding the crap out of me. "Hello?" A chuckle comes from the other side of the phone, and I squint at the name with a sigh.

"You know, I'm very offended."

I get up, stretching slightly as I look at the slight stubble growing on my face in the mirror. "Mm, pray tell?" I answer sarcastically and switch the phone's speaker to my earbuds, missing half of what Chase said.

". . . you know?" I mutter a mild grunt. "You didn't listen to a word I said."

"What do you want, Chase? You bored without me or something?"

He doesn't answer the question directly. "How's it going with Harrison?" His use of a nickname still doesn't sit right with me, and I finally realize what this phone call is for.

"That's between me and her, don't you think?"

He laughs. "Oh, come on, dude. I did help, sorta."

I roll my eyes and run a hand through my hair, the strands at the nape of my neck suffering their usual. "Why are you so nosy?"

He scoffs. "Because I finally get to talk to you after two years of trying, sue me for wanting to bond with my roomie, bro."

You know, a couple of weeks ago, I wouldn't have even considered being something more than just roommates with Chase. Yet, he's never given up, he's always tried to reach out. Maybe it's about time I do too.

"It's going well, but fair warning, I don't kiss and tell."

"Makes sense," he says.

"How's the dorm been since I left?"

He gasps, and I instantly regret asking him anything. "Did Liam 'Campus Grouch' Parker ask me something? I'm shocked. I think I'm gonna faint."

That earns him a chuckle against my own will. "Don't make me regret it," I say.

"Yeah yeah. Well, I unfortunately have to take some intro to finance classes for Summer B, courtesy of father dearest, and I'm dreading them."

I make a sound of acknowledgment, and not for nothing. *Am I actually enjoying talking with him?*

Half an hour later, I'm washing down a couple of painkillers thanks to the discomfort from the tattoo I got a couple days ago. I grab my car keys and twirl them around my pointer finger while smoothing down my better-looking sweatshirt. Jogging down the stairs, I walk into the kitchen for some more water and find Mom and Dad.

"Hey, guys." I wave before my phone rings, and I pick it up, not bothering to look at the caller ID. "Hello?"

"Hey . . . Are you busy?"

As that amazing voice flows through my phone, a smile comes onto my face and I clear my throat. "No. Nope. Not busy," I say. She giggles slightly and a blush comes onto my cheeks. Mom and Dad look at me suspiciously.

"Oh okay. Well, I was calling to . . ." She trails off while I wait with bated breath. Grabbing a water bottle, I move out of the kitchen, faintly hearing my parents laughing as I leave. Bianca clears her throat and confusion flows through me. "W-well. I remember you talking about helping me with my driving permit. I've always known it would be hard for someone I don't know to teach me, and Mom and I aren't really . . ." My heart jumps, and I rush to stop her rambling when I already know my answer.

"If you're comfortable, I'd love to teach you, Frec—Bianca." She doesn't say anything, but there's a low rustle. "Bianca?"

She inhales. "Yeah?"

I grin at the pull between us. No matter how much time, no matter how much has happened between us . . .

"I know Jamie's visiting, but if you're up for it, we can start today." There's a *thud*, followed by a playful giggle.

"She'll be ready in five." Jamie's voice floats through the speaker before she hangs up and a small chuckle leaves me. Even though the call ended, I'm still holding the phone to my ear as my heart takes off in a sprint. Glancing over, I see my reflection in the hallway mirror, noting a sparkle that only a certain person can bring out. My eyes have been dull, pained, and yet . . . having her in my life, even if we avoided each other in the beginning . . .

Yeah, that part of me she's got?

I don't ever want it back.

Walking back into the kitchen, grinning my butt off, my parents both look at me like I've grown another head. "What?"

"That smile definitely seems brighter," Mom teases.

Dad adds, "Maybe it has something to do with a certain *girl?*"

I roll my eyes and go to kiss Mom on her temple and give her a small side hug.

She looks up at me. "Have a good day, amor." I wave at them as I turn to leave. Eagerly closing the front door, I get in my car and roar it to life, ready to drive to her house. I walk up her driveway in time to see Bianca walking out. Jamie stands at the doorway and sends me two thumbs-up, causing me to chuckle. Bianca's wearing mid-thigh black shorts and a flowy pastel-purple shirt with embroidered tulips on it. She looks up at me and smiles and I mirror the expression. Though, as she gets closer, the fear and anxiety she hides behind her eyes is clear.

"We can do this another day if—"

She interrupts, "I got it, I promise."

"Are you sure?" She doesn't answer for a bit and rolls her shoulders. I move to give her a hug, but then back away, realizing I don't know if the circumstances are the same. She wraps her arms around me and sighs, almost expelling all her nervousness. I hug back, glad I can help her feel a little better. The accident is still very much a trigger for her, and I hope that I can be a good teacher. I drop my keys into her hand and she exhales sharply. "At your own pace, okay?" I reassure once more, and she nods.

"I promise not to damage your car," she says, nerves getting the better of her, and I shake my head.

"I can get another car, but I can't get another you, so don't focus on that, okay?" She nods, and we walk to the driver's side, causing a confused glance to be thrown my way. "After you." I open her door, and a blush comes onto her face. I can't help but smile at that. She climbs in and I close the door for her before jogging over to the passenger side. "Alright, when you're ready to start the car, put your foot on the brake and press that button right there." I point, then look back at her. She isn't paying attention at all.

Her posture is stiff and she's trembling slightly as she fidgets with her thumbs. I look at her, concerned. I slide my thumb against her straining forearm, and the touch seems to relax her a bit.

"I just—I freeze when I'm in the driver's seat. Give me a second." There she goes, always overexplaining when she has no need to.

"Take your time. If you want, we can learn the basics without actually driving."

She shakes her head. "No, I can do it." I nod, hoping she knows I think she can do anything she sets her mind to. She closes her eyes for a brief moment and grips my hand tighter. I rub my thumb across her knuckles, one by one, not knowing if this is crossing a line of our friendship.

"You've got this, okay? You're the bravest person I've ever known." Her head tilts as if she doesn't believe me, but I don't break eye contact, hoping she feels as reassured as I can possibly make her feel.

"Really?"

I caress the back of her hand once again. "I wouldn't lie to you, Bianca." She gives me a small smile and I return one of my own. "I'll be here."

"Anything else?" I ask, hoping she hasn't been holding out on any questions. We've been sitting here for about an hour, and while we haven't moved a single inch, I couldn't care less. She asks about things I didn't even think of when it comes to driving, and I nod when she goes on her little cute tangents.

"You're giving me a look." She rubs the steering wheel and I widen my eyes.

"What look?"

She sighs, waving me off. "This is stupid, I'm not ready. I don't think I'll ever be ready." I move to encourage her before she keeps going. "I just want to be normal and not have to wait when Mom goes out. Sometimes, I wanna go for a ride, but I can't do that because my stupid screwed-up brain doesn't let me."

My eyebrows crease as tears well in her eyes, but she blinks them back. I feel useless—I don't know what to tell her so that she won't believe she's any of the things her brain tells her she is. "Bianca, you suffered something really traumatic, and I've always marveled how you still give the world your smile. Even as kids, I'd complain about such stupid crap, and you'd treat it like it was the most important thing." She chuckles, and my heart warms as I see her little smile.

I motion to the car. "This is a trigger, and that's fine. I mean, look at what you've accomplished so far. You used to only ride in the back seat, and now you can be up front. *That's huge.*" I have a feeling Bianca's never really celebrated how much she's progressed. It's almost as if she believes they're not wins because everyone else does it.

She turns to face me. Her alluring eyes lock with mine, and I place my hand on the console more confidently while smiling at her, hoping to do away with those nerves.

"If you're not ready, it's okay. That doesn't mean you never will be, but I'm not gonna push if sitting there hurts you mentally," I say, honest as can be. I can tell in the way her body sags that there's something else she isn't saying.

"What if I hurt you, though?" A tear slips down her face and she catches it. "I'm scared that I'll lose control or . . . I don't know," she whispers. I stop my internal overthinking and look at her.

"Bianca, I get it. That's a very valid fear for every driver out there, and to be honest, it never goes away. But we're not gonna be leaving the neighborhood. Baby steps, okay?" I'm hoping it reassures her as I try to ignore the racing of my heart at her being worried for me. "I know you're scared. Hell, *I'm* scared. I'm scared I won't teach you everything, but I'm willing to face it . . . with you." I hope she can see all the trust I've always had in her. Smiling, she finally puts her hand on the wheel and takes a deep breath. She puts the car in reverse, using the camera and looking over her shoulder, then shifts into drive. We're off.

The car is moving slowly, but moving nonetheless. She speeds up slightly and a sense of joy for her washes over me. A stop sign is coming up and I hold on, waiting for the harsh brake we all do when we're learning. The sign gets closer, and I watch her as she shakes slightly with her eyes open, but has seemed to miss the sign.

Maintaining composure, I try to talk calmly, as I know she's really stressed. "Bianca, I know you're scared, I do, but there's a stop sign. I *need* you to brake." She whimpers, and I hate myself that I might've pushed her to do this when she doesn't seem all that ready. She brakes harshly at the last minute and I take a deep breath, thanking heaven above there wasn't anyone coming this way.

I give her a minute before I move the gear stick into park. She visibly exhales as she raises both her feet on the seat, putting her face between her knees.

"Hey." She lifts her head. "I'm so proud of you. You did it," I say, hoping she gains more of the excitement I saw briefly, but she scoffs.

"I left from the front of the house."

"Technically, yes. I know it may not seem like a lot, but baby steps are better than no steps," I reply.

"I guess," she says softly.

"Come on, what do you say to a celebratory snack?" Her little frown morphs into a small grin, and my heart skips a beat.

"You know I can't say no to food."

We swap seats and I start our way to the nearest fast-food place. Getting to the drive-through, I roll my window down and order our usual from way back when. She looks at me, shocked, and I clear my throat as I can already feel the blush starting on my face. They hand over our order and I pull into a spot as she's yet to say anything.

"I just realized I didn't even ask if I got your order right."

She stares at me for a solid five seconds. "It never changed, actually. This is perfect," she says, almost in disbelief, and I nod, desperate to rid myself of this burning across my face.

"To your first time on the road," I say, holding up my burger, and she touches hers to mine, rolling her eyes.

"You're a dork," she says.

"You loved it then, so I assumed you still might, five years later." She freezes as I unintentionally bring up something we've both tiptoed around. "So, how did we feel today?"

"It was good, Liam," she answers in a daze, not touching her food. My shoulders drop, realizing I must've put a damper on the whole thing.

"Bianca, look, I'm sorry."

She looks up. "You didn't do anything wrong. I forget sometimes, but five years is hard to completely ignore." I take a bite, not wanting to answer, even knowing the truth in her statement. "Even if my fast-food order didn't change, a lot has. And no matter how much we wanna sweep it under the rug . . . How I felt during it won't go away. As much as I want to freefall into this, there's still this fear . . ." My heart constricts at the word and my appetite wanes. "And with that comes everything else that I never associated with you, and never want to." She looks down, but my eyes don't leave her.

"Bianca—"

"Can we go back home, please?" she mumbles, and as much as it pains me, I understand her stance. Putting the car in drive, we make our way back to her house. A suffocating silence is present in the car, and neither one of us breaks it. Reluctantly, I turn onto her street, pulling to a stop in front of her house. I turn toward her as tears fall down her face.

"Thanks for the lesson today, Liam," she says with finality in her tone, getting out of the car, closing the door behind her. Her figure gets farther and farther away, and I want to run out and beg her to talk to me. *For us to talk.*

We talked about what happened all those years ago in the shelter, but not how we move forward now.

Or if she even wants to.

Leaving her street, I pull into my driveway. Bursting through the bedroom door, I plop down onto my bed, Bianca's words running through my head until I get sick of them.

They never stop circling, breaking my heart over and over again.

CHAPTER TWENTY-FOUR

Bianca

"GIRLS!"

I hear Mom before I see her. Jamie and I look in the direction of the door before she saunters in with Olivia. A smile on both of their faces causes apprehensive ones to start on ours. Mom has her beach hat on and Olivia wears a light sundress, and trailing behind them is Ana holding a boom box, with said boom box being way too big for her shoulder.

"Beach trip!" she says, and I sprint off the bed, hugging her as she puts it down to hug me better. I pull back to see Jamie behind me, and I turn around, ready to introduce them.

"Jamie, this is—"

She points at her. "Ana, Liam's mom?"

Ana looks at me with that smirk that I see all the time from her son. "Talking about me? I'm flattered." We laugh, and Olivia looks at me with an annoyed glance. As she leaves, Mom looks over sadly at the closed door. Jamie hugs Ana, and it fills my heart with warmth.

"I love you already, Jamie." A huge grin grows on Jamie's face and she looks at me happily. She always loves it when parents like her. Ana chuckles, giving her another side hug. "Okay, now come on. Everyone's waiting for us outside." She looks at us, frowning at our pajamas, and we chuckle sheepishly.

"I'll give you guys five minutes. Come on, Kate, let's hurry along that fiancé of yours." Ana drags Mom by the arm as they both laugh, causing smiles all around.

They close the door and I look over at Jamie. "Brought a swimsuit?" She chuckles and walks over, throwing open my closet as I raise a questioning eyebrow.

"I did, and I know just the one for you to wear."

A blush comes on my face, but then I think about the past couple of days. This is going to be awkward.

"Okay, you need to talk to him." I sneak a glance at Liam, only to find him still looking in my direction as Jamie and I lie on our towels. Thank goodness he drove in his own car because it would not have been fun. I mean, I get it, we're kind of in a weird place. But he's looking at me as if he's lost, and I've got to be overthinking that. I slide my sunglasses down from my head.

I shrug. "I messed it up, Jamie. Besides, if he wants to talk, he'll come over." Jamie sighs, going back to her magazine, a small mumble of annoyance leaving her that I pretend to ignore. I never realized I missed the beach until Ana and William invited us. The sun is shining and the clear water is practically begging for me to take a dive in.

I move my head from side to side, making it seem as if I'm cracking my neck. I catch a glimpse of Liam once again. He's wearing a light beige linen shirt, all buttoned, which makes the tattoos on his arms and neck look delectable as always. Though, I do my best to seem nonchalant. He has dark blue swim shorts on, the tattoos continuing their descent down his legs.

Gosh. He's really handsome.

Some girls whisper behind him, and I roll my eyes as I don't seem to be the only one who's noticed him. I huff, pissed at myself as all get-out, when a volleyball rolls toward me. Confused, given I didn't notice anyone at those courts a bit ago, I pick it up as a guy jogs over.

"Sorry, miss, we—" I freeze as he raises his head and tilts it as he looks at me with familiar blue eyes. "Harrison?"

"Chase?" He lets out a hearty laugh and hugs me. Squinting, I spot more familiar faces behind him. He pulls back, a smile mixed with shock on his face.

"I didn't know you'd be here," he says, playfully knocking me against the arm as he turns back, waving over the group of people. He shakes his blond hair out of his face.

I let out a laugh of disbelief. "Me? You live like five hours away." Goose bumps form all over my body as a warm presence comes up behind me, and I don't have to look to know who it is.

"Chase? What are you doing here, man?" He smirks, his eyes darting between us, and my smile drops when I notice a familiar girl jogging over and shrieking. Vanessa crashes into me and my eyes widen.

"Bianca! Oh-em-gee! So good to see you again, girl!" She shakes me back and forth in her embrace as I see Liam upturning his head at the bunch of guys; I'm hearing slivers of their conversation.

"What are you guys doing here?"

She shifts her weight. "It's summer break, and this beach is beautiful. I was, um—" She looks off and meets the eyes of a tall guy with black hair, brown eyes, and a smile on his face. "Hanging with a friend at the frat house, and they were all coming down, so I thought I would join."

I nod in all the right places, smiling even though it's not real. She's standing here in the smallest bikini known to man, and while I'm an advocate for showing off what you got, I hate that it makes me feel so inferior.

Her eyes flit for a few nanoseconds and finally focus on Liam.

"I can't believe he's here," she whispers, and Liam looks over at us, his eyes meeting mine. His expression drops when she raises a hand, waving at him, and I look away from that.

Yeah, today's shaping out to be a *great* day.

She giggles while a pit in my stomach forms. I excuse myself as she goes to where all the guys are, her eyes trained on Liam, causing my head to hang a bit. Jamie looks up at me, confused, and I blow out a breath in disbelief.

"Do I wanna know?" she asks when I make my way back to her.

With a sigh, I say, "Those guys are in the fraternity Liam's in. And that girl—she's the one who hooked up with Liam a couple years ago." Her eyes widen and she mouths the words "well, goodness," and I nod self-deprecatingly. "Yeah, so on top of Olivia's little looks toward Liam, I have to deal with Vanessa's." She gives me a saddened expression, and sits up, hugging my arm. I lean my head on hers, the beach day not shaping up as the best. Someone sits next to us, and I look, hoping it's Liam, but am surprised to find Chase.

"Is this seat taken?" I shake my head and smile. Chase was the one guy who was sweet to me during orientation. Jamie stiffens and his eyes drift toward her. "I'm Chase Collins." He gives her that suave smile and an outstretched hand that Liam has told me he gives to a bunch of girls. His platinum nose ring that I swore he didn't have before shines under the bright sun.

Jamie rolls her eyes, giving him her hand regardless. "Jamie Beckett." He repeats it, savoring each and every letter, and she takes her hand away. I glare at him.

He raises his hands in surrender. "Nice to meet you, Jamie." She nods before someone calls him over, and I turn to see that they moved their net closer, as they probably invited themselves to hang with us. He looks over and smirks. "We need another person, you up for it, Harrison?"

I shake my head before I elbow Jamie lightly. I point at her. "She was captain of the volleyball team for a bit in middle school." She slaps my arm and I rub it, pouting.

He laughs and stands, offering a hand. "Well then, *Cap*, you've gotta show us what you got." She sighs as she grabs his hand. Upon standing, she snatches it back and he walks them toward the game. Behind his back, she runs a finger horizontally along her throat toward me, and I giggle. Glancing around, I find Olivia and Vanessa talking together, sighing at that potentially becoming a thing. My eyes then lock on Josh saying something to Mom, causing her to roll her eyes at him.

Hm, that's new.

A shade casts over me as Liam sits. He crosses his arms and I fidget with my fingers.

"Didn't know they were gonna be here," he mutters.

I nod. "Coincidence. I'm glad Chase came."

Liam's head snaps toward me, his gaze heating at the simple sentence. "Why?" he asks, and I look at him, confused.

"He's nice . . . and my friend. One of the first ones I made at Mella Colta." He hums, but looks as if he didn't even listen to what I said. He doesn't say anything for a bit and I sigh. "If you're here to give me the silent treatment, you can do it somewhere else." He looks at me in disbelief—no, that doesn't make any sense, *disbelief about what?*

"I thought it's what you wanted. You haven't exactly reached out the last couple days either since the driving lesson." I don't bother defending myself because that statement is utterly true.

Resigned, I hang my head. "Why's this so hard?"

He shrugs, sighing. "I don't know."

I glance up. "I'm sorry for that day. Maybe if I didn't say anything . . ."

He stops me. "Hey, don't blame yourself. You went through a lot that day, and my comment didn't help either." He pauses. "Sorry, I've been acting kinda like an idiot."

I raise an eyebrow, shaking my head. "We both have." We chuckle at that, and he smiles at me while scanning me from head to toe.

"You know, I don't think I've seen a swimsuit like yours today."

I nod. "Yeah, it's not the most flattering on me either." Jamie swears that this thing is the best swimsuit I own, accentuating my features and using other fashion-related terms that I don't know the meaning of. I fuss with material and he stops me.

"That's a damn lie." I raise an eyebrow and he looks at me like he can't believe I think otherwise. "Bianca, you look gorgeous. You've outshone everyone on this beach, *sun included.* You're beautiful. When aren't you?" His voice stays reverent, but I stay stunned.

I'm wearing a simple dark green tankini. On this part of the beach alone, I'm practically fully clothed compared to the other girls here. He rubs a thumb over my cheekbone before someone calls his name, and the little bubble we're in pops. I look around to see everyone's eyes on us, most of them with smiles, except Josh.

Liam opens his mouth, but before he can utter something, someone pushes his shoulder jokingly. "As much as you wanna keep giving heart eyes to Harrison, the guys are trash-talking. We got Jamie, the badass captain—"

Jamie sits next to me. "No, I'm out."

Chase looks at her. "What, why? You're the only reason we're even winning. We need you on the team, Becks."

She rolls her eyes. "Swap me with Liam."

He groans. "I need you both." He's basically begging Jamie to keep playing, but she's stubborn. "Back to you, then, come on, you owe me." Liam looks appalled before Chase smirks.

"I mean, I *did* convince you to—"

"Fine, I'll play," Liam interrupts, standing as he looks at me. "I'll be right back."

I nod and Chase gives me a small smile before he follows Liam, who is currently dragging his feet in the sand. I look down at Jamie as she's grabbed her notebook, sketching something along the lines of a cute swimsuit.

"How was beach volleyball?" I ask.

She continues to draw as if the inspiration is oozing out of her. A small smirk comes on my face as she rolls her eyes at my implication. "Fun. I had fun, okay?" she finally admits.

"I saw, and by the looks of it, I think Chase likes you," I whisper, and she flashes me a deadpan stare.

"He's the type of guy who likes *everyone*." I shrug at that, and we turn around to watch them play.

Did I think volleyball was hot before? Not particularly.

But now . . . *Wow.*

Liam's muscles flex with every hit and his beautiful ink travels down the length of him. A hand covers my mouth, and I cough, embarrassed. Pretending to be looking at Jamie drawing while taking occasional glances, I don't miss when they finally finish.

He instantly makes his way back, but doesn't make it far before Vanessa stops him. My heart tugs painfully once again, but I ignore it as I've done so far.

CHAPTER TWENTY-FIVE

Liam

I MOTION FOR CHASE TO follow me, walking across the street, opening the villa Mom and Dad bought a while back. Pushing through the kitchen doors, he raises his hands in surrender. "I know what you're gonna say. I swear I didn't invite her to tag along."

Ever since Chase and I got a little close, I've told him more about Vanessa—including her swinging by the tattoo parlor and coming to every single event the frat has.

"Tommy has a thing with her, I couldn't say no." I understand this, but hate how it's making me feel, and I hope Bianca doesn't realize anything. I want her to hear it from me. Vanessa and I slept together *once*, and I wasn't in the right headspace. I was stupid, and thought that was the only way I could forget Bianca, the only way she wouldn't show in my mind. I consented, I wanted to forget her, but I didn't.

I never have.

Looking up, I catch Chase staring at me, feeling the decency to be somewhat remorseful. "Look, I get that this is extremely uncomfortable." He sighs and I raise an eyebrow, urging him to continue. "Liam, man, Bianca already knows about you and Vanessa." Something passes over me and my heart drops at that statement.

"What, how?" For a moment, I look at him, but deep down, I know Chase wouldn't do that.

He raps his knuckles on the counter. "Vanessa asked her to the frat party saying she wanted her to wingwoman for this guy she had hooked up with once. She's a smart girl, I know she's probably put two and two together." My body almost recoils in disgust at Vanessa's words before guilt overtakes me. No wonder Bianca had a weird look when Vanessa approached me earlier.

"Great," I grumble before leaning against the kitchen counter. "I *just* got her back, and even now . . . We're fragile." He nods thoughtfully and I can't believe I'm saying this, but he's actually a good listener. I chuckle sadly. "I feel like we're making some type of progress, and now. . ." I put my head down, my forehead connecting with the cool marble, my heart stuttering at the words that can't even come out. "Maybe this will be the thing that keeps us from moving forward." A frown stretches over my face as I look out the window and spot her laughing with Jamie. "And I wouldn't handle it well if it were."

I look back out the window and see them coming toward the villa. I give Chase a look to be done with the conversation. As I start to walk out, he stops me. "Look, knowing Bianca, she's probably the type to appreciate honesty. Just get everything out there."

I nod, pushing open the French doors, finding Vanessa on the other side. I step back, shocked, given I thought she was still on the beach. "What do you want?"

She looks up at me with glazed eyes and I pinch my nose when I notice that she's a little tipsy.

"Have you seen Tommy?" she asks.

"No."

She scoffs at that, sliding her hands into her back pockets of the shorts she's now wearing, then sighs. "Truthfully, I came looking for you." She reaches to grab my arm, but she huffs in annoyance when I pull away. Chase nods, leaving when he sees us, and I run my hands through my hair, frustrated.

"Vanessa, we've talked about this. Please *leave me alone*," I whisper sternly, hoping Bianca or Jamie doesn't see this for something it isn't. She looks up at me, her eyes glossier than before.

"Look, I know it's been a while, but I thought . . ."

I shake my head. "Vanessa, you're drunk, and like I told you already, we're *done*. We weren't anything to begin with. It was *one* freaking time *two* years ago!" I shout, but then lower my voice. "*I've moved on*. You need to as well. Tommy is nice, go for him."

She rolls her eyes and comes closer. "Oh, come on, Liam. We had fun, didn't we?" she says, a chuckle escaping her lips, and anger fills me.

"Stop." She flinches at my voice, but still tries to get close. I step back as much as I can before my back hits the counter. "You and I—*mistake*. I regret the night we slept together. I wish it *never* happened. So have some dignity for yourself because I want absolutely nothing to do with you." Her eyes widen and she looks as if she'll start to cry, but then she attempts to lean into me. The hairs on the back of my neck stand and I turn to see Bianca.

She looks startled and I push Vanessa off me. I try to move closer to Bianca, but she walks out, mumbling something along the lines of, "I'm sorry for interrupting." I let her go, and remain hopeful this is the last time I have this conversation with Vanessa.

"If you cost me the most important relationship I have, I'll make sure you're never allowed in any fraternity house, kicked out of the sorority you're in now, and I'll file a complaint against you for harassment, *do you understand me?*" She looks up at the menacing tone I've had to resort to, and for once, she hangs her head and nods. She then walks out without looking back, and I let out a sharp exhale as I go looking for Bianca.

Chase is trying to make conversation with Jamie. Moving toward them, she turns to me with a glare. "Where is she?" I ask, and she shrugs. "Jamie, come on," I beg, but she takes a long sip of her drink. I look at Chase for some help.

She scoffs. "I think she saw something that hurt her." I flinch at that. "Give her a minute."

I nod, sighing because she's right. Though, it doesn't mean I stop looking for her. My heart plummets at the thought of her thinking that I've been sleeping or flirting with someone while we almost kissed the other day.

Have I forgotten about that? Never.

I know we're not dating, solely making baby steps to being friends, I guess. Technically, it's fine if I did move on with someone in that way, but I still feel like I've betrayed her . . . us. As I rush out of one of the bedrooms, I bump into her as she's exiting the bathroom. Her dazzling eyes stare up at me, a blush painting her face.

"Bianca."

She pushes away from me. "Yeah, what's up?"

"It wasn't what it looked like," I say, getting right to the point.

She shrugs. "It's okay if it was, I assumed a while ago, besides we're not . . ." Her words trail off and my shoulders drop.

"Bianca, don't shut down because of this. What happened between her and me—one time, years ago—it's insignificant to me. Okay?" I try to catch her eyes as she ducks her face. "I hate that it happened. I thought by doing it, I'd forget about how you weren't in my life anymore." She looks up at that as if she can't believe that's why I did it. I sigh. "I'm not perfect, Bianca. Far from it." I chuckle bitterly, reaching to grab her hands, elated when she lets me. "But I'd never lie to you, and I'm not starting now. And if you don't believe me, Chase can tell you all about Vanessa's . . . persistence."

Her eyes widen at my use of the word, and I hold her gaze, willing her to believe me. She nods after a bit, and I wonder at what that could mean. "Okay," she replies.

"Okay?" I ask.

She sighs. "You're many things, Liam Parker, but a liar has never been one of them. I believe you." She gives me a small smile and I let out a laugh in disbelief. I rub her hands and she moves to take them out of my hold. "I just . . . kinda need to process everything. But we're cool. It's fine, and even though you don't wanna be with Vanessa, you can do whatever you want with someone else if you wanted. You don't have to stop on account of me."

My eyes close in pain. Why would she want to push me into someone else's arms? Before I can even grace her with a response, wanting her to know that the only person I want a relationship with—even if it's just best friendship—is her, Jamie joins us and throws an arm over Bianca's shoulders.

"I have the best idea." Bianca laughs, rolling her eyes while Jamie leans in to whisper in her ear. Chase follows, finding a spot beside Jamie.

Bianca looks at her, wild-eyed. "No, we *couldn't.*"

"Yes, we *should.* We always talked about it, I'm leaving in a couple of days, why not? Besides, *you* need a pick-me-up," Jamie says while giving me a dismissive look. I look at Bianca, hoping she at least tells me what they're going to do. They both leave and I'm not ashamed to admit I follow them out. Chase trails behind me as we head back to the beach. The thumping of music gets stronger and the knot in the pit of my stomach doesn't lessen any.

"Mama Kate!" Jamie shouts while Ms. Kate looks over. Josh does too before he rolls his eyes, and I raise an eyebrow. They walk over to her while I spot my parents having the time of their lives in the water. "Can we use your car to go to a tattoo parlor?" My ears perk at that and I walk over to them. All our expressions turn to ones of surprise, except Josh's. His is of pure disgust. Ms. Kate seems to mull it over while I still stand there in shock.

Putting his sunglasses back on, Josh says, "Nope."

Ms. Kate responds with her own, "Sure."

Bianca freezes when Josh and Ms. Kate say two different answers, and I get closer to her, hoping to see why she looks so tense. Though, she pretends not to notice me.

Ms. Kate turns to look at him in disbelief. "Honey, they're eighteen. Let them have fun." He takes his sunglasses off again before he stares her down.

"No, Kate. I'm not letting my stepdaughter ruin herself more than she already has. God. The influences you two have," he mutters, and my body recoils at the comment. Mom and Dad have made their way out of the waves, her face scrunching up in annoyance, his with an expression of subtle anger, obviously having heard what Josh said. Ms. Kate lets out a sound of disbelief before she grabs her keys and hands them to Bianca, Josh sitting up as he looks at her in shock.

"Have fun, girls." Jamie squeals happily while she drags Bianca away, but she turns to glance at her mom as Josh stares holes into the side of Ms. Kate's face. She sighs and then looks at me. "Liam." She signals with her head toward the girls, and a weird tug-of-war begins in my head. This guy. This Josh Callaway is *not* the perfect gentleman people make him out to be. But he wouldn't do anything to her, right?

They're in public. She wouldn't take that from him anyway.

I sigh and look at Chase as we start behind the girls, and I nod toward my parents. They nod back, understanding. I catch up with Bianca and Jamie, snatching the keys.

"Hey!"

Jamie turns toward me, but I hold the keys out of her reach. "I'm driving you both in *my* car."

Bianca steps forward. "You can't take my mom's keys."

I step forward too. "Bianca, I'll drive you both to a tattoo shop. A *good* one. Let me tag along." I shift my focus to Jamie, begging her with my eyes to let me do this. If being their chauffeur helps me be near Bianca, I'll take it.

"Oh, me too," Chase adds, and we all look at him. He shrugs. "Come on, you guys are way more fun." Out of all of us, Jamie's the only one who scoffs. I look at him knowingly.

Oh, this is gonna be interesting.

Jamie sighs, relenting, and Bianca nods nervously. I let them inside my car, going back into the villa and hanging Ms. Kate's keys on the hook where she can find them later. Jogging back outside, Bianca's in the front seat and Jamie and Chase are in the back. Through the rearview mirror, I watch him look at Jamie, and I realize it's the first time I've seen him really *look* at a girl. He's not ogling like he usually does, but admiring. I know because I do it to Bianca every time I see her.

My Freckles has yet to say a word.

I turn on the car and start toward the parlor. All I hear are the tires running along the road and the low conversation between Jamie and Chase. I sigh, merging into the left lane as we come to a stoplight. I open my mouth, then close it as the light turns green.

I remember when Bianca and I would get into disagreements; after such a short amount of time, we both demanded to talk. It was refreshing that we both valued communication, but now, she retreats. She goes back into her little hidey-hole while I work on coaxing her back out. I'm a patient guy, and I don't mind, but I refuse to believe that something so insignificant will ruin the little bit of progress we've made.

CHAPTER TWENTY-SIX

Liam

THANKFULLY, THE PARLOR ISN'T THAT far, and as we walk in, I'm met with familiar faces.

"Is that little Liam Parker?" A small smile starts on my face before I wave shyly. The tattoo parlor I work in near Mella Colta is owned by two brothers, one of whom lives and works here in LA. Randall smiles, given I saw him a bit ago for my most recent tattoo. "Back already?" He slaps my shoulder affectionately and I chuckle softly.

"You know me." He rolls his eyes and I extend my hand. "This is Jamie, Chase . . ." I stop for a bit as she looks at me. "And Bianca. They're wanting tattoos . . ." He gives me a look before nodding and then points with his head to Tyler, the owner.

He comes over to me, laughing, before he locks eyes with Jamie. "Alright. I got—" He glances down at her, a wolfish smile starting on his face. "—Jamie, was it, sweet pea?" She nods somewhat absentmindedly and something passes over Chase's face.

A woman that I don't recognize comes over, grabbing his arm. "I got—" Chase slips his arm out of her grasp and she glances at him, shocked.

"I'm not getting a tattoo." He goes to stand next to Jamie. "I'll join you guys, if that's okay?" He looks toward me and a smug smile starts on my face before he rolls his eyes. Bianca stands there, rubbing her arm nervously. She looks at me, something I can't read bubbling in her eyes.

"Liam?" Randall gives her a once-over, then looks back at me. He points. "Grab a machine." Bianca's eyes widen, as do mine, and I'm quick to shake my head. "Look, kid, my brother told me that more than half of that ink on you is your doing. I know you got all your licenses in order since you're working up in San Jose." I glance at Bianca, trying to gauge how she feels about it. "Trust me, he's probably better than all of us combined."

I hold my breath until she mutters a small, "Okay." Though, for a moment, I wonder if she really does trust me or if that's gone away too. We walk into Randall's tattoo room and I close the door behind me. I admire how she spins, looking at all the designs and photos he's got posted up everywhere, before I hear a little laugh come from her. My head snaps up and she's rubbing her hand across something.

liam parker waz here.

I prep the station for what is to come. "I did that when I was eighteen." She turns around, a small bloom of hope starting in my chest. She's looking at me as if she wants me to elaborate. "I was dumb, and wanted to leave my mark here. After I got my first tattoo, I realize I wanted more afterwards." The corner of her mouth quirks up and she shivers slightly, so I move to turn up the thermostat a bit.

"Which tattoo was it?"

I face her again and smile, gesturing at myself. "Can't you tell?" She shakes her head with another quirk of a smile. Progress, I think. I get closer to her and hold out my hand, pointing at the small yet most precious piece of art I have on my body. "This was for a dare back in senior year . . ." She seems interested, so I keep going. "The dare was to get a tattoo that means the absolute world to me." Senior prom. The worst night of my life. My tux was too tight because I had hit a growth spurt, some girl kept bothering me, and the guys on the team were on my case the whole night. Thankfully, I got the best dare, and I'm not stuck with some weird design the other guys got.

She eyes the tulips, then reaches out, softly tracing the design, and I command my body not to react to her touch.

Stay freaking calm.

She smiles. "You know, tulips are my—"

"Favorite flowers," I finish for her.

I grab a pair of nitrile gloves as she stands by the tattoo chair. "Why haven't you called me Freckles again?" she asks shyly. I turn around slowly, almost unsure I heard her right. I give her a confused look and she clears her throat. "The other night at the shelter." A blush comes on at the mention of that night. "You called me that, and then when I had my bad dream, but you haven't since then."

I grab the portable table, hoping it shows I'm not nervous. "I didn't know you wanted me to." She raises an eyebrow and I switch on the machine. "Sit down, *Freckles.*"

The cutest reddish hue starts on her cheeks under those adorable freckles that I've been practically staring at all day. She sits and looks at me, worried. "Wait, I haven't even told you what I want."

I chuckle as she really doesn't know how much I pay attention to her.

My thumb rubs over the back of her hand, the black color from the glove contrasting with her slightly tan skin. "Ursa Major constellation on the back of your shoulder, right?" Her eyes widen almost comically. A smile starts on my face and I bite down on the corner of my lip. "I heard you with Mom that one day you came over." Her jaw drops and she shakes her head, almost confused. My heart stutters as to why she would ever be surprised that I remember everything about her. I run a finger over the healed scar from when the fence scratched her, sighing at the conflict running around in my mind, taking a deep breath.

I quickly fix up the stencil, already knowing how I want the design to look, and before I can even show her, she grips my hand and gives me a shy smile. "I trust you." Three words that I've been waiting to hear again ever since we reconnected. Well, besides those *other* ones, ones that I would say to her every moment of my life if I could.

"Relax for me, okay?" I gulp at seeing the bare skin of her back, and for a bit, I freak out. Taking a deep breath, I place my hand, curving around, trying to be respectful. Once the stencil goes over her skin, I push through, the idea coming to life. I grab the tattoo machine as she stays as still as possible. "Ready?" I ask, and she nods in confirmation. Touching the needle to her skin while holding a breath, she stays as still as can be. I move my thumb in comforting circles along her shoulder. She relaxes, causing me to smile as I focus on the outline. There's nothing but the buzzing, but I find the silence rather comforting. It isn't awkward, but therapeutic. I smile as I trace another line, remembering when I sketched this exact same design for it to be tattooed on . . .

She tenses slightly and I remove the needles from her skin, the reddening much more apparent. I take a breath. "You alright?" My voice comes out much hoarser than I intended, she doesn't answer, but nods regardless. I place the machine back in its holder. "We can st—"

She shakes her head. "No." I let out a chuckle at her stubbornness. "I'm good."

I nod and return to her back. I keep going with the design, and she doesn't move a muscle after that. I finish the last bit of shading about an hour later and then switch off the machine. She sits up slightly. I spread ointment across the fresh ink, marveling at it.

"Can I see it?" she asks, and I point over to the mirrors Randall has in the room. She stands and walks toward them; I wait anxiously for her thoughts about it. She looks at me and gives this small smile. "It's beautiful," she whispers. Afterward, I apply an adhesive tattoo bandage, biting my lip a little.

"Can I show you something?" Nerves course through me and I run my hands through my hair, tugging at the strands. She stands with a focused expression, moving closer to me, but leaves enough space between us. "Remember when you asked how many tattoos I had?" She nods, one of her well-defined eyebrows arched. "Remember how I said I would show them to you one day?" I study her face to see if that's still something she wants. I look toward the door, hoping Chase or Jamie—or anyone else—doesn't burst in here. She nods once more, and I inhale deeply before reaching behind me with one hand, pulling off my shirt.

She gasps when the shirt falls and she drinks me all in. I'm buzzed off the way she's looking at me. She inches toward me, almost as if asking for permission, and I give it to her. She scrutinizes me as my breathing crescendos, but I make sure to keep my eyes on her. Her eyes flit between the drawings on my skin as if she doesn't know where to look first. She settles for a quote on my bicep and I shiver involuntarily. My skin ripples under her touch as she looks for something to further analyze before settling on the tattoo between my pecs. Her mouth drops open, a breathless sound escaping her. Her eyes widen slightly before she looks up at me. My eyes hood at the expression swimming in hers.

"Is that . . ."

I nod as she trails off. She traces the same Ursa Major constellation she now carries. I got mine a couple of days after I heard her say what her next tattoo would be. I added to mine a small cursive "B" interwoven in the stars and lines—something I didn't put in hers.

"This looks fresher than the others," she notes, and I let out a nervous chuckle, wanting to wrap my arms around her, but don't want to risk putting pressure on her new tattoo. She places her head on my chest, and I lay my head on top of hers, melting in the small action of affection.

"Freckles?" She looks up and I give her an honest smile. "It doesn't matter what girl wants my attention. I *only* look at you. You're the only one who will always have it." *Have me.* I hope she finally understands that it doesn't matter if Olivia or Vanessa or some other girl wants to flirt with me. My heart belongs to her, it always has, even when she broke it all those years ago. Her eyes fill with an emotion I can't read, and she hugs me tightly, my arms tightening around her. We stay like that and she probably can hear my heartbeat pulse rapidly under her ear. She pulls back, her face a breath away from mine.

"Liam?" She sighs while I hum in question. "We have so much to talk about." My shoulders sink with the truthful statement.

"I know," I add before she slowly blinks.

"I'm so confused . . ." She starts to push away, but I don't let her. "I don't even know what we are to each other anymore."

I sigh. "I know it's hard to trust me after what happened. I hate that we were dumb teenagers and didn't fight for our friendship before, but I wanna at least try. We're friends now—best friends before—maybe we can try to get there again, if . . ." I trail off, not wanting to voice even the thought that she thinks differently. Hesitation blooms on her face and stays there as she contemplates my offer. Her eyes refuse to meet mine. Little cracks make their way down my heart the longer I wait, but I don't dare rush her.

"Promise I won't ever lose you again," she almost begs for reassurance, and my heart tugs.

The way I felt for those five years—hell, the day I found out she had shut me out—courses through my mind. I remember all the times when all I wanted was those alluring eyes to connect with mine.

It comes with no hesitation. "I promise."

She sighs, relieved, and stands on her tiptoes while I slouch so she doesn't have to reach so much. Placing her forehead on mine, she whispers, "I promise you'll never lose me either."

Her words settle deep in my bones, soothing the slight cracks in my soul. I close my eyes in bliss as a trace of salt and summer overwhelms my senses, content with what we promised. I push down my true feelings where they won't bubble up right now. They stay locked up in my imagination, a place where I can fantasize about her being mine, and only mine. *Dreaming of the day when I can finally be honest with my best friend about how I'm in love with her.*

CHAPTER TWENTY-SEVEN

Bianca

WHY IS IT THAT WHEN I promise not to cry, it's the first thing I do? I hug myself as Jamie rolls her suitcase to a stop in front of us, turning around to look at me. I place a bag at her feet; I filled it with every single thing I bought for her this past week because I have no idea if that care package is still at her house. Even though it feels like she just got here, it was time for Jamie to go back to Philly. She waits with an expectant look on her face and I hug her with a small smile.

"I'm gonna miss you so much, J." She squeezes me in return, then pulls back, muttering the same thing. Josh rolls his eyes and goes to take a phone call as Mom looks at him, shaking her head. Ever since the other day at the beach, their relationship has been getting tense. He's barely home and Mom has started to roll her eyes around him more.

"Have a good flight, and take care of yourself, Jamie girl," Mom adds as they hug, and my eyes water that much more. Mom excuses herself, heading in the direction Josh stalked off in. Jamie's phone dings and she looks down at it in confusion.

A small smile starts on her face. "Isabelle again?" I ask, since they've been texting regularly. She turns off the screen quickly, nodding, but I swear I see the name *Chase* before the screen goes black.

"Mhm, yeah." I raise an eyebrow as the clear bandage over her butterfly tattoo peeks through the sleeve of her hoodie. I thought it was the cutest thing she could've picked, and that night was honestly the highlight of her trip here.

Mine too.

"So, have you talked to Liam again?" she asks, and I look at her in exasperation.

"You're about to leave for who knows how long—to a place almost three thousand miles from here—and that's what you ask me?" I say, crossing my arms while she barks out a laugh.

"You know me. I need to hear that my bestie is getting her guy. Besides, you're my *only* source for guy info." I roll my eyes at her, knowing that's not true, and she bumps her shoulder with mine. "B, I hung around that man, and even though he's a guy, and they do stupid stuff, I know he really, really likes you." She stares at me. "And you really, *really* like him." She raises an eyebrow, daring me to say otherwise.

"Chase seems to be on that track too. I saw those looks he was giving you," I counter, and I swear a blush starts on her cheeks. We trade smiles, but hers fades when her phone buzzes, the notification being that she needs to get going as they'll be boarding and she still needs to get through security.

I pull her into a tight hug. Reluctantly, she releases me, and I wave as she walks off. She rolls her suitcase behind her, wiping at her eyes.

I stay here, though.

I stay here until I see her walk through security. Mom hugs me from behind and I grab her hands for comfort. Tears prickle at the corner of my eyes, and I have no idea how long I stand there, but Josh comes back, sighing.

"Can we go now?" he asks, almost sounding like a petulant child, and I turn back to see Mom glaring at him.

Mom *glaring* at Josh?

As we walk to the car, she lets out a tired huff. Her eyes slide to mine, pleading, before I blow a kiss to the last place Jamie had been. We get in, and Josh's car hums as it comes to life. My air vent blasts cold air as Josh turns the volume for the radio down. My phone buzzes and my eyebrow raises, as it might be Jamie, but instead, it's a confirmation that I'll be volunteering at the shelter in a few days. I smile at that, ready to go hang out with those little guys. Mom's hushed voice comes as she looks at Josh while he merges onto the freeway, heading back home. Their voices start to become less hushed, and I look up to see Mom waving her hands around.

"I said *no*. Besides, we have to go to the Parkers' event." Mom sighs and nods. My heart starts to flutter at that, my emotions bouncing from sadness for Jamie and excitement for Liam. My middle ground being I get to see the one person I have to cheer me up in a couple of hours.

As I wrap my curling iron once more, I hold it for a bit and release it. The flawless piece of hair falls right into place, and I turn off the wand and start to fluff my hair a bit, hoping the hairstyle hides the clear bandage on my shoulder from my healing tattoo. I then slide my hands down my dress, smoothing out the invisible wrinkles.

Two hours later, I'm proud of myself for finishing with half an hour to spare. My makeup makes me look some years older, plus the hair makes my face more seductive. As a tribute to Jamie, I wear her gift with pride: the long, classy, deep-emerald dress with glittering crystals. They catch the light ever so slightly, complementing my skin tone nicely.

Tonight, I'm going to a fancy ball for William's promotion where I'll see *him*: Liam Parker, the guy who causes almost all my emotions.

The other night at the tattoo parlor . . . I don't even know how to describe it. It's like our hearts want to be the way they always were, but our minds . . .

We have so much to talk about.

I sigh. As much as I wish I could forget about the past, I can't. That girl who cried almost every night for her best friend deserves answers. Besides, what's to say he won't be cold again? Shaking my head to rid myself of the damaging thoughts, a door shuts, and I look at mine in confusion. Curiously, I close it behind me as I hear voices. Walking down the hall, the voices cease.

Did they leave me here? Did Mom?

I walk a bit faster and see Mom standing there before she places her eyes on me. She smiles and I give her a shy one back. I notice Olivia and Josh aren't with her, and looking through the window, his car is nowhere in sight. "Josh left early to get something, so he'll meet us there," she says, reaching for her keys. Without a reply from me, we walk out of the house and get into the car. Since this morning at the airport, Mom and I have been walking on eggshells around each other. Her face wears a solemn expression that she drops when I come around. "Bianca?"

"Yes, Mom?" I mumble, and we slow to a stop as she twirls her engagement ring, almost worriedly.

"Have you noticed Josh acting . . . more stressed than usual?" Her fingers drum on the wheel and I roll my lips, figuring out how to answer.

"He's been acting different from before," I say, and she sighs before pulling into the valet line.

"Okay, so it isn't just me. I mean, you're my daughter, and I'm in no way using you as a therapist or anything, but ever since we've been hanging out with the Parkers . . ." I nod, knowing how his mood, while sometimes not the best, tends to worsen around Ana and William, let alone Liam. "I mean, I don't think I've done anything."

I cut her off at that. "Mom no. It's not your fault, he's been a bit of a jerk for a bit now. I didn't wanna say anything, but he's gotten worse."

The moment I say that, the valet knocks on our window. Startled, we both leave the car. Josh stands at the entrance with Olivia. He's looking down at his watch, impatient, and when we get close, he asks, "You had to be this late?"

Mom recoils, not expecting that. "I'm sorry." He shakes his head before grabbing her hand. She follows behind while Olivia catches up, wrapping an arm around her dad's, and I scoff, walking past them.

Without any sense of direction, I stalk off to where I see everyone going. People are looking at me, causing me to look down at myself, hoping I'm not over or underdressed. As I'm trying to look for someone I know in this gigantic place, I hear my name. Ana comes over, crashing into me, sucking me into a huge bear hug, and I happily receive it, especially with all that's been happening.

"Oh my gosh, cupcake! You look *bella*," she says as she spins me around, puts her hands to her lips, and smacks them together.

I giggle. "You look amazing, Ana." I eye her satin maroon dress, which sparkles under the ambient lighting.

"Kate!" she shouts, and walks over to Mom, giving her a big hug while going in for the polite handshake with Josh and Olivia. A corner of my mouth quirks up at the sight before someone's arm snakes around my shoulders.

"Hey, pumpkin."

"Hey, Will."

"Will, Bianca, over here, *mis amores*," Ana says, waving us over. We stand there as Josh looks at us, and I wish I could wipe his and his daughter's dumb smiles right off their faces.

"Kate, how are you?" William asks, letting me go to gather her in a small side hug. Then, he looks over at Josh and sticks out a hand with a semi-friendly smile. "Josh," he simply says as Josh reaches for his hand and shakes it, distaste swimming in his eyes. I mean, at least William is trying to be nice.

William then looks over at Olivia to smile and she returns the gesture. He then pulls back and wraps his arm around my shoulders and squeezes, almost as if he knows.

"Alright, everyone. I'm so happy to see all of you here and I'm glad that you could make it," an older man on the stage says, and we all clap as he clears his throat. Everyone goes to their seats. I grin when I see that we're all sitting together. I frown when I see Liam's placard next to mine, but he's nowhere to be found. Sitting, I look around to see if I spot him, but to no avail. Someone starts talking into the mic, though I'm not even paying attention.

Ana leans toward me. "I think he's running late." I freeze like a deer in headlights and can only nod while she smirks.

There's some microphone feedback and he apologizes before continuing. "As you know, I started this company over forty-seven years ago, and it's now my turn to retire. Five short years ago, I was gifted with the most dedicated employee I have ever seen, and it is my great honor to bestow the title of CEO on William Parker!" Applause roars to life from every corner of the room. Josh whispers something to Olivia and she puts her hands down. I roll my eyes, glancing back to see William climb up on stage.

He hugs the guy, and everyone laughs as the older man stands there awkwardly. He then pats him on the back and gives William the microphone. "Hi, everyone. Wow—I'm speechless, and if you know me, that usually *never* happens," he says, and we start laughing at that. "I want to thank Mr. Palacios for this amazing opportunity. I promise I won't let you down. Let's enjoy the rest of tonight, shall we?" He walks off the stage as a nice, slow song comes on. Couples get up to dance, leaving me by myself as they all walk to the dance floor. Olivia's nowhere to be found.

I fidget with my thumbs as I think about where Liam might be, my mind being the dumb traitor it is by saying he might not even come.

CHAPTER TWENTY-EIGHT

Liam

"THAT'S WHAT I MEAN! I mean, she must've felt *something*!" Chase yells through the speaker, and I wince at that, setting the phone on the counter as I start to fix my hair. "Hello?" he asks, and I roll my eyes.

"I'm still here."

"Well? Has Bianca said anything?" I smirk as he refers to her by her first name, no nickname. I mean, they *had* found us in a bit of a compromising position the other night at the tattoo parlor.

In his head—she's mine. Just like I like it. I scrunch the strands of hair as I add in some conditioner to make my hair fluffy, how she said she liked it.

"No. And even if she did, I wouldn't tell you. Stop being a wimp and text Jamie."

He scoffs. "I did. Twice." He sighs in frustration. Poor guy's never had to pursue , and now getting to know Jamie a bit . . .

Yeah, I wish him luck.

"Dude, a couple of weeks ago, I was chilling. Hanging with girls, living the life. And then I see Jamie . . ." He doesn't elaborate, and I know exactly what he means. That's how I've felt about Bianca since I was eight years old.

"I feel you, man," I mutter, pulling at my suit, feeling a bit self-conscious. I close my eyes, hoping I don't regret this as I tap the option to video call him. He picks up, giving me a confused look. "How do I look?" I back up, showing him my all-black outfit with a deep emerald tie. He whistles.

"You look fly, dude. What's with the green tie, though?"

My face flushes in embarrassment. "I may or may not have found out what color her dress is."

Chase bursts out laughing at the admission. "Never thought I'd see the day. I mean, the Campus Grouch *this* whipped?"

"So, I look good, then?" I ask, receiving a nod.

"Someone's getting some today."

I cringe at that. "Oh, come on. Is that all you think about?" Honestly, I'm nervous. I mean, obviously I am if I'm asking for Chase's opinion.

"It'll be fine, man. You got this," he says, and I nod as I sit, rubbing my hands on my dress pants subconsciously. "Hey, quick question." I glance at the camera. "What time does the thing start?"

My eyes dart to the clock and grimace before hanging up without a goodbye. I quickly shrug on my tux jacket before grabbing my keys and sprinting to the door. She's going to think I didn't want to come, or worse, that I wanted to avoid her. I was so nervous that I didn't even notice the time. I speed along the road, my eyes looking at the GPS and the road simultaneously.

I'm coming, Freckles.

I toss the keys to the valet, muttering a "thank you" when I finally make it there. Thanking everything above, I didn't get stopped, even though I may or may not have broken a few traffic rules. I start walking quickly, looking for the only girl who makes me want to smile.

I struggle with the entrance to the ball. After a bit, the company banner outside a set of doors comes into view and I walk in to find a bunch of people dancing. Thankfully, there's a huge board with a diagram of the name plaques, and I find mine.

While we've been texting and calling, I didn't push too much, wanting her to spend as much time with Jamie as possible. Tonight is the first night I actually get her all to myself in this new stage of giving our friendship another shot, hopefully one day working up to the trust we had before. Scanning the room, I notice someone with their head down. Focusing my eyes on the person, they widen when she lifts her face to stare out into the crowd.

There she is.

An emerald dress, *thankfully*, that looks so gorgeous on her. Her hair is falling over her back in cascading waves, and I want to twirl one of the strands around my finger. She seems not to notice me as she's looking toward the dancing couples. I take a deep breath, readjust my jacket, and slide into my chair.

Her head snaps to me and I can't stop the way my mouth turns up when I say, "Hey."

She looks at me, shocked to see me here, and I don't miss the opportunity to really look at her. Her adorable freckles are on display, making me want to kiss every single one of them.

"Hey," she whispers back, and my mouth widens into a full-on grin. She looks at me and my whole body erupts in butterflies. My heart beats quickly as she does a once-over, zeroing in on my tie.

"What?" I ask coyly, and she rolls her eyes, but there's a hint of a smile as she shakes her head and blushes. I glance at the dance floor when Mom spots me. She waves, as does Dad, and I send them a curt nod.

Blowing out a breath, I ask, "Freckles?" When her blue eyes meet mine, my train of thought derails, and I'm left a stumbling idiot. "Would you, uh—maybe—well," I stutter, and she giggles at me. Goodness, if I thought I would get my thoughts back together, that sound right there throws me off again. "What I meant to ask is if you wanted to dance with me?" I hold out my hand and she looks at me, confused.

Am I a good dancer? More or less.

Will I do anything to hang out with her? Absolutely.

She nods and slides her dainty hand in mine, and I smile as I stand us up. We walk to the dance floor and I exhale sharply. We stand there for a bit, nervous, for my part at least. She looks as lost as I am and I gently guide her hands to wrap around my neck. I pull her flush against me, my arms curving around her waist.

Butterflies erupt in my stomach as I keep Bianca close. Her eyes hold mine in a way that makes my heart race. As we sway together, she melts into my arms, and I find myself losing track of everything else. Pressed against each other, every inch of contact sends warmth surging through me. My entire being responds to her presence.

The world around us fades, leaving only her captivating eyes that seem to hold infinite galaxies within them. When her hand moves, she unknowingly releases a thousand more butterflies into the already dizzying mix. When she rests her face against my chest, I hold her tighter, never wanting this moment to end. Her cheek against my heart feels right, and I can't help but notice how rapidly it beats beneath her touch.

"Why's your heart racing?" she asks, and I can't hide the blush that creeps up my cheeks.

"I could ask you the same thing," I counter, realizing mine is keeping pace with hers. Her blush matches mine and I lift her head, gently brushing my thumb against her cheekbone. "You look stunning tonight."

"You're not too bad yourself," she replies, a smile lighting up her face.

"Really? The tattoos don't ruin the look?"

She raises an eyebrow. "Of course not. You do realize I have tattoos too, right?"

I smirk. "Tattoos? So, you have another one besides the one I did on you a bit ago?" I coyly ask as if I don't already know. I trace her side, feeling her shiver under my touch. "Will you show them to me someday?" My voice betrays the emotions stirring within me. I can't help but smile as I tuck a loose strand of her hair behind her ear. Not knowing what else to do, she nods. I smile as my hand goes back to her waist, rubbing my thumbs along her sides, and she gulps.

"I actually think you look more handsome with your tattoos." Honesty drips from her words, and there's an instant rush of dopamine.

"You think I'm handsome?" I tease, reveling in her embarrassed giggle. "You're the most beautiful girl in the world to me," I admit, watching her eyes sparkle slightly. The song ends and I look at her, disappointment on my face. "Wanna take a walk with me?" I grip her hand, running a thumb over every one of her knuckles. She looks at me, biting her lip in thought, then glances back at the table. Everyone seems to be busy in conversation except for Lydia or Olivia or whatever her name is, who is staring directly at us.

"Okay."

I pull her toward me, finding the exit. Holding the door open, a little gazebo catches my eye. Sliding my fingers in with hers, I lead her to it. As we leave the concrete, she stops because her heels seem to dig in the grass. Without a second thought, I bend down and pick her up, and she squeaks, shocked.

"Is this okay?" Her minty breath, along with her sweet perfume, invades my senses. She nods and I walk us the rest of the way, setting her down when we get there. She looks up and begins to trace the stars with her pointer finger, and like all those years ago, I watch her. She smiles, and I hate that what I might say may ruin that, but I know it's time to get it off my chest, and put this to rest . . . for good.

"Look, Freckles," I say, angling my body toward her. "I wanna talk about something that's been on my mind for a while." She sucks in a breath, and even though I hate how uncomfortable this is, we'll never move past this unless we talk about it. "You were right." Plain and simple. She looks at me suspiciously. "We don't know a lot about each other anymore." I sigh. "I knew twelve-year-old Bianca like the back of my hand, but these days, I'm still learning the new Bianca." She looks up and I continue. "I've been learning about how much you love animals and that's why you volunteer at the shelter. You really wanna become the best vet for them. Learning how even now you still love looking up at the stars and tracing the constellations with your finger." She laughs at that, and I look at her, smiling. "Realizing that something happened in Philly, and it's why you used to wear a lot of makeup at first. I could go on forever, Bianca. I know we have so much to discover about each other, and I know it was dumb of me to think we could push away those years apart. To think we could get over five whole years of no contact when we were attached at the hip." Then, with a little bit of courage, I fully open the can of worms.

"That game, five years ago, was probably one of the hardest I had. I was still new, and Coach called me in since Andrew was injured. I was out of my mind nervous, I mean, it was all on me. The guys invited me out after the win, and I promised to be there for a bit, but then one thing led to another." I sigh. "I'm sorry, I lost track of time, I wasn't planning on standing you up." She shakes her head, but I hold her hands as I look into her forgiving eyes. "I blew it, I know, and I'm so sorry you were waiting for hours for my call. But then, you said I was leaving you behind . . . That I was replacing you with football when it was the only thing keeping me afloat after you left. I was like a robot for most of the day, yet our phone calls brought me right back. You lit up my life, and when you left, you took that light with you."

She covers her mouth, a slight sob echoing, and I hate the sad look in her eyes.

"Then, we fought, and when I tried to talk to you, the phone call didn't go through, and that's when I knew . . ." I trail off, inhaling shakily. "Some friend I was."

She puts her hand over mine. "Stop." I look up once again. "You're not the only one at fault. I blocked you out of hurt because you didn't talk to me for a couple days after. But when I undid it, I never got anything, so I thought you were done with me." I shake my head, appalled that she thought I would ever be done with her.

"I know that now, but I was hurt, Liam. You didn't talk to me about anything you were feeling. I would always ask how you felt when I moved away, and you would always say you were so happy for me. I guess, I felt you didn't miss me as much as I missed you each and every day."

She sighs, turning to face me fully . "Then, on my birthday, I thought you'd forgotten about me, and I lashed out. I know what football meant for you at the time now, and I'm sorry . . . I'm sorry I blocked you and you thought it was me cutting you off. I'm so sorry." Her voice cracks and my heart splinters at that. Shaking my head, I wipe a tear from her cheek. I wrap her in my arms, hugging her even though we're both hurting, and she tries to push me away. "Get off, Liam," she begs, but I stay hugging her. She calms down and hugs me, fully embracing me. Her sobs echo in my head and I rub my hand up and down her back. I whisper that it isn't her fault over and over. We were dumb kids afraid of getting our hearts broken. She sniffles, and I hope this hug conveys everything I feel for this girl.

My Bianca. My darling Freckles.

She pulls back and we look at each other, our hearts bleeding.

"Liam, I promise you with everything I've got, I *really* didn't mean to make you feel left behind. I'm sorry I didn't hear you out like I should've. For what it's worth, I'm sorry for back then, and I'm sorry for right now."

I nod. "I'm sorry I inadvertently made you feel that way too. It was never *ever* my intention. And I'm sorry for acting like a jerk when we saw each other again. I was upset. I thought if I kept you at arm's length, you wouldn't hurt me again. Turns out, we were hurting each other," I say, and she nods solemnly.

She leans against my shoulder. "Some friends we are, huh?"

I chuckle lightly, threading my fingers with hers like I used to always do. "On the road to being the best again." She smiles, and I look down as she glances up at me. "You're amazing, you know that?" Her smile widens. Her eyes are a bit red, her makeup still intact, and even if it weren't, she would still be the most beautiful girl in the world to me.

"I guess I am, huh?" she retorts, and we both laugh at each other, and at this moment, the fact is confirmed.

I have always been, and will always be, head over heels, irrevocably in love with Bianca Everly Harrison.

CHAPTER TWEMTY-NINE

Bianca

WE START TO WALK INSIDE and I'm smiling. *Truly* smiling. It's like I feel free, *free* of the pain I've been carrying for five years. Though as I'm walking, a familiar voice stops me.

"Well, well, well. If it isn't the *lovebirds.*"

I turn around to see Olivia leaning against the wall, a thin vape pen in her hand, and I scoff.

"Goodbye, Olivia," I say, but as I start to leave, she grabs my hand, pulling me away from Liam. I try to pull back, but she doesn't let up.

"Hands off," he says, and she glances at him, then throws my hand back at me.

"Why do you care so much?" she spews. "She's gonna be my stepsister, so I think I can do what I please. Besides, we don't want Daddy to find out about this, do we?" My eyes widen as I realize how deep Olivia's contempt for me really runs. Though, before I can even come up with a response, Liam beats me to it.

"I don't care. You can tell him whatever your little heart desires, and that won't change a damn thing. I'm actually sad that Bianca and

Ms. Kate have such shallow, spoiled people in their lives. But that's none of my business." He gets closer to her. "No matter what your dad says or does, I'll never let Bianca go. She's everything I want, and since the first multiple times weren't enough: *Leave. Me. Alone.*" He emphasizes every word, and my whole body flushes with a pinkish hue as he gently pulls me toward the venue. "You okay?"

We walk through the doors and I nod and squeeze his hand. He squeezes back as we weave through tables, finding ours. I quickly let go of his hand and take my seat, only to see him frowning at me.

"Liam, where have you been?" Ana asks.

"Outside, but I'm sorry for getting here late," he says.

"No problem, son. No problem at all," William mumbles, and zeros his gaze in on me while smiling, causing me to look down, trying to avoid his eyes altogether.

"Ms. Kate, how are you?" Liam asks, and Mom makes small talk. Josh clenches his jaw. "Mr. Callaway, is it?" Liam asks even though he fully knows Josh's name. "Nice seeing you again." Liam looks solely at Mom, and I cover my mouth as I smile. After the pleasantries, waiters come around with the food, and we get ready to say grace. I interlink hands with Liam, and he smirks at me while I roll my eyes. His thumbs rub on the top of my hands as William does the prayer. His rings create goose bumps, shooting sparks up my arms. We dig in, and Olivia finally joins us, sitting next to Josh. She says nothing, but she has a face as red as a tomato. I look over at Liam and he smiles, winking at me. Olivia looks up at me, and the usual annoyance or displeasure is replaced with pure and utter hatred. She leans over to Josh, and then he looks at me, anger covering his features.

"So, where did you two sneak off to?" Josh asks, cutting a piece of his rib eye, and I roll my eyes.

"We didn't *sneak* off, we were talking outside for a bit," I voice.

He clears his throat. "Uh-huh, well, I looked out the window down that way and didn't see either one of you. *Try again.*" Liam clenches his fist in his lap, and I put my hand on his to calm him down.

Before I can answer, Liam asks, "Why does that bother you, *Mr. Callaway*?" I shake my head at him.

"It just does."

"Why's that, Josh?" William's looking at him intently. Everyone stops eating and Ana tries to get William's attention, but he doesn't look at her. "Why is it bad that Liam was hanging out with Bianca? Do you have a problem with my son?" Ana scolds him, but he doesn't back down.

"I mean, have you seen *your* son? I don't want him corrupting my stepdaughter." A smug smirk comes on his face as he stretches his neck, almost as if he's asserting his dominance.

Ana shakes her head. "William, *amor*, don't."

"Josh, how about this? You can leave if you have such a problem with him," he says, then glances at Mom and me. "You both can stay if you want."

Josh seethes at that. "The hell they will."

"Josh!" Mom scolds, and he stands and throws his napkin down. Olivia stands too.

"Would say it was a pleasure, but it wasn't, and it hasn't been," he says angrily, and William waves him off, making me choke on my lemonade. "Kate. Bianca. Time to go." He starts to walk, but Mom doesn't move. He looks back, and after a bit, she relents before giving us an apologetic expression.

I don't move, though.

Josh glances at me in shock. "Bianca? What are you doing?"

"I'm staying here. You guys can go," I say before he storms out, Mom in hand. I look down.

"Well, *that* was something," Ana says after a couple silent minutes.

I put my face in my hands. "Ana, William, I am *so* sorry. I have no idea what got into him." But they both wave it off. "And Liam, I'm sorry for what he said to you."

He shakes his head at that. "It's okay, Freckles."

I nod, my face heating up against my will. "Speaking of the argument, so where did you both run off to?" Ana asks and I blush.

"I *knew* it!" I glance at her in confusion, but she looks at us happily. "You're dating."

"No, no, no. Ana, you've got it all backward," I rush to say, refusing to look at Liam. "Nothing like that. Liam and I—we're just best friends, right?" I glance in his direction, and something akin to sadness comes over him as his shoulders sag, his confident posture seemingly dropping, and I can only look at him in confusion.

"Right, what she said. *Best friends*," he repeats, and I look back at the group, nodding. Ana and William still look at me like they don't believe us. To be honest, I don't think I do either, but it has to be this way.

"If you guys say so," Ana says as she glances between us, and everyone starts to eat once again. William and Ana start a side conversation, but then someone comes over to steal them both away, leaving Liam and me. He's tapping his fork on his plate, lost in thought. I push against him playfully and he looks at me, smiling weakly. I look into his forest-green eyes, trying to read him, but they display nothing. I mean, all I said was the truth: We *are* best friends, even if my not-so-friendly feelings are currently bubbling up to the surface.

"William!" I yell as he drags Ana and me to the front of the line to dance the Macarena. To say the least, I have two left feet when it comes to dancing, but even I know that what William is doing is something worse. He seems to be getting tripped up every so often, and then I glance over at Ana. She's got it down to a T, and I burst out in laughter at them. Her dancing genes definitely did not come to play. Thankfully, the whole Josh fiasco has been forgotten and everything is the way it should be.

Another familiar shriek later, and now Ana has dragged some other ladies over to dance with her, showing them the moves as rows and rows of people are almost in sync. I glance around, spot Liam leaning against the bar, and I raise an eyebrow at him. He smiles at me. Slipping away from the dance party, I walk toward him as he looks me up and down, causing a strong blush to come onto my cheeks.

I cross my arms. "And what are you doing here?"

"Oh, you know. Throwing back shots. Getting drunk. The usual." His words drip with sarcasm and I roll my eyes as the bartender listens to our exchange.

"He's not twenty-one, so don't serve him. Or me, for that matter," I say, rather embarrassed as I drag Liam from the bar, a groan coming from him.

"Oh no, you're *not* taking me to do the Macarena," he says, stopping us, and I pull at him, but he stands his ground.

I give him my puppy-dog eyes. "Come on, please?" He sighs in exasperation, offering me his arm to drag him once again. Ana squeals when she sees us and I smile at her.

"Okay, dance lesson! Put your hands out, then flip." I follow her instructions meticulously, and after a few failed attempts, I get it, while Mr. Perfect gets it instantly and he guffaws at me.

"Stop laughing at me!"

"It's funny!" he retorts. "I wish you could see yourself."

"Alright, everyone! Loved the coordination. Well, some of you," the DJ says. Everyone laughs while Liam and I lock eyes and immediately point to one another. "Unfortunately, this ball's coming to an end. So, thank you all for coming!" Applause breaks out, and some attendees head to their tables to get their things while others start to leave.

"William, Ana, thank you so much for inviting me. Again, I'm so sorry for . . ." I can't even finish the sentence without the shame eating me up inside.

"Of course, cupcake," Ana says.

"I'm glad you came, pumpkin," William says, opening his arms, and I smile at that. I hug him, the sense of comfort William always transfers to me warming me inside and out. We pull back, and I see Liam coming out of the venue, eyes finding mine as always.

"Bud, I'll see you at home, okay?" Ana murmurs, squeezing his arm before walking away.

"So, tonight was fun," Liam says, and I look around, not knowing what else to say.

I chuckle. "Yeah, besides the whole—you know." He drapes his suit jacket over my shoulders.

"I'm glad we had it," he responds.

I nod, mumbling a small, "Me too."

"Want me to drive y—" he starts to ask.

A black sedan with a rideshare logo pulls up and the driver rolls down the window, interrupting him. A woman with shoulder-length, curly hair smiles. "Looking for a Bianca Harrison?" I wave, then my phone buzzes with Josh saying he sent someone to pick me up because Mom was *busy* with something. I sigh nervously as I have no idea how this woman drives, and Liam unfortunately picks up on my unease. I turn back, holding up a finger, and she nods. The window rolls back up as I come face-to-face with Liam once again.

"I can go with you, if you want," he instantly says, and I smile at the suggestion, but shake my head.

"I'll be okay."

He nods, resigned. "Good night, Freckles," he whispers, his lips pressing against my forehead. I look up, his face mere inches away. I raise onto my tiptoes, pecking his cheek, and pull back to see a pained expression.

"Night, Liam."

I start to take off his jacket before he stops me. "Keep it. Maybe it'll help ease your nerves a little." My heart stutters at how sweet he, and the gesture, is. I nod and grip it tighter, the scent of his cologne enveloping me. I turn, walking toward the car. I open the door, but before climbing in, I look back to see him giving me that sweet smile, his hands in his pockets.

Looking handsome as ever in his black long sleeve and tie that he conveniently matched with my dress.

Shutting the door, I look out the window as the driver pulls out of the parking lot slowly, leaving Liam in the rearview.

CHAPTER THIRTY

Liam

THE CAR PULLS OUT OF the lot and I exhale as it drives farther and farther away. Sliding into mine, I don't even input directions, taking myself anywhere besides home. I get closer to the field, needing its peace right now. Parking in the empty lot, I make no move to leave as my thoughts run through my head.

We talked about everything tonight.

Well, almost everything...

We finally brought it all to light, and yet, something still tugs at me. Something doesn't let me fully enjoy this. Raising my hand, I map the constellations one by one, hoping it does away with this feeling. After an hour or so, my heart doesn't let go of this emotion, so I suck it up and head home. After the longer drive back, as the field is farther out than the venue was, I turn right as I get closer to my house, slowing down when I reach Crystal Pines. I shouldn't tell her. I mean, we just patched up a wound from five years ago. Talking about feelings now?

Drumming my index fingers on the wheel, I worry that it's not the right time. Maybe months from now, maybe we can . . . I have to wait for the perfect time.

The thing is, when's the perfect time?

Finally fed up, I push my foot to the gas pedal as I rush to my destination. I used to believe that if I ever told Bianca my feelings, it would strain our friendship, but communication is what's helped us thus far. I told her my truth today, but I didn't tell her everything. After going through the visitor's gate, I park at the curb in front of her house and turn off the engine quickly before hustling out. I get to her front door and knock, but no one answers.

I knock again. But *nothing*.

Glancing at my watch, it's eleven thirty. I nod in understanding. As I start to walk away from the front door, I notice a light turns on in the only window along the side of the house, and I freeze for a moment, but then walk closer to it to inspect. The curtains open slightly, and her eyes widen. The window swings open and I smile at her.

She's got on teal satin pajamas, the shorts coming to mid-thigh, stirring something in me. Her hair is tucked into a messy bun, tiny strands framing her face. What makes her even more radiant is the lack of makeup. Her freckles are on full display.

Honestly, she's so gorgeous.

"Liam? What are you doing here?"

"I couldn't let tonight end without—" I start, and the words melt in my mouth. She looks at me, confused, and I scold myself mentally.

Don't chicken out now. Say something. Say it.

"Without?" she prompts.

Sighing while pinching the bridge of my nose, I look around. There's not a single soul awake right now. It's her and me.

Like it's always been.

"Without . . ." I continue, and she runs her hands over her arms, the wind blowing, no doubt going right through her thin pajamas. Instinctively, I reach out, wrapping her in a hug, thanking my height for once in my life. The window comes up to the middle of my torso, making this the perfect height difference. She wraps her arms around me, her face burying into my neck. Small puffs from her mouth land on my skin, making me break out in goose bumps.

Pulling back slightly, I rest my forehead against hers. My heart speeds up, as does my breathing, and I open my eyes to see her looking at me with concern.

"What's wrong, Liam? Tell me, please," she pleads. She must think something is wrong when she couldn't be further from the truth.

"Bianca, you killed me tonight," I confess, watching her expression, hoping she'll understand. Placing my hands on her face, my thumb rubs along her cheekbone.

She asks, her expression puzzled, "What do you mean?" A beautiful pink starts to color her cheeks, and I smile, feeling the rapid pulse under my fingertips.

"Every time you've kissed me on the cheek in the past, you've killed me," I explain, our gazes locked. "*Every. Single. Time,*" I continue, moving closer until our lips are almost touching. Our breaths mingle, tangling together, and her eyes widen slightly. She grips my wrists as I cup her face, our noses sliding against each other. I keep eyes trained on her, hoping she wants this too . . . that it isn't only me. Her blue eyes fill with nervousness.

But then, they fill with something else akin to longing and when her eyes flutter down to my lips and shut slowly, I close the small space still keeping us apart.

"Please, *please,* bring me back to life again," I whisper, my lips brushing hers. When we meet, a symphony plays in my head. She's warm against me as my tattooed arms wrap around her waist. It's an *electrifying* first kiss.

Our first kiss.

Kissing her slowly and tenderly—the passion behind it unmistakable—millions of butterflies take flight in my stomach. Her lips part slightly as my tongue teases her mouth, and I immediately sense her surprise. Moving my hand lower, she melts into it when my hand grazes her lower back, a gasp escaping her lips. Taking advantage of her distraction, my tongue slides into her mouth. She startles, but sinks into it. Her fingers tug gently at the hairs on the back of my neck, causing a satisfying sound to fall from my lips.

Forget my sounds—what catches me off guard are *hers*. All of them having hints of surprise and pleasure only spur me on. The tentative embrace of her tongue slowly sliding against mine. Her inexperience peeks through, making this kiss feel that much more special. I trace her tongue once more, causing her head to tilt slightly, and my hand entwines in her hair. I have no idea how long it continues, but I pull back as my chest tightens. I pant slightly, as does she, but she doesn't say anything, and my mind starts running.

Did she like it?

Did she not?

Oh no, she didn't, and now I've ruined everything.

I knew it, I knew it, I knew . . .

As my mind continues its downward spiral, her hands wrap around my neck and she crashes her lips against mine again.

Surprise takes me, but then is replaced with longing, yearning . . . *Love.*

I mash my mouth with hers and she runs her tongue along my bottom lip, seemingly more confident. My heart flutters at that, a satisfied sigh leaving my lips. Her mouth swallows the sound and I smile into the kiss.

"Wait, Freckles," I say, knowing we need to talk, and we separate. She opens her eyes and they seem to sparkle slightly. "I—" I start, and she raises her hand to her lips, tracing where *my* lips had been.

"You kissed me."

A blush comes onto my cheeks. "You kissed me back," I retort, and she nods while biting her lip; my eyes drop to them.

"Wait. *You kissed me?*" Her dazed expression drops and the obvious overthinking begins. I wrap a hand around her cheek, wanting her to see the truth in my eyes.

"I kissed you because I wanted to, Freckles. I kissed you because I've been waiting *years* to do that," I confess, and she gasps. "I was driving back home tonight, and I thought about you, naturally. I thought about us, how we decided to give our friendship another chance, but I don't want that. *I want us to be more than that.* I always have." I look at her, and her mouth hangs open in shock, and I put my hand under her chin, closing it. "Please say something," I mutter, defeat coming over me.

This is it. The day I'd dreaded since I realized I was in love with Bianca.

"I've always wanted that too, Liam." My head snaps up and my mouth spreads in a wide grin. She smiles back and I lean my forehead against hers again.

This whole time, she's wanted me too?

"Freckles, you have no idea how long I've waited for you to say that," I say while rubbing my thumbs over her knuckles. She blushes. I look into her enchanting eyes and feel myself being pulled in.

"That was my first kiss," she mumbles, and my eyes widen at the confession.

"I'm your first kiss?"

"Yeah. I'm sorry if it wasn't good or anything. I prom—" I press a quick kiss to her lips, shutting her up.

"Freckles, if you had kissed me better than you did, I would've had a heart attack," I truthfully say, and she giggles. The sound flows through my ears, making the swarm of butterflies attack my insides. Though, they stop in their tracks when my phone buzzes, the vibration unique to Mom; she's probably asking where I am. Bianca glances up at me, her face drops slightly, and I suddenly wish that I didn't have to go home.

Do I live five minutes away? Yes.

Can I see her tomorrow? Yes.

But do I wanna spend the rest of the night with her right now? Heck yes.

"I have to go," I mutter reluctantly as I link my hands with hers. She takes a deep breath while I look at her. "I just don't want to." She gives me a shy smile before her face lights up. "What, Freckles? I know that face."

She giggles and gets close to me, our lips a millimeter apart. I want to push our lips together for the third time, but she pulls back when I lean in more.

"What if you left tomorrow morning?" she asks, and I mull over the idea.

Technically, I could text Mom I'll be home soon and she'll fall asleep eventually. Plus, leaving Bianca right now sounds like downright torture.

"And where would I stay?"

She blushes and then motions with her head inside, and surprise washes over me. She smiles, biting her lip.

"Your Mom and Josh will see my car, gorgeous." She frowns at that, her slight blush glowing deeper, probably due to the pet name. She stands there pursing her lips in thought and I think about it too.

"Got it. Park at the little playground we hung out at the other day, and then we'll get it in the morning." I look at her in disbelief and she pouts at me.

"The things I would do for you," I whisper while kissing her forehead.

I follow through with the plan. It's so funny to think that a month or so ago, we wanted nothing to do with each other. And now? I bite my lip as my head swarms with thoughts of Bianca, and I lock the car before making my way back to her house. On the way, there's a patch of small daisies growing along the sidewalk, and I smile at the memories I've had with these flowers. Picking one, I continue my way back home.

Home to her.

"Hi," she says, color flushing her skin, and mine heats up as well. She smiles at me, and I hop onto the ledge, my heart speeding up more than usual.

This girl is gonna be the death of me.

I tuck the daisy behind her ear and rub her cheekbone. "You know, a guy usually doesn't go into a girl's room until later on."

Getting closer, she wraps her hand around my tie, pulling me in, and I bite my lip at her cheekiness.

"It's later on."

Bianca

He crashes his lips on mine and I revel in the way his mouth moves.

"Damn, beautiful," he whispers, and I press myself closer to him. He traces his hands down my body and he tugs my thigh slightly. I have no idea what he wants, so I lift it and he grabs hold. Then he moves his free hand to my other thigh, and I raise that too. He picks me up, a surprised sound leaving me .

I wrap my legs around him. His hands become locked under me so as not to break the kiss. He turns us around as one of his hands drops from my body, looking for something. He finds it, and I briefly hear the window click and lock in place, and I smile at him. His large hand then runs up my back and I sigh at the feeling. He pulls back and we breathe in unison. He flashes his pearly whites at me as his eyes gaze deep into mine.

"Freckles, you're amazing," he mumbles, and I can't help but smile.

"I know, right?"

He rolls his eyes and carries me as he looks around my room, and I let him snoop. His fingers run against the spines of my books before he freezes when he gets to my Polaroid photo wall. At that, he gently puts me down. Something like a small chuckle comes out of him and I recognize the picture he picks up. One that I recently put up.

He turns around with the picture in his hand. "You still have this?" he asks, his voice tight with emotion, and I nod at the question. Grinning as he chuckles lowly, rubbing a thumb along the picture, he pulls me closer to him.

"I put them up recently, something was missing without you."

He blushes slightly, kissing me on the cheek. "You were and are so beautiful." My heart skips a beat at the compliment and a blush comes to my cheeks. He laughs before I shush him. "Sorry, it's so cute when you blush."

"Shut up," I mutter, and he kisses me on the cheek, nuzzling my neck after.

Warm in his embrace, I stifle a yawn, but he feels it anyway.

"Let's get you to bed." Nodding, another yawn makes its way from my throat as I stretch. My fingers link with Liam's as I guide him to the bed before he stops us. He wears a shy expression. "I'll sleep on the floor. Let me freshen up. You go to bed, you're tired." His voice sounds sweet, but I refuse, shaking my head.

"Liam, we've slept in the same bed before."

"That was *back then*. And it's been years. Besides, what if Ms. Kate comes in?"

I look at him, crossing my arms, and he sighs while running a hand down his face. "Yeah, it's somewhat different, but it's okay. I don't mind. I'll lock my door, you sneak out in the morning, and no one will know."

He clears his throat and looks down before mumbling, "Hm, so I'm your dirty little secret now." There's a hint of uncertainty in the words and I shake my head again, giving him a reassuring smile.

"One that I will shout from the rooftops when we *both* feel it's the right time. But for right now, you're all mine," I say, and he smiles.

"All yours, Freckles." He wraps his arms around me, molding our bodies together, our noses rubbing. "And you're all mine, right?" He asks it almost as if he believes this is a figment of his imagination. After a quick kiss, his expression changes to one of pure happiness, and I hug him harder. He walks in the direction of my en suite before turning back and kissing me senseless. He smiles before actually heading to the bathroom, leaving me panting. My brain starts running a mile a minute and I realize what's all gone down.

We kissed.

Liam and I kissed!

He's staying in my room . . .

I giggle at my thoughts, and even though that voice—that *malicious* voice that makes me overthink—wants to break free, I keep it at bay. I'm not letting it ruin this moment.

I just hope this isn't only a moment.

The bed dips and I turn around and gasp. Liam's lying there, *shirtless* with boxer shorts on, his tattoos all on display. I look at him and he glances back sheepishly. "There was a pack of extra toothbrushes, I used one. I also realized I don't have any clothes with me, and the ones I had aren't comfortable to sleep in. I mean, I have some back home . . ." He must realize how that sounds, so he shakes his head. "If you want me to drive there and back, I can. I want you to be more than comfortable, and don't worry, I'll stay on my side." He makes good on his promise as he scoots as far as he physically can away from me, and I whimper at the loss of warmth. This man truly doesn't understand that I trust him more than myself. Scooting closer to him, I wrap an arm around his waist, burying my head in his neck.

"Freck—"

I mumble, "Good night, Liam." His otherwise tense body loosens and he wraps his arms around me. I sigh in contentment.

"Sweet dreams, Freckles," he whispers, followed by a kiss on my forehead. And with that, I pass out, having the best sleep of my life.

CHAPTER THIRTY-ONE

Bianca

I GROAN LOUDLY AT THE knocking, deciding whether to ignore or answer it. Letting sleep be more important, I roll over, snuggling with my pillow. The knocking seems to continue and I huff annoyance. I rub my eyes as I hear another sound in my room: the bathroom door opening. My eyes open a bit before I let out a small scream when I see him, scooting backward, landing on the floor with an *oomph*.

"Bianca! What's wrong, honey?" My eyes home in on the locked door, and I think quickly about what to say.

"Sorry, Mom, just a spider." The words slip out as casually as possible, staring at the six-foot *spider* in my room, who is currently half naked, an amused look on his stupidly handsome face.

"Okay. I wanted to let you know Josh bought breakfast."

He whispers, "Are you okay, Freckles?" Sparks run through my body as he moves to lift me up, and I gasp at them. Nodding, I breathe a sigh of relief as Mom's footsteps get farther away. I stay frozen as everything hits me all at once. His face is still the picture of concern as I look at him, bewildered. I trace the tattoo on his chest and he shivers a bit.

"I'm fine. I was startled." I drag a finger along the letter B as he looks at me with adoration in his eyes. "I keep feeling this is fake," I murmur, looking up at him, and red stains the tops of his ears. His hand reaches for the back of his neck in embarrassment.

"Well . . ." he starts as he places his hand over mine, "it isn't." He looks at me, certain yet shy, and I have no idea how to process my feelings, so I push his shoulder. "Good morning to you too." I smile, but then see his state, and I look down. A sexy, deep chuckle erupts from him, his hand curling around my chin, raising my head so that his eyes meet mine. "Don't tell me you've gone shy on me, Freckles."

His fresh, minty breath fans my face, and I curse out as mine is probably the complete opposite. I gulp, but he flashes his pearly whites at me, and my stomach does thousands of somersaults. "Well, I—" He rubs his thumb over my cheekbone, effectively shutting me up.

"Freckles?" He cups my face, bringing ours together, but stops just shy of my lips brushing his. "Do I have permission to kiss you again?" Embarrassment courses through me, and he must see something because he backs away instantly, not wanting to crowd me. "Got it. Don't worry, I know that because we kissed yesterday doesn't mean I have infinite permission."

My eyebrows dip before reaching out to him. "Liam, it's not because of that." I point to my mouth and he looks confused, but then realizes what I mean and rolls his eyes.

"That's *normal*, Freckles. And I couldn't care less, but if it bothers you . . ." He scoops me up and I gasp. He takes me to the bathroom and I can barely focus as he hands over my toothbrush with toothpaste slathered on. He leans against the doorway with his arms crossed in a sexy little stance, and waits like the gentleman he is before he comes over, his finger twirling a strand of my hair.

My heart is filled with so much love in this moment. I rinse my mouth and reach around his neck to bring him down to kiss me. A satisfied sound leaves him and my heart warms at that. Our lips meet and my body becomes light at the feelings running through me. We don't talk much about what this is, but if he kisses me like this every time, I'm willing to do anything to keep him.

After a bit, we realize that it's definitely time for him to go back home. Though, before he leaves, he gives me yet another one of those dizzying kisses, and I slide the back door closed. Feeling comfy in my pajamas, I walk into the hallway to start my day like always.

"I know, Liv. You'll be back soon, though."

I stop at the words, turning around the corner to see Olivia with suitcases next to her, and I can't stop the smile that comes on my face.

"Hon, I'm glad you're here. We're about to leave to drop Olivia off, if you were wanting to . . ."

I force my lips into a frown, but it's no use. "I'm okay, don't let me stop you. Olivia, have a nice flight." She smiles at me, and I send a fake one back for Mom's sake. I resist the urge to roll my eyes, and as much as I want to forgive Mom for how she's been acting, she takes us right back to square one. They all head out like the picture-perfect family, and as soon as the door closes, my shoulders lower.

I mean, how do you cope with the idea that your mom, your *best friend* in the entire world, is marrying an idiotic jerk who loathes you, and won't stop until she one day loathes you as well?

What then? She's all I have, and while I don't want to compromise her happiness, I can't help this feeling I have about him and his daughter. I used to consider my home a haven, but when Mom becomes *Mrs. Callaway*, this house will no longer be my home.

Then what?

Losing my appetite, I put down all notions of wanting to eat, and instead grab my phone to check the time. As the phone lights up, I gasp, seeing my background changed. It's a montage of all the photos Liam and I have taken. Our second more fun trip to McDonald's, when we hung out at the park together, and one where he's kissing my forehead as I cuddled with him last night. I click on the screen and it changes to every single one individually. I smile.

Even when he isn't here, he always knows how to cheer me up. As I continue tapping, the photo transitions to a screenshot of a note from my Notes app.

I've always wanted to do this for you, and I hope that you like it. I don't think you'll ever know how much happiness you bring me, Freckles. Now every time you're feeling sad, you can see this, and maybe grace the world with your beautiful smile.

Never ever be sad, gorgeous.

P.S. I'm sorry for using your phone without your permission. I hope you still love me, though. <3

Tears threaten to come out of my eyes, but I smile through them.

Liam Jax Parker, I have never and will never stop loving you.

It was a shorter shift at the shelter today, but I still feel exhausted. I was able to shadow our head vet, Penelope, and they weren't kidding when others said she takes her job very seriously. Liam didn't volunteer today, but we did talk over my break. He was playfully upset that I didn't tell him I was volunteering today. Now, I'm back home, scrolling through movies. The doorbell rings and I'm too tired to move from the couch to open it for Mom . I'm waiting for the familiar sound of her keys, but hear nothing. Confused, I go to the door and open it. My jaw drops when I see the tall shadow of my man leaning on the doorway with grocery bags in hand.

Liam smiles when he sees me and sets down his things, engulfing me in a hug. I sigh, hugging him back. "You're here," I murmur, then pull away as he looks at me weirdly.

"Why wouldn't I be?" He reaches down, grabbing the bags with one hand and my hand with the other. I smile sheepishly, shrugging, trying to play it cool.

"I don't know. I thought . . ." Liam looks at me knowingly as we enter the kitchen and sets the grocery bags on the counter. My favorite chips peek out.

"You must know by now that the only place I love to be is where you are." I smile as he kisses my forehead softly. "Josh is gonna have to do a hell of a lot more to keep me from you, *love*." He pulls me in, my grin growing wider.

"What about your ca—"

He interrupts, "Parked it at the little park." I nod and he smiles. "I missed you," he says as if we haven't seen each other in forever.

I grin and hug him once more, whispering a small, "I missed you too."

He then pulls back and our faces are close together, but I see hesitation in his expression. "Bianca, can—"

I don't let him finish. I wrap my arms around his neck, pressing my lips to his, and after a moment, he reciprocates, pulling me in closer by my waist. Our mouths move with ease as if they know they're right where they belong. There are no awkward pauses, but a smooth and continuous rhythm.

I pull back, his lips slightly pink, color flushing my cheeks, a small smile coming onto his face.

"You are gorgeous, Bianca Harrison." Not knowing what to say, I kiss his nose. He sneaks a chaste kiss once again. "Where's Ms. Kate?"

"With Josh, dropping Olivia at the airport," I respond, and he sighs almost in relief. I stifle a giggle. He starts taking out my favorite snacks and I look at him in surprise as he has that cute little smirk on his face.

"How about a chill Friday with a movie? Maybe our all-time favorite?" His eyebrows raise and I look at him, confused, but then understanding comes over me.

"Cinderella?"

He nods at that, and I smile at how, after all this time, he remembers my favorite movie.

"Yep. Years later, and I still hate the guy," he confesses, and I slap his shoulder, giggling. It's been about an hour or so, and we're in my room on my bed. He's lying behind me as I lean against his chest, his heart beating softly under me. And like before, this is the time where Liam grumbles the most, while I'm fantasizing about Prince Charming.

Just like old times.

As Cinderella and Prince Charming sway to the music, he chuckles, sneaking a hand into the popcorn. "You're such a hater," I say, looking up as he looks down at me. He sticks his tongue out, making me return the gesture.

"I don't get why you like him so much. Prince Eric, I get. Prince Phillip? Great choice. But *him*? The guy most likely had a foot fetish and could have done something else besides sending his guards to try a *glass shoe* on every woman in the kingdom." I giggle, and he nuzzles my neck, muttering, "Yeah, not really at the top of my prince list."

"I love the fact that you have a prince list."

He raises his head, his lips tickling my ear. "Well, I had to research my competition. Make sure I was better." I roll my eyes, and he gives me a kiss on the side of my neck.

"You never had any competition."

"Neither have you," he retorts, and I smile at him. He starts to rub my cheekbone, bending down to rub his nose against mine in the most adoring gesture. He pulls back and my eyebrows furrow. "You're the most gorgeous woman I know, inside and out," he mumbles dreamily, and I roll my eyes, returning my focus to the movie. Every time I'm with Liam, I'm at peace with the *now*. The future is tomorrow's gamble, and I know I'm safe in his arms.

I eventually feel bad as I subjected him to his usual torture, so we watch one of his favorite action movies. He digs his hand into the cheesy popcorn as I trace the tattoos on his neck. I look over and see *another* beautiful set of tulips over his pulse point, and I have the most brilliant idea.

"Liam?"

He stops the movie, turning to give me his full attention. "Yes, Freckles?" A blush warms my cheeks, but I shake my head, trying not to be distracted.

"I wanna ask something, and if you don't want to, you can say n—"

He puts a finger over my lips. "Just ask, love."

"I wanted to ask if I could color in your tattoos." I take a deep breath as he raises a questioning eyebrow. "I thought the work you have done is *beautiful,* but it's all black outlines, and I don't know . . ."

He smiles. "Color them how?"

I shrug before I think. "With markers?" Something crosses his face before he looks at me, giving me the gentlest smile.

"Go get 'em, love." I squeal in excitement, and he lets out a deep chuckle as I get my washable markers. Grabbing my desk chair, I put it next to the bed, but Liam has other plans. He lifts me easily as if I weigh no more than a feather and sets me on his lap. He takes off his shirt and kisses the tip of my nose. "Color away, Freckles." I giggle again and start on the ones on his neck while he presses play on his movie. He doesn't move a single inch while I shift around trying to find which ones to continue with. His skin ripples under my touch, a couple of goose bumps arise, and I give him a raised eyebrow.

"It's cold," he mumbles shyly, and I laugh as he shakes his head. I swipe the light purple over one of the tulips, and his hand comes to rest around my waist as his thumb rubs comforting circles. I eventually get down to his arms, and my eyes home in on one I didn't even notice he had.

Señora Bearington in all her blank ink-traced glory. A smile starts on his face, but he continues to watch the movie, pretending he doesn't know what I found. I start to color her, the red bow on her ear, her pink little nose, and her dark brown fur. Satisfied with my handiwork, I get off him slowly and run over to my closet to grab her.

Her fur and precious stitching are my favorite things. I walk to find Liam, looking right at me, and his eyes soften that much more when he sees the teddy bear. I smile as I sit back in my spot in his lap, and he pauses the movie as he glances down.

"You kept her all this time?" he asks.

"I needed something to remember you by," I respond.

A hint of sadness creeps through before he shakes his head, looking back down. "I remember that day, ten years ago. I came home, angry at myself when we played hospital and I accidentally cut a hole in her. I needed to do something to fix her for you." I listen intently to the story. "Mom asked why I was frustrated and crying, and I explained the situation, and that's how I learned stitch lettering." A small smile graces his face. "You know I still have mine too. Señor Bearington has been missing the love of his life for a while now."

I giggle. "We have to get them together again."

He smiles, and I look at my guy with color bursting from his skin. I then look down at Señora Bearington. Even as my best friend, he was always the sweetest boy ever. I trace over the stitching, the wobbly letters of a trying ten-year-old showing.

"Besides the star plush from Dad, it's the most important thing I own," I continue. There's a somber smile from him as he rubs his thumb over my cheekbone. A delicate hue is already starting on my skin under his attention.

"I never knew your dad, but I've always known that he would be so, so proud of you." He drops his hand, interlaces our fingers, and brings my hand up to kiss it. "I know I am." Tears well in my eyes, but I blink them away as he gives me a sweet smile.

"Honey."

I groan at someone shaking me, and I push another pillow over my head, though that gets ripped away. Huffing, a headache starts forming at how fast I get up, and blink to see Mom. She's giving me a confused look, a ghost of a smile on her lips. I tilt my head slightly, scrunching my eyebrows at the warm arm slung across my waist, and I shut my eyes in panic.

She asks, "Something you wanna tell me?" I look down at Liam, who's sleeping peacefully, as I try to find a way to explain this away.

"Well . . ." I trail off.

She chuckles. The front door slams and her head snaps toward the hallway. A look of unease comes over her face. "I'm okay with it. Let's not tell Josh yet, though." I sigh, Liam snuggling into me more, a sound of adoration coming from him. Mom smiles down at us as she heads to leave. I lie back down, hugging him, feeling safe in his arms.

I wake up at the feeling of little shapes being drawn on my skin, warmth enveloping me.

"Freckles. Wake up, love." Peeking with one eye open, Liam's looking at me adoringly, a small smile making its way onto his face, and slowly, one comes on mine. He runs his fingers through damp hair to get it out of his face. "Good morning, Cinderella," he whispers teasingly, and *my goodness*, it's true what they say about guys in the morning.

Their voice is truly that deep.

"Hi, Prince Charming." He groans, rolling his eyes, wrapping his arms around me. Sighing contentedly, I play with the little bits of hair at the nape of his neck, puffs of his breath causing my skin to litter with goose bumps. "I wish I could stay here every day."

I pull back, and he's wearing his signature pout. "My mom knows, meaning it won't be long before she lets it slip to Ana, so *you* need to get going."

He nods as he gets up, stretches, and I stay down, looking at him. His back muscles flex, the tattoos moving back and forth, and my mouth waters at the sight. I gawk shamelessly as I trace over each one with my eyes. He then leans back on one elbow, turning around to look at me, a smirk tugging on his lips.

"What are you looking at, you little perv?" he jokes, and I giggle at that. He leans in, and we're close to touching lips when his phone rings. Ana's picture appears on the screen.

Pulling back, he reaches and mutes the ringtone and I make my way to stand.

"What do you say about coming over tonight? I can pick you up at nine," he suggests, sitting to make himself be somewhat at eye level with me. I smile as I wrap my arms around his neck.

"Aren't you sick of me?" He looks at me as if I've offended him. He circles his arms around my waist, molding me to his body.

"I'll never be sick of you, sweetheart," he says. I rub my nose against his. "So, is that a yes to coming over?"

"That's a yes." A chuckle escapes him as he gives me a chaste kiss in return. We stay there for a bit, and I run my hands over his neck and shoulders, my fingers skimming little red dots. "These weren't here yesterday." I observe them more intently.

He winces, stopping my hands, and a sheepish smile forms on his face. "I, uh, this is gonna sound dumb." I raise an eyebrow as a blush of embarrassment starts on his face. "My skin's very sensitive, which is why only *certain* ink can go on it." He doesn't say the rest, merely alluding to it, and I gasp.

"Liam! Why didn't you tell me?"

He shakes his head, shrugging. "They don't hurt, they're a little itchy, but that's it. They'll go away after I put something on them." A frown comes on my face and he sighs. "You were so excited, so that's why I didn't say anything." He cups my face. "I would put up with anything to see you smile."

My heart stutters at this *stupid, adorable* man who is *all mine*. I move to kiss him, his phone ringing once again, and I know Ana must be worried out of her mind.

"You need to go." Grabbing his stuff, he holds it in one hand, his fingers lacing with mine in the other. We walk to his car without a word, and he unlocks it before placing his bag in the trunk. I turn around to face him and he seems lost in thought. The ground suddenly seems a lot more interesting. "Liam?"

He raises his head and sighs again, making me more confused. "Is it stupid to say I'll miss you even though I'm seeing you later?"

he asks, the red reaching all the way to the tips of his ears. A choked laugh escapes me as I shake my head.

"Not at all. I'll miss you too." He pulls me into his embrace as my arms loop around his neck. After a bit, we pull back only a few inches, our faces still incredibly close together.

"Since the night at the shelter, multiple scenarios have gone through my head of how I was gonna do this. I know I've said this before, but I can't help myself. Never in my entire life have I ever only wanted to be your best friend." My eyes widen, and he grabs both of my hands, interlacing our fingers. He smiles at me. "The day when I learned what a girlfriend is, you've been that in every single one of my thoughts." He blows out a breath. "Now, I know it's gonna be interesting to explain this to my parents and yours. And Josh not liking me is definitely a setback, but I have faith in us. This"—he signals between us—"is real. We're not only best friends, we're *so* much more. There's no one else for me, like I *hope* there's no one else for you," he finishes, and then kisses me, sealing his words, my heart soaring. We kiss desperately, and he pulls back, laughing breathlessly as he plants his forehead against mine.

"As much as I want this to keep going, my mother is gonna kill me if I don't get home soon." I nod at that, and he pushes a strand of hair behind my ear, whispering, "Perfect," and my heart explodes in fireworks. "Wear something a little fancy because I have a surprise later tonight." If he keeps this up, I'm going to pass out. He smiles, kissing me once more. He then places a finger under my chin, his pearly whites making their grand entrance.

"I love you," he whispers, giving me a final kiss. He walks away as I gasp at the confession. He gets in his car as I basically stand there, shaking my head, unsure if this is all real. He drives off, not before sending me a kiss with a flirty wink, and I walk back as I think about tonight, delicious nerves tickling me.

Once at the front door, I hear hushed voices, so I hurriedly push my way inside.

"Are you serious, Kate? That family . . . that boy . . . *You accept that?*" My heart stutters at the icy chill in Josh's voice, and a sniffle rings out.

"Josh, they're close friends."

He scoffs. "Because I allow it. Besides, you don't know that. I mean, because of him, she already added another piece of filth to her body. *Another damned tattoo.*" I stop at that as I listen behind the wall. "Oh, and William stopped by the office to *apologize* for the other night. That family is a bunch of hypocrites. You can tell they aren't as refined as us. I'm telling you, darling, we *need* to cut them out."

My heart drops at the venom spouting from Josh's mouth, and I peek to see Mom visibly stressed. "Josh . . ." She reaches out to grab his arm.

"If you're gonna defend them"—she whimpers as his hand wraps around her wrist—"don't." He lets go harshly as she looks at him, bewildered, and he stomps off. She breathes, gasping every once in a while, when I creep up to her, hugging her from behind.

"Oh—hi, honey." A smile is plastered on her face as she wipes her eyes, her hands subtly rubbing the skin around her wrist. I look down, barely seeing the imprints of Josh's fingers, but she pulls it back before I can get a better look. "I'm fine. Look, Ana called asking if Liam was here, but I couldn't confirm."

I close my eyes at that. "Yeah, he left to go back home." She nods, and I can't help but look at her, worried. "Mom, are you—"

She steps back. "Will Liam be coming over later today too?" Her posture is closed off; she's backing away.

"Um—I'm actually going to his place later today."

She smooths down her dress, nodding over and over. "Good, good. That's better, given that Josh is . . . you know." I dip my head in agreement as she smiles. She then puts her hands on my shoulders. "I love you, Bianca."

She walks off before I can say a word, but I still mumble a soft, "I love you, Mom." Though, she's too far away to hear it.

CHAPTER THIRTY-TWO

Liam

"LIAM JAX PARKER!" MOM YELLS the moment I attempt to close the door softly. Her accent rolls the Rs in Parker, and I close my eyes in awaited pain.

Oh yeah—big trouble.

I walk to the kitchen to find her pacing angrily, Dad sipping his coffee, looking at her worriedly. They both make eye contact with me, and he looks down at his phone, not before giving me the look that says *you're dead.*

"Donde estab—" she starts in Spanish, bringing out her native tongue. "Where have you been?" She crosses her arms, and even though I'm over a foot taller than she is, I can't help but feel a little intimidated.

"I—"

She cuts me off. "I understand. You're an adult, *you're twenty.* But I have one rule: Let me know where you are. I think I'm a chill mother." She looks over to Dad. "Aren't I a chill mother, Will?"

He nods vehemently. "The chillest, my love." She looks back at me.

"All I want to know is if you're alive at least." She sighs. "I don't want to nag, or treat you like a kid, but *eres mi niño*, and I will always worry about you." I drop my head like a kicked puppy when her voice lowers. Dad glares at me and I clear my throat, uncomfortable. She runs her hands over her hair, smoothing it down as she takes a deep breath. "So?" I glance up as she looks at me expectantly, and a heat starts up my spine. "Where have you been?" She sits upright on the counter stool, looking taller than she actually is, and the heat spreads over my neck to my ears, probably showing across my face.

"Um—I was at . . ." I sigh, rubbing a hand over my eyes. "I was at Bianca's." Dad drops his phone and Mom's eyebrows shoot up in surprise. I look back down as I let them process the information.

"At Bianca's?" She gets off the stool, and I await the rest of her yelling. I look and see smiles on both my parents' faces. "I *knew* it. I mean, I called, but Kate didn't confirm."

The blush burns ten times brighter as I shrug. "I'm sorry, I know you worry."

She comes over to me. "You're lucky I love that girl, or else I'd be yelling more at you right now." I chuckle when she pins me with one of her stares, and I shut up. "I accept your apology, just let me know beforehand so I don't freak out again, hm?" She cups my chin, making me look at her, and I nod, causing her to smile again. "So, Bianca?"

I roll my eyes. "Bye, Mom," I say as I walk to my room, buzzing with excitement for tonight.

I used to always consider myself a patient guy, except for when it comes to spending time with the person that I love most in the world.

Well, it's an hour earlier than I asked her to come over, and I'm at the Crystal Pines gate as the guard opens it. Rubbing my eyes semi-aggressively and then running my hands through my hair, I try hard not to mess up the style. My anxiety escalates bit by bit. My heart starts to beat faster and faster as I get close. It beats even faster as I roar through the gate, her house mere minutes away. I park in front, the tiniest bit of sunlight still shining through my windshield. A couple of beads of sweat merge together on my palms, causing me to rub them against my slacks, hoping the flower stems don't smell of sweat. I set the white tulips I bought earlier today on top of my hood as I run my hands down my face.

Should I have come early?

Should I have just waited until nine to come get her?

In the middle of my overthinking, the front door opens and she steps out. She's wearing these beige linen pants that curve around her waist. My eyes skim her bare arms at this loose vest that makes her slightly tanned skin—from the other day at the beach—look ethereal. Her hair falls in those loose waves, the same hairstyle she wore to Dad's work ball, and I smile a bit at that. She looks up and her eyes widen as she sees me, a grin gracing her pretty face.

She asks, "What are you doing here?" I catch her in my hold and her arms wrap around my neck. I chuckle as I see a slight shimmer on her eyelids, her blue eyes popping as they bore into mine.

"I couldn't wait anymore," I whisper, and she smiles, kissing me lightly.

"Me neither." I make a move to deepen it when she pulls back. I huff in disappointment and she giggles softly. "Lip gloss." I roll my eyes. I look down at her, seeing that she doesn't cover her freckles as much as she used to, and it causes me to let out a small laugh.

I ask, "You ready to go?" while reaching over and grabbing the bouquet, her eyes twinkling ever so slightly as she takes it from me, nodding. I know that while she loves Los Angeles, the rural parts of Pennsylvania are something she misses. So instead of a fancy dinner at an upscale restaurant, I've planned something that's utterly and truly her. We're driving down a smaller road, but the scenery is truly to die for, and I do have a bit more time to kill. From my peripheral vision, she leans her head on the window, and I reach over to interlock our fingers together. I look over for a split second, and she gives me a beautiful smile that makes my heart skip a beat.

Ever since I met her, I've written down almost every song that reminded me of her, and when I was old enough, I compiled them into a playlist. I mentally curse at how I should've already had the music playing, but well . . .

"Freckles, would you mind if we play some music?"

"Of course not." She grabs my phone, already knowing the passcode I told her the other night. "Which playlist should I . . ." Her words trail off, and I already feel the blush warming my body. I can see she's smiling before she lets out a small chuckle.

"You're adorable, Liam." She leans over, kissing me on the cheek.

"This isn't fair, you know I can't kiss you right now." She laughs at that, and I squeeze her hand as she squeezes back when the low tunes of the Bianca-centered playlist fill the car. I haven't told her where we're going, and I'm taking her the long way in hopes she won't remember. Yet, as we get closer, I genuinely can't think of a better place to have my very first date with the love of my life.

I stop a bit farther out as I know she has walking shoes on, and she looks around in confusion. Getting out of the car, I swing open her door, open the glove compartment, and take out a blindfold.

"I kinda need you to put this on for the next part." She looks at me, arching one of her perfect eyebrows, defiance on her face, and I sigh. "Please?"

Her demeanor falls as she gives in and a hint of a smile graces her face. My heart speeds up at the tiniest bit of emotion from her. She takes it from me and ties it over her eyes

She murmurs a small, "Done," and I wave a hand, making sure she doesn't see a thing.

"I got you, Freckles. I promise," I vow. She puts her hands in mine and I carefully guide her. After another bit of walking, I stop right in the middle of where we should be.

"Now what? Can I take—"

"Not yet." I reach for a small remote from my pants pocket. I click a button as she takes her blindfold off. A hundred fake candles glitter throughout the field. Trust me, I counted them, and the cashier had a field day with me. White tulip petals are scattered all around us and a lone telescope sits on the hill. I look over to her as I wring my hands and a couple of tears are coming down her face. I resist the urge to wipe them off, kiss them away. Instead, I patiently wait for her response.

I get closer while I say, "This is the field we used to come to as kids." I look around. "The one where we would go s—"

"Stargazing," she finishes, and I smile. *She remembers.*

She turns around, backing up again, and I let her look. She bends, her hands brushing the candles, and I chuckle.

"Can't have a fire, so we settle for fake ones," I say, and she softly laughs. She keeps walking the path I made for her with the candles, going up the little hill like she used to always do, and I follow. Her hands drag across the length of the telescope and she glances at me with a curious expression.

"Look into it."

Pursing her lips, she bends down and does as I suggest, and I pull a paper out of my back pocket, carefully unfolding it. "Okay, I don't wanna ruin the moment, but I have no idea what I'm looking at."

Rolling my eyes at her with a smile, I hand her the paper. Our fingers brush together, and I marvel at the different emotions crossing her face until they all explode and land on excitement.

"You always said you wanted a star," I mumble, and her head snaps up.

"You didn't."

"Of course I did," I say.

Her eyes stop as they zone in on the date. "And you bought this *five years ago* on—" She hiccups slightly, her eyes widening in realization.

"On your birthday."

I put my hand on her face and smile. Thankfully, she smiles right back at me. She takes a deep breath and I finally get to rub the tears from her cheeks while hugging her. She hugs me back, the paper crinkling as her hands wrap around my neck. The wind blows by and the crickets chirp. Then, little fireflies come closer to the light the candles give off, making the place even more magical.

"Liam," she starts, but I put a finger on her lips and she scrunches her nose. I let out a low chuckle at her cute expression, easing away some of the nervousness.

"That day, I was the most nervous I had ever been. I was your *best friend*, and for once in my life, I was stuck on what to give you for your birthday. I racked my brain that entire week, and leading up to my game, I got it. The most brilliant idea . . . I would get you that star you were always looking at, and even named because you said it looked lonely." She chuckles, shaking her head. "Bianca, I don't know if you've realized that my entire life has revolved around you. As much as I wanted to believe it didn't when we stopped talking, you've always been in my heart. *You never left.*" I roll my shoulders. "These past couple of days have been the best of my life. We both spent so much time building our walls against each other, but I'd like to think it was a matter of time before they were supposed to come down. So we could love each other." I cup her face gently, wanting her to look me right in my eyes.

"I know I was cold at first, and you found out some things about my past. Freshman year of college was the worst. I still couldn't fathom that I was living a life that you weren't in anymore. I listened to some guys, and one thing led to another . . ." I close my eyes in pain, but I open them back up. She deserves to know everything. "The night with Vanessa meant *nothing* to me, and I felt so disgusted afterward. Even though you weren't in my life, and we weren't dating, I felt like I betrayed you—betrayed myself. *Betrayed us.* I hate that she was my first . . ." My voice catches at the idea that I so carelessly gave away my first time, and I close my eyes, hoping it doesn't make Bianca look at me any differently. "I want you to be my last." Pulling back, I raise her face, hoping she knows what she means to me.

What she's always meant.

"Bianca, you're the most radiant woman I've ever had the privilege of knowing. You're the one I'm irrevocably and pathetically in love with. You're the girl whom I'll *always* love. I always have since I was eight years old. It's always been you from the very beginning. So, I want to ask you one more question, and hopefully you say yes." My nerves bubble up, but I push them down. "Would you do me the greatest honor of letting me be your boyfriend? Not because you need me, but because I *desperately* need you. I always have, and always will, Freckles."

I stand there, heart in hand, waiting to see what she does with it. She looks up at me and I take a deep breath, sweat building up again. Then, she wraps her arms around my neck.

"Yes."

A simple word, yet it explodes my whole world. She pushes her lips against mine and my heart thunders. My inner child jumps for joy and I wrap my arms around her waist, spinning her in a tight circle. She giggles, pulling back, and the reflection of light hits her from all angles.

Putting her down, I kiss her once more, the love pouring out between us. She smiles against my lips. "The signature Disney spin."

"I told you I did my research, baby." She blushes at the pet name and reaches up.

"I love you, Liam Parker."

I sigh, those words being the sweetest harmony I've ever heard. I lean down, my lips brushing hers ever so slightly. "I love you more, Bianca Harrison." I kiss her again. My arms bring her closer, the flickering lights casting the most beautiful glow all around us. I pull back and smile as she turns back to the telescope. I've been planning stargazing dates in my head for years, never believing they would actually happen. I mean, I've been waiting most of my life to be with my soulmate. Even if I hoped, I don't think I ever believed that this girl who's joyously looking at her star would finally become mine, and I hers.

CHAPTER THIRTY-THREE

Bianca

THE BELL OVER THE FRONT door of the animal shelter jingles, and I smile at the familiar doggy smell. I get some smiles my way, and then the bell jingles once more, and someone grabs my hand, interlocking our fingers. Looking up at Liam, he smiles down at me as we walk hand in hand for the first time toward the back to clock in for a shift.

As we walk into the break room, Rachel waves at us, then her eyes drift down. "And when did this happen?" She's wearing a huge grin, and a blush spreads across my face when Liam moves to answer.

"Unofficially, ages ago. Officially, last night."

She chuckles and nods. "Well, you guys look pretty cute." At that, her radio rumbles and we look at her, knowing who it's about. "This dog will be the death of me." She sighs as Liam and I laugh. He gives me a sweet kiss as he heads to the kennels and I go to the vet room. I put on some paper scrubs, moving to wash up. I observe Penelope and the technicians helping Daisy, our momma dog, give birth. The heat of the moment causes sweat to drip down my back, a drop smudging my notes a bit. The fan above us does nothing but provide a creaky sound every couple of seconds. Penelope mumbles something, and one of the techs hands her a tool in an instant, efficiency being of the utmost importance.

"You see, Bianca," she acknowledges me, and I make a move to get closer. "The most rewarding thing I can do is save a dog's life, but most importantly, it's when I help our pups get from there to here, safe and sound." At that, small whimpers fill the room and I smile when I see four little border collies, all whining as they settle next to their mother.

The vet techs begin to write their reports and I look down at the little puppies, joy filling my heart.

I lean against Liam's side as Sam huffs and moves his head on my lap as I continue to pet him.

"So, Penelope told me you were in the room for the birth today." Glancing up at him, he gives me a sweet smile when I raise an eyebrow. "Word spread really fast about you and me, hence her saying something." He gives me a kiss on my forehead.

I run my hands through Sam's fur and I look down at the sweet boy. His tongue is out a bit, his eyes are brighter than I've seen them, and my heart thumps. "Penny for your thoughts?" Liam asks.

"I wish I could adopt Sam."

His brow furrows. "Why don't you? I'm sure Ms. Kate would love—"

I cut him off, "I don't only live with Mom anymore, remember?"

Liam's smile drops into a frown and he looks off to the side. "Then, *we'll* adopt him," he simply says, and my head snaps up; Sam's does as well, even though he doesn't understand what's going on.

"What? No, we can't do that." I sigh, not believing this is a true proposition. "Liam, first off, the moment Ana sees him, she'll want to adopt four more, or keep Sam for herself. William practically has to pry her away from all the dogs she encounters."

He laughs. "That's not necessarily a bad thing."

"And we can't keep him at my house because Josh hates animals, said so himself. Besides, we're going to Mella Colta soon, and—"

"Then, we'll take him with us." I give him a faux glare and he sighs. "In all seriousness, Mom will love that we keep Sam at the house. We have more than enough room, and when we do go to college, I want to move in with you." I gasp at that and he gives me a smug smile. "Don't act like you didn't see this coming. Sure, we've been officially dating for a day, but we're not a normal couple. I've wanted to live with you forever, and besides, I can rent us a place close by campus. The best part being that I'd get to wake up next to you every day." My heart beats a little faster and I place my head on his chest, huffing at this stubborn boy. "So, is that a yes?" I rub Sam's face, cooing at him before finally looking up at Liam.

"Taking care of a dog is a lot of work . . ." He probably thinks that it's a no, but then I sigh with a small smile. "But in the meantime, I'll definitely consider it."

His face lights up and he whispers, "And the whole moving in with me when we start school?"

"I love how you snuck that in there."

"I saw an opportunity, and I took it."

I chuckle, grabbing his face. "I would love to spend my mornings with you, Liam Parker." He pulls me closer and kisses me, happiness thrumming in my veins.

"Mm, Freckles, as much as I wanna stay out here with you, it's late and you need sleep." I pull back, my body sandwiched between his legs as he leans against the hood of his car. We're parked in front of my house, and have been for a while, but I don't want to go inside. My nose rubs against his and he smiles at the gesture.

"I know, I know," I mumble, unable to resist leaning in for another kiss.

Can this boy get any more addicting?

I wrap my arms around him, my fingers drifting to the hairs on the back of his neck, and he sighs. Reluctantly, he pulls back, smiling as he rubs a thumb across my cheekbone.

"Just so you know, you're *never* getting rid of me. We're stuck together, Ms. Harrison," he murmurs, and I grin at him.

"You know, I think I'll be good with that, Mr. Parker." A small smile makes its way to my face, but then he pulls back a little more as we see a car's headlights approaching quickly. Grabbing my hand, he walks us up the driveway as the person driving weaves around.

"Josh's car," I mutter. Josh steps out, and Liam's guard goes up as the smell of alcohol wafts through the air. My jaw drops at that, as I've never seen Josh drunk, *ever*. He sneers when he sees us, his dress shirt untucked, tie yanked low.

Something isn't right.

He passes by us without saying a word and we don't say anything either. As the front door slams, I take a deep breath and Liam looks at me, confused. The lights flick on and I hear Mom's voice from inside.

A cold sweat breaks out across my back and a coil of dread starts in my stomach. I push away from Liam and he stalks behind me as we get closer to the front door. The yelling grows and I swing the door open. Josh's eyes are red, Mom is cowering slightly, and I freeze.

I don't think there's been a single moment in my life where I've experienced fear as intense as when I got into a car accident. I was only five years old, but to this day, I remember *every single thing*. The feeling of dread, of impending fear, and it all comes rushing back when I see Josh's hand connect with Mom's cheek, the sound echoing through the space.

I gasp and Liam shoves me in a dark corner of the foyer. "Stay here. You understand me?" I nod shakily and he kisses my forehead before moving into the living room. Mom looks up at Josh, shock and fear alive in her features, but before he can hit her again, Liam interrupts.

"Don't you dare put another hand on her." He stops Josh's arm, throwing it back at him as he stands in front of Mom, her hand cradling her cheek.

"This is my family, and I will do as I please."

I can't move a single inch and a warm tear runs down my face.

"I'm done." Mom's voice is crystal clear, and my head snaps up at that. She moves from in front of Liam, but he stays next to her while Josh stands there like a predator ready to pounce.

He lets out a calm chuckle. "What did you say?" Liam shifts to move closer, but Mom holds out a hand.

Pulling out my phone, I text Ana.

I need you and William to come to the house. Bring the police, please.

Pressing the record button, I hold it discreetly, still staying hidden in the shadows. Liam looks at her, confused, but her stare doesn't waver from Josh as he breathes heavily.

"I am done." She laughs bitterly. "I've put up with a lot of things because of you. Smiled and nodded because after so long of being alone, I thought this is what I deserve." She shakes her head. "Growing apart from my daughter." She looks down, and my face crumples when I see the pinkish hue on her cheeks. "Losing who *I* am . . . to satisfy *you*. I thought that was what I was allowed to have."

She looks down at her hand and Josh speaks up. "Kate, I'm sorry, honey. We can talk about this. We can fix it." He reaches out, but she steps back, tears running down her face. Liam is at her side—at the ready—should anything happen. Though Josh has the most heartbroken expression on his face, I finally realize how manipulative he's been.

How he continues to be.

She slides off her ring and looks up at him. "You have five minutes to get out of my house, or I'll have you arrested on domestic violence charges."

At that, his face contorts, and it's a look I've seen when he's in the courtroom. His features are sharp, his words unyielding, and the look he possesses sheds instantly as if it were a mask.

"Your house?" He chuckles. "Kate, you have *nothing*. *You* are nothing. Everything in this house, everything including you, belongs to me."

I faintly hear sirens as Josh starts screaming, a vein throbbing in his forehead. Breathing harsher, I stumble in sight, and his darkened eyes connect with mine.

"You did this." He seethes as he comes closer, leaving Mom's side as she sobs softly.

"Don't touch her, Josh," Liam threatens.

He ignores Liam, still looking at me. "*You* ruined our engagement. *You're* always what we fight about!" I shudder as his voice grows louder and louder. Mom stays frozen, tears streaming down her face as she trembles. "And you . . ." He lets out a sinister laugh as he points at Liam. "You think that because you're all tattooed that you're some big man." Josh rolls his eyes. "You're *pathetic*, a little boy that should've stayed away from *my* family." He scoffs, a demeaning look coming over his face as he wipes under his nose. He tries to get close to me, but Liam stops him. Angered, Josh whirls around, punching Liam, stunning him momentarily. Quickly bouncing back, Liam pushes away, but Josh doesn't let up, his posture ready to strike. There's a ringing in my ears, and it feels as if this isn't happening. Muffled voices make their presence known and Liam lands a shot on Josh, knocking him down. Blood drips from Josh's nose as he staggers up. My vision starts to blur.

I texted Ana forever ago, didn't I?

Why aren't she and William here?

What if they didn't see the message?

With more questions bubbling up, I begin to feel afloat in my own body, my breathing becoming more erratic by the second. Everyone starts to resemble blurry blobs, and I try to calm myself down, but nothing's working. I brace myself against the wall, the phone clattering to the floor as my other hand cradles my chest. My name is being called as Liam makes his way over to me. I keep breathing harshly as he shifts in and out of focus. Then, the door opens wide as deputies rush in, and I finally move right when Liam's ripped away from me. More tears run down my face as one of the officers separates the men.

"Wait, my girlfriend's in a state of shock. She can't handle seeing blood, please let me—" Liam says as they click cuffs on him.

"This is a huge mistake—I'm an attorney!" Josh's screams fade away, only leaving me to glance at Liam as I catch tears start to prickle his beautiful green eyes. They hold worry and concern and I try to run toward him, but a cop keeps me back.

"Miss, we can't allow you—"

"Please, he didn't do anything wrong. Josh *hit* Mom, and wanted to hit me. Liam was trying to defend me," I plead with the man, but he isn't having it. I look over to find two women officers going over to my mother, a red mark starting to show on her cheek. Though, I stand there helplessly as I watch the officers drag both Josh and Liam outside.

As they pass by me, I reach out to grab Liam's arm at the last second. At my touch, he turns back, shaking his head. He looks more concerned for me than himself as he pleads with his eyes for me to stay back. My head moves between going toward Mom or my boyfriend, who's currently detained. I go under the arm of the officer keeping me in place, trying to find out where they're taking him.

They sit him on the sidewalk, taking Josh to the back of a police car. Liam glances at me, trying to put on a brave face.

"I love you," he mouths, and I give him the saddest smile.

He nods for me to go and I run to Mom. I knock into her as she wraps her arms around me. She's shaking and shivering, and I cry alongside her. Neighbors start to leave their homes to see what the ruckus is about, and I close my eyes in embarrassment.

A familiar-colored Jeep speeds in front of the house, and I sigh in relief when I see Ana and William. Ana stands on her tiptoes, and when she locks eyes with us, she covers her mouth in shock. She dodges through people and comes over, hugging us both.

"Cupcake, I got your text. Are you two okay?" She gasps when Mom raises her face, and the red and blue lights accentuate the mark on her cheek. Tears well in her eyes. "Oh, Kate," she whispers as she wraps her arms around Mom, both of them breaking down in each other's arms. More tears fall down my face, and I look over to see William talking to the deputy near Liam. My eyes stay glued to the scene and I inhale shakily as they take off his cuffs. William hugs him as Liam stands there, seemingly numb, up until he looks around desperately.

I yell his name, hoping he can hear me, even though it's doubtful with the loud murmuring of nosy neighbors. I keep pushing and pushing, getting shoved back in the chaos of moving bodies. Liam's face is the picture of distress as he tries to catch a glimpse of me somewhere. I finally make it out to the open and yell his name once more. He turns around and I crash into him as he wraps his arms around me, my whole body shaking.

"I'm here. I'm here," he mumbles in my ear, rubbing my back as my tears soak his shirt. His hands trace my face as he lifts it. "Hey, hey, breathe with me, baby. It's gonna be okay." But despite his sweet words, the tears keep coming as I look at the cut he has on his eyebrow. He catches on and places a finger over it, the sight of red coming back on his index finger. His eyes widen as large as saucers and he holds his hand to it, preventing me from seeing the blood. "Look at me, not up there. I'm here, Freckles." I crash back into him right when the cruiser that's holding Josh begins its departure. Josh's eyes lock with mine, and they look murderous. A shiver courses through me when we finally lose sight of each other, and I take a deep breath as Liam starts to tremble. "I'm here," he whispers again. Everything fades out as I let myself fall fully into his embrace.

CHAPTER THIRTY-FOUR

Bianca

SOMEONE'S SHAKING ME GENTLY AND I blink rapidly, coming back to reality. The sun streams through the curtains, and I sigh at what happened last night. My eyes dart around the space, remembering that I'm in Mom's room. Liam looms beside me, mumbling my name, and I hum, pretending I'm listening.

"*Bianca*." That catches my attention. He's been calling me "Freckles" this whole time, never my name until now. I must've spaced out again.

He brings a hand to caress my cheek and I smooth out the crease that forms between his eyebrows. "You're gonna get wrinkles."

He gives me a look. "What can I do for you, Freckles?" I open my mouth when he stops me. "We can talk if you want to . . . or not. I can sit here with you—not that I don't want to be here."

I let out a small laugh and he smiles sadly at me. "I think you might be the world's worst rambler."

He hooks a finger under my chin, a delicious tingle shooting down my spine. "Well, I need to beat you at *something*," he retorts and rubs his nose against mine. I glance over, seeing Mom fast asleep.

273

It's been a hard night, and we were told that it would be best if we stayed here and rested. Of course, the Parkers decided they would stay with us, and I slept next to Mom, holding her till she fell asleep.

"I'm sorry about last night," Liam starts, his eyebrows furrowing in sadness.

My eyes narrow a bit. "You didn't do anything wrong. It was his fault, not yours, okay?" He looks away as if he doesn't believe me, but seems to accept it somewhat as he reaches to hug me once more.

"Thirteen years ago, when you were in your accident, I wish I'd known you then so I could've comforted you." I pull back at that.

My heart drops for my soft man.

"Well, you're here now," I say. I look toward Mom, then back at him. "You weren't there that night, but you've been there for me since then. Last night you defended me, you comforted me, you love me more than I deserve." He moves to say something, but I stop him. "Just you being beside me is all I'll ever need. Get me?" I grab his face so he knows I'm serious. He nods at that, and I kiss him on the nose, snuggling into him right after.

Ana and William walk in, and I shoot up to hug them both. William holds a tray with an assortment of teas, and I smile, knowing it was all Ana's doing.

"We brought something to drink," she says, briefly looking at me. She heads over to my mom, softly waking her. "How are you, Kate?" Her voice lowers to a whisper while Mom sits up, wincing. She sighs while we all look at her. Fresh tears spring to my eyes as I see the purple hue on her cheek and a look of defeat swimming in her eyes.

Ana throws her arms around her and Mom whispers a frail, "Hi, everyone." Her head swivels toward me and her eyebrows furrow in concern. "No crying. I'm okay, I promise."

I shake my head as my mind takes me back to last night where she was at the mercy of her fiancé, a man who was supposed to love and protect her from violence, not be the one to introduce her to it. My heart cries for Mom because no matter what she says, she's *not* okay. Liam hugs me to his side. I lay my head against his arm after I see him grip Mom's hand gently.

"Mom, I'm so sorry. I feel like it's my fault—"

She waves me off. "Bianca, never ever think this was your fault. Doesn't matter what happened, a man should *never* put a hand on a woman or vice versa. As much as I want to lie and say it came out of nowhere, we've been fighting for weeks ever since—" She looks toward Ana and William, and their eyes widen in realization, and that confirms what I suspected.

Of course, having them in our lives bothered Josh.

Tears fill her eyes again and I rub my thumb under them when Ana speaks up. "But that doesn't give him any reason to"—Ana's voice cracks slightly—"hit you." The room grows quiet and she clears her throat. "I knew I hated that guy for a reason." At that, Mom is the first one to burst out laughing, and we follow her lead.

Leave it to Ana to break the ice.

"I second that," William speaks up, and Liam loudly agrees too. He sneaks his arms around my waist. Mom's eyes seem to dart to the action and a small gasp erupts, and I look up to see Ana with a smirk on her face, shock apparent on William's.

She fans her face as if she can't believe what she's seeing. "So, you're dating? *Finally?*" she asks, and I look at Liam for help, but he only shrugs, making a scowl come over my face.

Traitor.

"Yes," I whisper.

"You guys are so cute," everyone says harmoniously, and Liam and I groan together, causing them to let out more small chuckles.

Mom then reaches out and I grip her hand while her eyes go to Liam. "Thank you for defending her, Liam, and me too." He nods and his arms tighten a bit, almost as if his mind is going back to that moment.

"Of course, Ms. Kate." My heart lurches, and there comes a gentle but promising kiss on my temple.

After a bit, William and Ana head home to freshen up while Liam goes out to grab us some food. It's Mom and me as my head rests on her shoulder, comforting her as best as I can. We're talking about anything and everything when I catch a tear slipping down her face. She looks up at me with red-rimmed eyes and my heart breaks for her. Her eyes are downcast toward her now bare ring finger and she sighs.

"How could I ever even think about marrying . . ." She stops herself, rubbing said finger. She shakes her head almost as if fighting with her conflicting emotions.

Conflicting emotions about who she thought Josh was, and who he turned out to be.

"I know, Mom. I mean, I knew he wasn't amazing, but to do something like that . . ." She nods, and I stop as the solemn look on her face grows more and more. She looks at me as I grip her hand. "It wasn't your fault, Mom, and I'm so happy you stood up for yourself." Her shoulders droop, but I continue. "Honestly, I hated that we were drifting apart. You're all I really have left, and Josh was getting in the way of that. For a minute, I thought he had convinced you to forget about me." I chuckle sadly as she shakes her head.

"No, honey. I'm sorry you felt that way, and I'm sorry for not being the mother I've always been with you. I'm sorry I brought . . ." She doesn't continue as she presses a closed fist to her mouth, then she takes a minute to let out a shallow breath.

"We're gonna get through this, like we always have," I say, and a small smile graces her face.

"Just you and me," she finishes. I hear some cars pull up to the house. We both look out the window and watch as the Parker clan brings bags of food and other things.

"Not anymore," I mumble as footsteps draw closer. Ana rushes to Mom while William gives me the biggest bear hug, his *twentieth* in the past twenty-four hours—but I don't complain. Liam comes in a second later with some muffins and smoothies, and I can't help the small grin that blooms on my face. William pulls back as he looks behind him, clapping Liam on the shoulder when he gets close enough. A small laugh escapes me while Liam proceeds to wrap his arms around me, muffins and all.

He gives me the much-needed sustenance as he wraps his arm around my waist, and I smile up as he bends to give me a peck. "How are you feeling, Freckles?"

"I should be asking you that. You haven't gotten any rest." He gives me a look, and I sigh, being truthful. "I'm processing. I'm happy Mom's okay, but I'm in shock at everything that's happened. So, processing is the best way to describe everything I'm feeling." He nods and gives me another kiss on my forehead before I whisper, "You know, I realize I haven't thanked you for being there yesterday."

Arching an eyebrow, he chuckles sadly. "You don't have to thank me. I'll always be there to defend you." His hands gently cup my face and another small smile graces his lips. "You, my darling Freckles, are the love of my life. They're gonna have to take me kicking and screaming away from you. I'll always be wherever you are, no matter what." I lean forward, hoping he never ever feels like I don't love him.

"Guess you're stuck with me, *boyfriend*," I say, a smirk spawning on his face at that last word, and I giggle.

"I'm pretty good with that, *girlfriend*," he says, and a dorky smile comes onto my face.

We join the circle of adults, and my mind goes back to the whole whirlwind that's been my life. Josh called my cell phone from the county jail, but I refused to pick up. I told Mom about it, especially concerning the email she got from his lawyer. There's a trial date coming up, but she's refusing to go. We provided all the evidence to the police necessary to put him away. She broke the engagement and filed a restraining order against him, in case there was a chance he would make bail. The thing is, Josh made us sell the house back in Philly, pocketed all the money, and paid for everything here.

So, now, we basically have nothing, and that's what I think she's most afraid of.

Starting over from zero again.

"You have no idea how sorry I am." At that, my ears perk up, and Mom starts to sniffle. "I thought . . . I didn't know Josh would ever . . ." An agonized sound comes from her, and my heart aches as tears slide down my face. William and Ana try to comfort her, but she doesn't let them. So we all stand there as she finally lets herself fall apart. "I had gone into his office and I heard him talking to someone over the phone. He saw me, and for the first time, he *yelled* at me. Told me to get out. I stood there, and he came close, trying to make me leave. For *once*, I fought back, and we started arguing." Her voice wobbles and I close my eyes at hearing Mom in pain once again. "Then, like always, he started talking about you guys. How you were a bad influence on me, and how Liam was to Bianca. Saying I needed to tell you guys to stay away from us. I told him no, and he got so angry, and then he said I either cut you guys off or he would."

I open my eyes to see Ana and William embracing her. Walking over, we all hug as emotions are at an all-time high, but after a bit, Liam speaks up.

"Ms. Kate?" We pull back and Liam grabs my hand and hers. "Please come live with us until you figure everything out."

Her bottom lip wobbles slightly and he squeezes my hand in reassurance as I wipe tears from my face.

"You shouldn't stay in this house any longer," Ana says.

"We have more than enough room for you both. Kate, you're more than welcome to stay as long as you need, even after Bianca and Liam head up to college in the fall," William finishes, and we wait a beat before Mom nods shallowly, and then nods more vigorously as she covers her mouth with her hands. Liam hugs her.

"You're truly something else, little man."

He chuckles as he pulls back, smiling at her. "That's all you, Ms. Kate."

She grabs my hand, glancing between us. "You got yourself a good one, Bianca." A slight blush comes across the tips of his ears.

"I really do, Mom."

He looks down at that and Mom shakes his hand to make him look up at her. "You love and cherish her, you get me?" He smiles and looks into my eyes, making me see every swirl of green in their depths.

"Always, Ms. Kate," he promises, and I can't help but smile. For once, I'm not scared for the future because I know . . .

I know he'll always be by my side. Bianca and Liam —forever and ever.

Bianca

"BABE, YOU'RE GONNA BE LATE," I whisper, and he groans, but makes no move to disconnect his lips from mine. Laughing, I push him back as he makes another noise in protest.

"You know they could mail me the diploma," he says, trying to pull me back into his arms, and I laugh in faux exasperation. "Fine," he drawls out. I hold out his cap as we walk out of the elevator, seeing everyone waiting for us, *as usual,* in the lobby.

"How is it that we're the ones waiting for you when it's *your* graduation day?" Ana looks at him, crossing her arms, and Liam blushes, as he knows why. Mom looks at me knowingly and I blush at her scrutiny, making her giggle.

William clears his throat. "Alright, you two, we'll see you there. Liam, you better not be late."

We both nod, heading to Liam's car in the parking garage down the street from the busy hotel.

"You know, I could've driven." He slides into the passenger seat of the car and I close my door.

"Not on your day, babe. Today, *you* will be spoiled," I say, adjusting the mirrors, causing him to smile at me. I wink, a nervous cough leaving him. Backing out of the spot, we make our way to Mella Colta's campus, thankfully only a ten-minute drive from the hotel.

"Liam Jax Parker!" His name is called and he walks to the stage. The entire Parker clan stands, and we absolutely make him thoroughly embarrassed. He takes his diploma, waves shyly at us, and sends a wink in my direction. As he goes to his seat, my legs bounce up and down, and I can't wait for the ceremony to be over. A half an hour later, I spot Liam talking to Chase, and I creep up on them.

"Congratulations, babe!" I say as I wrap my arms around him, making him turn in place.

"Thanks, Freckles," he murmurs.

"Nice to see you, Harrison," Chase says while Liam glares at him due to the nickname. I slap Liam on his chest playfully, turning to then smile at Chase. When I started at MCU, he became one of my closest friends. During my first semester, Liam had told him that we would be moving in together, and in true Chase fashion, he was able to get a fully furnished place that accepts pets at a great price. We all hung out whenever we could, and Jamie was able to fly over a couple times as well. As much as Liam wants to roll his eyes and doesn't want to admit it, I know he has a little soft spot for Chase. He has truly been a great friend to both of us.

I'm surprised to hear that he's thinking about coming back for graduate school for finance. Afterward, his family comes to take him away, and we wave goodbye as Ana calls us over.

"Alright, crazy kids, are we ready to go home?" Interlacing my fingers with Liam's, we nod happily, and I can't wait to go get Sam. I also can't wait for what I planned for Liam tonight. Giddiness comes over both of us, and in the parking garage, I turn to look at him. He smiles.

"You graduated!" I screech, and he lets out a rich chuckle as he lifts me against him, my legs wrapping around his waist. "I'm so proud of you, you know that?" Color flushes his cheeks. I rub a hand against his face, feeling the slight stubble over his jaw.

"You need to stop looking at me like that," he says, and his eyes darken slightly.

"Like what?" I taunt, and he closes his eyes, mumbling something along the lines of, "*You'll be the death of me, Freckles.*" I let out a giggle, leaning my forehead against his as he takes a deep breath. "We're gonna be late getting back home."

He doesn't listen and instead places me on the top of his trunk. "We can be a little late." The words flutter against my lips, and without missing a beat, he slams his mouth on mine.

"That drive is atrocious," Liam mumbles, a yawn escaping him, causing me to giggle as he grabs Sam's leash.

"I was the one driving. Besides, don't remind me, I have a bit more left of driving that route."

He looks at me. "You suggesting the scenic route did not make it better."

I roll my eyes. "Come on, it was *definitely* worth it," I add as his face morphs into a deadpan look. Grabbing my bag from the trunk, we make our way into his house.

"You make it all worth it, baby," he says, moving to open the front door of his parents' house, and my heart stutters at that. Blushing, he chuckles at me, turning the key, seeing all the lights off. He looks back at me, confused, as we walk farther inside.

"*Surprise!*"

I reach down, letting Sam off his leash, and he barks excitedly as if saying "surprise" too. Liam's eyebrows raise and he drops my bag on the floor at seeing everyone there to congratulate him for his secret graduation party. He's speechless, but then looks at me as I smirk smugly at him.

"You did this?"

I nod proudly. "Of course I did. It was the hardest thing to keep it a secret, you know." He smiles at that while scooping me up, giving me another kiss. Everyone starts making kissing noises, causing us to pull away and laugh.

"Let's get this party started!" Liam's head whips around and Chase makes his way over; they share a hug. Sam runs to them both, licking Chase's face, and my heart warms at that.

"Cupcake, this looks amazing!" Ana squeals in true Ana fashion, making me chuckle as I stand to my full height.

I glance around. "Ana, you're the one who hung it all up. I just had the idea." My eyes trail over the familiar faces when I catch the back of an unfamiliar person. I tilt my head, but then they turn around to reveal none other than the guard from the Crystal Pines front gate. I glance toward Ana, the person in charge of my guest list, and she shrugs. "Is that Matthew?" He locks eyes with me and sends me a shy wave, the barely perceptible smile that he shows Mom and me.

"Why's he here?" I ask, curious more than anything.

His eyes jump from me to the side, and I look to see him *staring* at Mom as she talks animatedly with Jamie. My jaw drops and I look back at Ana who has a little devious smile.

"I noticed how he looked at her, and one thing led to another . . ." Ana shrugs. "Wouldn't hurt, right?"

Looking back over, Jamie is heading my way, leaving Mom alone, but with sure steps, she won't be in a minute by how fast *he's* moving toward her. Jamie opens her arms and practically crushes me.

"Thanks for being here, girl."

She smiles at me. "Wouldn't miss it for the world. I'm sorry I couldn't make his actual graduation." I shake my head, showing her that it's fine. A little trail of heat climbs up my spine and I catch a smirk on Jamie's face as she lets out a sigh.

"Now, as much as I would love to actually have a *full* conversation with you, you better get. Even though your boy was with you, he's already looking lost over there." We both giggle. "He is *so* in love with you, girl." Turning around, Liam's talking to Chase, but glancing over at me pretty frequently, and my heart flutters.

Two years so far, and he still does this to me.

"Go, Bianca," Jamie urges, and I look back to see Chase also looking at someone—*her.*

"Chase likes you, Jamie," I counter, but she rolls her eyes. "C'mon, it's been years and he hasn't even *looked* at anyone, much less done anything else. I would know, I see him practically every day." She sighs and I place a hand on her shoulder. "Don't write him off yet." She nods and I hug her before she pushes me playfully. Another pair of arms wrap around me and my eyes lock onto those familiar tattoos, the tulips and Señora Bearington looking up at me. Smiling, I turn around, and there seems to be sparkles in his eyes.

"What's that look for, Mr. Parker?"

"Just thinking about our future," he simply says. My heart stops and he smiles. "I mean, I wanna marry you." My jaw drops, and he chuckles almost nervously. "Not at this very moment, more so for *your* sake than mine, because if it were up to me, I would've married you the day I met you." I look at him shocked as he gives me that little smile. "But since we're waiting, promise me this." He gulps, and I've yet to even utter a word. "Promise me we'll always talk things through, even if I do something to make you angry at me. Promise me that we'll never let anything break us. That even when life gets tough, we'll always rely on each other. That no matter what, you'll be here, holding my hand, like I always will yours. Promise me that we're *forever.*"

My eyes water and I nod, wrapping my arms around his neck. I put our lips as close as possible, uttering the simplest, truest words: "I promise, Liam Parker. You always have been—and always will be—my forever."

And with that, he kisses me until my brain fries, my heart melts, my mind clears, and love consumes me.

THE END

ACKNOWLEDGMENTS

With that, years of no sleep, pushing through writer's block, self-doubt, procrastination, and sometimes writing only half awake, *His Darling Freckles* has been a story I've had on my mind since I was fifteen years old, and the only reason it is in your hands is because of the overwhelming amount of support I've had when it comes to my writing. Bianca and Liam have gone from my phone notes, to Episode (iykyk), then Wattpad, to end up a real book!

Mom: You are my biggest inspiration, always have been, always will be. The only reason I even have the sense that I can accomplish anything I set my mind to is all because of *you*, and for that, I will always be so appreciative, and I love you more than you will ever know.

Siempre seré su fan número uno, su otito precioso.

Dad: You came into my life later than expected, but you have nonetheless been such a positive voice in my head. Due to you being an author yourself, and seeing how you put your writing out there, you inspired me to write. I will always thank God for bringing you into my life, and I thank you for always being my father in *all* the ways that count.

Aliyah & Gracie: You guys are the best sisters I could ever ask for, and I'm thankful for the love I get from both of you each and every day. Also, after begging me, I did give you a proper acknowledgment, thanks for letting me yap about my books. Love you both!!

Mae: You are my literal lifesaver, and only you know what this book has grown from . . . That we will utter to no one lol. Thank goodness I booked with you—fifteen-year-old me was definitely out of her mind. I'm so happy I finally got the opportunity to meet/ work and get to know you. You're freaking amazing, and I know this is only the beginning! All my love to your family, they're precious. <3

Kasey: Not going to lie, I was very nervous to work with someone else because it meant showing my manuscript to another person . . . oh no lol. But, I feel it was the best decision, and you took that unnecessary anxiety and threw it out the window. Your thoroughness is astounding, and you've shown me so much! All in all, I can't wait to keep working with you, and thank you for putting up with me and when my common sense seems to fail for the simplest things lol.

Anja, Ishika, Meghan, Meka, Rutuja: You guys are the reason why this book is better than ever before. Your feedback, whether critical or a simple text saying you fell in love with the story, made my day because y'all genuinely just want the best for HDF, so I wish you all the best!

Last, but not least, to all my online friends and supporters: You guys are freaking amazing! From the reels, to TikToks, posts, and DMs, among other things, you guys are the reason this is all happening. You guys are my motivation, and if I have any readers who are aspiring writers, this is your sign.

Write your book! Never forget you have a unique voice, and you have the potential to reach your writer goals if you just believe in yourself!

If you liked *His Darling Freckles* or have any suggestions, please consider leaving a review on any platform(s) you want. Reviews are the best and will help other readers.

Love with everything I've got in my hopeless romantic heart,
Alecsa

ABOUT THE AUTHOR

Alecsa Kayser is a simple girl who decided to put her hopes and dreams about her future husband onto paper. She's a hopeless romantic, but knows one day, love will come knocking on her door. When she's not busy with her nose in a book or typing away on her computer, planning books ten years in advance, she's working on programming, utilizing her data science degree.

In addition, if there is one thing she wishes for you to take away from her books, let it be this: *Your forever person is out there.*

Get connected with me: